ATTENTION ALL SURGEONS!

**MED-TEK IS NOW OFFERING
A REVOLUTIONARY TECHNIQUE
THAT WILL LET YOU
SEND PATIENTS HOME IN A DAY,
TRIPLE YOUR PROFITS,
AND CUT YOUR RISKS.**

INTERESTED?

(The only hidden cost
is your soul.)

LIFEBANK

A heart-stopping medical thriller

LIFEBANK

A NOVEL OF MEDICAL SUSPENSE

HOWARD OLGIN, M.D.

A Dell Book

Published by
Dell Publishing
a division of
Bantam Doubleday Dell Publishing Group, Inc.
1540 Broadway
New York, New York 10036

ISBN: 0-440-21878-0

Printed in the United States of America

Published simultaneously in Canada

October 1995

10 9 8 7 6 5 4 3 2 1

RAD

For Aviva Bette Olgin

With special thanks to:
My friends, Donald T. and Shelly Sterling
Lance Walker
Toni Lopopolo

Additional thanks to
Quinton Skinner for his
contributions to the book

LIFEBANK

PROLOGUE

DR. KERRY NORDSTROM MOVED QUICKLY THROUGH MED-TEK, waving his all-access key card at the steel and glass doors that isolated every unit of the complex. In place of knobs, the barriers housed electronic eyes, which barred entry to all those without high-level security clearance. At this time of night, the research labs were under total lockup; only the manufacturing wing was open and populated, the round-the-clock production continuing without rest or cessation.

Each click of an unlocking door, each silent recognition of the invisible beam, took Nordstrom farther into the complex. He passed through the private operating suite, in which he and his staff tested new surgical instruments that had yet to hit the market. He strode through the darkened surgical lab, where fifty gleaming stainless-steel tables waited for test subjects, usually pigs. After passing through this foreboding room, he reached a final unmarked door: his own laboratory.

The door shut and automatically locked behind him, the automated lights revealing that nothing had been disturbed. His bank of computers was activated, processing information from the previous night's data collection. A long operating table, scrubbed clean and disinfected, sat inert, surrounded by metal carts covered with the full range of surgical implements that he himself had developed: long gleaming surgical microscissors, internal staplers activated by the index finger like a gun, lasers and electrocauteries that sliced through living tissue quicker and cleaner than a scalpel.

On the strength of inventions like these, he had become a millionaire several times over. He was director of Med-Tek and had overseen its construction. His innovations had landed him a place on the board of Endicott, Med-Tek's parent corporation. These particular instruments, however, would never be used by the surgical community. They represented years of work for a different purpose.

In the middle of the room stood three glass and chromium canisters, each large enough for a full-grown man to climb into. They waited like silent sentinels, each warmed to a perfect temperature by heating units and lit by overhead spotlights that revealed their contents. The first tank contained purified water. The second was filled with porcine blood, obtained over time from test specimens.

The third canister was filled with a slightly greenish-yellow solution he had developed over the last five years: hydrocarbon-adjusted fluocil. It was a substance he had first experimented with long before his current prestige and position, but this tank would be the place where ordinary fluocil became something different. It would be his ticket for passage to a new higher level of power and wealth.

Donning a white lab coat and buttoning it over his bulging belly, Nordstrom opened the door to a room containing the animal pens. The pigs and rhesus monkeys were kept in a central location, affording easy access for both research and teaching staff at the complex. With a flick of the light switch, the monkeys began to chatter with their usual manic anxiety. The pigs lay in their cages: sedated sleepy-lidded beasts that seemed inured to their plight.

Nordstrom rolled three specially marked cages into his lab and closed the door behind him, sealing off the din of the monkeys. He hated the sound of their babbling; normally, he would have an assistant fetch his research animals, but he had decided weeks ago that this critical juncture of his research would pass unwitnessed. No one must know of the special preparations these animals had undergone. It was time to begin keeping secrets.

The pigs were now fully awake and started to make slight grunting noises, scared by the glow of the lab and the strange objects. Ignoring their complaints, Nordstrom walked to the fluocil-filled canister and began to make the final preparations: he activated the trio of argon, KTP, and CO_2 lasers set into the base of the tank, creating a swirling mixture of green and orange hues within the murky liquid. The lasers hummed softly in the quiet of the room, their beams diffused in the fluocil.

For a moment, he allowed himself to stare into the tank, transfixed by the colors as they danced across his vision like a will-o'-the-wisp or an underwater aurora borealis. His mind reviewed the adjustments in the organic carbon compounds that were taking place on a submicroscopic level. He was not a religious man, but thoughts of the unthinking molecular play within his tank led him to ask: Is this what God felt like?

The time had come. He walked to a bank of speakers and removed a digital audiotape from his hip pocket. After he placed it in a portable tape deck and activated the machine, the twangy steel of an electric guitar filled the room. The high-pitched instrument was followed by Nordstrom's own voice, warbling a country-western song about stormy nights and rain-slicked roads. I'm a man of many talents, he thought, fussily analyzing the tape's sound quality before returning to the task at hand.

Nordstrom arranged thick nylon straps to the underside of the pigs' cages, hooking them to identical remote-controlled hydraulic lifts. His action took him closer to the third tank, allowing him to take a deep breath of the fluocil. He never got used to the smell: like blood, but less brackish. The lasers created an odor of charged ozone, the crackling sizzle of a primordial stew that this world had never known until now.

The pigs made deep whining complaints when the cages were lifted above the three tanks. Using the simple joystick control, Nordstrom maneuvered the animals over the canisters, then halted. He allowed himself a final look at the instrument panel: temperature, frequency, voltage, radiation levels—all were perfect.

"It's time to make history," Nordstrom said. He looked at the animals. Hours before, he had injected them with substances that had already begun to kill them, eroding their immune defenses and poisoning their blood. They wouldn't survive the night without intervention, he thought.

Before commencing the experiment, there was his audience to consider. He removed a wide-lensed camera from a padded leather satchel and propped it on his computer. Looking through the viewfinder, he noted that the camera angle took in all three tanks with ease. He activated the recorder and plugged a small microphone into the machine's shiny black casing.

"We will begin the demonstration," he said in a hushed, breathy voice, holding the microphone close to his lips. "These animals have been contaminated with pertinent toxins. In order to provide adequate control data, I will submerge one specimen in purified water, one in blood, and the third in my own solution. Please watch carefully.''

He threw a switch on the remote-control panel. Without ceremony, the first pig was dropped into the water. It sank to the bottom and began to bob toward the surface. The top of the tank automatically sealed before the beast could reach fresh air. Within moments, the dumbstruck animal had drowned.

Nordstrom threw a second switch. The pig dropped into the dark red blood, which swirled and bubbled with the impact of the thrashing animal. It had more fight than the first, and it butted against the unyielding side of the tank before the final bubbles of air escaped from its nose. The blinking eye of the video machine recorded the pig's death throes.

He threw the third lever. The bottom of the last cage opened slowly, giving the startled pig a moment to take stock of its predicament. It clumsily tried to stand on either side of the receding steel panels, which stubbornly continued to pull away. Finally the animal had no purchase and fell splashing into the fluocil solution. Nordstrom heard his own voice and guitar erupting from the speakers. It was another song, about lost love and childhood memories. The sound of the music would show up on the tape, Nordstrom thought, but what the hell. There was no need to shut off the microphone. Those people didn't know anything about American music.

Its hooves scratched against the sides of the tank, but the pig swiftly discovered that its thrashing served only to suspend it helplessly in the liquid. As it began to choke, its snout reddened and its eyes opened wide with uncomprehending fear. Bubbles began to appear around the creature's face as the last traces of oxygen disappeared from its lungs and burst on the roiling surface of the fluocil.

Nordstrom leaned over his instrument panel, his glasses reflecting the odd hues within the tank, his mouth set in an expectant grin. The bubbles of air were gone, but the pig's eyes remained open. Both ears on the long head perked up as it continued to bob and float. The human walked to the tank. His gaze met the animal's.

The pig lived and breathed. The poisons in its body could not kill it. He had created perfection.

11:40 P.M., April 1993, Cincinnati.

HOMICIDE DETECTIVE CARL WILLERS RODE THE ANTIQUATED elevator to the basement of the Cincinnati medical examiner's office, cursing under his breath at how quickly the evening had gone to hell. The timing had been perfect: in the middle of an argument with his wife over his late nights on the job and time away from his family—an argument that he knew he was losing, and deserved to lose —the telephone rang. Another person had died.

Only Willers and a few others at the department knew about the Keyhole Killings. When dispatch told him that another victim had been found, he knew the secrecy around the murders couldn't last. The media would soon find out the details of the bizarre cases. Once they did, they would publicize and sensationalize the killings and the whole city would end up in fear, waiting for answers. He would have to admit that he had no leads, no clues, no way of even knowing how the killer worked. His wife was right: The job took too much out of him.

After fourteen years as a policeman—five years in Homicide and nine before that as a beat cop, trying to raise a family and stay alive—Willers prided himself on maintaining a tough professional attitude toward his work.

At times like these, though, his veneer peeled away. He was back in the academy, a puzzled recruit trying to fathom how, and why, a criminal could perpetrate deeds that would never have crossed the imagination of anyone with even a modicum of sanity. He had driven his wife crazy the week before, running out of the bedroom in the middle of the night to check on his newborn daughter. It was hard for him to explain what these murders had done to him, how he woke up in the middle of the night thinking about the mangled bodies that had been washing up on the banks of the Ohio River.

The creaking elevator jolted to a stop, and Willers underwent the routine of donning surgical scrubs and a mask before entering the examination room. He locked his revolver away with his street clothes. There was nothing to fear from the dead, only from those who made them that way.

"Carl, come on in. As you can see, we have the place to ourselves," said Al Belle. The tall older forensic pathologist stood alone in the middle of the darkened room, snapping on a pair of latex surgical gloves.

The main source of illumination was a series of hanging lamps suspended over the stainless-steel examining tables, creating stark cones of light amid the general gloom of the long rectangular room. A set of bleacher seats sat in gray darkness, unoccupied. Belle stood on the periphery of a lamp's range. His slender frame was hidden by his long plastic gown, which gave him a stocky appearance quite different from his street clothes: then he looked every one of his fifty-seven years.

"I hope you waited for me this time, Al," Willers said.

"Seems like every time I get in here, I miss out on the good stuff."

Belle laughed. He knew of Carl's dislike for witnessing autopsies. In fact, there was a grain of truth behind the sarcasm: the toll of the Keyhole Killings was now at five, if the corpse on the table proved to fit the pattern, and Willers had yet to be present for an autopsy on any of the victims. When he was assigned to the case, he put in a standing request to be called in for the next examination.

"This is the first Keyhole victim I've worked on, Carl, but there's been a lot of talk going around. I'm glad I was on call when one of them came in," Belle said, checking the balance on the hanging scale next to the occupied table.

Willers didn't respond, instead bracing himself for what he was about to see: the cutting and peeling back of the skin, the removal and weighing of various internal organs and tissue. His weakness embarrassed him. He had trouble watching the methodical way in which the human body was disassembled by the pathologist like a car in a strip shop.

"I'm working on my own tonight, so let's just go ahead and start. I should have an assistant, but they've cut so damn deep into the budget I almost expect they'll be asking us to reuse gloves and masks. I have to work in this inadequate light to save money, without help, and there's a car accident in the cooler waiting for me after I finish this one. I'll tell you, the bean counters in city hall have no concept of the importance of this department."

Carl ignored Belle's litany of grievances. He had long ago grown used to hearing them from everyone in the examiner's office. Instead of responding, he moved closer to the dead body as Belle pulled back the white sheet that covered it. He immediately focused his attention on the abdomen of the victim, looking for the series of small incisions that characterized these cases.

The corpse was a female Caucasian, approximately twenty-five years old. She was an attractive blonde, young, and worked for a design firm downtown. She was the first victim not to fit the previous pattern: homeless, indigent, hard to identify. This detail chilled Willers: the killer was starting to go after upscale "respectable" victims.

On her belly was a series of small but conspicuous wounds; the five cuts were approximately an inch in length, in an elongated box pattern that reminded Carl of a basketball-play diagram. A longer, deeper incision appeared on the victim's side, just under the ribs.

"Is this what you're used to seeing?" Belle said, searching around on his instrument tray.

"More or less."

"Well, we got pictures when they brought her in, so there's nothing to save for posterity." Belle produced a long-handled scalpel and unceremoniously cut into the patient's chest. With a few confident strokes, he cut a Y-shaped incision that sliced open the flesh from the collarbones to the groin.

"I checked for rigor," Belle said, beginning to peel back the flaps of skin created by the long cut. "It's worked all the way down to the feet. Nysten's Law: Rigor mortis progresses from the head to the feet. This one's been out of action a while."

"So I heard," Willers said. It annoyed him to listen to Belle repeat what he had read in the report from the scene, but he let it pass. Coroners tended to be chatty types: it kept their minds off the unsavory aspects of their job.

"We're both lucky on this one, you know," Belle said, picking up his scalpel again to cut loose a strand of skin he missed with his initial swipe. "This is the first one they didn't fish out of the river. It's a lot harder to find those little marks when the body's been submerged for a while. The flesh tends to just peel away when you touch—"

"Please," Carl said. "Let's just get on with it."

It was an act they had been through before on other murder cases: Belle playing the wizened old medical examiner telling stories about the mortification of the flesh, and Willers playing the queasy cop who tried to hide his disgust.

"Here we go, just like I thought," Belle said. He had pulled back the skin, and the inside of the dead woman's body was exposed to the air. What they saw looked more like a gutted carcass than a typical human anatomy.

"Patient has been partially eviscerated by unknown means," Belle said, speaking monotonously into the microphone hanging near his head. "Visual examination indicates removal of both kidneys, liver, spleen, pancreas, portions of upper and lower intestine. Gross injury to the stomach, partially removed. Let's see . . . uh, trauma to surrounding tissue and arterial structures."

He switched off the recorder. "What I really mean to say is that someone ripped her guts out."

Willers stepped away from the table and walked to the darkened bleachers. He sat down and took a series of long deep breaths as Belle began to cut out and weigh the organs and tissue that remained in the victim's body.

"Queer as a three-dollar bill," Belle said absently. "I heard about it, and now I've seen it for myself. You know, I worked on a case like this once when I was in New York City. I did the remains of a man who was disemboweled with a bread knife by his karate teacher. They had a fight over drug money. Damnedest thing. I could never figure out why the guy didn't just karate chop him or something."

"Al," Willers interrupted, "how do you account for this girl being gutted without being cut wide open?"

"That's the million-dollar question, isn't it, Carl? How, indeed. This wound on her side is large enough to pull the organs out of, but it's not like you could just put your hand in and grab a handful. There's a degree of precision involved in what's been done here."

"Well, what do you think?"

"What do I think? I think we have a sicko out there who knows something we don't." Belle switched on the microphone again. "Heart is intact, statistically normal. No damage to surrounding structures."

"Do a solid report on this one, Al. I have a feeling a lot of people are going to be looking it over."

"What's your profile on the killer?" Belle asked, plugging in a rotating power saw.

"Standard serial killer profile: white male, twenty to fifty years old, above-average intelligence. Possibly no prior record. Maybe a professional health care background. Nothing specific."

Belle nodded and turned on the saw, drowning out the end of Carl's comment. Willers knew that Al's line of questioning on any case was largely academic: like many forensic pathologists, he was interested mainly in the effects of death rather than the motivation or drama that created it. He liked Al Belle but found his profession morbid and strange.

The guard that Carl had passed when he entered the building peeked into the room, holding his hand over his mouth in a concession to the supposed sterility that was to be maintained at all times. He was a young kid that Carl had never seen before, and he waved his hand for Carl to come over. The bleachers creaked as Willers walked across them, stepping over a rail to get to the door.

"Thought you'd want to know," the guard said. "There's about a dozen reporters out there. I guess someone in your department blabbed about the details of the case you have in here, and the press picked up on it. They want to ask you some questions when you get a minute."

Willers sighed deeply. This was exactly what he feared would happen. "Tell them to wait," he said. "The examination isn't finished."

"We got a back door you can sneak out of if you want," the guard said, smiling.

"No, that's all right. Maybe it's time to go public with this."

Carl thanked the kid and walked back to the examining table in time to see Belle remove the young woman's brain, then weigh it on the hanging scale. He averted his eyes.

"The press is here, huh?" Belle asked, his eyes creasing into a frown above his mask. "Just what we need. From what you've told me, it's going to be a pretty short interview."

"Maybe. What's your final cause of death going to be?"

"Are you kidding? Where do you start? Blood loss from surface wounds, wholesale havoc in the visceral cavity. Take your pick."

"One thing, Al. What's the quality of the work?"

Belle was occupied cutting slivers of brain tissue and placing them into small plastic bags, which he fastidiously marked for identification. "What? Quality? What do you mean?"

"I mean does this look like a professional job, or the

work of a psychopath who cooked up a unique way to kill strangers?''

Al put down the bags and pondered for a moment. ''Well, I'd have to say the organs were severed with a surgical-quality instrument, judging from the clean condition of the connecting tissue left behind. I could show you the renal structures in here—''

''No, that's all right. Go on.''

''It seems that the killer had a knowledge of anatomy, and some basic skill at extracting organs. That takes good hands. Of course, a physician would have tried to save the patient, which takes even better hands. By the way, what did toxicology find out on the others?''

''I only have one report back. They say they're backed up until the Fourth of July.''

''Figures. Goddamned budget cuts,'' Belle said bitterly. ''Well, what did they find in the one you got back?''

''No illegal substances, no alcohol. Carbon dioxide and pentathol.''

Al looked up from his scale. ''What? That's an anesthetic combination.''

''I know. Knowing hasn't helped me catch him, though.''

''At least these poor people weren't conscious when it happened. Tell me something, Carl. Are you the only detective working on this case?''

''At the moment.'' In fact, it was highly possible that others would be brought in, especially after the story hit the press. Carl planned to use his seniority and track record as leverage to stay on the case. It would be too injurious to his pride to let it slip away.

''See what I mean, Carl?'' Willers looked at Al quizzically. ''Bean counters. Late test results, understaffed examiner's office, no support for you. And you know why I think it is? Because all of these victims have been the underclass. Homeless, bums. Nobody cares.''

"Well, Al, maybe that'll change. This young lady doesn't fit the profile.''

"Maybe, but I bet it'll take even more. I'll tell you, nobody loves you when you're down and out. They even wrote a song to that effect.''

Carl could feel a speech coming on Belle's second-favorite subject, after the foolishness of the city budget: the inequities of American society. He decided he would rather face a horde of reporters than listen to another harangue.

He stepped out of the room and took the elevator up to the lobby entrance. It was really an old freight elevator: he could see the bare walls of the elevator shaft, and a number of places where they had been spackled and patched. Al had a point: the entire facility was aged and out of date. It made it harder than it should have been to solve homicides and keep the killers off the street.

The reporters waiting for him in the lobby were more polite than usual: they allowed him a second to brush down his short-cropped Afro before snapping pictures and shoving video cameras in his face.

As usual, they all asked him questions at the same time, as if he could discern anything rational out of a cacophony of screaming voices. The guard leaned against a far wall, watching Willers's discomfort with a sardonic grin. To the kid, Carl was downtown brass, the kind rookies love to watch squirm. He had been that way himself once.

"I'll make a short statement and then answer a question or two," Carl said. "It's late, though, and I'm tired. Let's keep it brief.''

"Is there any truth to the rumor that these killings have

been linked to satanic rituals, officer?'' a reporter asked from the rear of the crowd. He was a lanky young man with a beard, wearing a jeans jacket. Ignoring him, Carl composed a statement on the spot.

"We have a body in the examiner's office that was discovered this evening,'' he began. "I have come to believe that it is part of a series of killings, of which there have been five to date. The cause of death has been partial or complete evisceration, through unknown means. That is all."

"Channel Nine News, officer,'' a young red-haired woman said, flanked by a cameraman. "What is the name of the victim you found this evening?"

"Detective, not officer. And we can't release the name until we contact the family."

"Do you have anyone in custody?"

"Not at the moment. At this time, we are in the process of reviewing the evidence before moving forward."

An older man stepped forward. He held a notebook and pen, a marked contrast to the other reporters, who relied on tape recorders.

"Detective,'' he said, "can we get more details on the murder method involved in these cases? What do you imply when you say, 'unknown means'?"

Willers took a deep breath. This was the question that would reveal that he knew nothing. He would look like a fool.

"All the victims show small incision wounds in the abdomen and the side,'' he began, "through which the organs were removed."

Then he had an idea. In the Farm Hill killings back in the seventies, the police had deliberately released misinformation to the media. It ensured that deranged individuals couldn't duplicate the killings or make false confessions. It created a trap; only the police and the killer would be privy to certain information. In some cases, serial killers were angered by the false reports and made fatal errors by contacting the police to correct the public statements. It was a strange aspect of a lot of serial killers, Willers knew: they often took a fiercely grotesque pride in their work.

"We aren't sure how it was done, but it was pretty sloppy," he said. "It was, you might say, the work of an unskilled amateur. We're putting together a profile at the moment that will take a lot of factors into account, including the fact that this individual, in addition to being extremely deranged, is also clumsy and under the impression that he possesses a great deal more medical knowledge than he actually does."

"Detective, you say there have been five killings to date. Why is it that no information has been given to the media?"

"Because we were trying to determine if it was a series. If you didn't report the individual deaths, then that's your problem."

The reporters began to ask more questions, again speaking like a great multiheaded babbling beast, but Carl waved them off and walked out to the parking lot to drive home.

Along the way, he began to wonder what he might have involved himself in. He had finally gone public with this case. The lieutenant might be pissed off, but that would just be too bad. You can't hide behind your public relations department indefinitely. At some point, you always have to face the media and come clean. His years on the force had made that abundantly clear.

Of course, he hadn't come clean. He had lied and even insulted the killer in hopes of flushing him out into the open. The consequences could be deadly: a number of serial killers in the past had latched on to the investigating officers as a sort of flip side of the coin, their diametric opposite. Such relationships, almost symbiotic in nature, had resulted in the killer stalking the detectives and their families. Willers decided to put in for around-the-clock protection of his home when he went in to the station in the morning.

By the time he got home, Claudia and the kids had gone to bed. He knew tomorrow morning would be strained, as they tried to avoid resuming last night's argument. She was right: the job was too demanding, too dangerous. But Carl Willers had worked his entire life to be where he was, and he was proud of his work. Bring on the bastard, he thought. I'll be the one to catch him.

To his surprise, in the months that followed, there were only two more killings. They were further apart in frequency than the previous ones, and they eventually stopped altogether. The murderer never contacted Willers, and when the Keyhole Killings stopped, no helpful evidence had been gathered. As far as he knew, the atrocities would go forever unpunished.

SEPTEMBER

September 1, 1995
Satellite Microwave Transmission—Scrambled and Restricted Code. **<u>Do not transcribe. Commit to memory.</u>**

Executive Office, United States National
Security Council
The White House, by Permission and Acknowledgement
of the President of the United States

To:
All Active Intelligence/Security Operatives
South-Central Asia, Middle East, South America

Operatives report developments signaling potential destabilization in your areas. Attention particularly directed to recent activity in Nation Eleven **(attn: South-Central Asia intelligence).**

Alarming arms buildup in Nation Eleven necessitates status two alert for chemical/nuclear strike against its hostile neighbor to the west. Agents close to regime claim conventional mutual deterrence is threatened by promised delivery of technological X-factor. Is believed technology will inure military and elite class to effects of germ warfare and radiation from nuclear strikes.

Origin of this technological X-factor linked to the United States. Domestic operatives on alert. Technology is offered to nation able to deliver highest cash bid. Nations in regions listed above are involved in the bidding.

President is informed of current alert. He adds that we have delicate situation vis-à-vis previous sale of usable arms/technology to several bidding nations. Continue to gather information. U.S. forces stationed globally prepared for worst-case scenario. Under no circumstances are domestic or foreign civilians or press to be informed of any part of situation.

Transmission complete. Reset receiving and scrambling equipment to standard security settings. Out.

CHAPTER ONE

9:00 A.M., September 2, 1995, Los Angeles.

MARTHA SANCHEZ AWOKE EARLY IN THE MORNING AND, WITH A momentary lurch of fear, found herself in a strange unfamiliar place. Then her memory came back to her: she was in the hospital for treatment of the nagging pain in her lower abdomen. It had come and gone for weeks, finally becoming so severe that her mother had to carry her to the car and rush her from their house in Palms, California, to the hospital.

Her fear was attributable to several causes. First, although her grasp of English was sufficient for her job at the day-care center, it wasn't enough for her to comprehend all of the instructions and requests made of her by the parade of nurses and orderlies. The only bilingual nurse on the ward was harried and overworked and had been available only for brief moments to help her fill out the forms and information sheets. All the medical language and terminology was gibberish to her.

The entire experience had been disorienting and chaotic, and she became more and more frightened of her upcoming surgery. There seemed to be no one she could explain her apprehension to.

Now she lay on a table, covered only by a thin gown, bright lights shining on her from above. She was surrounded by strangers in blue masks and gowns, none of whom seemed to even notice that she was there. She scanned their faces, searching for the shining green eyes of Dr. Donald Page—her surgeon. He had been gentle and understanding when he explained to her that he would have to operate to remove a cyst on her ovary and was receptive when she voiced her special needs and concerns through the interpreter.

The bank of strange machines behind her head beeped and pulsed in a steady rhythm. With a momentary flash of shock, she realized that the noises from the devices perfectly matched the pace and speed of her heartbeat. The door to the operating room opened, and a man walked in dressed like the others: from the green eyes, she recognized Donald Page.

"Do you have the patient under yet?" he said.

The young Asian woman sitting next to her looked up from the notebook in which she had been fastidiously writing. "Ready to go, Donald. Just give the word."

"Since when do I have to give the word, Jennie? Let's get going. I have two hernias after this, for chrissake."

The doctor sneaked a guilty glance at Martha. "Everything will be fine, Ms. Sanchez. Jennie is one of the best in the business. She flew in from the People's Republic just for the occasion." The Asian woman and Dr. Page shared a brief laugh, both looking at Martha as if the levity had been arranged for her benefit.

From what she understood of his words, Martha knew that Donald's joke was meant to make her overlook his blasphemous reference. It was all right, though. She had become used to that kind of thing, especially from the people at work. Page was actually more considerate than most. When she told him that she was a Jehovah's Witness and would have to refuse blood transfusions because of the strictures of her faith, it didn't seem to bother him. In the first place, he said, the procedure is an exploratory laparoscopy with little bleeding involved. In the second, he said, there is fluocil.

She had heard of fluocil before, when Carlos Herrera from her church was operated on for his bad knee. He had received fluocil instead of blood and mentioned it at one of the Wednesday night worship meetings. The chemical blood substitute had been in limited use for transfusions for the last twenty-five years, particularly for Jehovah's Witnesses. Someone had brought an article, which was read aloud to the group, in which fluocil was referred to as a "magic solution."

Dr. Page had tried to dispel that notion. He told her that the substance had come into being after the discovery that some perfluorocarbon compounds had the property to dissolve as much as 40 vol of oxygen per 100 vol of perfluorocarbon, which led to clinical use. She had nodded and smiled, feeling that she was in good hands, even though she didn't understand a word he was saying.

He told her through the interpreter about the safety and effectiveness of the laparoscopic surgery that she would undergo: there would be only small incisions, not a cut through the muscles of her belly, and she would be able to go home in twenty-four hours if everything went well.

Then he started talking about possible side effects of the fluocil—pulmonary complications, oxygen toxicity, adult respiratory distress syndrome—and again he lost her. Besides, she didn't want to hear about the possible harmful implications: she was lying in a hospital bed with a pain in her belly that she had begun to feel even through the pain-killers they had given her. As long as no one else's blood entered her body, she was happy.

Martha saw Dr. Page walk out of the operating room, a little surprised by the way he had snapped at the young woman, Jennie. Still, she trusted him. She tried not to listen to the voice of doubt in her mind, the voice that told her that she would be asleep and they could do anything they wanted to her, even ignore the needs presented by her religious beliefs.

"You're going to go to sleep now," Jennie said, holding an object where Martha couldn't see it. She was doing something to the intravenous tube in Martha's arm. "Don't you worry about a thing. We'll take real good care of you." Jennie leaned over her, looking into her eyes. She heard a roar in her ears as her vision dissolved into darkness.

Within minutes Martha Sanchez's personality and humanity had been converted to a disembodied abdomen, a stripped belly covered with viscous orange jelly. Blue cloth drapery, held in place by metal clips, surrounded the field, obscuring her face and lower body.

The only member of the surgical team who could see Martha's features was Jennie Oh. The anesthesiologist had administered a mixture of chemicals, recorded them in her log, and had begun to read a fashion magazine. She idly monitored the rhythmic beep of Martha's heart and the regular compression of the intubating respirator, which kept the young woman breathing: otherwise, the anesthesia would paralyze her central nervous system, and she would die of oxygen deprivation in minutes.

Donald Page impatiently held his arms before him in

what could have been mistaken for a messianic pose. Nurse Anna Anderson rapidly pulled a gown around his tall frame and fastened it behind him. She received no acknowledgement of her actions and didn't expect any. She took her place near the feet of the patient, reviewing the instruments that she would hand to the surgeons.

"Dr. Kernowicz," Page said in a dry tone. The other doctor, a slight brown-eyed man, nodded neutrally. It was no secret that the two had little affection for each other: Kernowicz was there to assist, a standard return of favor for a series of patient referrals in the past months.

"Veress needle," Page said. He took the long perforator and, after lifting the loose stomach flesh of the thirty-four year-old patient, plunged it through skin, fat, the abdominal wall, and into the cavity underneath. "CO_2," he ordered.

Nurse Anderson turned the dial on the gas line. The abdominal cavity of the patient began to fill, inflating the patient's belly like a balloon. There was nothing for anyone to do but wait patiently while the filling proceeded.

"By the way, Page, we need to wrap this one up as quickly as possible," Kernowicz said. "I'm leaving for a ski trip right after the operation. Got the car packed up and waiting outside, and the wife'll kill me if we leave late. The traffic's going to be hell as it is."

"We'll see what we can do," Donald said, nodding. He knew that the comment was meant to get under his skin, but it was delivered with a faint trace of humor that took into account Donald Page's position as director of laparoscopic surgery at Community Hospital in Culver City. Kernowicz was just a general surgeon and was in the OR for the experience as much as for the money he would make. Precious few surgeons had any extensive experience in laparoscopic surgery. Donald accounted for the faint antagonism he always received from Kernowicz as the product of professional jealousy.

"Six liters, Donald," Anderson said.

The patient's belly was distended to the point needed for the laparoscopy: she looked as if she were seven months pregnant, the skin stretched taut and rising in a mound above the rest of her body. "What's the word on this one, Page?" Kernowicz said.

Donald held a knife an inch above the patient's exposed skin. "Routine ovarian cyst. The work-up gave all indications: there was a small shadow on the X ray. Technically I'm calling it an exploratory, just in case we find something else while we're in there." At the end of his sentence, he cut into the taut skin of the distended belly, a minute one-inch incision that yielded only a small bead of dark blood. "Number-ten trocar."

Within three minutes Donald had cut a series of incisions across the lower abdomen of the patient and pushed trocars—long metal tubes—into the holes. He inserted the microcamera into the trocar just under the navel, which he handed off to Kernowicz, the day's "cameraman." At the end of the minute instrument was a powerful light, which illuminated the interior of the body.

The camera was activated, and an image appeared on twin video monitors placed at the patient's head and feet. The operating team saw the inside of Martha Sanchez's body, magnified twenty times.

"The liver's all right," Donald said. "And there's the gall bladder."

On the screen was the robin's-egg-blue sac of the gall bladder. "Looks healthy as well. Nothing unusual showed up on the upper GI series. Let's turn it around now," Donald said.

Kernowicz rotated the angle of the camera 180 degrees,

revealing the patient's lower abdomen and reproductive structures. Donald worked around the cecum and closely examined the uterus: a hollow pear-shaped structure, partially covered by peritoneum. His actions were reflected in vivid color on the video monitors, on which the surgical team's attention was fixed.

Their hands worked with precision and care, but their gaze was aimed ahead and above them. To an uninformed observer, it would have appeared that they had decided to operate on the patient without looking, instead opting to watch a television program. Below the monitors, on the lower shelves of the large steel cabinets, videotape recorders silently taped the progress of the surgery.

"Left ovary, normal," Donald said absently as Kernowicz moved the camera to examine Martha's ovaries and fallopian tubes. "Right ovary . . . here it is."

There was no answer from the team; they could all see the small cyst attached to the right ovary, which oozed a small quantity of clear yellow fluid. The visibility of the area was still slightly clouded by the angle at which Kernowicz held the camera. Donald mused that Kernowicz shouldn't give up his practice to become a Hollywood cameraman. His skill level was definitely geared toward home movies.

"Just like I thought," Donald said. The surgical team peered at the picture of the cyst on the almond-shaped ovary. "I think we ought to take it out," he said, and looked at Nurse Anderson. "What's your advice?"

The nurse laughed softly at Donald's joke and reached to the instrument table for the miniature scissors and clip that would be used to seal off and remove the cyst. She was interrupted in her search by Donald.

"No, not the scissors. I want to try out an instrument

that Endicott sent me. It's a new laser. I put it to the left side of the table. Power up and bring it to me."

Kernowicz's eyebrows raised over his mask. "Endicott, huh? The big boys been sending you some samples?"

"This is just a trial model they sent me. One of the perks of being chief of endoscopic surgery, I guess." Donald took the opportunity to remind Kernowicz of his position, even though he knew his comment reeked of self-promotion.

But why not? After all, Endicott was a corporate giant in the field and put out a good line of instruments. Whatever Donald's feelings about the high levels of corporate command there—and they ranged from ambivalence to suppressed hatred—he was excited to try out the new laser. It was an improvement on earlier KTP models, which showed a tiny greenish beam on the screen but tended also to create a reddish discoloration that impeded the surgeon's vision.

"Pretty flashy. The man whips out the high-tech equipment. Going Hollywood on us, Page?" Kernowicz said. He had looked away from the monitors to examine the laser that Donald was about to insert through the trocar. It was small and compact, as it had to be, and had the silver high-technology sheen that characterized all Endicott products. Kernowicz silently calculated the probable cost of the instrument, guessing that it was upward of a quarter-million dollars.

Donald first began to dissect the cyst with a small grasper, suctioning fluid away with purified water and a vacuum tube. He then inserted the laser with one hand through an open trocar, holding a clamp with the other hand to secure the cyst and prevent it from spilling into the cavity.

"Did I tell you about this patient?" he said to no one

in particular. "Jehovah's Witness. That's why I brought in the fluocil."

"Fluocil? Now I know you've gone Hollywood," Kernowicz said. "Anyway, we won't need it. We could do twenty of these and not have that kind of blood loss."

As long as you're holding the camera and not anything sharp, Donald thought. He began to work in earnest, aiming the laser at the precise spot where he wanted to sever the cyst from the ovary. He had been waiting for a week to witness the purported efficiency of the laser; the accompanying literature claimed that it had less field-obscuring flash and produced a narrower, better-defined beam.

Even with the benefit of the technology, though, there were many immutable constants to surgery, one of which was the perpetual hazard of injuring surrounding structures. Page took a look at the ovary and the ovarian artery that maintained its blood supply. Any damage to it, or to the utero-ovarian ligament, could result in sterilization of the patient. With an intake of breath, he pushed down on the floor pedal that would activate the beam.

Nothing happened.

Donald held his hand steady and pushed again on the pedal. "What the . . . ," he said, his voice betraying his dismay. The surgical team looked at him warily.

He pointed it at a slightly different angle and pushed again. The beam flashed for an instant, in which he saw that it fired slightly off the mark, almost striking the suspensory ligament that held the ovary in place to the pelvic wall. The field on the video monitor turned dark red as blood from the wound splashed on the camera's microlens.

Donald pulled the malfunctioning laser from the trocar and threw it on the table behind him. He blindly shoved endoclips into the empty tube and tried to apply clamps to the bleeding area. "We have to open. Scalpel, now!"

Jennie Oh threw down her magazine and grabbed her log. "Pressure dropping, doctor. Seventy over forty."

After the trocars had been pulled out, Donald made a long incision into the lower abdomen of Martha Sanchez. A hiss came from her body as the gas rapidly escaped.

"Fifty over thirty," said Jennie.

Donald cursed and reached into the patient's abdominal cavity. Without asking, he was handed clips, which he hurriedly attempted to apply. Nurse Anderson irrigated the area, trying to clear away the still-spurting blood.

The patient would wake later to find that a twenty-four hour hospital stay with minimal scarring had turned into a week in bed, a long convalescence, and extensive scarring across the lower abdomen.

All of this if the laser hadn't cut an artery. If that was the case, Martha Sanchez would never wake up.

Two hours later, Donald sat in his office filling out postoperative reports. He had gone over the time allotted for Martha Sanchez's surgery and was waiting for word from the surgical traffic desk telling him when he could reschedule the first of the two laparoscopic hernia repairs he had intended for the late morning and early afternoon.

He had been able to save Martha Sanchez's life by opening her up and performing traditional surgery, but only after a harrowing rushed effort to stop the bleeding in the abdominal cavity. Damage to the tissue surrounding the ovary had been minimal. Martha would, in all probability, be able to bear children.

When it had finished, and the surgical team knew they had saved the patient, relief turned to puzzled looks all around the room. The unspoken question: What had happened? Where did the fault lie? with Donald Page, or with the prototype instrument he had used?

Donald had personally pulled both of the videotapes from the recorders in the OR, planning on viewing them at home that evening. He would have to figure out what happened before calling Endicott with a complaint; anyway, if he called them now, there was no telling what he might say.

He tried to separate the corporation from the people who worked for it. After all, Endicott had been at the forefront of laparoscopic surgery since its inception. They had invested massive resources in development and training throughout the country and, in fact, the world. Ostensibly, he and Endicott were on the same team.

But he and Kerry Nordstrom weren't. That had become apparent long ago. Nordstrom headed the Med-Tek research facility in Indianapolis, a giant corporate edifice owned by Endicott and dedicated to research and training for laparoscopic surgeons. In his capacity as head of the facility, Nordstrom earned well over three million dollars a year. It was a job that could as easily have gone to Donald.

Donald tossed the reports on the corner of his desk and looked out the window to the packed parking lot below. These were memories that he normally tried to keep at bay, banished to the remotest part of his consciousness. It was irrational, but the trouble with the new laser had brought it all back to him: the feelings of betrayal, the sense that all his work in the past had been for nothing.

He had endured that series of Minnesota winters, the endless testing and the lack of support from his colleagues and from the university surgical department. When was it, he thought—could it have been that many years ago that he and Nordstrom had last worked together?

Kerry was a gifted surgeon, there was no denying it. Without him the work on advanced laparoscopic diagnostic techniques, as well as the initial series of gall bladder and appendix operations, would never have happened. They were a team: they were research scientists as well as doctors, secure in the knowledge that their work would revolutionize surgery as the world knew it, and brought together by a friendship that had endured since medical school. Most of all, they were equals, each stimulated by the other's talent and innovation.

Donald stirred in his chair. Something in the light today, he mused: winter is coming, or at least what they call winter in California. If he tried, he could remember the chill in the Minnesota air on the day when the university convened an international panel of surgeons for a three-day conference.

Kerry and Donald were allotted fifteen minutes to present their research findings. When they got the news of this breakthrough, they toasted each other with champagne and danced on their laboratory table (Donald with a clumsy, knock-kneed jig, Kerry with a grinning, burlesque tap dance). Finally: a chance to make their mark, to reveal to the world that they had taken laparoscopic technology beyond its lowly station as a diagnostic tool.

They agreed that Kerry would deliver the findings. Donald was shy and hesitant of speech, while Nordstrom was a born salesman. Donald sat in the audience and watched his friend up on the stage, dressed in a bow tie and professorial glasses. He delivered the findings of the research series, never once mentioning Donald. The slides projected above the audience attributed the data to "Kerry Nordstrom, et al." The initial splash of that conference began a series of repercussions that changed the face of medicine, like concentric circles moving ever outward from a pebble tossed into a pond.

Weeks later, a network news team came to the hospital and set up in the labs. Though few words had passed about the betrayal at the conference, Donald saw the national coverage as an opportunity to finally receive credit for his work. Then Kerry had taken him aside.

He wore the same glasses and bow tie. "Donald, this is incredible. After all that work, the world is going to know what we did," he began. Donald nodded, trying to straighten his tie, wondering how he would look on television.

"But I was just talking to the producers. In fact, well, I've been talking to them for a week. They say they only want one doctor to speak about our research and, well, that doctor ain't you."

Donald left the hospital at once, walking through the stinging cold along the picturesque banks of the higher Mississippi River. Later, he found that Kerry had been lying to him, and that the producer had been nonplussed at Donald's absence. It was the end of his professional, as well as personal, relationship with Kerry Nordstrom.

Now Donald worked at a small hospital in Los Angeles, performing twenty-five surgeries a week on often uninsured indigent patients. Nordstrom was renowned as the pioneering force behind laparoscopic surgery, which had quickly become big business. Kerry operated very little these days, only for audiences at Med-Tek in carefully promoted showcase surgeries.

There were rumors that Kerry had built a state-of-the-art recording studio in the Med-Tek basement, where he recorded country-western songs in indulgence of a dream that had been with him since his Tennessee childhood.

It was part of his charming persona as far back as his

college days. Even Donald's wife, Liz, had been attracted to Kerry when she was a medical student at Minnesota. Eventually she saw through him and fell in love with Donald. She was the one thing that Kerry hadn't been able to take away from him.

Donald looked at the tiny laser, apparently so harmless. He tossed it on a pile of files atop his desk, trying to assuage his guilt at having used the instrument. It was really unnecessary to have used it at all, but then, he had no idea that he was endangering the patient by doing so.

Adding to his guilt was the fact that the hospital, for some unknown reason, had an inadequate supply of fluocil on hand. Donald had to use human blood to transfuse Martha during the surgery. He had violated her religious beliefs and broken his promise, but it had been necessary to save her life. Donald did not look forward to telling her what had occurred.

He considered calling Liz but knew what her reaction would be. Liz hated what Nordstrom had done and, by association, was caustically skeptical of the entire field of laparoscopic surgery. This kind of news would only confirm her prejudices. Besides, it wasn't as if he found her all that sympathetic about anything lately. Their relationship had grown strained, and he wasn't sure that they thought of each other first when they had problems.

Liz, also a surgeon, was somewhere in the hospital. Her practice was in the east wing of the building, not far from his office. He would have liked to go to her, but the distance between them was more than could be bridged in a five-minute walk. Donald watched the parade of cars in the parking lot below, trying to determine if what he felt was anger or sorrow. At times it was hard for him to tell the difference.

CHAPTER TWO

6:05 A.M., September 3, Los Angeles.

LIZ DANNY DRESSED FOR WORK, AS SHE DID EVERY MORNING, IN front of a full-length mirror that she and Donald had bought years ago in Koreatown. At the time, she had been attracted to the ornate wood carvings that ran along its frame; now she was grateful for the slightly warped and distorted glass within it. She didn't feel particularly attractive this morning, and she hadn't in some time.

She took a step back and pressed down the pleats of her skirt. Her eyes were ringed from lack of sleep, her long black hair was flat and lifeless in its utilitarian barrette. Even her tall slim frame didn't look right until she remembered to straighten her posture. God, she thought, I look like a first-year resident: frazzled, plain, just getting by. I thought private practice would make me come alive again.

But she knew there was more to it than that. A lot of the problem was Donald. The man she married—the tall considerate charmer who was engaged in groundbreaking research while she struggled through her internship and residency in Minneapolis—hadn't shown his face in their

Santa Monica household in quite a while. They had wakened together and made love that morning, both coming to awareness before the alarm began its insistent buzz. He was still a good lover, but the experience lately had become bittersweet; it seemed that only in bed could they communicate without complication or unspoken recrimination.

Her parents had told her that their age difference would be a problem; if not when they married, then later, as Donald grew older. Her father, who had died four years ago, had been very adamant about his disapproval, saying that she was squandering her youth on an older man. Now Donald was forty-two and she was twenty-eight. Their differences had grown more distinct with the passing of time, to the point where she had to struggle to remember what they had in common.

It didn't help that her professional reputation was growing so quickly. As a general surgeon, she had attracted the notice of her older and more established colleagues, who told her she had "good hands" and limitless potential. At first she took these compliments as the by-product of old-fashioned, condescending medical sexism —for medicine certainly was still a boy's club—but recently she had grown in confidence and accepted the attention with grace, truly believing that she was deserving.

And as her star rose, Donald's fell. The bright young surgeon, full of life and belief in new surgical techniques and technology, who would proselytize to anyone within earshot about the virtues and advantages of laparoscopy and how it would forever alter the future of medicine, had turned tired and distant. It was no mystery when his downturn had begun: in the years after he started his practice, when his work turned routine and dull, at the same time that Kerry Nordstrom became a millionaire. It had defeated Donald and taken something out of him, something that hadn't returned.

But it wasn't as if she didn't try to help him. She urged him to step forward and take his deserved share of the credit, offering to bear witness to the medical boards about Nordstrom's misrepresentations. After they moved to Los Angeles, she even offered to take time off from her own fledgling practice to help Donald receive the credit and prestige that was coming to him. Donald merely said that he hadn't gone into medicine for politics and fame and that he would continue on his own as best he could. At that moment, it felt like a door had closed between them.

Liz could hear the burps and gurgles of the coffee machine downstairs. Always an early riser, Donald had already performed his morning rituals and was in the kitchen setting out the cereal boxes and toast that constituted their breakfast. It was often the only meal they ate together; it seemed that one or the other always had some pressing commitment to fulfill in the evenings. For a time, she had thought Donald was having an affair, but his lackluster approach to his work and his life made it a slim possibility. She intuitively knew that she couldn't attribute his lack of interest in their shared life to a dalliance with another woman.

She took a last look at the mirror, trying to be kinder to herself. The dancer's body she had attained through the University Jazz Ensemble was still hers, though her lithe figure was something she had learned to downplay as long ago as medical school. It was easier to get through her education and career without the omnipresent stares and whispered comments of her colleagues.

One thing she had discovered early in her career was that her male colleagues lacked a certain maturity and development in their attitudes toward women. When they weren't feeling threatened by an attractive woman, they were trying to get her into bed.

Donald's maturity had been a very attractive trait when they met. Then as now, Liz had looked younger than her years. Even though she was approaching thirty, she was often asked for identification when ordering a drink. She tried to figure out what it was that made her look young: the small, upturned nose, or the optimistic energy in her face and movements? Whatever it was, she hoped it wasn't waning. She had problems, but she wasn't ready to be helped across the street by Boy Scouts. Not yet.

Downstairs, Liz found Donald spreading cream cheese on a slice of toast, peering uninterestedly at the headlines of the *Los Angeles Times*. She decided to skip the cereal that morning, pouring herself a large cup of coffee.

"You were home late last night," Donald said.

"I had coffee with Ronnie. We were catching up." Veronica Wilson was an old friend of Liz's, a psychologist she had known since she moved to Los Angeles. They had spent much of last evening talking about Donald, in between Ronnie's laments about single life.

Donald grunted in acknowledgment. "It was a rough day yesterday," he said after placing a slice of bread in the toaster. "I had an equipment malfunction." He told Liz about the faulty laser and the emergency open surgery he had had to perform.

"I can't believe it," Liz said. "Has that ever happened before?"

"Never," Donald said. "I have never had a laser misfire—or refuse to fire, for that matter. The worst part is that it wasn't absolutely necessary for me to use the laser. I could have used a more tried and true model, or just scissors and electrocautery. I wanted to try out the new laser because the literature said it had a more concise beam.''

Liz stared out the breakfast nook's bay windows at the garden outside. She had taken up gardening as therapy after the death of her father, planting colorful rows of dahlias and tulips in the back yard. Several vases of fresh flowers served to brighten the dim kitchen, but the morning was still gloomy. The sun was obscured by morning fog, and there was an unseasonal chill in the air.

"It just confirms what I've always thought," she said. "There's too much margin for error. At least you had the traditional techniques to fall back on. It doesn't surprise me that a company like Endicott would rush faulty product out to doctors. Anyone who would employ a shark like Nordstrom is capable of anything.''

Donald was silent, his eyes turned down to examine the headlines of the sports section. With his gaze averted, Liz had the opportunity to take a good look at him. What she saw was worrisome: horizontal creases lined his broad forehead. His cheeks were sallow, and he had more gray hair than before. She felt that they were slipping into an argument that they had gone through many times before.

"I don't really blame Endicott," Donald said. "They put out a good line of product. It could have been a manufacturing problem, or it could have been damaged in shipping.''

"You always insist on defending Endicott," Liz said, exasperated. "I'll never understand it. It's as if you just want to passively accept whatever happens to you. How can you act like nothing ever happened? You deserve to be the one running Med-Tek, and if you were, I'll bet there wouldn't be the kind of slipups you experienced yesterday. Nordstrom has no morals, no professional ethics.

God, he's barely even a surgeon anymore! He just a businessman!''

She was shocked to realize that her hands were trembling with anger; some of her coffee had spilled out on the treated wood of their breakfast table. Wiping it off with a towel, she almost wished she had said nothing. After all, she was just repeating what she had said a million times before.

"You'd better have something to eat," Donald said. "You shouldn't drink coffee on an empty stomach. You'll burn a hole in it."

Liz shot Donald a dirtier look than she had intended, but she took his advice and pulled a box of bran cereal from the cabinet. The heavy mood in the room was broken for a moment by the arrival of Daisy, their Irish setter, who had characteristically slept later than her owners that morning. She entered the room, tail wagging, and immediately found the dish of food that Donald had set out for her.

Behind Liz, Donald had pulled his briefcase from the floor under the table and was rustling around amidst its contents.

"I know this isn't the best time to bring this up, particularly after this conversation," he said. "But I wanted to show you this. I think we should seriously consider the offer."

Donald shoved a glossy pamphlet across the table. It bore the sleek Endicott logo. The futuristic lettering across the front of the flier touted an extensive laparoscopic training seminar to be held in Indianapolis at Med-Tek, under the auspices of Endicott and supervised by Kerry Nordstrom. Taped at the bottom was a handwritten note on thick high-grade stationery. It said: "Please come and see the latest developments. It would be good to catch up. Bring Liz and maybe we'll show her the light. K. Nordstrom.''

With a snort of derision, Liz waved the pamphlet in the air. ''The gall of this man. As if we would have anything to do with him. And for his information, I do not need to see the damned light. I'm proud to be a traditional surgeon.''

''Come on, Danny,'' Donald said. He always called her by her last name when he was becoming impatient. It served as a reminder of his irritation when she had announced, shortly before their marriage, that she intended to keep her maiden name.

''I don't care if Genghis Khan is running the program, I think we should go,'' he said. ''Read it. They're going to be giving training and demonstrations on advanced techniques like vagotomy, splenectomy, hernia repair. I owe it to my patients to attend. And you need to go to get more training than the little bit you've had at the hospital. You can't continue to avoid an entire range of treatment just because you have a grudge against Kerry Nordstrom.''

Liz had to admit that the program for the training sessions was advanced and exciting. She chewed on her cereal as she read. Hundreds of their peers from around the world would be there, learning new techniques in a highly competitive field. She owed it to her patients, as well as to herself, to stay abreast of the latest surgical advances, even if she opted not to use them.

Then her memory filled with Nordstrom's betrayal. She seethed at the images of his stealing credit for the initial research and rigging the network news story. ''What I don't understand,'' she said, looking up. ''is why you don't have a grudge against him.''

''Oh, I do, Danny. Believe me, I do.''

She had to take a moment to allow her anger to fade

away. Donald was staring at her with a sad petulant expression, one that allowed her, for an instant, to share in the anger and frustration that he had denied feeling for the past several years. Then the look was gone. He picked up the newspaper again.

"I guess I could use more hands-on experience. You know that I've used laparoscopy as a diagnostic tool in some cases, so it's not like I'm completely opposed to the possibilities. I just feel that . . ."

"I know, I know," he said. " You think it's gimmicky and expensive. You want to wait for more clinical trials. You think 'real men make big incisions,' right? It's not an operation unless you cut the patient wide open?"

An edge of bitterness crept into his voice. Liz knew that these comments were the ones that Donald had had to endure when he was doing the first basic research into laparoscopic surgery. He had faced a lot of tacit and explicit opposition from other surgeons, particularly the older traditionalists. Many of these criticisms persisted, and she had to admit, she agreed with many of them.

"All right, Donald. I'll go. I just wish you would have shown this to me sooner. It's coming up in a little over a week. I'll need some time to find someone to cover my patients."

"Sorry," Donald said with sincerity. "I've been putting off talking to you about it. I thought we'd just get into an argument."

Liz sighed heavily. She didn't know what bothered her more: Donald's assumption that they would be incapable of talking over the situation rationally, or the fact that he was right.

* * *

Liz left for the hospital, dreading the usual hassle of her brief morning commute on the Los Angeles freeways. When her drive had taken her some distance inland, the fog cleared and the morning haze over the city began to collect above the rooftops, obscuring the high mountains in the distance.

The drive from Santa Monica to Culver City took her from a sphere of relative affluence to one with mixed levels of prosperity. Like much of Los Angeles, the neighborhoods suffering from poverty and crime were harder to spot than in the eastern United States; here the problems lay under the surface, beneath the sheen of palm trees and the rows of medium-size homes with distinct individual yards.

She had come to love her surgical practice at the hospital in the short time since she opened it. Many of her patients lacked insurance or had neglected their health until they reached a critical point, but she was glad to be in a position to effect some real change in their lives. It made her feel that the long struggle through medical school had been for a purpose.

Pulling in to the parking lot, waving at the guard in the kiosk, she thought again about Donald. He had once had more ambition than Liz. He had wanted to be a great surgeon, a pioneer. He had had confidence in his destiny.

Now he relied on his wife for many of the surgical referrals that kept his practice in business. His position as head of laparoscopy was an administrative bow to his experience, but his reputation had suffered over the years from his lackluster attitude. She realized, with painful irony, that Donald might find himself with a severely shortened workday if she began performing laparoscopic surgery.

* * *

Donald watched Liz's Honda pull out onto their quiet residential street and round the corner in the direction of the freeway. When he was sure that she was gone, he put down his coffee cup and walked up the stairs of their comfortable home. He stood in the doorway of their bedroom for a moment, then turned on his heels and strode into his study, locking the door behind him.

After walking to the tall windows and closing the curtains, Donald took a small key from a ring in his pocket and opened the lower drawer of his desk. He cleared away a large pile of aged papers and medical journals and stacked them on the floor at his feet, then pulled a small red leather shaving kit from the very bottom of the drawer.

From the bag he produced a small glass vial with a label marking it the property of Community Hospital. He ripped the thin plastic wrapper off a disposable syringe and laid it on the desk next to the vial. Quickly, with experienced hands, he tied a piece of rubber tubing just above the elbow of his right arm and repeatedly clenched and unclenched his fist.

A small drop of blood from his vein entered the syringe before he depressed the plunger and, with a great sigh, removed the length of tubing from his arm. Then Donald sat in the dark quiet of his office, listening to the distant hum of a lawnmower engine somewhere outside. He distantly recalled that he didn't have to perform surgery until noon that day. Five and a half hours.

CHAPTER THREE

4:15 P.M., September 8, Malibu, California.

LIZ LEANED BACK IN THE ROCKY ALCOVE AND TOOK IT ALL IN: THE high cliffs behind her, the sparse crowd of relaxed sunbathers, the beach volleyball teams, the gentle swell of the emerald ocean as it crashed to the pristine sand. She closed her eyes and tilted her face to the sun, a breeze billowing through her oversize T-shirt.

"Oh, God. I think I left the keys in the car."

She opened her eyes, using one hand as a visor against the sunshine, and watched her husband fishing vigorously through the pockets of his baggy khakis, a panicked expression on his face.

"Donald, I'm sure you didn't. Anyway, I don't even remember if I locked my door or not. I'm sure we can get back in."

He towered over her, his exasperation growing. "For chrissake, you left the car unlocked? You saw the characters hanging around that lot. They're probably halfway to Oxnard in our car by now."

As he shuffled back and forth, comically checking the flap pockets of his safari shirt, his form passed back and

forth in front of the sun. Liz alternately squinted and relaxed at this alternating barrage of glare. Finally his face
went agog, and he produced the keys from a rarely used
shoulder pocket.

"What are you laughing at?" he asked, sitting down
next to her heavily. "It's not like people don't steal cars,
you know."

"I'm not laughing at you," she replied, rubbing her
mouth, trying not to reflect the hilarity she felt bubbling
up from within her. "I'm glad you found them, honey."

Donald sighed, adjusting his sunglasses and dragging
the heavy wicker picnic basket toward him. "Remember
when we first moved here? This beach wasn't half as
crowded." He peered disdainfully at the shore, at the
young people on beach blankets and a small pick-up football game that was rapidly deteriorating into a water fight.

"Come on, honey. We came out here to relax. Remember?"

"I know, I know. I'm trying. It's just there's always
something to worry about." He opened the basket and
began looking inside, ignoring the sandwiches and the
plastic container of cheese and pulling out the bottle of
wine he had stopped to buy in Santa Monica.

A cloud passed before the sun, and Liz shut her eyes,
feeling the momentary coolness like a palpable relaxing
hand. This day jaunt up the coast had been her idea, one
that Donald had only reluctantly agreed to. For most of
the way up, he had been game and cheerful, even upbeat
about the difficult parking and the frightening jog across
Pacific Coast Highway they had had to endure to get to
this beach. Now she felt him growing tense, distant, and
felt a quick urge to bring him close again.

"Give me a kiss, Donald."

He had the corkscrew halfway twisted into the bottle

and looked up with surprise. Staring searchingly into her eyes for a moment, as if looking for an understanding of her that he had forgotten he even desired, his expression softened. He took off his sunglasses, leaned forward, and kissed her tenderly. When he returned to the wine, he wore an embarrassed smile.

"What is it?" she asked, leaning back again.

"I don't know." He pulled the cork from the bottle with a grunt. "I felt strange for a second there, like someone might be watching us. Not in a bad way, you know, but like a kid. Like someone might tell my parents."

Liz laughed, sensing his good mood returning. "Well, you know my mother approves of you."

"And I approve of her, even though I'm old enough to be her kid brother." He poured out some wine into a plastic cup, securing it in the sand against the rising breeze. "Hey, you want some of this?"

"Sure. Anyway, you're also young enough that I could be your kid sister. I've known families that have had kids twenty years apart."

A young man, muscular and shirtless, suddenly streaked from the pack of players, a football held aloft in his hand. A couple of defenders tried in vain to tackle him before he reached an invisible goal line, but he easily avoided them, laughing and slamming the ball to the sand. His path led him close to Liz and Donald, and as he circled around to rejoin his friends, he passed a boldly appraising look at Liz before sprinting away.

"He's a good runner," Donald said, sipping the wine. "I'd be lying if I said I didn't wish I was his age. Look at him. His world is all sports and good times. I don't think I was ever like that."

Liz looked away, at the long winding path of the shore as it snaked toward the city. She wasn't sure how to handle Donald, whether to keep up an effort to buoy his spirits and try to enjoy an uncomplicated afternoon with him, or to really talk to him about his obviously troubled state of mind. There was some quality in his voice, however downcast, that suggested that he might be willing to open up to her.

"You always had qualities to compensate," she said quietly, her gaze still following the damp sand where ocean met land, the rhythmic wash of the waves like some primal pulse.

Donald was already on his second glass of wine. "I guess you must know that I'm a little apprehensive about going to Indianapolis next week." He picked up a rock and threw it into a patch of seaweed.

"I know. But the experience will be good for both of us. Community Hospital hasn't exactly been generous about sponsoring research seminars for the surgeons."

Donald nodded, still staring at the football game. "I think they don't want to waste the money. And they're probably right; I may well already be on the downslope of my career."

Liz stood up and looked down at her husband. He seemed so small, so vulnerable. "Now you're just feeling sorry for yourself. Come on, let's walk."

She offered him a hand, which he accepted hesitantly, stopping to refill his wine for the stroll. They walked to a relatively secluded section of beach, where the waves were taller and the forms of surfers rode the crests and breaks of the sea.

"I'm *not* feeling sorry for myself, incidentally," Donald said, taking Liz's hand. "I'm just being realistic. Community Hospital has the funding for noninvasive technology, but my department could easily become a liability in a budget crunch. And if the hospital is bought out, they would want to bring someone in with flashier credentials.''

Liz felt the warm pressure of her husband's hand, vainly seeking the reassurance and reliability that had been there in the past. Instead she felt nothing, as if there were a cold blackness next to her instead of the man she had loved for years. She blinked her eyes against the wind, trying to drive the feeling away.

"Kerry is bothering you, isn't he?'' she asked with as little import in her intonation as she could manage. ''You haven't even seen him yet and he's already getting to you.''

"I guess so,'' Donald said dryly. ''One part of me wants to see him so I can punch him in the stomach or something. But then there's another part that's sort of looking forward to seeing him.''

They stopped walking. Donald turned to face the ocean, the color deepening as it extended to the distant horizon. His hands deep in his pockets, Donald slouched and was silent.

"Looking forward to it? What do you mean? Kerry Nordstrom is as close to a purely bad man as anyone I've ever known. He's completely without a conscience, without—''

"I know that,'' Donald said impatiently. ''It's just that —remember when it was the three of us together, when we were all friends? Those were good times, Liz. Some of the best of my life.''

Liz dragged her foot through the sand, looking away from Donald. There was something too painful in his tone, an admission that went beyond nostalgia to a profound sense of sadness for the present. She wondered if there was really anything she could do for him.

"They were good times," she agreed quietly. "When I met you and Kerry I was pretty socially retarded."

Donald laughed eagerly. "That's not true. You were just young, that's all. And, God, the two of us taking you into our little clique of two. We were both competing for you, you know."

Liz looked around, ignoring Donald's comment. The only other people within a hundred yards were two young surfers knocking the sand from their wetsuits.

"We were all young enough for life to be easier. Simpler," she said.

"Remember the time Kerry sat on that morphine injection?" Donald asked, his features suddenly animated with humor. "Were you there?"

"No, I was in class or something. But you guys told me about it."

"God, it was the funniest thing. It was almost summer, I remember that. We always complained about the winters in Minneapolis, but the summers were just as bad."

"I remember. The mosquitoes and the humidity were awful," Liz said gamely. She felt a warmth from him that she somehow wanted to sustain. It was as if, in talking about his youth, he had recaptured some vital element of it.

"Yeah. Anyway, Kerry and I were both on call in the ER. This was even before we started the laparoscopic trials. We had this really nasty wound coming in by ambulance, so Kerry of course rushes out to take the case. I remember now: it was a guy who worked at the docks, and a gas stove had blown up in his face."

Liz tried to picture both men in their prime: Donald, with his bushy hair and guileless eyes, earnest and serious and forever talking about doctors repaying the trust granted them by society; and Kerry, the country boy set loose in the city, full of rough humor and always pushing those around him with his manic energy. Kerry had been good-looking then, athletic and vital. When she had met them, it was on his gaze that her eyes lingered.

"The patient was really in a lot of pain, and he was fighting us, so Kerry had me fetch morphine to calm the guy down. We were both in a state. There was blood everywhere, and we weren't used to that kind of thing yet. So I give Kerry the hypo, and he has to set it down in the ambulance while he tries to hold the patient down, trying to get him to sit still. Kerry took a step back, tripped and"—Donald made a wet piercing sound—"right in the ass. Enough morphine to zonk him completely for a couple of hours."

Donald finished his wine with a gulp. "And when he was going under, right there in the ambulance, he looks at me and says, 'Page, they got me. Carry on, soldier.' "

Liz began to laugh softly. "I remember one time when I was in the ER with Kerry. I told you about it—the man with the concussion, the broken arm, and the injured penis."

Donald nodded at the memory, a smile playing on his face. "Right, he had just gotten out of the shower and was giving his cat a bowl of milk. It got so excited it jumped up, and gave a love bite to the first thing it saw."

"Its owner's penis," Liz said, giggling. "And because he was kneeling under the kitchen sink at the time, he banged into it and gave himself a concussion. I still remember Kerry trying to keep a straight face when he asked him how he got the broken arm. The poor man told the ambulance orderlies what had happened to him when they got to his apartment, and they laughed so hard they dropped him and broke his ulna."

By now they were laughing together. "And Kerry said

to the patient, 'Well, it could have been worse. You could have had a Great Dane instead of a little kitty cat.' " Liz felt her laughter fading at her last mention of Kerry, as if a cloud had passed over her thoughts.

They began to walk back toward the alcove and their picnic basket. The afternoon had passed into a time of long, lengthening shadows. During their walk, many of the sunbathers had packed up and left. Liz shuddered with a surprising chill, trying not to allow herself to feel the passing of the day as a loss, as symbolic of anything. She was failing.

"Kerry had a good sense of humor," she finally said, after they had walked in silence for a while.

"That he did," Donald said, He pondered for a moment. "He was practically a member of my family for a time, you know. He never wanted to go back to Tennessee for the holidays, so he would come stay with us. We'd get drunk by the fire and pledge eternal friendship. College stuff, I guess."

They reached their basket. Donald looked inquiringly toward the parking lot, but Liz motioned for him to sit down.

"Donald," she said, "I don't know why Kerry betrayed you. I really don't. I've thought about it for years and I still don't have any answers."

He peered at the wine, draining the remainder of the bottle into his cup. "Me either," he said after a pause. "I guess he changed. Simple as that. Turned into someone I didn't know anymore."

Liz leaned against the familiar rock, somehow comforted by its touch. She sensed the conversation turning to a realm that she didn't want to discuss, but she felt helpless to prevent it.

"You know, I always thought that my relationship with

you had something to do with it, if you want to know the truth," Donald said.

The words hung in the air for a moment. Amazing, she thought, that we've never talked about this. Years later, and it's still an untouched subject. Liz turned to look at her husband. He was red from the sun, his fair skin already turning rough crimson. If she peeled away the wrinkles, the growing gauntness, the darkness in the eyes, there he was—the man she had chosen over Kerry Nordstrom. The man she had fallen in love with.

"Really," he said, as if she had disagreed. "I think it disturbed him that you left him for me. I think that's when our friendship fell apart."

She wanted to fight against him, to say that it wasn't fair to put her in the position of wrecking a friendship, to insinuate that they had merely played out a common script. But she saw there was no accusation in his eyes, just a tired acceptance.

"Maybe," she said. "I don't really know." But she knew he was right. Kerry would have enriched himself at anyone's expense eventually, she was sure of it. But the decision to betray Donald had been too bold, too callous. Too personal.

"How long were you and Kerry seeing each other?" A strange unfamiliar malice lurked beneath his words, as if he were allowing himself the luxury of indulging a jealousy he had never mentioned.

"A couple of months. Until I got to know you better. Remember, we were all friends for quite a while before anything happened."

"And what did happen, Liz?" Donald looked into her eyes with a quiet determination. "I mean . . ."

"I know what you mean, damn it." She pushed against

the rock so that she sat erect. "You know we were lovers. But I chose you. I'm your wife. What purpose—"

Donald suddenly reached out and grasped her hand. He leaned forward and gently kissed it. "I'm so sorry," he said.

"It's all right."

"Of course it isn't." He reached up and stroked her hair, his eyes alive with emotion. "I remember those days like they were yesterday. The three of us roaming around town, supporting each other through our studies. And Kerry was handsome, I know, and witty. I was so jealous of him. I guess I still am."

This frank admission stunned Liz for a moment with its obviousness, and its sadness. She tried to smile at her husband. "I chose you because you were a good man, Donald. And you still are. I was just a kid then, but I saw the difference between you and Kerry. A blind woman could."

Donald gripped Liz's hand tighter. "I'm really not looking forward to seeing him," he said, his voice strained and urgent. "Maybe I can forgive him for what he did to me. I don't know. Most of the time I don't even care anymore. But Kerry's worse than—he just doesn't *care*. About anything. The things that he—"

"What do you mean?" She reached out and took his hand in hers, caressing his open palm, trying to calm him. She realized with a lurch that he was on the verge of tears. "I don't want to defend him, but even he has limits."

Donald nodded. "I know. He was always terrified of physical violence and anger. But there are other ways to harm people."

"Donald, what the hell are you talking about?"

"Nothing," he said, obviously trying to compose himself by drawing into some deep familiar place that was his alone.

They sat in silence. Liz tried to look into her husband's eyes, to somehow find the thing within him that had made him tired, so fearful and full of regret. She suddenly hated that thing and wanted to destroy it forever.

"I do know this," he said. "That I was the lucky one. All of Kerry's money and fame can't compare to the pleasure you've given me."

The surf crashed beyond them, the sun beginning to tilt downward into night. Liz felt the moment as if she had lived it before, and she wished she didn't have to leave it. The comfort, the love that she had known, had returned. Now she feared it would flee as quickly as it had reappeared.

"We had good times back then," he said. "And we've had some good times since. Haven't we?"

"We've had good times, Donald."

He nodded in satisfaction, and she felt alone again. Why, she suddenly wondered, was there such finality in his voice?

"Donald, I—"

But he put his finger on her lips, replacing them with his own in a kiss full of tenderness and affection, the kind of kiss that used to transport her to an abstract place full of wholeness and purity. A place full of Donald Page and his good heart.

Then he picked up the basket.

"It's getting late. We should get home and check our machine. I told the staff to call me if there were any complications from surgery last night." He spoke apologetically, hesitantly. She could see that he was awash in emotion that he didn't know how to deal with.

Liz nodded, putting on her sweater. They walked up the

hill to the parking lot and drove home in silence through the beach traffic of Pacific Coast Highway. Among the messages on their machine was a confirmation of their reservations for the Med-Tek seminar in Indianapolis on September 13.

CHAPTER FOUR

IT WAS EARLY FALL, ACCORDING TO THE CALENDAR, BUT WHEN Donald and Liz stepped out the airport door into the Indianapolis chill, their southern California–acclimated bodies shivered in the gloomy morning as if it were darkest winter. A light mist fell from the dark oppressive sky. Most of the airport travelers walked at a relaxed, comfortable pace, their coats unbuttoned like vacationers in a more balmy climate.

Nordstrom had promised to extend the Endicott "red carpet" treatment to Donald and Liz, and the first sign was quickly visible: a long black tinted-window car waited for them in the taxi line. The driver, dressed in a blue jacket bearing the Endicott insignia, stood holding a stenciled sign that read: "Drs. Page and Danny." When they walked to the car, he said to Donald, "Are you Dr. Page or Dr. Danny, sir?"

Donald indicated his surname, and the driver loaded their baggage into the trunk. He helped Liz and Donald into the backseat, then resumed his vigil on the curb. Liz allowed him to stand in the drizzle for a few minutes, watching it intensify into a steady rain. She stuck her head out the window.

"Waiting for me?" she asked. The driver looked puzzled. "I'm Dr. Danny," she said, becoming a little cross.

Following an awkward series of apologies, the driver pulled out to the interstate and merged with the light Indianapolis traffic. Liz smiled at Donald mischievously, recalling the misunderstanding with the driver. He responded only with a tired grin before turning to stare blankly at the road ahead.

The flat open spaces of the city were a stark counterpart to the dense sprawl of Los Angeles. Instead of going to the center of town, the driver took them out into the undeveloped countryside, along the loop of freeway that enclosed the city. Fields and farms dotted the landscape, along with a series of green, well-tended industrial parks.

"There it is," Donald said, staring out the window. "Med-Tek."

Looming ahead was the huge complex, a low-slung warren of pristine white buildings linked by elevated walkways and covered sidewalks. The lawn was green and flawless, and manicured trees and hedges lined the grounds. It gave the impression of being an ivory city, perched on hundreds of acres of land, surrounded on all sides by chain-link fence and high guard towers. The overall imposing quality of the place was enhanced by the dark, foreboding sky. The institutional white of the buildings and the gray water in the long trench dug around the outer fence made it look like a modern, high-technology version of a medieval castle.

"It's astounding," Liz said as they drove through the gate toward the central structures. Donald barely responded, lost in thought. She wondered about him; he acted almost irritated with her, though that probably wasn't the case. She knew that his feelings upon entering the main center of laparoscopic study, and as a visitor, must be complex and bitter.

The driver pulled to a halt in front of high gleaming glass doors. "I'll take your bags ahead to the hotel," he said, his face impassive behind mirrored sunglasses. "Since you arrived a few hours late, I have instructions to bring you directly here." He walked to the door and waved a key card in front of an electronic eye. The doors sprang open with a hydraulic hiss, and they entered.

The reception area was staffed by a half-dozen attractive young women. They warmly greeted Liz and Donald and issued them glossy name tags, warning them that identification would have to be worn at all times. Donald was immediately dispatched to the south wing of the complex for the advanced seminars.

He gave Liz a peck on the cheek. "Stay out of trouble," he said. The flight seemed to have taken a lot out of him: his eyes were blurry and unfocused, his hair hung limp over his forehead. Liz thought for an instant that he looked older than his years, like a man who had grown world-weary. Without another word, he turned and was ushered by a guard through a set of doors. They automatically closed behind him, and she watched his form recede into the distance.

Liz waited for the attendant who would take her to the labs for the beginners' session. The place made her uncomfortable: as soon as she registered, the women ceased to take notice of her, resuming their paperwork behind the long light-colored desk.

A sterile atmosphere prevailed. The floors were carpeted in neutral beige, the walls were a starkly pristine white. The windows and doors were all gleaming glass, ringed with steel and equipped with what seemed to be motion detectors in addition to the electronic opening devices. Above her head, suspended by a lattice of wires, she spotted the impassive eye of a camera. A red light on its casing blinked monotonously, watching her.

"There you are," a voice said behind her. Liz turned to see a short mustached man holding a clipboard. "Sorry to keep you waiting, Dr. Danny. I was paged from the sessions. My name is Greg Harris."

Harris walked Liz through a set of doors with an experienced swipe of his security pass, then took her down a long featureless hallway. "The security here is amazing," she said.

"It's because of the research and the production lines," he responded brightly, picking up his pace. "And of course, the animal rights activists have taken issue with the use of porcine samples in our labs. There have even been death threats against Dr. Nordstrom."

Though Liz had a height advantage of at least five inches on Greg, his rapid steps made him hard to keep up with. Finally, he led her to a door marked "Women's Lockers" and pointed out the labs at the end of the hall. He wished her luck and headed off, his heels clacking against the tile floor as he bustled away.

She dressed in the unoccupied locker room, wondering if a hidden camera somewhere watched her undress. Quickly, she donned thin paperlike scrub clothes, tucking her hair under a cap and covering her shoes with paper booties.

A feeling of vague anxiety came over her, and she paused for a moment to sit on a bench. The sterility and high security of the place had done little to make her feel comfortable, and now she faced the research lab. She felt like she had in medical school when she had been late for class: butterflies in her stomach, tension in her shoulders.

Like the other surgeons in the session, her experience with laparoscopy was limited. Some came eagerly to learn; others, like Liz, came reluctantly, knowing that the new technology was revolutionizing surgery in ways they might not prefer. In either case, the knowledge they came for would be essential to keep up with the times, for keeping up their practices and their livelihoods. She knew, though she was loath to admit it, that eventually she would have to give up her traditional, almost old-fashioned prejudices.

There was still no one in the hall when Liz emerged from the lockers. As she had been instructed to do, she entered the door marked "Restricted Area." As if all the other areas were easy to get into, she thought. Her sarcasm vanished when she stepped into the lab, her breath drawing in with a quick gasp.

The room was dark and long, extending at least two hundred feet into the distance. The roof sloped up high above and was lined with thick windows that afforded a clear view of the dark rainy sky. Liz remembered seeing these windows, from the outside, in photos of Med-Tek. She remembered thinking it was one of the more sinister and intriguing views of the compound.

She allowed her gaze to wander down from the heights above to the scene before her. Discolored blotches danced before her eyes as her vision adjusted to the gloom. Instinctively folding her arms across her chest from the chill room, her eyes focused.

Two long rows of surgical tables extended the length of the room; counting quickly, she guessed they numbered seventy, perhaps eighty. Supine forms were strapped to the tables and draped with blue cloth. At first she thought they were children because of their size, but a glimpse of a snout on the table nearest her dispelled the unlikely notion. They were pigs, anesthetized and strapped down. Normally this sight wouldn't have bothered her. She had operated on animals many times in medical school. It was the magnitude of the lab that was disturbing, giving her a moment's dizziness.

Each pig was surrounded by three or four surgeons, who waited for animal technicians to finish their pre-op procedures. Trocars and instruments poked from the pigs' bellies. Intubation tubes protruded from their throats. Banks of machines monitored the animals' vital signs, heart rates and blood pressure readings silently tracing across tiny green screens.

Liz struggled in the dark to find her name on the sheet taped to the wall that bore table assignments. Seeing that she was stationed at the far end of the room, she walked down the center aisle, watching as attendants activated video monitors and fussily checked the abundant instrument trays beside every table.

A voice called out her name. She turned to see a robed and masked form walking toward her. It was a man, short and stocky, and he walked with quick confidence and purpose.

"Liz Danny?" he said again, and she recognized the voice before he lowered his mask. Nordstrom shuffled a pointer and thick stack of notes into one hand, extending the other. "Please come to my group," he said with a trace of a southern accent. "You're late, but you haven't missed much."

The cordial politician's greeting came as no surprise to Liz, nor did the fact that he had recognized her through her mask and head covering. It was just like Kerry Nordstrom to be solicitous and to attend to every detail; in addition to his medical expertise, he was an excellent public relations man. She was a little surprised that he had involved himself in the mundane work of teaching a low-level session, but she figured he was cultivating his image and laying the groundwork for selling more product. Each surgeon in the room, over time, could represent millions of dollars to Endicott.

Nordstrom paused at a dais and laid down his papers. The room was growing crowded with surgeons and technicians, as well as instructors. They could be recognized by their general disregard for the niceties of a sterile environment, eschewing masks and head coverings. An overall atmosphere of tension pervaded the room.

"Liz, I am so pleased to see you," Nordstrom said, his glasses shining from an overhead lamp. "I assume Donald is here as well?"

She took a moment to look him over. His appearance did nothing to dispel his reputation as an aggressive achiever: his mouth was set in an unchanging smile, his eyes fixed on Liz, his hair brushed back in a long wave to cover a bald spot that had been much smaller when she had last seen him. He wore cowboy boots, which stuck out incongruously from his scrub pants. Through his tunic he could see his belly, which had also grown over the years. A multimillion-dollar gut, she thought.

"Donald is at the advanced seminar," she said, though it should have been obvious. She took the opportunity to look away from Nordstrom's gaze, peering at a nearby tray of instruments. They all bore the ubiquitous Endicott logo.

"I'm sure he'll find it beneficial," Nordstrom said. "The panel is discussing acid-reflux disease and peptic ulcers. Not the most exciting stuff in the world, though. The real action is down here in the lab. Your first assignment will be to perform a laparoscopic cholecystectomy on one of the porkers here."

An attendant handed Liz a pair of sterile gloves. She was a pretty young girl who looked impatient to get started.

"To tell you the truth, Kerry," Liz said, "I've always done gall bladders open. I'm not convinced of the long-term efficacy of laparoscopy. There haven't been enough trials—"

Nordstrom cut her off. "But here you are, Liz, which means we have the chance to convince you of the error of your ways. I know I must have my work cut out for me, though, if Donald hasn't been able to show you the light."

That phrase again, Liz thought. Show me the light. He had the evangelical zeal that Donald once possessed and now had lost. She looked at Nordstrom in the murky light as he barked demands to one of the animal technicians. He had an aggression in his voice and body language that conveyed a sense of personal power and a confidence in using it. Though he hadn't changed much, his presence made Liz uneasy.

"Speaking of our Dr. Page, how is he doing?" he said in a loud, sonorous voice, walking back to Liz. Some of the surgeons looked up from their preparations to hear what the director of Med-Tek had to say to the attractive young woman at the edge of the room. "I have to admit, Donald worries me at times," he added.

"He's fine, Kerry. Why do you ask?"

"Oh, rumormongers. I should know better than to listen to people who have nothing better to do than to run their colleagues down. Anyone who says he's less than brilliant and at the top of his game must simply be jealous."

Nordstrom left her to take his place on the dais. Liz snapped on the surgical gloves, irritated and deep in thought. What rumors? What jealousy? Donald was now a simple community surgeon; she was sure he was the topic of few conversations in a cosmopolitan group such as the one assembled at Med-Tek.

There was no time to follow this line of thought. She had to join her group at the operating table. After a quick round of introductions she found that she was working with a tall dark-eyed surgeon from Lyons, France; a heavy-set, boisterous surgeon from Boston; and a third man from Dallas. The American men went first, and Liz was impressed with the dexterity they gained with the instruments in the relatively short time they had to complete the procedure.

The pig's belly was inflated, its nipples stark against its gray, wrinkled flesh. The surgeons' movements and the interior of the pig's body were shown on a monitor overhead. The Texan aimed the camera while the larger surgeon worked.

Liz, comfortable for the moment to be a bystander, watched the swift movements of the technicians as they ran to fetch particular instruments at various surgeons' request. The majority of the assistants seemed to be young girls, and some of them were extremely attractive. Liz wondered if this was part of the marketing plan.

She took the opportunity to have a closer look at the room. Long electrical cables extended from the machinery into the darkness above. At the station next to her, a technician roughly cranked a lever under the operating table, which tilted the body of the pig to a more agreeable angle.

A door behind her opened with a hiss. Before it could close again, she had a look inside: on a long row of stainless-steel tables, at least two dozen pigs had been laid on their bellies. Some seemed to be awake but too groggy to move. A man moved from animal to animal, injecting them with long needles.

A cry came from behind her: it was from her table. "Shit!" yelled the Bostonian, his eyes wild with anger.

Liz stepped closer and looked at the monitor. Apparently, the grasper with the cautery edge used to clear away adhesions had slipped in his hand, and he had cut into an artery. Blood spilled through the pig's abdomen, a crimson pool growing at the base of the cavity.

"Damn it," he said, stepping away from the table and bumping loudly into the instrument tray. The vital signs on the monitor bank became erratic as the pig's blood pressure sank. It was quickly bleeding to death.

Nordstrom stepped down from the dais to join their table. "A rookie mistake," he said to the surgeon. "A simple matter of not having your hand-eye coordination down yet."

His words did little to mollify his student and didn't appear to have been intended to. An air of superiority crept through his comment, as well as an element of contempt.

"That's easy for you to say," the Boston surgeon said, ripping the mask from his face. "I have one of these scheduled on a patient the day after tomorrow. I have to get this right!"

The desperate edge to the man's words momentarily astonished Liz. He sounded like a man racing against time, trying to gain a precious edge of knowledge before the other surgeons in his city surpassed him. How strange, she thought, that these men with years of experience and schooling should be in this position: fanatically straining to learn new ways of doing old procedures, reduced to the status of students.

A young girl came to unhook the pig from the respirator and monitors. When the task was complete, she transferred the animal to a gurney. "I'll have another one set up for you in a few minutes," she said, and wheeled the pig through a set of double doors.

"You gentlemen can take a break and consider the delicacy and skill that you will have to master. Dr. Danny, I'd like to talk to you in private," Nordstrom said, watching the pig being wheeled away.

"I thought I'd take the opportunity to show you something, if you have a moment," he said. She felt that he was standing too close and took a step backward.

"Sure, Kerry. As long as it's above board," she said. She was torn between conflicting impulses, between her gut dislike for the man and the respect he commanded on his own turf.

Nordstrom rolled his eyes. "Please, Liz. I'm a respectable man these days. Nothing like the rogue you knew when you were in medical school." He smiled with self-satisfaction and looked back at the room. "David!" he suddenly barked at a white-coated assistant. "Get some of those new circular staplers out there. The blue ones." The young man scrambled to a white metal cabinet and fetched the instruments, which he began to distribute to all the tables.

"Sometimes I feel like I'm the only one here who knows how to sell product," Nordstrom said in disgust. He led Liz out a back door to a short passage, pausing at an unmarked door.

"I had my people prepare a demo of some of my flashier research. I wasn't sure who I wanted to impress with it, but you seemed like a good candidate," he said, smiling.

He opened the door with a black key card unlike the generic models the other staff carried. Gently guiding Liz with his hand on the small of her back, he led her into the darkened room.

"Kerry, what's going on?" she said. What am I doing?

Liz thought. I knew I couldn't trust this guy, and here I am alone in a dark room with him. She tensed up, prepared to knee him in the groin if he tried anything.

Suddenly the lights came on. "What do you think," Nordstrom said from behind her. "Impressive?"

Liz tried to speak but found that the words were trapped somewhere in her throat. Before her was a seven-foot glass and metal canister, glowing softly in the middle of the room. A long chaotic series of wires and electrodes ran from the edges of the container to a computer. The soft hum of active electronics pervaded the room.

"Let me shed some more light on the situation," Nordstrom said, activating a switch on the wall.

The interior of the tube was suddenly flooded with light, revealing it to be filled with a blue-green viscous liquid. Within it floated a pig, its eyes open and its hooves gently pushing against its watery environment. Somehow it was living and breathing, not drowning, not struggling.

Nordstrom switched off the lights and led Liz out into the hall, looking at her expectantly. She masked her amazement with a defiant look of nonchalance.

"Swimming pigs, Kerry?" she said, wondering why he had chosen to show her the bizarre tank.

He let out a loud laugh. "Teaching pigs to swim might be a by-product of my research. Who knows." He leaned against the wall and folded his arms across his belly. "Hydrogen-adjusted fluocil under low-intensity laser treatment. It's a liquid that mammals can breathe. Not indefinitely, but for a surprisingly long period."

Liz had to allow some of her surprise to show. "Kerry, you developed that here?"

He nodded, pleased that he had broken through her reserve. "I've been working on chemical modifications of fluocil solutions for several years. I thought it might interest you, since Donald and I did some preliminary work in the field before we were swept away by laparoscopy.''

"It's incredible," Liz admitted, shivering in the chill of the air-conditioned hall. "What do you intend to do with it?''

Nordstrom shrugged and laughed. "Oh, a lot of things. There are lots of possibilities. I'm thinking about sterile conditions for burn patients. Who knows? They might even be able to use it for space travel. I'm pressing forward, trying different permutations of the laser frequency and combinations of argon and KTP. The floating pig represents just the smallest fraction of what I will accomplish.''

They walked back into the pig lab, where Nordstrom flagged down an animal technician. "Janet, show's over," he said. "Why don't you go and rescue Porky in the lab.''

Lunch was served in a huge ballroom deep in the inner recesses of the complex. Liz was amazed at the relative opulence of the place, and admired it in spite of her own more modest tastes. Long chandeliers hung in a zigzag pattern from the ceiling, and the walls were papered with an obviously expensive William Morris pattern much like one that she had considered for her own living room.

A long stage rose above the diners. Waiters hovered constantly around each of the large round tables, refreshing water glasses and attempting to clear each course of the meal as soon as it was finished.

Liz was stuck at a table with the surgeons from her work group. The doctor from Boston, in between laments at his earlier failure and expressing his anxiety about being ready for surgery on Monday, tried out his remedial tourist's French on the surgeon from Lyons.

She looked around the room, trying to spot Donald, but couldn't see him. She hated to admit it, but he would have blended in perfectly with the crowd of two hundred white men in glasses, white shirts, and short hair. Bald spots were in abundance. Taking a look around, Liz guessed that about ninety to ninety-five percent of the guests were men; among the small number of women, many were nurses who had come along with surgeons to learn how to effectively assist in the new technological environment.

Just as Liz spotted Donald walking in uncertainly from a side door, the lights dimmed a fraction. The crowd responded by ceasing the low rumble of conversation that had dominated the room. Donald sat at an empty seat near the door he had entered, staring at his plate of food, seemingly oblivious to his surroundings.

Kerry Nordstrom strode to the podium at the head of the stage, which elevated him about six feet over the diners. He cleared his throat for attention and beamed his patented smile at the audience. The effect was chilling to Liz, her memory still dominated by the sight of the submerged pig. However intriguing the research may have been, it was certainly ghastly to look at.

Nordstrom began to speak. "Greetings and welcome to Med-Tek. I'm overjoyed to see such a turnout for our humble seminar. It speaks well for our profession that we're willing to make the effort to learn new procedures and challenge the stale prejudices of the old guard. As you know, I am a great proponent of laparoscopy. In fact, I have such a warm feeling for it that I just bought a ranch near Aspen."

The crowd laughed heartily at Nordstrom's line, delivered with deadpan timing. Liz noticed the men sitting behind Nordstrom at the table of honor. They were all dressed expensively and sat with the calm assurance of the rich and powerful. They chose not to laugh at Nordstrom's joke.

He glanced back at the men. "My colleagues know that I'm kidding. Sort of." Another laugh.

He leaned over the podium and gestured at the audience, finally warming to his subject. "What I want us all to keep in mind," he continued, suddenly serious, "is that we are here for one purpose: for the safest and most effective treatment of our patients. We must continue to earn their trust and respect, and we have to grow with the times.

"Laparoscopy *is* the future, gentlemen. Anyone who does not see this will be left behind. They will lose their practices and their jobs. They will go the way of the dinosaurs. On behalf of Med-Tek and the Endicott Corporation, I welcome you to this three-day session."

Nordstrom stepped from the podium and retreated to a chair. He was followed by an older man, just this side of elderly, with thick white hair and an unassuming manner. Liz dug into her dessert before eating the main course of her lunch, eager for the sugar. The Frenchman at the table observed her doing this and, with a smile, began to do the same.

The old man at the podium cleared his throat and spoke in a deep, soothing voice. "For those who do not know me, my name is Malcolm Endicott IV. You have my permission to call me Malcolm." A murmur of recognition ran through the room, followed by laughter at the self-deprecating style of the giant corporation's owner.

"I have ventured out from corporate headquarters to see the good work that Kerry is doing here, and it pleases me to no end to see the surgeons of our nation, as well as those of other nations, attending such a seminar. We have a responsibility to our patients. We must never forget it.

This is the Endicott mission, and it is my personal ethic. As such, I have committed the resources of my company to research and development for laparoscopic surgery. I am convinced that the results will make us all proud. Thank you.''

Liz reflected on the demeanor of the sweet old man. Donald had told her about him: born into a massive fortune, he pursued a medical career and quickly earned a reputation for compassion and skill. After his father's death he retreated into the affairs of the corporation he had inherited. A multibillionaire, he now was one of the leading corporate proponents of laparoscopy. If someone such as this, she thought, was willing to commit himself to that degree, perhaps she should reconsider her reservations.

Endicott appeared to lose his train of thought for a moment, then yielded the stage to Nordstrom.

"Thank you, Malcolm," he said. "Allow me to say how pleased I am that you could attend. Before our luncheon concludes, I would like to introduce my second-in-command here at Med-Tek, Dr. Calvin D'Amato. Please feel free to contact him with any questions or comments." He pointed to a smallish bulldog-faced man, who rose and scowled at the audience.

"And Dr. Irwin Ross, head of the Endicott Project and, I should add, my boss." Nordstrom smiled and pointed to Ross, who rose. He was younger than any of the other men on the stage, having made his name as a pioneer at a very young age. Not yet thirty-five, he had already become Malcolm Endicott's second-in-command.

He was also very good-looking, Liz noted, and he obviously knew it: his blond hair was swept away from his chiseled features, and he looked down to acknowledge the audience as if he were a prince receiving subjects.

"Finally, please welcome some of my personal guests from abroad. They are here to observe the proceedings today and take information back to their home countries." Nordstrom proceeded to introduce four men, from China, Argentina, Pakistan, and Turkey. They nodded gravely and declined to stand.

"What is this?" the surgeon from France asked Liz. "I am an international guest, and I get no such welcome." He said it with a smile and looked suggestively into her eyes. It was an occupational hazard of being one of only several women in a place like this, she thought. She looked up at the stage again.

As the lunch was breaking up, the speakers descended from the stage to speak with surgeons in the audience that they knew. Only Nordstrom remained, deep in conversation with the four foreign visitors and their translators. He was smiling and patting backs, and the group retreated to the back of the stage to sit and talk at length.

For some reason, something about the men gave Liz pause and a general sense of dread. They all had a definite aura of authority and power, but none of them appeared to be medical people. They looked more like politicians or government officials. Liz dismissed the thought: it was probably a financial matter. Perhaps the men were investors. She had to remind herself what a big-money game modern medicine was.

Donald spotted Liz after lunch broke up and came over to talk to her. He complained of a headache. "I thought the food would have helped, but I think it made me feel worse. I think I'm coming down with a migraine. I'm sorry I didn't sit with you, but Kerry set a special place for me. He remembered my food allergies from medical school and had a special meal prepared for me."

"That's odd," Liz said. "I wanted a vegetarian dish,

but I just ordered it from the table. I guess vegetarianism is a lot more common than your allergies.'' Donald nodded in agreement, wiping sweat from his forehead.

Liz kissed him on the brow. ''Feel better, hon. I'm off to cut up some more pigs.'' He laughed softly and left for the next advanced seminar.

Watching him walk away, Liz realized to what extent her feelings were in a state of flux. She had to admit that she was excited about the things she was learning: she would have to rethink the very foundations of her surgical philosophies. This should have brought her closer to Donald, but he seemed as far away as ever. For some reason, nothing seemed to work between them. At times such as these, he might as well have been a stranger.

The afternoon was an exhilarating series of discoveries for Liz. Her main criticism of laparoscopic surgery—that the surgeon's hands were metaphorically ''divorced'' from her eyes because of the video screen—disappeared. She gained a rapid proficiency with the instruments and the techniques for working within the unopened body of a patient or, in this case, a laboratory pig. Before long, she became the unofficial leader of her working group.

With the French doctor holding the camera in place, Liz carefully isolated the violet sac of the gall bladder, cutting away adhesions and clamping the cystic duct. She took great care not to nick the right lobe of the liver.

''That's where I went wrong,'' the Boston surgeon said ruefully, peeking over her shoulder at the video monitor.

Liz overheard the comment and tried not to think about the man's poor patients. She inserted a vacuum tube through a trocar to retrieve the organ from the abdominal cavity. It came out of the tube and flopped on the pig's belly. Looking at it, Liz felt profound relief. She had performed her first laparoscopic cholecystectomy.

Dr. Irwin Ross came to the labs to make an appearance, looking like Alexander the Great surveying recruits for one of his campaigns. He stood against one wall of the huge room, joined by Dr. D'Amato. They made quite a pair consulting together, the younger Ross with his expensive suit and obvious self-confidence, flanked by the older D'Amato, a squat and overweight man who wore what was apparently a perpetual look of worry and disapproval.

Before resuming her work, she noticed that Ross had pointed at her. D'Amato had nodded, as if she were the topic of their conversation. Liz looked away, examining the pig's appendix in the video monitor. The animal's vital signs held steady; she decided to go ahead and perform an appendectomy.

When she had finished and was snapping off her gloves, D'Amato motioned for her to join him against the wall of the room. She stepped away, giving up the table to the Texas surgeon, who was having difficulty perfecting his hand-eye coordination to a point where he could operate without killing the pig.

The new perspective was even more startling than that she had seen when she first came in. The surgeons and technicians, engrossed in their work, looked like assembly-line workers. The strangeness of this sight was quickly replaced by curiosity over why the gruff man had called her over to speak.

"Dr. D'Amato, I'm very pleased to meet you. This is quite an impressive complex you have here," she said, trying to take a tactful approach with him. He looked at her as if he were ready to have her thrown off the grounds.

He waved his hand dismissively. "The best in the

world. The real revolution in all abdominally located surgeries is taking place right here.''

He leaned against the wall and looked absently through
a glass door that revealed a long hallway veering off to his
left. ''I understand you work in Los Angeles. I can't say I
envy you.''

''A lot of that is just negative publicity,'' Liz said. ''It
has its problems, like any big city, but I've come to feel
that it's home.''

D'Amato coughed into a handkerchief. Liz saw a glaze
of red around his eyes and a ring of purplish veins around
his nose and realized, with a shock, that he appeared to be
a heavy drinker. She hoped that most of his duties were
administrative.

''Well, I'm sure it has its good points. Indianapolis is
my kind of place, though. Quiet, sedate. I've been told
that you're making a lot of progress here.'' The quick
change of topic surprised her, but Liz smiled at the compliment and to her surprise, she was met with a thin-
lipped grin in return. She was unable to stop thinking of
him as a bulldog; the idea gave her a terrible urge to
laugh.

''But some of the things I've heard about your husband
aren't so fine,'' he continued. ''In fact, I don't like them
at all. I came here to see if you could shed any light on the
rumors that have been going around.''

His words shocked Liz. In the context of their fairly
harmless conversation, they felt like an attack. She looked
at him quizzically and asked him what he meant.

''Well, don't take any of this the wrong way. It's just
that I've heard that Dr. Page has been inattentive and distant. He took a practice turn on some pigs in the advanced
seminar and killed off about five of them before he went
back to his hotel.''

Liz gasped. "All of this happened today?"

D'Amato nodded. "Listen, it's probably nothing. The guy's having an off day. They said he was sweating and complained of exhaustion. I just wondered, if he has the flu or something, we could have him checked out."

"I think he's getting migraines, actually."

He clapped his hands, making a startlingly loud noise. "There we go. He'll probably be better in the morning. I was concerned for him, but Kerry told me not to worry. In light of what happened with him today, I hope you won't think that I . . ."

His words trailed off and he looked up at Liz sheepishly. She made a point of smiling at him because he seemed genuinely embarrassed. She appreciated this kind side to this previously gruff man and realized that she had actually taken a liking to him. "I appreciate your concern, Dr. D'Amato."

"Call me Calvin."

"Calvin. It's good of you to be so considerate, especially since I know that you have foreign investors here and you want everything to go smoothly."

D'Amato's eyebrows raised, making him look more like a bulldog than before, if that was possible. "Investors? What the hell are you talking about? Endicott is entirely privately owned. You'll give the old man a heart attack if he hears you talking like that."

"Oh, I'm sorry, I just assumed that's who those men on the podium today were. I couldn't care less about the business end of what goes on around here."

"Those men are guests of Kerry," D'Amato said. His stern manner had returned. "They have to do with the foreign expansion, I suppose. I haven't been told why they're hanging around. In case you haven't noticed, I'm the second banana around here."

Liz seemed to have touched a soft spot. "In any case, Calvin, I'll talk to Donald tonight and make sure he's all right. He'll be flattered to hear that someone was concerned about him."

Donald and Liz's hotel was in downtown Indianapolis; Liz neared it after a forty-minute ride from Med-Tek, past the famous racing track and the domed football stadium. The driver encouraged her to see the Indiana Medical History Museum, but Liz begged off. She was in a hurry to get to Donald, alarmed that he had been so sick as to leave early.

Nordstrom had made lavish arrangements: they stayed in a three-room suite overlooking a large courtyard. A swimming pool and Jacuzzi nestled below amidst greenery and artificial waterfalls.

Liz found Donald on the huge bed, his eyes closed and a wet washcloth draped over his forehead. He was too ill to go out. After receiving reassurances that he just needed to sleep, Liz took a soak in the Jacuzzi and relaxed in the hotel sauna. She lay out naked in the private chamber, feeling her tension flowing out in the waves of steam.

Feeling refreshed, she joined Donald in their room. Before she could lay out her towel to dry, Nordstrom phoned and asked if he could visit. Donald muttered a vaguely affirmative reply from the darkened bedroom, and Kerry hung up before she could ask his reasons for coming.

Liz was still in her bathing suit when she answered a knock at the door: she quickly covered up with a towel after receiving a boldly appraising look from Nordstrom. Donald had retreated to the bathroom and was taking a long soak in the sunken tub.

"Ms. Danny," Nordstrom said with pointed emphasis,

"you are as beautiful as ever. Donald is a very, very lucky man." When Liz met his stare with an icy look, he continued.

"Anyway, darling, I have a proposal for you two. If you've checked the schedule, you will have seen that there is an exhibition surgery tomorrow morning, performed by yours truly."

Nordstrom was smiling and rocking back and forth on his heels as if they were old friends. Liz felt acute embarrassment that she had ever gone out with him. The fact that she had been young and naive then made no difference.

"I haven't looked at the schedule, Kerry. To tell you the truth, I've been too worried about Donald to really care."

Nordstrom's eyebrows raised. "Really? Too bad. Tomorrow is going to be historic. I'm performing my combined approach for severe ulcer disease: vagotomy with seromyotomy and congo red testing. A few people in France and the States have got out in front of me on this one, but I'm ready to run ahead of the pack and do them one better."

Liz had heard of the operation: it was aimed at easing the suffering of ulcer patients by dissecting out the vagus nerve, which triggered acid production that created and exacerbated the ulcers. It was a highly complicated and difficult procedure when performed laparoscopically, one that was indeed exciting in its possibilities.

A loud thunderclap sounded from outside, followed by an intense flurry of rain. A storm had arrived, though Liz hadn't noticed it in the indoor courtyard.

Nordstrom sat back on the sofa and put his shiny leather shoes on the table. "I would like you and Donald to assist me. You, of course, would have less of a technical role, but I'd like you there nonetheless. I think it would be a good opportunity for Donald to get some of his reputation back, if you know what I mean. Working in the public eye once again.''

Liz flushed red. ''How dare you say that. You don't give a shit about his name or his reputation.''

Nordstrom smiled. ''I know we've had our differences, but please say yes. I'd like to have old friends there. I want to extend the olive branch to you and Donald. Life is short, Liz. There's no reason to hold grudges forever.''

A splash came from the bathroom, followed by Donald's voice echoing against the wet tile. ''Is that Kerry? Send him in here.'' Then his voice lowered. ''Kerry, bring me some water. I'm thirsty.''

Nordstrom took his hand from his pocket and looked at Liz with a hint of alarm. He filled a plastic cup with water from the refrigerator and walked to the bathroom.

She heard low voices speaking: Nordstrom's clear and intent, laughing occasionally and cajoling; then Donald's, low and indistinct. Finally, she heard both say good-bye.

''He's agreed to do it,'' Nordstrom said. ''And he agreed for you. I hope that's all right.''

He rinsed out the water glass he had brought to Donald. ''The whole thing will take about two hours, tops. Donald can take the expertise back to his practice, and it may go a ways toward convincing you, my dear, that these procedures are not quackery.''

Donald's slurred voice called for Liz from the bathroom.

''And it might go some ways toward bringing our Dr. Page back into the real world,'' Nordstrom said, rolling his eyes. He stepped out into the night, closing the door quietly behind him.

Outside the hotel room, Kerry Nordstrom walked confidently toward the elevators. He softly whistled an old country tune to himself. When he came to a garbage can, he retrieved a small yellow packet from his pants pocket. It was caked inside with a pale blue powder.

The drugs had already begun to take effect: Donald would feel sick and disoriented. The long-term effects would include an inability to concentrate and, hopefully, memory loss. Between the packet he had just slipped his old friend and the doses placed in his "special" meals, Nordstrom guessed that Donald might soon have a complete breakdown of his faculties. He would suffer confusion, acute clinical depression, even problems with his central nervous system.

"What a shame," he said, looking back at the room. Brushing his hands off, he pushed the button for the elevator that would take him to his waiting limousine.

CHAPTER FIVE

IT WAS A SPLENDID MORNING: THOUGH FULL DAYLIGHT WAS STILL a short time away, the city below Liz's hotel window had been washed clean by the storm and rain of the night before. She had arisen for a hot shower and, invigorated, begun to dress for the trip out to Med-Tek. Donald slept on.

"Honey, wake up," she said, nudging his inert form. "We're running late. A limo will be downstairs for us in fifteen minutes."

Donald turned over, drawing the pillow over his head. His voice, low and husky, said something in an unfriendly tone. Liz pulled the pillow out of his sleep-weakened hands, laughingly tossing it out of his reach to the other side of the room.

"No more sleep, Donald. You've told me before you wanted to learn this surgery. If you sleep in any later, someone else will have to hold the camera and listen to Kerry talking about his plans for world domination."

With this, Donald stood up out of bed, cradling his head in his hands. Liz turned on the light. His eyes were settled back in deep caves of purple skin, and his cheeks were pale and bloated. She rushed to his side and took his hand.

"God, you look terrible," she said. "Is it still the headache?"

He brushed her hand away and walked to the bathroom. "Funny thing. The headache is almost gone. I just feel like I got run over by a truck in my sleep last night."

Liz stood in the doorway as Donald stuck his head under the cold-water tap. "Maybe you did in your dreams," she said, trying to keep the conversation light. "And your body's trying to catch up with your imagination."

Water dripping wildly from his hair, Donald fumbled for a towel. Liz tossed him one. "Listen," he said from under the towel. "You go on without me. I'll call for another car in a little while. I need some time to regroup. Could you please call room service and have them send me up a pot of coffee? That'd be a big help."

"You know, you lose all sense of humor when you're not feeling well," Liz said. Her husband ignored her. "Donald, I'm really worried about you. You look like hell. I can call Kerry and arrange to have someone else assist. I'm sure they can—"

"Just go," he snapped. "I can't back out on this. It disgusts me that Kerry Nordstrom has to be the one handing me a break, but this will be good for my career. You're new to this, but believe me, the exposure in the medical community will be invaluable. Anyway, I've worked under worse conditions than this."

"Suit yourself," Liz said, angry at Donald's patronizing tone. She called room service for his coffee and went downstairs to catch the car. She passed through the lobby, where some other surgeons were also preparing to leave for Med-Tek in shuttle buses. As was always the case at medical conferences, the action started early. Stepping outside, she realized she hadn't even had an opportunity to tell Donald about Nordstrom's bizarre fluocil tank. In his mood, he probably wouldn't have been interested.

Finally alone, Donald leaned against the sink and examined himself in the mirror. He was so sick that he couldn't stand up for long without feeling that he was going to vomit. It didn't make sense: he had been trying to wean himself off the drugs with lesser dosages. Anyway, this feeling was unique—it went beyond the first tentative pangs of withdrawal. He sank to his knees, trying to gather the strength to get dressed. He had no idea what was wrong with him. Whatever it was, it was terrible.

An Endicott limousine was waiting by the curb, outside the hotel. Liz told the driver she was going alone and climbed in, watching the sleepy city shake off its morning drowsiness. The air was crisp and smelled of vegetation after yesterday's rain.

Before they left downtown for the expanses of the city's edge, they passed a large colorful building with a high glass arch trimmed in yellow: the children's museum. Why is it, she wondered, that when things aren't going well, I always have to be reminded that we haven't had children yet? For the last few years, Donald always had a convenient excuse for putting it off. Now she wondered if it would ever happen.

At least he was showing some interest in his professional standing. She had begun to think he didn't care about anything: his work, his life, his wife. She said a silent prayer that everything would go well at Med-Tek. While the laparoscopic vagotomy was a new and difficult way of performing a very delicate operation, she had to believe it would be a success. Failure was something she had never been able to accept.

As a medical resident in Minneapolis, she had gained quick notoriety as a skilled professional and a potentially great surgeon. Donald had been engrossed in his work on the first laparoscopies when they met, but she had also been working hard. The discoveries she made for herself on seemingly trifling cases gave her as much pleasure and satisfaction as if she had been performing a heart transplant on the president. Every scrap of information seemed important, and every obstacle was a challenge to be conquered.

A near-obsession with practice and perfection had distinguished her to her teachers and peers. She used to compulsively practice her knot-tying on the bed post in her cramped hospital quarters. She was single then, and younger, convinced that perfection was hers to achieve. The knots seemed symbolic of this quest. *Over, under, over, pull. Over, under, over, pull.*

She must have tied thousands of knots on that post, perhaps millions, even during the increasingly frequent visits from Donald. He had taken an early interest in the attractive young resident from Virginia. Though his youth was so much further in the past than hers, he fascinated and amused her with his stories of growing up in Brooklyn in the fifties.

It was as a resident that she was first told that she had "good hands," a tag she was so proud of, she had written about it to her mother, who had written back (in her motherly way) that it was quite a compliment. Her reputation as a rising star was cemented when she extracted a long needle from the leg of a patient under fluoroscopy. She had worked in a sure-handed fashion that caught the eye of the chief of surgery, who happened to be on the floor on a different case.

These were just memories. Now she was a skilled general surgeon who took great pride in her work, but she no longer sought the praise of her superiors. Watching the influence of politics and money on medicine had convinced her that she could be truly happy only by thinking and caring exclusively about the work she performed, not what others thought of it.

One of the elements that was so appealing about private practice was that she could feel accountable only to her own value system. In a way, she was glad to be liberated from the constant search for approval that had followed her through her life: first, she had achieved to please her father; then she had achieved to prove that a woman could be a superior surgeon. It had been a long fight to reach the point where she worked to please herself.

But in fifteen minutes she would be scrubbing in on an operation conducted in the huge public amphitheater at Med-Tek, under the glare of lights set up to videotape the work for the inevitable corporate promotion. Billionaires and millionaires would watch her and her husband working, ready to mete out their approval or disapproval depending on their success. And Kerry Nordstrom would be in charge of it all.

A security guard whisked her in the front door of the building and past the reception desk. She was greeted by Greg Harris, who looked refreshingly enthusiastic and alert.

"Dr. Danny, good morning," he said, a clipboard and pile of papers in his hand. He was dressed in a stylish suit and tie for the occasion. "I don't see Dr. Page. Is your husband with you?"

"He's running late," Liz said. "I think the time difference has worn him down a bit."

Greg smiled. "Always happens when we have surgeons in from the West Coast. I'm sure he'll wake up when he sees what we have waiting for him. The assistants are already seating the audience. In addition to the group here for the course, we have medical personnel in attendance from all over the Midwest. This surgery is a real event. We're going to fill up the amphitheater, and it holds a thousand."

Liz smiled at his contagious good spirits. Though she found Med-Tek eerie and odd, the employees were generally pleasant and helpful. She wondered what they really thought about working under Kerry Nordstrom.

She was a little early, which she regretted. It gave her time to think. She wondered if Nordstrom's crew was truly ready to perform the vagotomy. The operation had been performed successfully by Dr. Jean-Luc Germand in Paris, and by a select handful of surgeons in the United States, but it was by no means a commonplace procedure. It was still exotic and exciting. In a sense, it could even be considered elegant: unlike many other surgeries, vagotomy sought to correct an acute condition without removing a part or the whole of an organ.

Greg brought Liz a cup of coffee and a pastry, which she hungrily ate while waiting for Donald. She wandered over to the entrance of the amphitheater, looking down the stairs that led to the sunken room. The stage was dark, though the room was noisy with the chatter of surgeons who had arrived early.

They were there to see a show, an exhibition. They couldn't possibly be more removed from what was at stake: the life of the patient, the careers of the surgeons, perhaps even the future of laparoscopy. A voice within her warned her that something was wrong, that this wasn't the way to save lives. This was show business. Unfortunately, it was too late to pay heed to inner doubt. It was nearly time to begin.

The surgical team was scrubbed in and dressed for the operation, wearing gowns that had been created specifically for that day: they were clad in a deep crimson fabric, the color of blood. Even their masks were red, rather than the neutral blue disposable models one normally found in a modern OR.

The effect was at once spectacular and disconcerting. While the vivid color was a stark contrast to the pristine white tile floor and gleaming walls, the hue gave the gowns an oddly ritual aspect, as if they were a group of priests or initiates about to perform a ceremony. Liz looked down at her attire, wondering whose idea it was to dress in such a way. She knew it had to be Nordstrom.

Donald stood beside her, having arrived at the last minute, while the team waited for the audience to settle into their seats and for Nordstrom to begin his address. Liz had a sudden urge to take her husband's hand but restrained herself, knowing that it would violate the sterile operating conditions.

She wished she could feel his support, but it wasn't there. She stood on the sunken surgical stage, her eyes burned from the bright lights trained on the group. She could see only the vague shapes of the audience, along with rows of stairs receding up into the distance. For a moment, she felt as she had in her elementary school production of the Nativity: frightened, nervous, and frozen in the oppressive glare of spotlights.

"Thank you for your attendance," Nordstrom began.

He wore a microphone affixed to his gown under his chin, peering up from the sunken pit at the audience. He beamed with confidence and energy. Above them, tall twin video monitors suspended from the ceiling showed Nordstrom's face, covered by the crimson mask.

"I am very pleased to conduct this revolutionary procedure in the company of my colleagues and our respected visitors." He bowed toward the front row, where Malcolm Endicott, Ross, and D'Amato sat, then nodded toward the foreign visitors, who occupied a small booth to the left of the audience. The men briefly acknowledged his greeting with grave nods.

Liz looked again at the men. She didn't think they were surgeons: they hadn't participated in any of the workshops. Why are they here? she wondered. Even D'Amato had had no idea.

"Our patient today is Mr. Raymond Barker. I will briefly inform you of his medical history," Nordstrom continued, pointing to the man lying supine on the operating table.

Barker was still conscious, listening intently to Nordstrom. He was obviously uncomfortable with his role as guinea pig before the gaze of hundreds of observers. Liz felt pity for the man, who had to endure this indignity in order to have his suffering eased.

"Mr. Barker has a particularly severe history of stomach ulcers," said Nordstrom. "His previous treatment history is very conventional, comprising a variety of pharmaceutical approaches."

Nordstrom cocked his head up at the audience, glancing briefly at his own image on the video monitors. "The medicine has been unsuccessful in treating the patient. He has been to the emergency room in grave pain five times in the past three months. This inadequate medicine has cost this man two to three thousand dollars a year," he said. His voice resounded in the cavernous, otherwise silent auditorium. Liz looked up at the ceiling. It must have been fifty feet high. The lamps suspended over the table hung from thick white cables that disappeared into the heights above.

"His insurance company is paying for medication that is ineffective and can cause highly undesirable side effects: nausea, vomiting"—he paused for emphasis—"and impotence. But we feel that our latest advances in research and technology can help this man and many more like him. Let us proceed."

Nordstrom signaled to the gastroenterologist to begin his part of the procedure. Liz stepped to the back of the stage with the rest of the team. She stood next to Donald, watching him. Soon after his late arrival, he had begun to sway slightly on his feet, once even having to catch himself from leaning too far over and falling.

"You don't have to go through with this," she whispered. "We can have someone take you back to the hotel."

"I'm fine," he said. "Please stop worrying about me." His eyes looked slightly clouded above his mask. Liz pondered whether she should let him go on. By then Nordstrom had continued his narration.

"The congo red dye test will be conducted before and after the vagotomy in order to prove how effectively we have cut off the flow of acids to the stomach. Dr. Basu, a member of our staff since 1990, will conduct the test."

Basu, a middle-aged Indian man, went to work on the hapless patient. Basu turned Barker over on his side, then ran a tube into his mouth and down his esophagus, finally threading it to the stomach. The still-conscious but lightly anesthetized patient's eyes blazed and teared.

"How are you doing, Mr. Barker?" Basu asked. Barker, his eyes wide open with shock, weakly held up a hand. "He says he's doing so-so," Basu said. "Don't worry, we will soon be done."

A camera attached to the tube showed its descent into Barker's body on the video screens. The audience watched raptly as red dye was introduced to the stomach. It splashed around the vivid interior of the organ like wine inside a cask and quickly turned black.

"This color change to black," Nordstrom suddenly said, his amplified voice shocking the team and most of the audience, "will occur as a property of the dye when a level of pH3 is present in the stomach. We will see a retention of the red color after the vagotomy, when we have stanched the flow of acids."

Nordstrom motioned to a young bearded anesthetist to put the patient under. While this procedure was performed, Nordstrom walked back to the surgical team to introduce them individually to the audience.

He mentioned Donald last, adding that he was "a pioneer spirit in laparoscopy, one that we are glad to have back in the fold." Donald gave no reaction to this comment, merely staring ahead of him and ignoring the audience's scrutiny.

Liz noticed that the cadre of Endicott, Ross, and D'Amato had stopped talking to one another and were staring at Donald. Ross shook his head and said something to Endicott. What were they saying? she thought. Had rumors about Donald's condition spread to the highest level of Endicott's management?

The anesthetist sat on a stool at the head of the patient, in front of a cart of electronic devices monitoring Barker's vital signs. The surgery was finally ready to begin. Liz, with a growing feeling of misgiving, looked on the instrument table for her sole responsibility during the procedure: the babcock retractor, used to hold back the patient's liver. It was a long thin plastic device that fanned out after passing through a trocar into the patient's body.

Liz resolved to insist that Donald take a vacation when they got back to Los Angeles. He could even go without her. The time apart might help them value each other more.

Watching Nordstrom examine the instrument table, she thought that they might even need a trial separation. Whatever it took: as things stood, Donald looked like an absolute wreck. She repeated her earlier prayer, a plea for the operation to proceed without complication. Whatever passed between them, she loved Donald.

Jed Everett motioned for Nordstrom to come to him. As director of the film crew, he had a special status that enabled him to be blunt and direct with the Med-Tek director. Nordstrom's preoccupation with media and public relations made Everett a power at the complex greater than his bureaucratic rank.

"Remember, Kerry, we'll want to get close-ups of the equipment. When you're using the new KTP laser or the hot scissors, hold it up in the air and keep it there for about fifteen seconds. I'll see that we get the shot." Even under the uniform red scrubs, Everett managed to exude a Hollywood mien.

CO_2 gas was injected into Barker's belly, distending it to the required point. Nordstrom inserted five 10mm trocars in a scattered pattern across Barker's upper abdomen with a swift, almost violent twisting motion. He grunted, pressing heavily on the patient's body.

The camera was the first instrument inserted. It was passed through the trocar inserted above the navel. The image of Barker's insides was displayed to the audience, magnified on the surgical monitors and passed along to the twenty-foot screens suspended over the stage.

As she fanned out the babcock retractor's fingers inside the patient's body and pushed back the liver, Liz noted that there were six VCRs recording the screen's image. That was several more than in a routine case. The Med-Tek people were leaving nothing to chance.

Donald aimed the camera while Nordstrom began to gently push aside the esophagus, the first stage in locating the section of vagus nerve. From the surgical stage, the team could feel the palpable presence of the audience's fascinated interest.

"Your first experience with this procedure will be to-morrow in our animal labs," Nordstrom said, a slight wheeze in his breath. "You'll find that the pig's esophagus is easier to manipulate than a human's, but the porcine model is a good step in your preparation."

Liz stood to Nordstrom's left, only a step away from him. She could feel his tension and focus. He continued to breathe heavily, finally ceasing his sales pitch to the crowd. Donald leaned over the patient, holding the camera and focusing his attention on the monitor. He seemed fine at first, save for a line of sweat on his brow, but then his hand shook. The image on the video monitor danced crazily before the eyes of the team and the audience.

"Hang steady there, Donald," Nordstrom said, chuckling.

"I have located what I think is the appropriate section of vagus nerve," Nordstrom said in a voice intended for the audience, indicating a white, shiny, tubular structure peeking out from behind the esophagus.

He inserted a long white instrument through an open trocar. It was a long fingerlike coil, which closed into a circle around the nerve when Nordstrom pulled a triggering mechanism on the handle. "I have trapped the posterior vagus nerve in the hooking instrument you see on your monitors."

Following a pause for close-up, Nordstrom inserted a microscissors into a trocar, snipping off a piece of the vagus nerve for specimen and retrieving it with a grasper. A nurse left with the sample, leaving Nordstrom to continue his work.

"Donald," Nordstrom said, "for the seromyotomy, I'd like to ask if you can assist me on the laser. I'm going to finish on the vagus and wait for confirmation from the lab." Donald nodded.

"Colleagues," Nordstrom continued, addressing the audience. Liz realized that all of their comments were captured by the microphone on Kerry's gown. Perhaps Kerry had truly changed his ways; he had explicitly asked Donald to share in the latter stages of the operation, a chance for him to show off his skill before his peers.

"You will have noticed that there is some delicacy in finding and isolating the appropriate section of posterior vagus nerve. This is due to the area in which we are working—near the heart, lungs, stomach, esophagus, and several major arterial vessels—as well as to the critical nature of our job. If we remove too much of this nerve or locate it incorrectly, the results would be catastrophic. One major hazard is paralyzing stomach motility, in which case the stomach would be permanently unable to evacuate its contents. Imagine the patient's reaction to such a condition."

A voice crackled through the intercom on the wall of the operating arena. "Dr. Nordstrom. This is the lab. We confirm that you have the vagus." Nordstrom thanked the disembodied voice and continued dissecting out the section of nerve, clamping and incising the innocuous white tube with a laser.

"Liz, let's get some better retraction," he said. "The liver's falling in my way." She strengthened her hold on the retractor, knowing that she couldn't do more than she already had. She felt as she had years ago in school, when she was assisting in surgeries and subject to the whims and demands of the older surgeons. She pledged to be more considerate of her OR staff in the future.

"Donald," Nordstrom said, "get a laser and join me in here." Kerry again addressed the crowd. "At this point, we will be cutting the serosa and the muscular layer of the stomach down to the submucosa. We use Endicott laser technology to cut from the GE junction at the top of the stomach down to the crow's-foot series of nerves, sectioning the remaining branches of the vagus nerve and permanently stanching the flow of harmful acids to the stomach."

He motioned to Donald to join in. A nurse handed Page a laser. He took it with one hand as she activated its power source, which began to hum.

"What about the camera?" Donald said. "I can't do both at once."

"I'll take it," Liz said. "Nurse, would you mind taking over for me on the retractor?"

It was no problem to pass off the retractor without losing hold of the liver; the instrument was well-made, manufactured to create little strain on the assisting surgeon's hand. Liz allowed herself a second to glimpse at the audience. Their attention was uniformly focused on stage, and she had become the momentary focus of their interest. She took the camera and rapidly adjusted to its thirty-degree-angled lens, zeroing in on the surgical field.

*   *   *

Jed Everett stood to the side of the table, careful to keep away from the sterile operating area. He wore a wireless headset, which he used to communicate with his three cameramen and sound man, a form of discourse that amounted to a series of whispered admonitions and obscene epithets. Four video monitors sat at his feet, three corresponding to what each of the cameramen was shooting and a forth displaying the image captured by the laparoscopic camera.

Every time he found himself at one of these damned operations, he had to give a chuckle at how far he had come in his career. From filming baby food commercials and public-service ads for the government's war against drugs, he found himself the head producer of marketing films for Endicott International. Sure, he had had to move from L.A. to Indianapolis, but for the money they paid him, he'd be able to retire early.

The hardest part was getting used to the surgery itself. He had almost not taken the position, knowing that the sight of blood made him instantly queasy and lightheaded. Soon he found that Endicott focused primarily on laparoscopic surgery. Once he found out what that meant —that he wouldn't have to watch someone bleed or be cut wide open—he knew he was the man for the job.

Recently, he found himself extolling the virtues of the new surgeries, just like a real company man. If his gall bladder or his guts went on the fritz, he told his wife, he'd go straight to Med-Tek. Nowhere else. This hardened cynic realized that he'd started to believe in his job.

"All right, Camera One: Zoom on that laser Page is going in with. Damn it! I told them to hold for close-up," he whispered into his headset. "Forget it, it doesn't matter. I'll film a shot with a stand-in after this is all over. Camera Three, get in tight on the surgeons. Let's see some sweat on those brows. Come on! Get off your ass! All right, good job.''

Everett remained silent for a while. He really did have a good camera crew, even though he'd never let them know it. Reward them too much, and they get soft on you. He'd seen it happen time and again with this corporate stuff. Commercials were where you found the real hard-asses. He once had to refilm an entire spot because a framed picture in the background didn't hang at a perfect horizontal angle.

Nordstrom's voice resounded from the speakers. ''My colleague Donald Page and I will proceed to finish the operation with the seromyotomy. I want to add that souvenir T-shirts and posters will be available in the lobby after the show.''

The audience laughed loudly, relieving some of the tension that had filled the auditorium. A sense of anticipation and glee had developed in the crowd: the operation was nearing its final stages and was going perfectly. The groundbreaking expensive production was going to be a success.

''What a ham,'' Jed whispered into his mouthpiece. The cameramen discreetly smiled in response. Jed felt that his word choice was actually pretty generous; in fact, he thought, Nordstrom was a complete pompous ass, a real bastard, and an impossible man to work with. His demands and condescendingly abrasive manner were the only negatives to an otherwise plum job.

Everett watched the monitor at his feet that displayed the surgery in action. He never could figure out when they were going to finish one of these things, and he still didn't have his anatomy down. It looked to him like they were poking around in a pile of red meat.

The outsider, Page, had started making tiny cauteries with the laser, moving at an excruciatingly slow pace along the stomach. Everett was surprised to see him performing such a vital and delicate task; Kerry had warned him that Page was a head case and a has-been, and that he was working that day only out of Nordstrom's charity. The couple of times that Donald had shaken the laparoscope meant that Everett would have to do some fancy editing when he got the tapes back to the studio.

In the quiet auditorium, the only audible sound was the dual activation of Donald and Nordstrom's lasers. They pressed on floor pedals, which responded with a plastic click followed by an electronic hum and a high-pitched warning beeper indicating the laser was in use. Nordstrom performed mop-up work in an area millimeters from Donald's. Jed stifled a yawn and looked at the shots his crew was getting. Not bad, he thought. Really not bad.

A sudden cry from the surgical team brought his attention back to the laparoscopic screen. Something was wrong. He too yelled out at what he saw: the operating field had gone completely red. The patient had been cut and was bleeding. The situation had instantly gone out of control. Everett rose to his feet as the room broke out into chaos.

"Page, goddamn it!" Nordstrom said, stepping back from the table and pulling out his laser. "You perforated the damned stomach! You just killed the fucking patient!" The polite silence of the auditorium erupted into a spontaneous din: the voices of hundreds of surgeons witnessing their worst nightmare.

"Open him up! Open him up!" Malcolm Endicott

shouted from his seat. Irwin Ross put his hand on the older man's arm, trying to calm him down.

Nordstrom reached around the nurse and fetched a scalpel from the steel tray, knocking over a dozen other instruments in the process. He made a hasty, broad cut across the patient's upper abdomen. A hiss resounded in the room as the escaping gas hit his lapel microphone, and the blood began to pour out onto the table, spilling over onto the pristine white floor.

In five minutes Ray Barker was dead. The coeliac artery—the branch of abdominal aorta supplying blood to the stomach, liver, spleen, duodenum, and pancreas—had been ruptured by a brief flash of laser beam.

In the initial moments of chaos, Liz pulled out her now-useless camera. Donald yanked his laser out of the trocar and looked at it in genuine astonishment. His apparent calm was so incongruous to the panic erupting among the surgical team that Liz called his name to see if he was all right. He ignored her and stood there motionless, watching Nordstrom's futile efforts to stanch the bleeding and save the patient through conventional open surgery.

The immediate implications of what had happened were staggering: she knew this would cost Donald what remained of his professional reputation. She felt an anguished mixture of dread and anger as she watched the final efforts to resuscitate Ray Barker. Finally the life-support indicators flat-lined.

Not even sure what she was doing, Liz crouched behind the operating table. She felt that she was hiding like a little girl, but the sight of the audience yelling out to

Nordstrom as he stood over the patient was more than she could take.

At her feet, she saw the row of six videotape machines. For a reason she couldn't quite fathom, she pressed the eject button on one, pulling out the tape and tucking it into the back of her scrubs. She untucked her scrub shirt and adjusted her crimson gown to cover the contraband. No one had noticed.

The atmosphere of collective panic quickly dissolved into a somber pall. Nordstrom leaned against a wall, shouting obscenities, while Donald remained standing in the position he had occupied since the fatal incision. She looked up at him from behind the table, realizing that he was stunned with shock.

He turned, looked around the room to see all eyes fixed accusingly on him, and began to leave. Everyone watched him walk away through a side exit, mumbling to himself and stripping the surgical gloves from his hands. A nurse came forward and pulled a sheet over Barker.

A terrible disappointment and sadness settled over the amphitheater. It seemed impossible that all the pomp and ceremony could have come to this. One of the scrub nurses began crying, then busied herself with restoring the fallen instruments to the metal tray.

Ross and D'Amato jumped the rail separating the audience from the operating stage and tried to talk to Nordstrom. D'Amato looked regretful and worried, while Ross wore an expression of barely controlled fury. Nordstrom ignored them both, walking behind the operating table and fussing with machinery on the floor. His mask hung around his neck as he walked to the front of the stage clutching five videotapes in his hands.

"We'll need these," he said. He held them away from his surgical gown, which dripped with Barker's blood. It blended perfectly into the color of the fabric, appearing only in beads on the floor.

"Nothing went fucking right today," he said. "Someone forgot to put a blank tape in one of the decks. Where's Everett, damn it? Get Everett over here this very second!"

Nordstrom turned to look around the room. He seemed to be searching for something. His gaze traveled through the auditorium, finally fixing on Liz Danny's back quickly retreating through the operating room doors. For a moment, he thought he saw her hiding something in the folds of her gown. His expression changed from one of anger to perplexity, and he stared at the empty doorway long after she was gone.

CHAPTER SIX

6:30 P.M., September 29, Los Angeles.

LIZ COULD BARELY BELIEVE IT HAD BEEN ONLY TWO WEEKS SINCE their return home from Med-Tek. The trip had been an unqualified disaster: Donald was roundly condemned by the Endicott management for his fatal lapse during the surgery, and word quickly spread back to Community Hospital about what had happened. It all happened very quickly, and the consequences were painfully obvious. Donald's reputation as a surgeon had been shattered.

The Indiana State Board of Medical Quality Assurance sent a notice to Donald within a week that he was under investigation for gross negligence. A board of inquiry would convene in October to determine whether he was still fit to hold a surgical license. The letter also contained the ominous news that the possibility of criminal charges couldn't be ruled out.

Donald had offered little in the way of explanation upon their return, only mentioning that his headaches had finally cleared up and that he needed time to rest. To help him, Liz assumed temporary control of his practice. She farmed out some of his surgeries to other staff or reassigned the patients to Cedars-Sinai. In a few instances, she herself covered for Donald in the OR, putting to use the new techniques and methods she had learned at the surgical seminar.

Sitting in Donald's office, reviewing all that she had tried to accomplish that day, Liz felt as if she were battling against the impossible. Worst of all, Donald had retreated ever deeper into himself since they got home. He never wanted to talk, and rarely left the house. He took up residence on his study sofa. It was the first time he and Liz had slept apart, save for when one or the other was on a business trip, since they were married.

She reviewed the case load for the next day. There was one laparoscopic cholecystectomy—she would perform that herself. She had done four of these basic procedures since her return from Indianapolis, gradually growing very confident in her work. Liz marveled at her patients' recovery time; they were able to leave the hospital within a day and suffered no complications. She even began to perform surgical cases from her own practice laparoscopically, raising a few eyebrows on the staff.

Suddenly, Liz found that she was one of only a few surgeons in Los Angeles regularly performing laparoscopic surgery. She appreciated the irony in light of her earlier prejudices and misgivings. She had to admit that it worked, and she realized that with little fanfare the entire nature of her professional methods had undergone a radical change. She just wished Donald could have been on hand to see it happen.

A hard knock at the door of the office made her jump in her chair, sending a stack of case folders careening to the floor where they fanned out in a chaotic mess. Before she could bend over to pick them up, John Rogers stood in the doorway sheepishly asking what the commotion was.

"I'm sorry if I scared you," he said, smiling. "You weren't in your office, and Donald's receptionist isn't around. I sort of just showed myself in."

"Unlike some of us, she works a sane schedule," Liz said, watching John pick up the papers and stack them in a haphazard pile. "What are you up to, anyway? Going around scaring all the poor women of Community Hospital?"

John put on his best innocent-little-boy look. She glared back at him, pretending to be angry. He was one of the few people at the hospital she felt comfortable joking around with; they acted almost like siblings. Liz took a long look at her friend in the fading twilight filtering in through the window as he helped himself to a cup of coffee from the machine against the wall.

She thought he could have been a model if he hadn't gone into medicine. With his thick wavy black hair and striking face, he looked distinctly Greek or Italian, perhaps Portuguese. A long distinct nose and deep black eyes gave him a look of mysterious elegance. It only added to his overall appeal that he had a reputation as a skilled and caring obstetrician and gynecologist and was known as a reliable and talented surgeon. He was a little short compared with her: at five foot nine, she stood two inches taller than him. That was one area they never joked about. He was sensitive about his height.

"Actually, I came by to see how Donald was, and how you're holding up," he said. "And to ask if there's anything I can do to help."

"Thank you, John. That means a lot to me," she said. "To tell you the truth, I'm not even sure what he's feeling. He barely talks to me anymore. I've tried, but he gets angry at me whenever the conversation drifts into medicine. They're convening a board to look into his surgical license," she added in a small voice.

Rogers took a seat in one of the old upholstered chairs in Donald's office and looked at the row of diplomas on the wall. He spoke in a deep modulated tone, with a precise and deliberate diction that Liz had always admired. He talked like a professional, with all the smoothness of a radio announcer, but without the hysterical hard-sell attitude.

"It's really a shame, and over one mistake. In any other profession, people make mistakes every day. When a doctor makes an error, it's as if they've never done anything right in their entire career. All the legal vultures start circling."

His voice trailed off, but he kept his gaze fixed on Liz's eyes. He had a habit of directness that she never got used to. She picked up her purse from the floor and started looking around in it for a stick of gum.

"Well, look," he continued. "Why don't you let me take you out for a cup of coffee? If I know you, you've been here since seven this morning. Maybe we could get a bite to eat."

Liz looked out at the darkening parking lot, where a pair of nurses talked excitedly under a lightpost. Finally they parted company and walked off to their cars, which were easy to find among the dwindling numbers remaining in the lot. "Sounds good," she said. "I can't keep sticking around until ten o'clock every night."

She followed John's car to the Beach Café in Venice. She had been to the restaurant several times, mostly with Donald but a few times in John's company. As a couple, she and Donald socialized with John quite often. For some reason, though, they had never visited each other's houses, and John never brought a date.

He rarely spoke of his personal life. Donald speculated that John was gay and kept his affairs private, and Liz had always assumed that was the case. She knew she was familiar with only one side of John, though it was a side that she felt close to and liked immensely. He was a man who clearly kept his life compartmentalized, his secrets close to the vest.

In any case, she was grateful to be in the company of a friend. It seemed that their colleagues had effectively quarantined Liz and Donald since the fiasco at Med-Tek. She had received only a brief call from Hal Bergman, the chief of surgery at the hospital, and that had been perfunctory and strained. Everyone else had kept their distance, perhaps fearing the vultures that John mentioned.

"How are you keeping up with the work?" John asked after they ordered. He had a filet of poached salmon, she the Chinese chicken salad. The waiter opened a bottle of white wine and poured two glasses after John sniffed the cork and nodded his approval.

"I'm not," she said, tasting the wine. "It's going to hell. I can farm out my general surgery cases, but the laparoscopies can only go to people with experience. That's a limited group. Actually, I've already done a few myself."

John raised his eyebrows in exaggerated shock. "Really? Old 'big incisions are for real men' Danny? That's a surprise."

"I guess I'm not a real man. Let's just say I saw the light," Liz said, wincing at her own words when she heard herself echo Nordstrom's phrase.

She looked affectionately at John: in his blue blazer and sculpted hair, he fit in perfectly with the upscale clientele and modern furnishings of the Beach Café. Liz thought that she must look tired and dumpy in her businesslike pantsuit. People probably wondered how she had snared such a good-looking man, she thought. If people could picture them together at all.

The food provided an appealing diversion from her thoughts. John was amazed at her gusto as she attacked it. When he filled their glasses with wine a second time, he said, "I don't want to say I told you so, Liz, but I'm glad to hear that you're working with laparoscopy. You're young and talented. You shouldn't cut yourself off from the future."

"Unlike an old dinosaur such as yourself," she joked, buttering her third roll. She tried to remember; how old was John? Thirty-three? Thirty-four?

"No kidding, though. Take this afternoon. I had a case of peritoneal endometriosis. I was able to go in laparoscopically and deal with the local sites with the same efficiency as with open surgery. The difference is: Patient goes home in a fourth the time."

Liz nodded, warmed by his enthusiasm. It was nice to hear him talk about his work. She knew he was trying to take her mind off her husband.

"You know, of course, that we OB/GYN surgeons were using basic forms of the technology for twenty years. Ahead of our time, as usual."

"Yeah, but you never thought to turn the laparoscope around and look up into the abdomen," she said, feeling that she was inadvertently turning the conversation back to Donald. Whatever happened, she was still proud of him.

"True," John admitted, sipping his wine. "That was a bit like discovering the axle after having the wheel around for a while."

He paused for a moment and looked around the restaurant. The place was becoming crowded with attractive people, affluent types dressed in a studied casual style. He waved shyly across the room at someone he knew, then turned back to Liz, his expression serious.

"I know you might not want to talk about this, but exactly what happened at Med-Tek? The patient died during a vagotomy?"

Liz paused, holding her fork in the air. "I don't mind talking about it, but there's not much to say. I passed off the liver retractor to a nurse and took over on the camera. Donald and Kerry Nordstrom both had lasers inside the patient, doing a seromyotomy. That isn't standard—usually one surgeon would do all the work—but Nordstrom asked Donald to pitch in. It was an opportunity for Donald to get his name back out in the front ranks."

"That's unusually magnanimous behavior for Nordstrom, from what you've told me about him," John said.

"Well, Donald's laser perforated the patient's coeliac artery. He died within minutes. That's really all there is to it," Liz said. "Just a very costly mistake."

They finished their meal in silence. John seemed to be quietly preoccupied with Liz's version of the events at Med-Tek. He watched her dispatch her dessert with a bemused expression on his face, nursing a cappuccino. "You can put away the food when you want to, Danny," he said.

She paused between mouthfuls. "True. Sometimes I don't realize how hungry I am. Before he died, my father used to say that I could eat a running horse. Anyway, that probably explains why I'm getting fat and flabby. My metabolism is finally catching up with me."

The smile disappeared from his face. "That's not true at all. You're as svelte and beautiful as ever. See, I can compliment the fisherwoman with the best of them." He laughed and motioned for the check. "But seriously, you never told me your father was dead."

"He died when I was in my residency. It was a very bad time for me. I couldn't get back to Virginia until two days after he passed away. My mother was very upset."

"Your family lives in Virginia?"

"Richmond," she answered. "But now it's just my mom and my baby brother. And my big sister in New York."

"I can't believe I didn't know that. I guess I just don't ask the right questions."

"That's okay. After all, I don't know anything about your background, Rogers. You've been pretty mum."

She meant her comment to be taken in good humor, but it made him visibly nervous. She immediately wished she had said nothing.

"Well, it's not that," he said. "It's just that there's not much to say. I had an all-American middle-class upbringing in suburban L.A. My mother is still alive. I don't know, I guess my family isn't what you would call close-knit."

They stood outside in the evening fog, waiting for the valets to return with their cars. An awkward silence had developed between them. John had grown distant since talking about his life.

"I hope Donald got something to eat," she said, trying to change the subject. "He isn't taking care of himself, and I really need his support right now. I don't know how much longer I can try to balance two practices."

John took Liz's hand in his and squeezed. The gesture pleasantly shocked her with its sudden warmth; she hadn't considered it, but he was one of her closest friends. "Just stay strong, Liz. Donald will come around. Tell him to give me a call if he wants to talk."

Liz saw her Honda rounding the corner. "Guess they found mine first, Rogers. You'll have to wait out here in the cold all by yourself."

"So, Danny, you're abandoning me to the wilds of the Venice streets? The first warm car that you happen to own comes along, and you just hop in and leave me," he said with a smile.

"Seriously, thanks for dinner. It was nice."

John gave her a smile and helped her into her car. His perfect white teeth sparkled as he stepped away. "The pleasure was mine. Remember to tell Donald to call me."

John Rogers watched Liz Danny's car turn right and head west on Main Street, in the direction of her Santa Monica home. Then his black Lexus, driven by a young Mexican valet, pulled up in front of him. *"Gracias,"* John said, handing the young man a five-dollar bill.

He skipped his chance to get on the freeway, opting instead to take surface streets to his West L.A. apartment. He had a lot on his mind: Donald and Liz's troubles, the conversation he had just had with Liz about his family background. For a moment, he had been almost ready to tell her the truth. He had been equally close other times but had never taken the leap. There was always a reason not to, and this time he simply felt that Liz had enough on her mind without finding out the reality of his past.

As he drove further inland, the night fog dissipated and the temperature became more comfortable, as if driving closer to the heart of the city brought him closer to some basic source of heat and energy. He opened his window to the pleasant night air and turned on his radio, listening to the jazz flowing from his speakers. The drive at that time of the night, the city was easygoing yet alive with the buzz and action of a sprawling modern metropolis.

John was thirty-four now, an age at which he had expected to be married and to have a family. Instead, he was alone. He loved his work, he respected his colleagues, but he had been truly close to no one in a very long time. And he had no one to blame but himself.

He parked his car and waved at the doorman as he made his way to the building's elevators. His apartment was dark and quiet when he stepped inside, and the answering machine indicated that no one had called. That was a little disappointing. He had hoped that Donald would have phoned by then. Deciding not to intrude on him or Liz by calling first, he poured a glass of wine in the kitchen and sat heavily on his sofa. He turned on the television, more to break the silence than anything else.

Liz pulled into the driveway of her two-story Spanish-style home, her spirits buoyed by her dinner with John. Though he stubbornly persisted in being mysterious and secretive, she intuitively knew that he was someone she could trust. And Donald, too; in fact, she was going to insist that Donald call John that very evening. John would be a steadying influence, with his calmness and reason, and perhaps they could talk man-to-man in a way that might help Donald.

With dismay, Liz saw that the mail was overflowing from their box. It must have been there all day. She knew Donald was home—his car, his pride-and-joy restored Porsche 914, occupied the far half of the driveway—but apparently he hadn't come out of hiding even to check the mail.

Her keys clattered loudly on the entryway table. She

looked at the mail, glad that Donald hadn't seen it. Lurking amid the usual appeals for charitable contributions, magazine offers, and medical flyers was another letter from the Indiana State Board of Medical Quality Assurance. No doubt it was a notification of when and where Donald's license hearing was going to be held. She would see what kind of mood he was in before delivering the news.

Before Liz had put down her purse, a sudden noise made her heart leap. A large shape moved quickly toward her from the darkness in the living room, and she raised a hand in the air as if to defend herself. It didn't do any good; the rambunctious Daisy leaped up on her and began to whine, licking her lips and wagging her tail with manic abandon. This overflow of attention was due to more than Daisy's usual avid affection: the dog ran to the kitchen and whined loudly by the door. She obviously hadn't been let outside in a while.

Liz let Daisy out into the backyard, annoyed. The dog acted as if she had been waiting all day. Even if Donald was depressed, he could have taken pity on the poor animal. She looked for signs of Daisy, but she had run off to the far part of the yard in search of rabbits or some other canine entertainment. Liz closed the door and locked it.

Donald hadn't appeared, but that wasn't anything unusual. Even under normal conditions, they had never been the most romantic or demonstrative of couples. When they first started living together, a year before they were married, they found it wasn't necessary to seek each other out the minute they got home. They would go about their business, waiting for the natural course of their actions to bring them together.

There was a certain logic to it, but at times it made her sad. She remembered how her parents used to sit at the table for hours after dinner, drinking coffee and talking about their days. Liz and Donald had been married for almost three years and had yet to spend such an evening together. The afternoon they spent on the beach in Malibu, even though it had been tinged with sadness and regret, had represented to her all of the things they had deprived one another of in the last few years: the togetherness, the communication, the hope that they could continue together for the rest of their lives.

Tonight would be different, she decided. Some quiet time together might help them both. She was tired, but she felt good, and she wanted to share her mood with her husband. The more she thought about it, she felt that Donald had a good chance to face the board and keep his license. He had told her about a malfunctioning laser before they left for Indianapolis. It was possible that the same thing had happened twice; perhaps the equipment was to blame.

And as John said, it was one mistake. A fatal mistake, true, but Nordstrom also deserved some of the blame. He may have rushed his team to perform the vagotomy. When he asked for Donald's help, he may not have been motivated solely by a wish to help his friend's faltering career. Perhaps Kerry himself had been in over his head. If that was the case, then Donald's error was the least of what went wrong that day.

Liz climbed the stairs, two long-stemmed glasses in one hand and a freshly opened bottle of zinfandel in the other. She felt her optimism and good cheer begin to fade when she found the place dark and silent. Donald was probably asleep. She turned on the hall light and made for their bedroom, hoping to find him there. The television set was turned on, but the sound had been muted. She watched a local newscast for a moment, alone. Donald wasn't there. He must have fallen asleep on the sofa.

Whistling softly, she walked the length of the hall to his office. It was strange for the house to be so quiet: she usually had the TV or the stereo going. His office door was closed, which presented a problem. Her hands were full, and she stamped her feet with frustration. She kicked the door and called out Donald's name. There was no answer.

Growing slightly irritated, she tucked the bottle of wine under her arm and turned the knob. The door creaked on its hinges as it came open, revealing nothing but darkness. Liz turned on the light and looked inside. What she saw caused her to drop the bottle and the glasses, which shattered on the hardwood floor. The sudden crash echoed horribly in the silence before the house resumed its unnatural calm.

She backed away from the door and walked back to their bedroom, as if retracing her steps could reverse the series of events. Like a child, she wished over and over for time to reverse, for it never to have happened.

"No," she said. "No." She sat on the bed, her hands shaking violently.

She wanted to cry but her eyes remained dry. Instead, her entire body shook: with clinical detachment, she realized that she was in a state of psychological shock. She closed her eyes but the image wouldn't go away. Donald had wound a length of rope around the ceiling rafters in his office. He had tied it around his neck and kicked away the chair beneath him. She saw his face, his gray skin, and his eyes lifelessly staring at her.

A line from Oscar Wilde entered her mind: "But it is not sweet, With nimble feet, To dance upon the air." A violent shudder swept through her body.

The tears finally came—gentle at first, then with a terrible force that wracked her body. Lying back on the bed, she looked around their room. She had never felt so alone. "Donald," she said. "How could you do this to us?"

OCTOBER

October 1, 1995
*Satellite Microwave Transmission—Scrambled and Restricted Code. **Do not transcribe. Commit to memory.***

Executive Office, United States National
Security Council
The White House, by Permission and Acknowledgment
of the President of the United States

To:
All Active Intelligence/Security Operatives
South-Central Asia, South America

Nation Eleven South-Central Asia regime nuclear/chemical capacities placed on full operational standby. Anticipated receipt of technological X-factor (code: Lifebank—from intercepts) enabling inoculation against nuclear radiation and chemical toxins.

Bidding now between Eleven and South American Nation Three. Middle Eastern nations no longer active. Situation advantageous to continued acceptable stability levels in M.E. region—potentially catastrophic to other regions involved.

White House assumes Nation Eleven will receive Lifebank secret, due to large cash reserves, advanced war technology, level of hostility between regime and nearest neighbor.

Full nuclear strike from Nation Eleven projects immediate counterstrike, global involvement. Informing Nation Eleven's neighbor of situation is forbidden, due to likelihood of precipitating immediate conflict. Pentagon running computer simulations of global/domestic fatality estimates, viability of nuclear-winter/large-scale extinction theories.

Operatives instructed to locate means of technological transfer. Courier, satellite transmission, database link-up possible routes of transfer. Mission status upgraded to Level One—non-political fatalities allowable, expected in course of directive.

Transmission complete. Reset receiving and scrambling equipment to standard security settings. Out.

CHAPTER SEVEN

10:40 A.M., October 3, Los Angeles.

PATRICIA DANNY STOOD IN THE PARLOR DOORWAY OF HER daughter's home, a stern but sympathetic expression on her face. She was a woman with a deceptive appearance: though she was fifty, her tall erect bearing and sparkling brown eyes led people to believe that she was ten years younger. It flattered her that strangers sometimes mistook her and her daughter for sisters. "Elizabeth," she said, "have you even heard a word I've said?"

Liz looked up from the television screen. It bore a graphic, disturbing image of the insides of someone's body. A variety of instruments pulled and cut at the red and white tissue. Patricia could barely stand to look at it.

"What, Mom? I'm sorry, I wasn't listening," Liz said. She sat on the floor in a long flannel nightgown. A cold unattended cup of coffee sat perilously close to her feet.

"I said, how many times are you going to watch that awful tape? Let go of your work for a while, darling. It will be there for you when you're ready to come back to it. It's time to get dressed."

Liz used the remote control to pause the videotape. For

what seemed like the thousandth time, she peered intently at the image of twin lasers in the abdomen of Ray Barker.

She saw the same scene in her sleep and when she was awake: identical lasers steadily made a series of cauteries as Donald and Kerry Nordstrom burned out the remaining branches of vagus nerve. Then the laser nearest the stomach made a quick motion in the open area of the cavity. The movement reminded her of a loop-the-loop made by a barnstorming stunt flyer. The daredevil was Donald, making a quick search for remaining branches of vagus. Then the laser fired into the stomach, and the screen turned red.

She stopped the tape, finally noticing that her mother was staring at her. Patricia's arms were folded, a fretful expression creasing her attractive features. "Elizabeth, honey, what do you expect to find on that tape? You've watched it almost constantly since I've been here. I didn't want to say anything, but it worries me. It's morbid."

"I don't know, Mom. Maybe I just think that if I stare at it long enough, I'm going to find some answers. I don't know where else to look."

She embraced her mother, trying to control her emotions. Patricia had flown in from Virginia within twelve hours of hearing about Donald's suicide and had been a godsend in helping her with the arrangements. Liz didn't know how she could have handled everything otherwise.

"I'll go get dressed now. I know I'm running late," Liz said. She walked to the foot of the stairs, thinking about the funeral she was about to attend. She realized that she was still in a state of emotional shock and that the true grief had yet to hit her. It had been the same years before, when her father died unexpectedly.

"Mom," she said, pausing on the stairs, "thanks for everything. Really. If it wasn't for you, I . . . ."

Patricia gave a weary smile. "Of course, darling. Ev-

erything's going to be all right in time. You have to believe in that. Remember, I went through the same loss
with your father.''

From the moment she entered the church, Liz felt that
she had made a mistake. She didn't know if she could
make it through the service. Instead of looking at the casket, she concentrated on the row of flowers lining the al-
tar. They were beautiful, she thought, trying to avoid the
glances and comments her entrance had triggered.

The presence of Donald's and her colleagues made her
anxious and uncomfortable. She knew that the autopsy
findings and recent testimony about Donald had shocked
the medical community, and she felt as if she had to answer for it all.

Donald's death was ruled a suicide, but a worse shock
came when the medical examiner's office discovered
traces of opiates and barbiturates in his blood. The same
day, a nurse at Community Hospital stepped forward to
tell the director that she had seen Donald inject himself in
an empty on-call room two months before. He had convinced her that he was giving himself an antibiotic, but
the scene had gnawed at her conscience.

Several others came forward and stated that they had
been suspicious of Donald's behavior on several occa-
sions. He had frequently been glassy-eyed, clumsy, and
distant in the operating room. Supplies taken from his
home by the police indicated that he probably had a daily
habit and had obtained the drugs from hospital supply.

Though no one said it, Liz knew the question on everyone's minds: Did she know about this? And if not, how
could she not have known? Sadly, she had no answer to
these silent voices of accusation. She had never suspected.
It was impossible to describe the relationship between two
people: how they could grow distant and inattentive, how

they could reach the point where they no longer knew each other's secrets. She thought of her optimism and ebullience in the moments before she found Donald, of her hopes for the future, and felt at once foolish and spent.

John Rogers slipped into the pew and sat beside Liz. Her mother introduced herself, and they fell into a polite conversation about his work and her garden. Liz slumped down in the pew, not even bothering to answer when Patricia asked her how she felt.

She wouldn't admit it to anyone—it made her feel strange and heartless—but she felt almost nothing. She felt lost and abandoned, but it felt as if she were playing the part of the grieving widow. More than anything, she felt numb. Her mind was filled only with videotaped images. She thought back to the arrangement in the OR, trying to find some way to explain how Donald could have made that meticulously precise looping motion, only to misfire the laser a moment later.

An absentminded count of the room indicated that about a hundred people came to the funeral. Donald would have been flattered: Hal Bergman was there, as well as most of the surgical staff. Even a few of Donald's patients showed up, people with whom he had developed a rapport.

They had come to pay their respects, but Liz couldn't forget the period of ostracism after their return from Med-Tek. Following that stinging line of thought, she allowed herself to steal a glance in the direction of Kerry Nordstrom. He sat on the other side of the room in a somber black suit, staring straight ahead of him, pausing from time to time to speak with one of the surgeons.

Although she had immediately thrown away the flowers and condolence card he sent, much to the consternation of her mother, Liz had agreed to allow Nordstrom to deliver the eulogy. She knew she wouldn't be able to control herself if she had to speak, and Nordstrom had written her a letter requesting the honor. He cited a long string of memories from his friendship with Donald, and even a few times the three of them had spent together.

The minister's remarks were brief, but Liz found it impossible to concentrate on what he was saying. The casket loomed at the edge of her vision, a great and terrible thing she couldn't bear to look at. It contained her husband's body, she thought. How strange, just a wooden box. Finally Nordstrom got up to speak, his head bowed solemnly.

"Friends and colleagues," he said. "I come to remember a treasured friend of us all, a man who brought warmth to those he knew and healing to those he served. I ask you to remember the considerable good that he did, and his skill and excellence."

Nordstrom paused, his head still bowed. His hands were clasped before him, and he spoke in a low, distant voice.

"My own life was greatly improved by knowing him, and I think that he would want to be remembered for his deeds. He was a caring healer who became misguided somewhere along his path in life. The history of our profession should remember him as one of our best. Let us leave the role of judgment to higher powers."

Nordstrom looked up at the audience, a single tear shining in the corner of his eye. He nodded to the minister and resumed his seat in the audience, pausing along the way to pull a silk pocket square from his jacket and dab the tear away from his cheek.

10:30 A.M., October 5, Indianapolis.

Irwin Ross stood on the thick carpeting in Kerry Nord-strom's office. He had exhausted the string of expletives he shouted at the Med-Tek director, triggered when an indignant Nordstrom had complained that he was on an important call and didn't want to be disturbed. After more than two weeks out of town, building his anger, the comment was more than Ross could take. Finally he stopped yelling and stood there, lost in thought. It looked as if he were checking his memory to see if he had forgotten any choice profanities.

"It's just . . . idiotic," he said. "I can't understand why I ever listen to you. You want to make a spectacle of surgery, make a Broadway production out of the first va-gotomy performed under the Endicott aegis, and what do I say? I say: All right, Kerry. You want to use your friend to assist, even though he looks like he can't stand up on his own? I say: All right, Kerry. What the hell was I think-ing?"

Nordstrom smiled at his boss, knowing it would infuri-ate him. If he had his way, he'd pluck off every button on Ross's five-thousand-dollar Savile Row suit and force him to eat them.

"I don't know, Irwin. What were you thinking?"

Ross looked at Nordstrom with an expression of ag-grieved incredulity, his cheeks and ears tinged red with anger. "I've listened to you for too long, Kerry. I won't let you make a fool out of me."

Nordstrom stood up and walked to his humidor, pulling out a cigar and sniffing it. "Look, your highness. It was a mistake. I shouldn't have let him assist. It'll never happen again. All right? Now, why don't you go figure out what you're going to say to the old man?"

"The hell with you," Ross said.

"The hell with me. That's an intelligent response, Irwin. Did one of your girlfriends think that one up for you?"

"At least I don't have to pay for sex, Kerry."

Nordstrom pursed his lips. "What are you talking about? What are you trying to say?"

"Relax, Kerry," Ross said. "None of your extracurricular pursuits are going to make the papers. I'm in so deep with you that I truly curse the day we met."

Nordstrom smiled a broad toothy grin. "Spare me. You're getting a fair cut. You had your chance to get out. You could have turned me in, you could have just walked away. But you didn't. Face it, Irwin. You're a slime."

"I'm warning you. Before long, I'm going so far away that nobody in the world will be able to find me. Even that won't be far enough away from you."

Ross left without another word, slamming the door behind him. With a metallic snip, Nordstrom cut off the end of an expensive Havana cigar and lit it, walking ponderously to the window. He had an an ideal view of Med-Tek, his kingdom. Below, Endicott trucks bustled in and out of the front entrance, and he could see the slanted windows of the pig laboratory, in which another seminar was taking place.

He reviewed the figures in his head. Two hundred and fifty surgeons at four thousand dollars a head: he had brought in one million dollars a week through his seminars, to say nothing of the future benefits of brand-name loyalty and long-term ties that would follow. He was doing his job well, bringing in money hand over fist. Even the old man, Malcolm Endicott, had to admit that he was a roaring success in his job, even though the old prig looked down on him. It was easy to say that money didn't matter when you were born into a medical empire.

He had made plenty of money for the old man and his white-haired board of directors. His three-million-dollar salary was almost insulting, given his value. But that was pocket change. Soon he would be richer than a king; then they could all go to hell.

It had been a long climb from being born a dirt-poor hillbilly in rural Tennessee. His parents had been worthless to him as a child: his father got himself killed in a bar before little Kerry was out of diapers. His mother was gone more often than not, leaving him in the care of his doddering grandmother.

It was then that he had learned about focus, about immersing himself in his work and eventually earning a scholarship to medical school. He also learned to hate: his mother, the kids who tormented him for being fat and bookish, and himself for being luckless enough to be born without means, without power, without all the things he would dedicate his life to obtaining. He had learned to let nothing get in his way. Sentiment, love, friendship—these things merely reminded him of the weakness he had been surrounded with as a child.

Of course there was the matter of Liz Danny. He was certain she had the tape. When he saw her rushing out of the operating theater after Ray Barker died, alarms went off in his head. So she had that advantage, and she was too intelligent to be underestimated.

The question was: What did she plan to do with it? One possibility was to buy her off. He liked the idea: greed was a motivation he could understand. There were other options: permanent and messy possibilities. But when the first stage of a plan meets with failure, the tactician moves on to the next. Seeing her in Indianapolis had been painful; he had been reminded of a time when he cared for her, when a few dates brought forth a rush of sincere emotion that had been dashed when she broke off with him before they had even started.

His performance at Donald Page's funeral had, of course, been worthy of an Oscar; it may even have gone toward rehabilitating his old colleague's reputation. It certainly helped solidify his own image, which was the important part. I certainly didn't get to where I am, Nordstrom thought, by neglecting to put forward the best image. Nor by failing to recognize threats to my position.

Human history will be changed by coming events, he thought. Changed by me. The course of nations, the nature of life and aging, all different. The power will rest in the hands of those who meet the price. And Kerry Nordstrom, in the middle of it all: wealthy beyond his wildest dreams of avarice.

3:45 P.M., October 12, Los Angeles.

Trying to keep up with Liz Danny was almost more than Ronnie Wilson could take. In fact, she was getting a little pissed off: she canceled her afternoon patients when her friend called needing to talk to her, then drove straight to Culver City from Westwood. Since then, she had spent the last two hours riding elevators, rushing down hallways, and standing in the background while Liz compulsively attended to her patients. Psychologists have feelings, too, she thought. This is getting ridiculous.

Ronnie stood in the doorway of a standard hospital room, waiting for Liz to finish a pre-op conference with her patient: a middle-aged, portly man with close-cropped brown hair. Veronica thought he was playing up his discomfort a little for the benefit of his young and attractive doctor.

"Mr. Bausch, I think the pain-killers you have already received should be sufficient," she said, checking his chart.

The man lay back on his pillow and stared at the ceiling. "Always the same. How long am I gonna have to stay here, anyway? I think I get sicker every day I have to lay in this bed."

"The laparoscopic repair should be routine," Liz said, smiling at the man's histrionics. "I guarantee you'll be back at work in a week, and without unsightly scars. How's that for a deal?"

"Hey, who said anything about going back to work? I just want to get the hell out of the hospital."

"You have to take the bad with the good, Mr. Bausch," Liz said.

"Oh, hell, I'm just fooling around. I'll be happy to get back. They're lost without me back at the plant. I basically run the place, you know."

"Oh, by the way, Mr. Bausch, I've had some complaints about you walking around the halls and distracting our nurses." The older man shrugged, a sheepish grin on his face. "I'm sure they're flattered, but they have a lot of work to do. In other words: stay in bed." Liz smiled and shook her fist at Bausch, leading Ronnie out of the room.

"Liz, stop," she said, gently holding her friend's arm. "You called to talk to me, remember? We can't talk about what's bothering you while we're jogging up and down the halls of this hospital. We need to go someplace where we can sit down for a moment's peace and quiet."

A high-pitched beep rang out. Liz and Veronica looked down at their pagers, neither of which bore a message. A young intern came from behind and elbowed between them, heading for an in-house phone with a harried expression on his face.

In the cafeteria, Liz relaxed and had a laugh at herself. "Sorry for the whirling dervish act. You have to realize that, in effect, I'm conducting two practices now: mine and Donald's. I'm still trying to balance the work load and get everyone taken care of."

Ronnie stirred her coffee and nodded. "As a psychologist, allow me to say that your pace worries me. I understand, though. Work is a good way to take your mind off things."

Liz looked at her friend quizzically. "I hadn't thought about it like that, to tell you the truth. But I see your point. Ever since Donald died I've been practically keeping the pace of a resident. I tried to take some time off, but it didn't work. My mind was filled with a million things."

"Like what?"

"Well, Donald, obviously. His drug use, which I still can't explain to myself. I also have questions about what happened at Med-Tek. I have this strange feeling that something was going on that no one knows about. Did I mention that Donald complained to me about a malfunctioning laser before we left?"

"No, you didn't," Ronnie said, staring at the table.

"And not only that, but the fact that Nordstrom was involved has me concerned. The more I think about it, the entire setup in Indianapolis had some strange, sinister qualities. I mean, who knows what happens on such a high corporate level? Those people could be capable of anything, and I mean anything. I might even go back there and have a look around; since I'm now a practicing laparoscopic surgeon with all of one month's experience, I'd have every right to just walk in and snoop around the place. Right?"

With a slow measured sigh, Ronnie looked up at her friend. "I understand that it's hard to come to grips with everything that's happened, Liz, but I don't think this is the time to start blaming others. I mean, come on. Endicott is a reputable company. They make baby food and surgical instruments. And from what you've told me, the evidence condemning Donald is very clear-cut. You have to let go of these . . ."

"Paranoid feelings?" Liz snapped. "Is that what you mean?" She ran her hands through her hair, pulling out a tangle.

After a moment's silence, Liz reached out to take her friend's hand. "Ronnie, thanks for talking to me. I understand what you're saying, and I know there's a lot of truth to it. The next thing you know I'm liable to start thinking that they're coming after me, right?"

Ronnie smiled weakly. Something in Liz's tone made her wonder how serious her friend really was.

Liz went back to her office after sending Veronica home with assurances that she would go home early and get some sleep. Michelle, her secretary, handed Liz a batch of phone messages even as she tried to slip into her office unnoticed.

"Come on, Liz. We can't keep neglecting the housekeeping," she said, handing her the messages.

Liz looked at them with little interest. One was from a colleague who had been pestering her for referrals. Another was from her mother. The third message made her purse her lips in consternation. She looked at it for a moment with surprise.

Dialing the long-distance extension, she waited for an answer. "Kerry Nordstrom, please. Dr. Liz Danny returning his call."

She waited for a moment until the familiar voice appeared on the line. "Liz! Thanks for calling back. I know you must be very busy these days."

"Swamped, Kerry. What can I do for you?" she said, trying to keep the edge of animosity out of her voice. So many of her recent thoughts had centered on him, and now the sound of his voice made her neck ache with tension.

"First of all, Liz, I wanted to check on you and see how you were holding up. I'm sorry we didn't get a chance to speak at the funeral, but I wanted to let you know again how shocked and saddened I've been since Donald's untimely death."

Liz took off her glasses and pressed on her eyes with her fingers. She struggled to maintain her composure, simply allowing Nordstrom to talk on.

"But to the present, Liz," he said. "If I may shift gears for a moment, I also called you in my capacity as head of Med-Tek and a vice-president of Endicott International. I have a proposal for you."

His voice had shifted from a tone of sympathy to ingratiating salesmanship. Something smooth and velvety came across in his voice, making Liz feel strangely dirty, almost violated. His trace southern accent and boyish zeal were sinister rather than charming. She grunted permission for him to go on, feeling angry at herself for letting him get to her.

"I heard that you've assumed Donald's practice, within limits, and that you're converting over to laparoscopic surgery. A little fly on the wall told me that."

"It's no secret, Kerry," Liz said, unwilling to allow Nordstrom the satisfaction of insinuating that he had ferreted out some sort of hidden information. "I've taken a lot of flack from some of my colleagues, almost like I deserted to the enemy camp, but I've come to believe that the possibilities of laparoscopy are limitless. That's why I've converted, as you say.''

"Well put, Liz. Well said. In fact, so well said that I know I've made the right decision in calling you today.''

Liz rolled her eyes as Nordstrom continued. He sounded like a satanic version of an infomercial host.

''I want to offer you a contract with Endicott for exclusive use of our line of instruments. In return, we are prepared to offer you a place on our national panel, with financial considerations and a variety of educational and promotional benefits.''

Liz had heard of the corporate panels: they were an honor highly sought after by surgeons, for the prestige as well as the money. They usually went to surgeons who had put in years of work on research and publishing data. There was a lot of political infighting for these positions, and they were often awarded to surgeons who campaigned the hardest. Something about this offer was wrong.

''Let me get this straight. I've been a full-time practicing laparoscopic surgeon for a month, and you want to offer me a panelist position? Do you mind explaining why?''

Nordstrom's raspy chuckle resounded into the telephone. ''Not at all, Liz. My decision was based on two judgments. First, there's you: You're smart, intelligent, and an excellent surgeon. I want to catch you while you're on the way up, and I think I can help you get there. Second, the chief of surgery at your hospital, Hal Bergman, has agreed to an exclusive contract with our competitor. Signing you would be a way to keep your hospital from falling completely under the sway of the enemy.''

It was a surprise to hear the hospital described in these terms, like a battleground, and a bigger surprise to hear that she was being asked to counterbalance Bergman's corporate affiliations. She certainly couldn't see herself pledging allegiance to Kerry Nordstrom.

"I appreciate your honesty," she said. "But I'm not sure this is the time to make a decision like this. To be frank, I need more experience with the instruments before I can decide which I like better."

"That's fine," Nordstrom cooed. "I have little doubt that you will decide that ours are superior. You see, I stand behind our product."

"Good, Kerry. If that's all, I have to be going," Liz said. She was eager to get off the phone and away from his voice.

"Give me a second to sweeten the pot, Liz. I can't let you get away from me so easily. It just occurred to me, because of a previous phone call, that there is another aspect of the deal that might appeal to you. Were you aware of our expansion into Latin America?"

Nordstrom's voice had risen in volume and insistency. He was straining so hard to keep her on the phone that she felt bullied. "No, I'm not, and I really don't have the—" Liz said.

"At the moment we have a facility in Mexico, and we're planning one in Uruguay. Our installation in the Yucatán state of Mexico is really up and running. We provide patient care to the local populace, and we're starting to train surgeons from all over the hemisphere in our techniques. On our equipment, of course. If you came aboard, I could arrange to send you down there for a few weeks. You could inspect the facilities, help out. It'd be more of a vacation than work, and we'd pick up the tab. I might also mention that we are looking for permanent surgical staff there, and we offer an outrageous salary."

Liz's mind reeled at this string of big-money offers: a high-salary position in addition to a panelist's spot. He was moving way too fast. He was intimidating when he was in action, and as he spoke, she knew instinctively that he would eventually ask for something in return.

"Kerry, I have to wait to think about all this. I have to get my feet wet for a while. I hope you understand."

"Of course, Liz. Forgive me for coming on so strong, but that's how I got to where I am: by taking advantage of opportunity when it presents itself."

"You can say that again," she said.

A moment of silence passed between them. It felt to both parties like an electric charge of understanding. Finally, he spoke again.

"Uh, one more thing, Liz. I know that the scene in the operating theater after the vagotomy, uh, incident, was very chaotic, but I wondered if you noticed anyone fooling around with the video recorders during the confusion."

His voice was cold when he asked the question, all trace of ingratiating solicitude and boyish enthusiasm gone. Liz's mind filled again with the image of the laser looping in the abdominal cavity, preparing to make the fatal cut.

"No, not really, Kerry," she said. "My mind was definitely elsewhere."

"Of course. Pardon my asking, but one of our tapes turned up missing. There are a lot of headaches regarding privacy laws and copyright if we lose one of the masters. I think one of those scatterbrained technicians forgot to load up the machine. I apologize for wasting your time by asking about it."

"No problem, Kerry. Thank you for your call," Liz said. Why don't I just hang up on him? she asked herself.

"Thank you, Liz. Please consider my offer. And don't take too long. I don't want to be overly blunt, but there is a time limit on this kind of thing. I assume you know what I mean.''

''Of course,'' she said.

''And, Liz, thank you for allowing me to deliver the eulogy. I hope it bodes well for our professional future and, I hope, personal friendship. We were close once, and I think we're the kind of people who understand each other.''

After they hung up, Liz sat in her office for a while without venturing out. Though she had surgery in a half hour, she wanted a quiet moment to digest what Nordstrom had said, particularly his final comment. She thought back to how he had looked at her in that Indianapolis hotel room, the way his eyes had made her feel that her bathing suit was invisible. So they had been close once, for the briefest of times—why would he play upon that now? And why did he mention that insignificant tape after offering her instant money and prestige?

The key had to be the videotape, she thought. But what about it? If it showed that the laser had been defective, it would implicate Nordstrom. But it didn't seem to be defective in the tape: it simply appeared to have been aimed improperly. Even if it was a prototype model, there was no reason to assume anything would have been wrong with it. Nordstrom had used the same device, and he didn't kill the patient.

Liz turned Nordstrom's offer over in her mind. He was ready to give her things that other surgeons would kill for. She hadn't really earned a panel position or any of those other things. It made her feel sick and anxious inside to think that Nordstrom might expect some kind of repayment for his favor, but she killed the thought before it could grow. She wondered if he was aware that she knew nothing about why the tape was important to him. It was impossible to tell what he might think. As always.

He wanted her for something. The thought echoed in her mind. Liz checked her watch; she was due in the OR, where things were simple and direct. There was a certain safety and security there that could be found nowhere else.

"What does he want with me?" Liz said to the empty room.

CHAPTER EIGHT

LIZ TRIED TO SIT PATIENTLY, FEELING THE IMPACT OF THE POWDER puff on her face as her makeup was fine-tuned yet again. Angela, a young woman in a leotard and sweatshirt, fussed and hovered over Liz's face as if putting the finishing touches on the ceiling of the Sistine Chapel. It wasn't easy to sit still. Liz preferred her face when it wasn't under four coats of thick, vigorously applied paint.

When she entered the set of the TV station, Angela had told Liz that her nose would come off shiny on camera and that she should wear her hair down rather than pulled back. Liz acquiesced to the air of authority and solemnity the girl projected in these matters but drew the line at changing from her navy blue suit jacket to a snazzier model. "I want to look like a doctor, not Madonna," Liz said, earning a perplexed look from Angela.

Andy Connor, the producer of the "MedNews" segment on the local network affiliate, approached from the rear of the set. With him was the reporter, Dr. Simon Weaver. They had been talking with the camera crew over the fine points of the segment they were about to film, and

from what she overheard, Weaver sounded more like a
movie star than a doctor. He insistently reminded the crew
that his left side was more complimentary and asked repeatedly for applications of styling gel to his elaborate
coiffure.

Even before she entered the building, though, Liz
pledged to herself to be patient and put up with whatever
Hollywood eccentricity she might encounter. Truthfully,
she had been flattered when Hal Bergman asked her to
appear on the segment, which would deal with advances
in laparoscopic technology. Hal said with a laugh that she
certainly was the most photogenic of the surgical staff,
and probably the most articulate. He reminded her to
mention the name of Community Hospital as often as possible, and to play up the fact that they were trying to
develop one of the best laparoscopic surgery departments
in the nation.

Liz agreed to appear but felt a sad sense that Donald
should have been the spokesman, not she. She began to
see the project as yet another instance in which she carried on his work for him.

"All right, Dr. Danny. I've reviewed the footage you
brought and I think it's spectacular," Weaver said. The
producer stood in the background and nodded. "What
we'll need is for you to provide a voice-over for what's
going on in the tape. Besides that, we'll have you on camera for intro and outro, the usual stuff. Do you watch my
segments often?"

"No, I don't," Liz admitted. The host seemed crest-
fallen. "But I've heard they're quite informative. People
at the hospital always speak highly of your work," she
added eagerly. Weaver seemed mollified.

"Well, good. Maybe we'll make you a fan," he said.
"You'll be able to see yourself in the monitors up above,

but in general you should look at me when we're talking. You look great—you'll show up on video like a pro. Won't she look great, Andy?''

The producer briefly looked up from a bank of monitors. ''She'll look great, Simon, Now sit still for a moment, Dr. Danny,'' he said.

Liz nodded and sat absolutely motionless as the sound technician stepped forward and unceremoniously pinned a microphone on her lapel. She peered up at one of the monitors that showed her image. Not bad, she thought. It was a good decision to wear her hair down, and the dark suit jacket made her look tall and serious. With a glance at Weaver's chair, she saw that it contained a large cushion. The shorter man wanted to maintain an illusion of being taller than his female guest.

The beginning of the show consisted of Weaver making general statements about laparoscopic surgery, alluding to the newness of the technology, the rise in the number of surgeons who practiced the procedures, and the range of treatments available.

When the time came for Liz to speak, she was amazed at how quickly her nervousness evaporated. In the moments before, she had stared transfixed at the red light atop one of the three cameras, but the frantic waving of the producer forced her to turn and face Weaver just as she appeared on the screen. In response to a general question, she told him that she had been performing laparoscopies for only a short time but had begun to shift the emphasis of her practice.

''This is what convinced me, Simon,'' she said, laughing inwardly at this stab at on-the-air, first-name-basis chumminess. ''The patient that once faced two weeks in the hospital, scarring, and muscle damage can go home in a day and be back at work in two. There is minimal scarring, and we have had few recurrences or complications, all within reasonably expectable levels of probability. The true revolution, you see, is in making complex surgery into an outpatient procedure. Currently, the technology is available for abdominally located surgery, gynecological procedures, even vagotomy for ulcer sufferers.''

She suddenly fell silent. Weaver spoke quickly to ease the momentary awkwardness. ''The amazing thing, Dr. Danny, is that this technology is less than five years old. Isn't that correct?''

''It is,'' she agreed. ''I reasonably expect that within most people's lifetimes, they or someone they know will reap the benefits of laparoscopic surgery.''

Footage began to run of a recurrent left direct inguinal hernia that she had performed on a fifty-seven-year-old patient one week before.

''The entire procedure takes thirty to forty-five minutes to perform,'' she said, watching the video of her work. ''You see here the dissection to gain access to the preperitoneal space, using hot cautery scissors.'' The screen showed the magnified interior of the human abdominal cavity, where the instrument steadily cut through red tissue that briefly became yellow as it gave way to the scissors.

''Working in the inguinal region, the hernia is repaired with a biological mesh screen, which is stapled directly to the posterior fascia. The peritoneum is closed over the prosthesis, and the patient can be sent home four hours after the surgery.''

On the screen, a long silver instrument moved through the abdominal cavity, dispensing staples to affix a piece of mesh that resembled a section of screen door. Liz winced when she saw the black Endicott logo on the instrument.

Though she hadn't intended to, she had provided great free advertising for the corporation.

After the taping, Liz was told that the segment would air on that night's local broadcast, with a possibility that it would be picked up by the network for the evening news. "It depends on how many car bombings and hijackings there were in the world today," Andy Connor remarked archly.

Back at her office, Liz tried to catch up on the small mountain of paperwork that had accumulated on her desk during the previous week. In addition to the stack of reports and forms, there was an ominous note asking her to report to the hospital surgical committee in two days. She guessed it had to do with her participation in the vagotomy death at Med-Tek. Everywhere she turned, there were reminders of what had happened.

As the hours wore on, she was able to reduce the papers to a manageable hill in her in-box and had amassed a huge pile of filing for her secretary to take care of. She rang Michelle into the office and was informed that the filing would have to wait: it was already five o'clock. Liz hadn't noticed, so engrossed had she been in getting the administrative details of her practice in order.

She decided it was finally time to get to her mail. Michelle filtered in advance all billing information, information inquiries, and obvious junk. The rest came to Liz, and on top of the stack she saw a thick envelope bearing the glossy Endicott logo in raised letters. Curious, she opened it and found that it was filled with brochures for the entire Endicott line of surgical products.

A note was affixed to a different booklet, which came in a plain white cover. The note read: "In light of our conversation, I'd like to have you aboard very soon. Don't dare delay. K.N.''

Looking inside the literature, she saw aerial shots of Valladolid, a small Mexican city. In the center of town was a huge colonial mission surrounded by a pretty flower-ringed square. Another photo showed a smaller, plain structure, surrounded by the thick foliage of the Yucatán. It was Endicott Mexico and was quite a contrast to the sparkling modern facility in Indianapolis. This hospital blended in so well with its surroundings that it could have passed for a school or a city government building.

Inside was a different story. The photos showed gleaming tiled hallways and laboratories filled with top-of-the-line Endicott products. A shot of the operating rooms indicated that they were entirely up to American standards. In one wing, local patients were cared for and treated, while another entire floor was devoted to instruction. Liz frowned at a posed picture of Nordstrom with the facility's management. They all smiled and clutched Endicott products.

Putting down the literature, Liz again wondered about the hard-sell technique that Nordstrom was trying with her. It made no sense: though they talked around it, she made no secret of her personal loathing for the man. And the more she considered it, it seemed improbable that the corporation would count on her practice as a linchpin against Hal Bergman's competition. She learned earlier that day that Benjamin Wilder, an older and respected surgeon at the hospital, had signed an exclusive Endicott contract a year ago, when he first expanded his practice into laparoscopy. He held a panelist's position in the corporation and wielded greater influence than Liz at Community Hospital.

She looked again at the note from Nordstrom. ''Don't

dare delay.'' But why? What was the hurry? She wasn't going anywhere, and she hadn't expressed any interest in joining with the competition. It was more than her practice that interested Kerry Nordstrom: he wanted her.

Shutting off the lights in the office suite, she decided to call it a day. She knew that soon, like most nights, she would find herself in front of her VCR, reviewing the videotape, trying to come to terms with the crucial moment that had shaken and transformed her life into a strange new shape.

Hank Mancini sat in his four-door Oldsmobile smoking his twentieth cigarette of the evening. It was now two in the morning, and he knew the doctor wasn't going anywhere. He reviewed his notebook entries: home at six-fifty, no visitors, lights out at eleven-thirty. This Dr. Danny did not lead a very exciting life. The only thing unexpected that had happened was when the big Irish setter ran out the front door when the doctor first came home. The stupid dog ran three laps around the front yard, barking and whining, then joined the lady inside the house.

Most jobs were a lot more interesting than this. True, the doctor wasn't a bad physical specimen: her suit was a little dowdy, but he figured that if she wore the right outfit he could have a little fun with her. Unfortunately, there probably wouldn't be much fun to have on this low-level surveillance job. The Beretta in his shoulder holster was untouched, and he didn't think that he'd have to use it.

He looked up and down the street. Nice neighborhood, not like the kind he usually frequented. But then, this wasn't a typical assignment. When he got called in from Chicago, he was told that the client would remain anony-

mous. As for the object of the job, all he had to do was
watch the woman's house, get a description of any visitors, and tail her if she went out. It was grunt work, the
kind of stuff you could hire a legit private eye to do, but
this time it paid as well as a hit. The only stipulation:
under no circumstances was he to make himself known.

That last part was typical bullshit. Of course he
wouldn't make himself known. What did they think he
was, an amateur? Mancini started up his car and quietly
pulled out onto the street. He'd have time for some coffee
before the doctor got up. He'd tail her until she went to
work, then he'd call in to his boss and finally get a little
rest. All the sleeplessness was making him irritable and
edgy, a feeling he liked. Sometimes, he thought, these
nothing jobs can turn out to be the most interesting. You
never knew what might happen.

The next morning Liz arrived early at the hospital to
perform surgery on an incarcerated right inguinal hernia.
The patient, a schoolteacher in his midfifties, had been
difficult all through pre-op, complaining about his pain
and the incompetence of the nurses. When Liz talked to
him, she plainly saw that he was petrified about his operation. She assured him that he was in no danger and would
be much healthier in the long run. Her pep talk didn't do
much good, but it distracted him until the anesthesiologist
was ready to put him under.

It was a challenging procedure, possibly the worst hernia complication and the most difficult to correct: a piece
of intestine was imprisoned in the hernia itself and would
probably have strangulated within the hour. Though she
had to pull a foot of intestine out of the hernia, she was
able to save the tissue. The operation went perfectly, and

Liz stepped from the operating suite in time to walk directly into Lawrence Cooke, a gruff surgeon in his midfifties who had been on staff for twenty years. Cooke wore an offended expression at having been bumped into, as though the contact had been intentional.

"Liz," he said. "I see you've just wrapped up a case." He adjusted his surgical cap over his graying hair. "What was it?"

Though Cooke was technically of the same rank as Liz on staff, he always behaved aggressively and inquisitorially toward her: it might have been his years, or the fact that she was a woman. She found it diplomatic to be polite to him.

"An incarcerated inguinal hernia, Lawrence," she said, moving toward the wall to allow an orderly to pass bearing a tray of heavy instruments that would be used to install a prosthetic hip. "It went well," she added. "He'll be able to go home this afternoon."

Cooke snorted. "So that's the criteria these days. Can they go home the same day. It's really a video game mentality, don't you think? Quick fixes, taking the easy way out?"

Liz stiffened at the condescending tone of the older man. "Not at all, Lawrence. I used to feel that way, but I'm getting in step with the times." She paused for the moment, realizing that her words might sound like a jab at his age. She decided she didn't care.

"Well, Liz, just don't come crying to me when your patients all start coming back with the same recurrence, or suing you because the prosthetics you used aren't stapled properly. You know as well as I do that a good surgeon gets his hands into the patient, does the work like an honest doctor."

With this, Cooke turned without saying good-bye and

walked into an adjacent operating room. And don't come crying to me, Liz thought, when you have no patients left because you needlessly want to cut into them. She knew that if she had performed her previous case in the traditional open manner, she wouldn't have had sufficient visibility to know that she could save the foot-long length of intestine. Cooke would have been forced to remove it.

Back at her office, she sifted through the usual pile of phone messages. Her mother had called, no doubt to complain that they hadn't spoken in over a week. Liz was growing frustrated with her mother's repeated inquiries into her emotional health, a topic that Liz was still trying to avoid by concentrating on her work.

Her phone rang, jarring her in her seat. Listening to it ring again, she felt her pulse racing in her ears. She had been jumpy and nervous the last couple weeks, and for no apparent reason. For a moment she considered calling Ronnie. Maybe it was time to put the high horse out to pasture and ask for some help.

"Yes?" she said, answering the phone.

"Kerry Nordstrom from Endicott International on the line, Liz," Michelle said. "I know you told me to screen calls from him, and I told him you're busy, but he won't take no for an answer. He's very pushy."

"All right, put him through," Liz said. She was at a loss. Nordstrom could be like an unstoppable force of nature at times.

"Liz, hello," said the booming voice on the line. He was in a state of high excitement, and his southern accent was more pronounced than usual. "I saw your performance on the news last night. Smashing, you looked tremendous. It was nice to see you there putting out the good word. And the placement of the Endicott instrument was truly perfect. Thanks so much for the plug: do you have any idea how expensive it is to buy time on the network news?''

''Network?'' Liz asked, confused. Apparently it had been a slow news day, and her piece had appeared on the national news. She couldn't believe she hadn't even thought to tune in.

''Don't be coy, Liz. It was fantastic. Everyone here is ecstatic. Malcolm Endicott even called me this morning to say that I had done a great job. I take this to mean that you've decided to accept my offer?''

The placement of the instrument had been an accident. It could as easily have been anyone's product, but now Nordstrom sounded like a shark given the opportunity to move in for the kill.

''No, not yet, Kerry. I'm still thinking about it.''

Silence on the line. ''What am I hearing?'' he asked, annoyed. ''You know, maybe I haven't been persuasive enough. Do you realize that a panelist position could bring you fifteen thousand dollars a month if you do the right things?''

Liz was shocked; she had no idea. For that kind of money, she could afford to pay off her mother's mortgage. Her father had convinced Patricia that they should buy a more expensive home for their retirement, then had died months after they moved in. Now Patricia was trying to hang on to the place out of nostalgia and habit.

What was she thinking? Her father had told her that there are no free rides in life. ''That's appealing,'' she admitted. ''But I'm still not ready to commit.''

''Liz, in two weeks, I could have you on the staff in Valladolid. I could start you at a base salary of a half a million a year. That kind of money goes a long way in Mexico, you know. And I would provide you with one of our company houses. I know you're not a stupid person,

Liz. Let's talk to each other honestly. I think the time has
come for that.''

"Kerry, I have to go. I have an important call. I'll think
about what you're offering. I can't promise any more than
that.''

She hung up without waiting for a response. To her
surprise, the phone rang again instantly.

"A Detective Carl Willers from the Cincinnati Police
on the line,'' Michelle said. The news of the caller's identity froze Liz for a moment: she thought the police were
calling about Donald. Then she realized: Cincinnati is in a
different state from Med-Tek.

"Detective Willers,'' she said, confused. "What can I
do for you? I hope this doesn't have anything to do with
my husband. He's recently passed away.''

"I'm sorry to hear that, doctor. Please accept my sym-
pathies.'' He had a deep rich voice and spoke with a kind-
ness that she didn't associate with her image of a grizzled
cop. She tried to visualize the man she was speaking with
but couldn't see him: she could only guess that he was
black, and older than she.

"Then what can I help you with, Detective? I have
patients to see.'' Talking to Nordstrom had rattled her
nerves: for a second, she considered telling Willers about
Kerry but realized she would sound foolish. There was no
criminal wrongdoing in making an extravagant offer, even
if the motive behind it was unclear.

"I understand, Dr. Danny. I'll try not to take up too
much of your time. I'm calling because I saw you on the
news last night. When I saw you, I said to myself, 'Now,
there's a lady who might be able to shed some light on an
old case of mine. Maybe she should be doing my job.' ''

He spoke with a sort of self-deprecating humor that
was appealing. Liz smiled in spite of herself at the comi-

cal light in which he portrayed himself. "What kind of detective are you?" she asked.

"Homicide," he said. Liz's smile vanished.

"Here's the story in a nutshell," he continued. "I don't know if any of this made its way out to L.A. or not. You see, I had the bad luck to be assigned to a series of killings about two years ago. Some bodies were discovered in the Ohio River over a period of eight or nine months. These bodies had been mangled internally. Gutted, or eviscerated, as you might say. Within a few months, the killer got more sophisticated. He began removing specific organs: kidneys, mostly, but also spleens and livers. The press found out about it and had a field day. Unfortunately, I never got any solid leads, and no one came forward."

"I don't see what the actions of a psychopathic serial killer have to do with my being on television."

"Hang on a minute, I'll get to that. You see, the odd thing about the murders is that it looked like the killer reached in and removed the organs without cutting open the bodies. There were only a series of small incisions across the victims' bellies, along with a larger cut along the side."

Liz froze, instantly seeing the connection. When she appeared on the news, her discussion on laparoscopy must have given Willers the idea that a surgeon killed the victims.

"Now, the victims weren't exactly Nobel prize winners," Willers continued. "They were the kind of people I usually meet in my line of work: prostitutes, drug addicts, homeless people. I think for that reason the department didn't push any harder than it did. The medical examiner didn't have any bright ideas, and we got more resources only after a couple of what you might call 'good citizens' were murdered.''

"Wasn't there any kind of reaction from the public?"

"Sure there was. Especially after the media got hold of it and called the sicko the Keyhole Killer. Well, that's not entirely true. Our own people came up with the name first."

Willers loudly cleared his throat. "Anyway," he continued, "people weren't too worried, since most of the victims were nonentities. When the bodies stopped coming, people just forgot." He paused for a moment, and Liz heard the sound of a match being struck, followed by Carl inhaling deeply on a cigarette. "Anyway, I taped your report, and I'm going to take it over to a coroner friend of mine today to see if it rings any bells."

"It's possible that a killer could use laparoscopy," Liz said. "But you said these happened a while ago. When did they stop?"

"The last body was found eighteen months ago, but the case is still open."

"You see, Detective, you have to realize that access to laparoscopic technology is limited. And a couple of years ago, it was even more limited. I suppose it's possible that a murderer could have come up with a sloppy form of the technique on their own."

"That's what I thought when I saw your report," Willers said. She could hear the sound of him snapping his fingers with the moment of inspiration. "If not a surgeon, then a copycat."

"Anyway, despite all appearances, I'm not a leading expert on laparoscopy. In Indianapolis, the Med-Tek hospital would be a good place to ask."

"I have an appointment to talk with them on the phone this afternoon, Dr. Danny. I called you because, if you'll pardon my saying so, you seemed like a nice and honest woman on TV last night."

At first she was shocked at his brash forwardness, but she warmed to the compliment. Then she had an idea. "If you send me copies of the medical examiner's reports, I'd be happy to look them over and give you a call."

"That would be very kind of you. I'll have them mailed out today. I'd fax them, but we count every nickel around here."

"I'll be looking forward to seeing the reports, Detective, and I'll give you a call as soon as I've had time to review them." They hung up.

Willers sounded as if he knew more than he was letting on. It felt as if the true substance of their conversation lay buried just beneath the surface. He reminded her of a TV detective, taking his time to chat it up with the suspects.

He couldn't possibly consider her a suspect. She had said on the news segment that the ranks of laparoscopic surgeons were growing daily, and that soon every surgeon would have to learn the techniques just to stay up with the times. Of course, two years ago that wasn't the case. She didn't buy the theory of a copycat, and she didn't think Carl did, either.

Certainly there were a number of surgeons in Cincinnati who could have performed the terrible murders, but that assumed the existence of a rogue doctor who had to be a psychopath, killing for the sake of killing. She hoped that wasn't the case, for the sake of her profession as well as for the reputation of laparoscopy.

This line of thought made Liz shiver with distaste. Serial killers and corporate sharks, she thought. This wasn't what she had had in mind when she decided to become a doctor.

CHAPTER NINE

8:30 P.M., October 29, Los Angeles.

THE PHONE RANG AGAIN BEFORE LIZ COULD LEAVE THE OFFICE.
She cursed in the semidarkness, putting down her leather
briefcase to take the call at Michelle's desk.

"Liz? Hello, it's Benjamin Wilder."

"Ben, hello. What can I do for you? I was just leaving
for the day."

"I'm calling from home, actually." Liz could hear a
television playing in the background. "I wanted to extend
an invitation to you for tomorrow morning at seven-
thirty."

Liz looked at her watch. These twelve-hour days had to
stop.

"I'm performing a laparoscopic bowel resection in the
morning," Wilder said. "And the Endicott people are
coming down to film it for a promotional video. I was just
firming up some details with Kerry Nordstrom, and he
suggested I invite you."

Liz could tell from the enthusiasm in Wilder's voice
that he was excited; this kind of film was a great promotional tool for a surgeon, and it was flattering to have

Endicott lay out the resources to fly in their audiovisual crew. "Of course, Ben. In fact, I've been meaning to invite myself to one of your surgeries for my own education. I'll see you in the OR."

After hanging up, Liz was hit with the full impact of Wilder's allusion to Nordstrom. It was beginning to feel like he was everywhere. From anyone else, this kind of attention and these offers would be exciting. From Kerry, they were simply ominous. In the small cone of light from Michelle's desk lamp, she checked her calendar for the week.

After the surgery tomorrow she would have to deal with the Community Hospital investigative committee. Though she faced no charges, she would have to account for the events at Med-Tek. She knew Cooke and others like him—old-school surgeons ready to condemn laparoscopy at the drop of a hat—would be at the inquiry.

Inked in for later was the ASPECTS conference in Phoenix. The American Society of Practicing Endoscopic Surgeons was the prime association for laparoscopic surgeons; it was also owned and run by Endicott, and their annual conferences were as much a running advertisement for Endicott products as a place to network with colleagues. Liz had accepted the invitation after returning from Med-Tek, before Nordstrom began his strange campaign to take Liz under his wing. He would certainly be there. Perhaps that would be the place to find out what was going on.

Tired and more than ready to call it a day, Liz thought about the prospect of going home to her empty house. She wasn't sure she could endure the solitude; she needed to see a friend, if only for an hour or two. It would be good to talk to someone outside of everything that was happen-

ing, someone who could tell her if she was getting paranoid or if her worries about Nordstrom were unfounded.

She left the freeway at Wilshire Boulevard and drove
east, checking the Rolodex card she had fetched from her
office. Her destination was easy to find: John's apartment
building was a huge high rise on the south side of the
wide traffic-filled street. This was as good a time as any to
make a first visit.

John held the door open as Liz hurried into his apartment. She didn't notice his surprise and discomfort at
having a visitor, instead hurriedly telling him about the
events of the day: the increasing pressure from Nordstrom, the call from Willers, and her growing suspicion
that the videotape held some kind of answer to what was
going on. John sat on the arm of his sofa and listened
while Liz gesticulated and paced. Finally she could think
of nothing else to tell him.

"That's all of it, I think," she said. "Am I crazy, or is
something going on? Should I be worried? I mean, maybe
I'm overreacting. It's not every day that the police call me
on a murder investigation."

"I don't know, Liz," John said, rubbing his eyes. He
looked tired and a little irritated that she had dropped in
unannounced. "The offer from Nordstrom is fairly
straightforward. He wants to buy you into the corporate
fold, so what's the problem? If he bothers you, don't take
his money. You'd probably be better off staying away."

"What about the detective, though? It was almost as if
he were calling me as a murder suspect. I don't like answering questions about a serial killer, and I think he was
suggesting that a surgeon had committed the crimes." Liz
took off her coat and sat in a padded chair in the middle of
the room, realizing as she talked how upset she was from
the phone calls.

"From what you told me, he didn't suggest that a surgeon killed anyone, just that the murder method resembled laparoscopic surgical techniques," John said. "Listen, why don't you stay here and relax for a while? I'll make you some tea."

Alone in the room, she had a chance to look around the apartment. She had never seen it before, but it was impressive: it was a spacious well-designed place, with large windows that looked down on the glittering circuit board of L.A. at night. What surprised her, though, was the way John had decorated. A series of framed travel posters with various scenic vistas of Mexico adorned one wall. In a curio case a series of small statuettes stared out at her: the brightly colored creatures she had seen in small shops when she visited Oaxaca. On a wall was a Spanish Catholic cross, and a small, ornate rendering of the Virgin Mary.

John returned with the tea. "I learn more about you all the time, Rogers," Liz said. He set the tray on the coffee table and stiffly took a seat on his sofa, pouring milk into generous mugs.

"What are you talking about?" he said. There was a strange edge of discomfort in his voice, as if he had been caught at something.

"You obviously come from a Catholic background," she said, indicating the cross. "So do I. 'Danny' is actually the name my grandparents came out of Ellis Island with. The actual family name was O'Danelyn. My family is as Irish as Guinness stout."

"How's that?" John asked. "You don't look Irish, you're too dark."

Liz accepted the steaming tea. "Well, my mother's side is mostly Italian. I guess I got the Mediterranean coloring."

The conversation reached a lull as John stared at the cross on the wall. He offering nothing to continue this discussion of their ethnic backgrounds.

Finally he stopped brooding. "I see you noticed the statuettes, and you can't help but notice the posters." He paused. "I've always been fond of Mexico. I go every year or so. Between the strength of the dollar against the peso, and the friendliness and goodwill of the people . . ." His voice trailed off.

"Do you speak Spanish?" Liz asked. "I see you have some Spanish-language books on your shelf."

"A little. I picked up the books on my trips, just because I liked them. I guess my Spanish is as good as any other American tourist's." He laughed, looking around the room distractedly.

"This is one of my favorites," he said, pointing to a framed Mexican bullfighting poster on the wall. Amid a brilliant array of colors, a toreador waved a red cape against an onrushing bull; all around him, the stands were filled with spectators.

"Look at him," John said. "The essence of ease, of mastery over the animal. Those men are incredibly brave."

Liz saw John's obvious enthusiasm and tempered her words to spare his feelings. "I saw a bullfight in Spain once," she said. "It was terrible. They butcher that poor dumb animal for sport. But I know people enjoy it, and they look up to the bullfighters."

"It's not a case of simple cruelty. The torero enters into a relationship with the bull; they come to understand one another. It's more than just sport. It's a way to show machismo, bravery, confidence. It represents so many things."

"I see. So they kill animals to show how macho they

are? Why don't they just chug a six-pack and call it a day?''

''I know you're kidding, Liz, but it's no laughing matter. I know *I* would have to search deep inside to find the bravery to face that angry bull.''

John was acting nervous and strange; she began to think she had made a mistake in coming and that she had hurt his feelings. ''John, I'm so sorry,'' she said. ''I just barged in on you like a maniac. Did I come at a bad time? Are you expecting someone?''

He looked startled; though he hadn't meant to, he had given her the impression she wasn't welcome. ''No, no. I'm thinking about everything you told me. It seems like that detective is leaving something out. Did he tell you about the level of sophistication of the murderer's technique?''

''Not too much. He did say that it increased over time.''

They sat in silence for a moment, both thinking about murder and mutilation. They were both chilled by the implicit concept of surgery perverted into a means of taking life.

Then Liz had an idea. ''I was thinking of something on the way over. Do you still subscribe to all those computer bulletin boards?'' She knew he was a bit of a hacker. A year before, he had spoken of a new computer he had just bought with all the pride of a new father.

''Sure. I don't use them much anymore, but I still subscribe to a nationwide network.''

John's office was as roomy as the rest of the place. A set of French doors led out to a small balcony with patio furniture and a dozen potted plants. This is a great place, even if it is a little large for one person, Liz thought. She looked over his bookshelf while he turned on his com-

puter and initiated the modem link. There were more
Spanish-language books and even a few current Mexican
magazines. She decided not to pursue it. If he wanted to
improve his rudimentary Spanish, that was his business.
Like everyone else that day, he didn't seem inclined to tell
her the full story.

"I have it ready," John said. "We're linked up to online subscribers throughout the United States. I used to
sign on to this bulletin board all the time, but the novelty
wore off. They give sports scores, news, travel information, things like that, but I found they didn't tell me anything I couldn't find out by buying a newspaper or turning
on the news. What exactly are we looking for?"

"You'll see. What do I have to do?" Liz asked.

"We'll start by watching," John said.

Slowly at first, then more rapidly, lines of disembodied
dialogue appeared on the screen. It was a five-party electronic conversation that had degenerated into an argument
over the relative crookedness and dishonesty of the
Republicans and Democrats.

"Pretty boring stuff," John said. "But we can switch
to another line. It's sort of like rooms in a house. A lot of
dialogue runs over others, so you have to sit and wait for
the person you're talking with to respond. Sort of like
when you hear other people's conversations on your
phone line."

He instructed Liz to type her message into the keyboard. She entered: *"Is anyone out there logged in from
Cincinnati?"*

They sat and watched the dialogue continue. A running
discussion had ensued over the merits of a new computer
operating system. A few insults were exchanged.

John chuckled behind Liz. "Some of this stuff gets
pretty passionate. Especially when they argue about com-

puters.'' Liz sat in the chair in front of the terminal, with John behind her. He allowed himself a discreet smell of her dark shiny hair and found himself staring at the smooth skin on her neck. He coughed and abruptly stood upright.

Then a message appeared: *"I'm in Cincinnati. What's up?"*

"Thank you," Liz typed. *"I'm in Los Angeles, and today I heard about a string of murders in your city. They went on for almost a year and stopped about two years ago. It wasn't in the papers here, or else I didn't notice. Do you remember anything?"*

"You shouldn't be so wordy," John said. "It takes too long. Most of these people type in a kind of shorthand." He stepped away from her and walked to the window, lost in thought while looking out at the city below. He was elated that she was in his home but was also filled with tension. It should have been easy to tell her his secret, but there never seemed to be an opportunity.

The return message came: *"Sure do. Someone killing hookers and bums. Ripping the guts out of them. Police called it the Keyhole Killings. Weirdest part was man in emergency room with no kidneys."*

Liz read the message aloud to John. "What does that mean, no kidneys?" he said.

He leaned over Liz and typed onto the keyboard: *"What do you mean, no kidneys?"*

There was another pause, then a message: *"Just what I said. Man went to emergency room. Went into coma. Doctor found he had no kidneys. Someone took them out but left him alive."*

John and Liz read the message with similar expressions of confusion. "That's horrible," Liz said. "Willers didn't tell me anything about the killer being that sophisticated.

You would have to know advanced surgical procedures to take out organs without immediately killing the patient. But it's so twisted and sadistic—"

Another message appeared from the person in Cincinnati: *"I figured a Hannibal Lecter type,"* it said. *"Evil cannibal genius doctor. Total psycho, eating them with fava beans and a good Chianti."*

John rolled his eyes. "You get all kinds on these networks," he said. They logged off the network after thanking their anonymous source of information. They retreated to the living room to talk.

"Willers is sending me copies of the autopsy reports," Liz said. "Maybe I can make something out of them."

"You shouldn't worry about it," John said. "Willers calling you was a shot in the dark. He just wanted the opinion of an expert. After all, you weren't in Cincinnati at the time of the murders."

"Then why didn't he tell me the entire story? I don't really think he decided I was involved, but why didn't he tell me about the man with the missing kidneys? It doesn't make any sense."

John shook his head and yawned. "I really don't know, Liz. I guess he's playing it close to the vest."

"I just wish someone would tell me what the hell is going on," Liz said, standing. "I won't keep you up any later. I know you weren't expecting me."

John hastily stood, gently touching her arm. "No, it's fine. I just think you shouldn't let all this bother you. With everything that's happened recently, you have enough on your mind. Just keep putting off Nordstrom until you've had time to look into it, and help out Willers all you can. You need to spend your energy taking care of yourself."

"I guess you're right."

She looked at John while putting on her coat. He was

trying to calm her down as if she were a hysterical woman. Maybe what was happening to her wasn't reasonable or rational, but it was real.

"Liz, don't be mad," John said, picking up on her feelings. "I don't mean to underestimate your worries." He took her hand. "Look, call me soon. Or come by. I keep a spare key outside under the edge of the carpet. Let yourself in. I—I'd like to see more of you."

He's so sweet, Liz thought. She mussed his hair with one hand, turning to open the door with the other. "I just might do that, Rogers. If the bogeyman doesn't get me first."

Downstairs, a black Oldsmobile sat parked across the street. Mancini had a hard time finding out what apartment she went into, but after turning on his hazard lights and parking in the bike lane, he was able to look through binoculars to see which number she buzzed. John Rogers. Probably her boyfriend. He looked for a legitimate parking place, expecting her to spend the night there.

He was surprised to see her coming out an hour later. She finally showed some leg, wearing a knee-high silk skirt with a slit in the side. Not bad. It took self-control to keep from visiting her late at night.

She walked out of the security gate with her boyfriend: a tall, dark, pretty-boy type who looked like he was dressed for the opera. Hank pointed his directional microphone at them and flipped on his recorder. He'd want to get this on tape before calling in to check on tonight's assignment.

"Call me if you need anything, Liz," Rogers said. "And don't worry about a thing. There won't be any trouble.'' Hank looked him over a moment, then jotted down his description in a thick notebook.

Liz couldn't sleep: the silence of the house was oppressive, and she lay staring at the ceiling for what seemed like hours. She finally got up, careful not to disturb the unconscious Daisy. Now that she lived alone, she indulged the dog by letting it sleep with her. It gave her a sense of security. Now, looking at Daisy's stretched-out form, she wondered if she was fooling herself. The dog probably could sleep through a hurricane.

The steps creaked as Liz walked downstairs. She tried to keep Donald out of her mind, keeping her sadness and isolation at bay. Wandering around with a glass of wine, she checked the locks on the doors. It had been years since she lived alone. Maybe I should have an alarm system installed, she thought. The security might be worth the cost.

She walked into the living room to fetch the videotape. There was no point in watching it again: its contents played against the back of her eyelids every time she closed her eyes. In the sleepy quiet, the tape looked innocuous, harmless. With the tape in tow, she walked to the office and dropped it on her desk. Nordstrom hadn't mentioned the tape since his first call, and she had denied having it. She still wondered if he believed her.

She had an idea: she would make a copy of the tape at the hospital's video lab the next morning, then store it in her safety-deposit box at the bank. ''All right, maybe I'm paranoid,'' she said aloud. ''But I'm a nut with a system. I'll have one tape to watch and another in a safe place.''

After rummaging around on the shelf, she found a cassette to copy over: it was last year's Super Bowl, which

Donald had recorded when emergency surgery kept him from watching the game live. She remembered him coming home that day, his hands over his ears and a silly grin on his face. "Don't tell me the score!" he said. "I'm in quarantine until I watch that tape. Don't you dare tell me who won!"

At the typewriter, Liz made a label for the new tape: "Med-Tek Vagotomy, 9/14/95, K. Nordstrom." Satisfied, she went to bed and tried to sleep. It was already after one in the morning.

Liz had just begun to drift off, thinking about John Rogers all alone in his roomy apartment, surrounded by souvenirs of his bachelor vacations. An image of him occupied her mind, his lean frame standing stiffly with his hands in his pockets, his face lit up with a sheepish grin. She was in a half-dream of affection and confused emotion when she distinctly heard a noise downstairs.

She struggled to wake up. At first she couldn't move, still immersed in her dreaming. With great effort, she wrenched herself into complete consciousness and sat up, trying to be absolutely quiet. The house was silent, though sitting there she imagined she heard other noises, indistinct bumps. It may just be the house settling, she thought.

Daisy slumbered on. Liz remembered Donald facetiously calling the dog "Killer" and saying with a laugh that no one had ever bought an Irish setter for a watchdog. The sound of the refrigerator grumbling and running came to Liz's ears, a familiar nighttime noise. She allowed herself to relax for a moment, thinking that her jokes about suffering from paranoia were becoming reality. The seductive beginnings of sleep pulled at her, and her eyes grew heavy. Her body relaxed, and her breathing became deep.

Then there was another noise, louder this time. Liz sat

up again. It sounded like the kitchen door. Quietly, she slipped out from under the blankets and groped around in the dark for her nightshirt. She remembered all the times she had thought about keeping a flashlight in the bedroom, but she had never gotten around to doing it. Her mind rapidly catalogued the contents of the bedroom: was there anything that could be used as a weapon? She picked up a solid brass paperweight from the nightstand, the heaviest object she could possibly carry with her.

She tried to open the door quietly, but it instantly burst out with a great creaking complaint. When she reached the hallway, she could hear nothing from downstairs, just an insistent throbbing in her ears that she realized was her own accelerated pulse.

The third stair from the top groaned from her weight. Whoever was downstairs had to have heard it.

Liz froze and leaned against the wall. Damn Donald, she thought. Every day something served to remind her that he was gone, and now a terrible fear was coming true: she was alone in the house with an intruder.

Liz peered at the pool of moonlight at the foot of the stairs. I'm being foolish, she thought. After several minutes of silence, she began to relax, walking down the stairs into the darkness at a normal pace. In the kitchen, she turned on the light. There was no one around. What a chicken I am, she thought. I'm like a teenager left alone for the night.

She walked through the house, turning on all the lights and quickly glancing into each room. She was alone. Placing the paperweight on the living room table, she allowed herself a bitter laugh. Maybe she was cracking up—seeing danger where there was nothing, hearing bumps in the night.

The house returned to inky blackness after she shut off

the lights, figuring that fear was no reason to run up an astronomical electric bill. Lingering for a moment in the kitchen, she thought: I forgot to check the closets. He might have hidden in a closet when I came downstairs. Suddenly, she felt a presence behind her.

It bumped into her from behind, brushing against her bare legs with a warm rush of impact that made her lose her footing and fall to the floor. She tried to scream, but fear had paralyzed her. Only a gasping sound came out, and her vision went red with mortal panic. The nearest phone was in the office, two rooms away.

A sound like tap shoes sounded on the tile of the kitchen floor, accompanied by a nervous pant. Daisy walked to her water dish and began to drink, her tail wagging in the semidarkness. When she was finished, she walked to the back door and began to whine, sneaking glances at Liz and turning circles on the battered floor mat. She was so clumsy that she loudly bumped into the wall at the end of every enthusiastic rotation.

Liz pulled herself up and leaned back against the wall, looking incredulously at the dog. She put her head in her hands and laughed long and hard. "Daisy, you're going to give me a heart attack one of these days. If you weren't so clumsy, I'd be mad at you."

It wasn't until the next morning that she discovered the missing videotape.

Benjamin Wilder's laparoscopic bowel resection was going well, in spite of Betty Riordan's protests. She felt that her territory as circulating nurse was violated by the presence of the film crew. The room contained fourteen people in masks and gowns, including a sales representative from a small firm who had attended the surgery merely in order to make business contacts.

Jed Everett, the head of the film crew, had tried to win Betty over by making small talk while the surgeons scrubbed up, but she was unresponsive and had since complained about every transgression on the part of the two cameramen and the sound engineer.

"For the last time, get out of the way of the ventilating wall," she yelled to Everett. He stepped away from the wall, where a gentle stream of fresh air blew through tiny holes. Particles of dust and debris flew from his clothing as he retreated, motes that lazily blew through the air toward the sterile operating field. "For crying out loud, Ben. It's like a damned circus in here."

The twin video monitors showed Wilder's instruments tugging at a length of intestine. Liz watched the surgery, struggling to pay attention, but she couldn't concentrate. The Super Bowl tape she had prepared was missing from her office, and she absolutely knew she had left it on top of her desk before going to bed.

At first she thought she was imagining things: the locks on her doors showed no signs of forced entry. But she was certain now that the house had been broken into. In addition to taking the tape, someone had gone through her briefcase, leaving its contents spilled on the floor. It didn't make any sense: why had they gone into her office and taken only the tape from her desk, ignoring the computer, the antique vase, even an American Express card lying in plain sight on a shelf?

Whoever it was, they must have come solely for the tape. Fortunately, they stole a useless video. The real one, as of that morning, was secure in her safety-deposit box. She had been lucky: whoever broke in wasn't interested in her. She shuddered to think that she hadn't been alone in the house last night.

She made a mental note to check on occurrences of equipment malfunction at Community Hospital over the last two years: perhaps Endicott had bad product out on the market, instruments that they had invested too much time and money on to recall. Maybe she had evidence that she couldn't recognize, and Nordstrom, or even someone else, wanted it in their possession.

Across the room, Shevaughn Lyons watched the proceedings with intense interest. A high-level sales representative from Endicott, she had been icy cold to Liz and the members of the surgical team since she arrived that morning to oversee the surgery. She barked orders at Everett and Wilder throughout the operation, telling Wilder to hold an instrument higher for a close-up, or ordering Everett to take still frames of critical moments.

Lyons was blond and diminutive, with forest-green eyes and a hauteur in the way she carried her shapely body. Though she was thirty at the oldest, she had been rapidly promoted through the Endicott corporate ranks. Liz mused about what she would have to deal with if she signed up with Endicott: being bossed around by people like this, who behaved as if the act of surgery were something to be manipulated and packaged like a laundry detergent.

"Hold on a second, Benjamin," Shevaughn said after conferring with Everett. "Camera two has a lens problem."

"This can't wait, Shevaughn," Wilder said. "Due to her age and condition, I have to limit the time this patient is under anesthesia." Liz glanced at the patient, whose head was barely visible under the drapery and the crowd of people around her. Before the patient was put under and her belly was inflated with gas, Wilder had explained for the cameras that Shelly Dent, age seventy-three, had a slight cardiac irregularity that made close monitoring under anesthesia a necessity.

"You're telling me what I already know, Benjamin," Shevaughn said, scolding him like a child. "This will only take a minute, and you know how important this film is to us. Just take a breath. Count the holes in the ceiling or something."

To Liz's amazement, Wilder pulled out the grasper and the laser from the patient's belly and sat them on the instrument table. He stood expectantly, waiting for the lens to be changed. Over the blue surgical mask, Shevaughn Lyons's eyes creased into a smile.

The remainder of the operation followed the same pattern: Wilder's authority as presiding surgeon took secondary status to Lyons's demands, which were delivered in a tone ranging from harsh command to affectionate cajoling. In spite of these interruptions, the surgery was a success, and the film crew applauded Wilder as he sat on a stool in the corner filling out postoperative reports.

Liz halfheartedly joined in the applause. Though the surgery had impressed and stimulated her, Lyons's behavior had been bizarre: never before had Liz seen the concern for human life take such a subordinate role to the demands of business.

Standing alone in the surgical area hallway, Liz decided that she needed to talk to a colleague. She didn't want to talk about the break-in until she had time to think, but the trip to Phoenix was looming, and John's reassurances had done little to placate her. She decided to call Hal Bergman to see if he was in.

Instead of calling from the crowded hall, Liz ducked into a little-used conference room to use the phone. The room was quite cool: the air conditioning seemed to have been set too low, and the lights were off. She felt around in the dark for the switch, her hand grasping in the darkness.

The bright fluorescent lights came on, and Liz blinked from the sudden glare. She saw the ancient low-grade conference table, surrounded by a hodgepodge of chairs and a couple of divans with stuffing leaking out of the arms. Then, in the corner, she saw them: Wilder and Shevaughn Lyons on the sofa, locked into an embrace. She was on top of him, her hands raking through his thinning hair as his hands greedily explored her body.

Liz excused herself and left the room before either of them could say anything. She left the lights on.

Hal Bergman agreed to meet with Liz that afternoon; in the meantime she would have to attend the board of inquiry, he reminded her. She had tried to forget about it, but at least Hal was on the panel. She thought about ducking out, going for a drive or something, but that was ridiculous: not attending the meeting would be tantamount to requesting a discharge from her affiliation with the hospital.

After grabbing a quick pastry and a cup of coffee in the cafeteria, Liz took the elevator to the fifth-floor conference room. The board meetings were always held there in its boring cut-rate corporate environment. The hospital had done well in procuring equipment, such as the new MRI machine on the lower level, but had compensated by decorating the meeting rooms and lounges in cheap pastel paint that had already begun to chip and fade. This room had a round oak table, surrounded by padded chairs, but its contents couldn't overcome the institutional quality of the walls and ceiling.

Liz arrived and took a chair. Hal Bergman had arrived

and was talking to Sandra Garrison, the administrative head of Community Hospital and the voice of the corporation that owned the facility. Hal winked at Liz as she entered, but Garrison ignored her. To their right was Lawrence Cooke, who frowned at a patient file he had balanced on his knee while he tore open a packet of sugar for his coffee. Completing the panel was D. K. Singh, chief resident and a notoriously aggressive player in hospital politics.

Trying to be inconspicuous, an impossible task in such a small group of people, Liz occupied herself by staring at a colorful painting on the wall depicting daffodils against an abstract field of greens and yellows.

Even under the best of circumstances, she hated these meetings. When general hospital business was addressed, surgical staff were strongly advised to attend; Liz had often found herself sitting through debates over billing time, office space allocation, and use of equipment. She never imagined one of these meetings, even on a smaller scale, would be convened with her as the focus.

A young man with a tape recorder and notebook walked into the room, seating himself next to Garrison. "Since we're all here, I'd like to call this meeting to order," she said. "My assistant will keep a record for future reference." Without looking up at the group, the young man pressed a button on the recorder and nervously adjusted his tie.

"We'll try to keep this brief," Garrison continued, looking at Liz. "I've read and distributed the statement you and Donald submitted following the accident at Med-Tek. The board merely wants to formally follow up on certain elements of the deposition."

Liz shifted in her seat, focusing her gaze on Garrison. Sandra was about forty and wore her hair in a tight bun over her perpetually pinched-up face. She was a physically tiny woman, known as a tough administrator and a real money-cruncher who had to answer to her corporate bosses for every nickel spent in the hospital.

Lawrence Cooke cleared his throat, looking at Liz over his glasses, which were perched on the end of his nose. "What troubles me about this statement," he said, "is that it insufficiently accounts for the patient's cause of death. I know it was from bleeding, that's obvious. What I want to know is how your husband fired that laser approximately three inches off the mark."

"I'm not sure what I can say about that," Liz said slowly. "As we know, Donald was under strain. I have my opinions: perhaps the instrument misfired, or maybe Donald just made a terrible mistake."

"But you were there," Singh said in his strong Indian accent. "How can you say you don't know exactly what happened?"

"And this bit about the laser not working," Cooke interrupted. "That's a serious charge. If you plan to follow up on it, you'd better get your facts straight."

"I said I don't know," Liz said, her voice rising. Her face felt hot. "I was holding a retractor, then later I took the camera. Kerry Nordstrom and Donald were both working inside the patient. As soon as the artery was cut, visibility was reduced to nothing. Isn't that enough for you?"

Liz realized she was shouting. The room was quiet for a moment, and everyone looked down at the table except for Cooke, who stared at Liz with a perturbed expression.

"Look, let's keep this friendly," Bergman said, pushing a pile of papers away from him to rest his elbows on the table. "I've reviewed this case and agree that it was negligence on the part of Dr. Page. I should remind you that, of the surgeons on this board, I have the greatest experience in laparoscopy. I'm best qualified to judge what happened in that operating room.''

''Maybe that's the problem,'' Cooke said, turning angrily to face Bergman. ''Everyone's running off half-cocked to do these operations with goddamned gimmick instruments like they were playing some kind of game. You people are ridiculous, jumping on the bandwagon with each new thing that comes along.''

''I don't have to respond to that. You know the excellent track record we've established here,'' Bergman said, his face reddening.

''The hell with that,'' Cooke said. ''You people don't know what you're getting yourself into. And a formerly good open surgeon like Dr. Danny, trained in traditional techniques with a strong foundation, starts doing these surgeries—they remind me of my kids playing their video games all day, staring at the screen. I'm telling you, there'll be hell to pay!''

Singh stared at Cooke, appearing somewhat aghast at his older colleague's fervor. ''One thing I do know,'' Singh said in a calm voice, ''is that the residents and interns have expressed some misgivings about these new technological advances. They wonder if they'll still be trained to do the traditional open procedures when their patients all want the same operation their cousins or neighbors down the street got—the fancy one with flashy technology, without scarring or pain.''

''And what about the changing political climate?'' Cooke blurted. ''If medicine shifts to a more managed care—''

''The expense involved in laparoscopy concerns me as well,'' Garrison interrupted, watching the assistant record her words. ''The instruments cost a lot of money. I've been instructed by the board of directors to monitor the expenses of our surgical staff. I'm sure you're all aware that the bottom line is—''

''Money, I know,'' Liz said, staring at the desk's wood-grain pattern. ''But the companies are moving toward more affordable surgical packages, kits of trocars and staplers that would cut our costs. We can't lose sight of the fact that patients benefit from new discoveries. I know we can agree that that takes priority.''

''Benefit,'' Cooke snorted. His earlier excitement had cooled to a seething bitterness. ''I'll tell you about benefit. I do the surgeries better, in the traditional manner, and it costs the hospital less. When this goddamned managed-care revolution takes place—and mark my words, it will—it won't matter who can do the operation better. Maybe your trocars and staplers will be in demand, who knows. But better will no longer be better: for the patient, the hospital, for the doctor, or anyone. Cheaper will be better.''

''Cheaper is better already. There's a surgeon advertising on the television in New York City,'' Singh said with a smirk. ''He has a phone number: 1-800-HERNIAS. Says he can beat the competition's prices. There'll be surgeons willing to stand up and do any operation for three or four hundred dollars to beat *your* prices, Dr. Cooke.''

A low titter of laughter came from the group. ''What the hell's wrong with that?'' Cooke said, throwing his hands up in the air. ''All right, it sounds ridiculous. Other than that, what's the harm? It's old-fashioned competition. When I got out of medical school, you hung a plaque on your office door and you were in business. Now everyone has to toe the corporate line of the HMOs— like *they* know how to do anything but make money. I'm telling you, when I sit here and listen to this, I know that my profession's dying. When the smoke clears, there won't be anything left but a bunch of technicians. We might as well be dental hygienists.''

"There will always be doctors," Singh said in a mollifying voice.

"Not the way we know them. I feel like I'm the last M.D., and I'll tell you who I blame: the accountants and the administrators. Where does the patient's money go in managed-care programs? Directly to the fat-ass administrators sitting in their offices—doing nothing.

"And," he added sullenly, "to the trendy fringe like you laparoscopic surgeons." Cooke pointed at Liz and Hal. "You people are evangelists, like some kind of high priests ordained by the god of technology. You want to throw aside years of tradition like it was nothing.''

Liz sighed deeply. "Just why do you think the doctors are jumping through hoops now for those administrators and managed-care programs?" she said. "Because we've always jumped through hoops. You worked thirty-six-hour shifts as an intern. You operated around-the-clock for five years in your training. You did the impossible, as we all did, just because we were made to. We were trained to be momma's boys, pleasing our parents, pleasing the authorities, pleasing the heads of our medical programs. And now we're asked to treat patients with accountants hanging over our heads. We're still jumping through hoops.''

"Momma's boys," Cooke said dryly, his face red with irritation. "Speak for yourself, Dr. Danny. Real surgeons make big incisions. Wounds heal from side to side. Laparoscopy is a gimmick.''

"But it works," Liz said.

"This board was not convened to hold a referendum on laparoscopic surgery," Bergman said coldly, "or on the future of medicine.''

"Indeed," Garrison said, standing and straightening the pleats on her plain blue skirt. "In fact, it's just a formality, but I have been assigned the task of expressing the concern of the majority holding partners in Community Hospital. Dr. Danny, your involvement in this accident leaves us with no choice but to place you on probation for six months."

"Probation?" Liz said, shocked. "But I—"

"You can, of course, continue your practice during that time," Garrison continued. "Your record is excellent, and your performance is superior. Consider this a warning not to move too fast in the future. We're glad you're expanding your surgical practice, but we won't tolerate malpractice."

She pushed a triplicate form across the table for Liz to sign. It was an acknowledgment of her probationary status.

"Before we go, allow me to express a more general concern on the part of the corporation," Garrison said. "We are pleased to be a growing center for laparoscopic technology, but at the same time we want to be cautious. Hal, I want you to monitor Dr. Danny and ensure that her work continues to be satisfactory."

Cooke leaned across the table as Liz was reading the form. "Look at what happened, Liz. If you'd have never messed with that high-tech bullshit, you wouldn't be here today. Remember tradition! We need real surgeons in this hospital."

"Lawrence, shut up," Bergman said in exasperation.

Hal Bergman was in his office after the meeting, behind the door reading "Chief of Surgery." He greeted Liz with a smile and ordered his secretary from the room, closing the door so they could talk privately.

His office was one of the largest in the hospital: high shelves filled with books lined the walls, and a matching set of sofas and chairs nestled cozily around a coffee table. A long series of diplomas hung behind the desk, surrounding generous windows that looked out onto a small row of trees planted on the edge of the parking lot. In contrast to the elegant room, his desk was littered with scrap paper and coffee cups, and a hand-held video game sat within reaching distance of his overstuffed chair.

"Don't let it get you down, Liz. The probation is just so they can say they've done something. I'm your monitor, and I believe in you. Larry Cooke is just a pompous old asshole," he said.

Hal had a kind bearded face, and his eyes shone from behind his glasses. He was a short man, but he dressed jauntily and carried himself with an air of energy and good humor that tended to make one not notice his height. That day he wore a blue blazer and a sloppily knotted tie over jeans and sneakers.

Liz was visibly upset about the board meeting. She hadn't expected to meet that kind of antagonism or to be officially punished for participating in the vagotomy. She also couldn't erase the image of Wilder and the young blond sales rep on the couch downstairs. Wilder was an aging dumpy man, and Lyons was a knockout. Maybe she was manipulating him with sex; in any case, it seemed that Endicott International went to elaborate lengths to control its client-surgeons.

"I've been getting offers from Endicott," she said, deciding not to mention what she had seen. "They're offering me a panelist position and want me to sign an exclusive contract to use their products."

Hal sat back in his chair, a huge smile on his face.
"That's pretty good, Liz. Not bad for someone on probation. You've only been at this for a little while, and they're
offering you the farm. So what do you look so worried
about?"

Hal's reaction surprised her. "The problem is that I
don't trust the offer, or the person it comes from. I'm not
thrilled about being associated with a company that em-
ploys Kerry Nordstrom."

"I see," Hal said, slouching back in his chair. "You
know, Liz, you have to separate the person from the offer.
Endicott hired Nordstrom for his talent and his public
relations sense. If he wants to give you money, let him.
Anyway, he's harmless, and Endicott is a good firm."

He looked at Liz, his glasses catching a shining ray of
sun from the window. "I know that what happened to
Donald is affecting your decision, but you shouldn't let it.
If you don't want to be affiliated, then refuse. If you do,
then Endicott is a good way to go. They're one of the big
boys."

"But you're with the other big boys, aren't you?"

Hal laughed. "Sure. Interscopic gave me a good deal,
and their products are as good as anyone else's. But that
doesn't mean I'm a company man. I told them that I
wouldn't use my position to influence the surgeons on my
staff, and I haven't."

"You have a good attitude, Hal. You always have. I
guess I could learn something from you."

"Now you're talking."

"Hal," Liz said, suddenly serious. "I've been invited
to the ASPECTS meeting in Phoenix."

"Of course you have, Liz. That's the number-one Endicott gathering. I'd be there to schmooze, but I'm the
enemy." Bergman's phone buzzed, but he ignored it.

"It's just that I . . ." Liz paused. She was on the verge of telling him everything, about the murders, about the break-in, about her feelings of dread, but she stopped. She was on her own. Maybe she would learn something in Phoenix, a piece of the puzzle that would ease her mind.

"Oh, I'm going," she said. "I should see what they have to say. Anyway, it'll get me away from here for a while. I could stand a few days without Lawrence Cooke and Sandra Garrison."

"Of course you should go," Hal said, standing up. It was the signal that their meeting was over. "Remember, Liz, Endicott is just a company. They exist to make money. You can take their offer, or you can leave it. Either way, life goes on."

Liz walked to the door. "I guess you're right. I'll talk to you when I get back and give you all the details."

"Please do. Oh, Liz?"

"What, Hal?" she asked, alarmed at the serious tone he had taken.

"Just don't let them get you alone. They'll brainwash you and make you into a corporate zombie-slave, bound forever to their service."

Liz stared at him from the doorway, shocked.

"Oh, come on, Liz, I'm joking."

CHAPTER TEN

8:50 A.M., October 31, Phoenix.

THE PHOENIX CONVENTION CENTER WAS A MAMMOTH CONCRETE box, taking up a city block on the edge of downtown. Though the city wasn't as hot as Liz thought it would be, the cement sidewalk had begun to absorb some early-morning sun. The threat of oppressive temperatures in the arid shifting desert wind hung in the air like a palpable menace. She stood in the shade of a tree outside, thinking about why she had come.

It may have been sheer stubbornness. John and Hal had tried to tell her not to worry, that everything was fine. At times such as those, she came as close as possible to re-senting being born a woman. They couldn't discount her anxieties without resorting to the old, chauvinist tactic of acting superior and rational. But this wasn't a rational situation. I'll show them, she thought. I'll simply march right in there and get some answers.

She hadn't called the police about the missing tape, and now she wished she had. Though a worthless item was stolen, an intruder had been in her house. Part of the

problem was that she couldn't believe anyone would bur-
glarize her home for a stupid videotape.

Nordstrom was the only person who wanted the real
tape and who suspected that Liz had it. But this didn't add
up either: Would he invite her to do business one day, then
have her house robbed the next? He couldn't be trusted,
but was he capable of those kinds of tactics? If he was,
then Liz was ready. The real tape was still in her safety-
deposit box, hidden and secure. If it was that important,
then she could use it as a bargaining chip.

If she was going to Phoenix, she decided, then at least
it would be on her own terms; this meant rejecting Endicott's offer of the red-carpet treatment in favor of making her own travel arrangements. Liz registered at a small
hotel two blocks from the convention center, away from
the posh accommodations the other surgeons would enjoy.

Inside the hall, the ASPECTS convention had taken
over. Two thousand doctors, all either affiliated with Endicott or targeted for recruitment, roamed the halls with
schedules in their hands. There was time before the opening remarks, and Liz stood alone in the swirl of humanity.

What she saw was typical: the doctors, mostly male,
milled about in their nondescript slacks and ties, some
forming loose groups and slapping each other's backs and
laughing with loud fraternity-house glee. As usual, Liz
felt the stares of far too many men and wished that she
had worn something more dowdy and form-concealing
than her light-blue, off-the-shoulder summer dress.

In addition to the surgeons, Liz noticed a number of
people in blue jumpsuits emblazoned with the Endicott
logo. Most of them were engaged in dealing with the lo-
gistics of the conference: manning the registration desk,
controlling human traffic, and answering the countless
questions of doctors suddenly separated from their secre-

taries and assistants. Standing back against a wall, Liz
noticed another class of staff that didn't appear so benign.

They were all burly muscular men who wore their uniforms differently from the others. Their sleeves were
rolled to the elbow, and their collars were turned up, as if
they had dispensed with the niceties of appearance. They
stood together in small groups around the main registration area, looking at the surgeons and speaking to each
other. Several congregated around a desk marked "Security" and spoke into walkie-talkies with calm unhurried
expressions. Suddenly Liz saw that she had attracted the
notice of a man at the desk.

He was over six feet tall, his blond hair pulled back into
a ponytail. He poked the ribs of the man next to him, a
short black man with extraordinarily wide shoulders, to
get his attention. They looked at Liz and continued talking, not bothering to avert their gaze when she stared back
at them.

"Tell me again exactly why I came here," Liz said to
no one in particular. She decided to duck into the grand
ballroom, which was being utilized as the exhibition area
for Endicott products. The men's looks may have been
typical, relatively harmless sexist aggression, but their attention disturbed her. Even though it was a public place
with thousands of witnesses, it was weird to be picked out
of the crowd the moment she arrived.

The product exhibition was a garish display of affluence and power. Two dozen young women, wearing straps
of cloth that could only generously be called bikinis,
walked through the hall. They put their arms around
small-town surgeons and kissed their cheeks, leading
them to tables where they could order an array of products.

Liz's worry about the security guard's stares was replaced by amazement at the full range of instruments displayed. Equipment for tissue retraction, ergonomically designed staplers and cameras, cholangiogram catheters, and hypersensitive graspers lined the walls and booths, which were staffed by more than a hundred sales representatives. Liz looked around the room for Shevaughn Lyons, thinking that she might be there somewhere.

Standing under the centerpiece of the display—a large steel Endicott logo under which twelve banks of television screens showed various advanced surgeries—Liz looked around the room. The only way to enter or exit was the way she came in. If those men wanted to come after her, for whatever reason, she would be trapped.

She folded her arms over her chest and took a deep breath. Hold it now, Liz, she told herself, this is getting ridiculous. There are at least five hundred people in this room. Nothing is going to happen to you. As if to verify that her imagination had run wild, she saw no sign of the two rough-looking men.

Then a hand tapped on Liz's shoulder, sending an electric charge of fear through her. She turned, squared up almost as if to fend off an assailant, and found herself facing the petite blond Shevaughn Lyons. The young woman wore a shy smile as she extended her hand.

"Liz Danny," she said. "Good to see you without a mask covering your face."

They shook hands. Liz was amazed at how open and friendly Lyons was, considering that the last time they had seen each other was a rather compromising moment. "I just got a call that you were here," Shevaughn said. "We've been on the lookout for you."

"Why is that?" Liz asked, trying to gauge Shevaughn's expression. Liz calculated that they were about the same age, but Lyons dressed to demonstrate all the things that Liz tried to play down. She wore a very short black skirt, heels, and a blouse that cut low into her cleavage. Somehow she gave off an air of complete professionalism, in spite of the call-girl outfit.

"I've been instructed to bring you into the fold. Stop at nothing, death or glory. You know, I'd hate to have you fall under the sway of my counterparts at rival firms," she said, an aggressive twinkle in her eye.

"I guess you're welcome to try," Liz said, warming to Lyons's honesty. She seemed like a genuinely well-meaning person, devoted to her job. Liz allowed herself to be led around the exhibits, wondering if this stop-at-nothing enthusiasm explained her behavior with Ben Wilder.

"Great turnout," Irwin Ross said, drinking coffee from a styrofoam cup. The brown liquid had spilled over the edge, staining the Endicott logo. "I love the competition at these things. My presentation is going to blow these people out of the water."

"Sure, Irwin," Calvin D'Amato said sarcastically. "It's your show."

"Don't you forget it," Ross said, no trace of humor in his voice.

They sat at a round conference table behind a one-way mirror overlooking the main area of the convention. They could see the thousands of surgeons walking about, pocketing free samples and gradually milling toward the main hall, where the opening remarks and initial seminars would be conducted. Kerry Nordstrom walked in, out of breath.

"What's the matter with you, Kerry?" Ross asked. He straightened his tie and brushed the lapel of his two-thousand-dollar Italian suit, purchased for the conference. The very sight of the plain chubby Nordstrom always made Ross want to adjust some part of his own attire, as if being in the same room with him somehow besmirched his own youthful glamor.

"Steep stairs," Nordstrom gasped, falling into an open chair. "For what it cost to rent this damned place, they could have put in an elevator or something."

D'Amato laughed harshly. "Too many steak dinners and martini lunches, Kerry." For his remark, he earned a sharp glance from Nordstrom. D'Amato shrugged, beyond caring whether his boss was in a good humor. Calvin loved that fact that Ross, who outranked Nordstrom and ran ASPECTS, was present. It was good to see Kerry outside of his kingdom.

"I hope you catch your breath soon," Ross said. "We'll be out there delivering our data in forty-five minutes. You know, justifying our jobs and sparkling reputations and all that."

"Yeah, no kidding, Kerry," D'Amato said. "We have to burn this place up. I've been catching nothing but hell from the old man since that disaster last month. You're always in the lab so you don't get the worst of it, but he's been really torn up about the vagotomy."

Ross nodded distractedly. "Our NYSE value fell right after that little mishap. We're almost back to where we were, but that's not the kind of development we want to see."

Nordstrom took a measured glance at his colleagues. "I've been meaning to tell you both, but I haven't got around to it." As he spoke, Irwin Ross's eyebrows lifted with a typical bemused impatience. Nordstrom ignored him. "For the last couple weeks I've been offering Liz Danny an exclusive contract with us, as well as a panelist post."

"Who is Liz Danny?" Ross asked.

"Don't be coy, Ross. She's Donald Page's wife," D'Amato said, obviously annoyed. His bleary eyes cleared up as he thought for a moment. "Are you saying you're doing that on your own? That's pretty generous."

"Liz Danny," Ross said, as if he hadn't heard Calvin. "That's the woman who assisted on the infamous vagotomy, isn't she? Why in God's name would you throw our good money at her? She should have been run off the map right along with her husband. That little mistake was extremely damaging to the company."

Nordstrom looked at the younger man. With his red power tie, his impeccable hair, and his Bostonian accent, Irwin Ross looked more like a movie producer's idea of a surgeon than the real thing. It irritated him to no end that the kid was so damned talented.

"Irwin," he said, drawing out the name to irritate Ross. "I have my reasons. First of all, she's good. Page was past his prime and full of drugs, but I'm convinced she had nothing to do with that. She's clean, she's talented, and she has a long money-making career ahead of her."

"She's at Community Hospital in Los Angeles, isn't she?" Ross said, still behaving as if he couldn't hear what was said to him. "We have Wilder there, not to mention Koshima, and that gynecologist. What his name, something Scandinavian . . ."

"Nooteboom. He's Dutch. And yes, we have those people, but Danny has an expanding practice. It's an investment. And to tell you the truth, I think she's a troublemaker. We might be better off if she's on our payroll."

D'Amato ran his hands through his thinning hair. His features thickened into a scowl. "What the hell are you talking about?"

"She's willful," Nordstrom said. "Look, I've known her since she was in residency, back when Page and I were working together. She's one of those militant types, a real ballbreaker. If you ask me, anyone married to her would have to take drugs, or do something, just to get away from her. She's one of those women who's always talking. Thinks she's as good as a man."

"So why in the world would we want to sign her?" Ross said, as if Nordstrom were the most ludicrous idiot in the world.

"For the money. And to keep her in line, if you have to know. I've offered to send her to Mexico."

Ross raised his eyebrows again, this time in alarm, and glanced at D'Amato. Calvin returned the glance with a blank stare.

"You can't really think she'd be good material for the Mexican facility. Not with what you just told me," Ross said.

"I had something in mind," Nordstrom said.

Irwin Ross rose from his seat and looked out the window. "They're bringing in the video equipment," he said. "Calvin, get down there and watch them. Make sure they get everything straight. This thing has to go off like a Hollywood production."

When Ross was satisfied that D'Amato was gone, he returned to the table. "What are you thinking, Nordstrom?" he said. "I can tell you're up to something."

"It's very basic. I sign her, and we can use her as a cash cow: we'll clear half-a-million dollars a year from her practice before long. We also keep an eye on her. If she agrees to go to Mexico, we can see how she reacts. Who knows, she might come along for the ride. I offered her a generous salary."

"She has something on you, doesn't she, Nordstrom?"

Ross said. "I don't see why she's such a threat, and I don't like this secrecy. Anything that affects you affects me. Don't think I'm not aware of that."

"I'm not playing games here, Irwin. Do you realize that she's talked to that Cincinnati cop?" Nordstrom smiled with perverse satisfaction, watching Ross turn pale. "That's right. He saw her on TV and called about the case. Does that change your impression of the situation?"

Ross stood and looked at his reflection in the glass. He was only thirty-one, but he looked twenty-five, he thought. He should have a very long career ahead of him.

"I knew Cincinnati was a mistake the minute I stepped in. The world is not a laboratory. You should have waited until the process was perfected."

"Such is life, Irwin. Imperfections abound," Nordstrom said, leaning back in his chair.

"Take care of this, Kerry," he said. "Try to buy her out, if you think that will work. Keep an eye on her. If it comes to it, it would be advantageous to send her to Mexico. For whatever purpose."

"My men have instructions to bring her to me as soon as she arrives," Nordstrom said, pleased at the deepening worry on the young man's face. "I'll talk to her alone. Listen, partner. I'm not going to let this bitch get in our way. I started this—it was my game before it was yours."

"Maybe so, but now I'm in it as deep as you. In any case, call me constantly," Ross said. "And don't underestimate me. Remember that. I will not go to prison."

Nordstrom laughed. This was delicious; the kid was losing his mind with worry. He had no idea that he was being left out of the real action. His worst nightmare would soon come true: the end of his career.

"Oh, please, Irwin, spare me. Nothing's going to happen to you. Your reputation and your good looks will last forever.''

Ross ignored the comment. "Just remember. I will not go to prison."

After walking around with Shevaughn for twenty minutes, Liz was exhausted. After a while she began to tune out the smaller woman's incessant sales pitch, trying to figure out where she got her energy. Though they were both nearing thirty, Shevaughn had the spark and ebullience of a teenager. If her personality weren't so appealing, it would have been disgusting.

They stopped in front of a large display devoted to staplers—advanced models of the small gunlike instruments used to affix mesh or bind together human tissue. A young woman in a one-piece bathing suit smiled and shot staples into a slab of veal, inviting the surgeons to step in and try the device. A ministampede ensued as the men vied to get closer to the shapely young girl.

Shevaughn shook her head and smiled at the combination of sex and commerce. "As I told you, whatever it takes."

Liz nodded. "I guess so. Money seems to be the great motivator."

A roar of laughter erupted from the crowd as an overexcited surgeon stapled his finger to the veal slab. "What you saw with Ben Wilder had nothing to do with money," Shevaughn said, suddenly turning to face Liz. "It was personal, and it's over. He's a married man. I don't know what got into me."

"It's really none of my business, Shevaughn," Liz said.

They looked at each tensely for a moment, then relaxed. "I just thought I should explain," Shevaughn said. "Now please tell me that you're ready to sign up with us. I'd be proud to say that I influenced your decision."

Liz was about to respond when a pair of men in Endicott uniforms approached them. She hadn't seen them at the security desk, but both were as tall and muscular as the others. The younger of the two had a wide scar running from his orange sideburn to his lip. They didn't look like typical corporate security: they looked more like hired thugs.

"Liz Danny?" the redhead asked. He was only about twenty, and his high voice sharply contrasted with his rough appearance.

"Can I help you?" Shevaughn asked, irritated.

"Dr. Nordstrom sent us. He wants to speak with you."

This was unbelievable. Nordstrom had sent goons to fetch her in front of a thousand people. Even some of the surgeons at the stapler display looked up with quizzical expressions at the two men, momentarily forgetting the beautiful creature in their midst.

Why send these guys? Liz wondered. Anyone could have come for her. Why the muscle? If he wanted to intimidate her, he had succeeded. This is a public place, Liz reminded herself. They can't try anything here. She left with them, walking out of the exhibition hall and through the sign-up area, leaving behind the evidently stunned and confused Shevaughn.

Liz turned to one of the men. "You know, he could have just had me paged." He didn't respond. "Well, at least tell me where we're going. I'm sure you have permission to do that."

"Upstairs," the older man said, pointing to a huge mirror over their heads. This wasn't the public meeting with Nordstrom she'd had in mind. The plan to walk in and demand answers began to lose its appeal. These men could be killers, she thought. Nordstrom might not even be up there; this could be a trap.

"Listen, guys," she said in her best waifish voice. "I have to go to the little girls' room before I go upstairs with you. Do you mind?"

The young man grunted and pointed to doors marked with symbols for men's and women's facilities. She walked into the empty room, her steps echoing off the spotless tile floor. She wished she hadn't left her course schedule in the exhibit hall: it included a map of the building.

A young woman walked into the bathroom, ignoring Liz and entering one of the stalls. Liz ran water and pretended to wash her hands, looking around desperately. In the rear of the room was a high metal door marked as an emergency exit.

A sign warned that a fire alarm would be activated if it were opened. She had seen the same sign as a teenager in Virginia, when she used to sneak her friends into the movies through a similar exit. No alarm had sounded then. She took off her name tag and threw it in a garbage can, walking quickly out the door. She smiled. Just like in the movie theater.

Instead of finding herself out on the street, she stood amid the noisy din of a loading platform. Several catering trucks were parked there, and a variety of workers bustled about, preparing for the lunch that afternoon. Peeking between the trucks, she saw several large men in Endicott uniforms talking and smoking cigarettes. Voices riddled with static sounded out from the walkie-talkie each carried in a hip holster.

Liz tried to think how much time would pass before anyone would start to look for her. Four minutes? Five?

She knew she had some leeway: they would assume she was fixing her hair or primping for her impromptu meeting. Men always expected women to take forever in the restroom.

Walking along the loading docks, trying to stay behind the trucks and hidden from sight, Liz slowly made her way toward the front of the building. She bumped past one of the food service workers, who looked at her questioningly.

"How do I get out to the street?" she asked, and was met with an uncomprehending stare. The young woman pointed to a door at the far end of the docks and said something in Spanish.

The door was unmarked, but it was a better option than dealing with the security crew. Peering between two trucks, she saw one of the guards, a muscular pot-bellied guy with a long beard. These men were different from the usual off-duty police officers hired as security. They all looked like criminals. Why in the world would a reputable firm need to hire a private army to police a harmless convention?

Walking through the door, Liz was greeted with an enormous clatter and a barrage of voices. She looked around, but none of the dozens of people in the room took any notice of her. They were preoccupied with unpacking crates, chopping vegetables, slicing bread, and filling up plates of appetizers. A mustached man stood in the middle of the chaos, directing the action with stern commands delivered in alternating snatches of English and Spanish.

It was easy to remain unnoticed; she walked through the room as if she belonged there, opening a freezer to take a bottle of orange juice. The chef noticed her but said nothing. Drinking the juice, trying to look calm and self-assured, Liz considered her options. Perhaps she could just go to Nordstrom and tell him she didn't care to be escorted around by hired felons. She could put a stop to all this before it got out of hand.

A voice resounded through the room, a familiar baritone that Liz recognized from Med-Tek. Malcolm Endicott. She knew that the kitchen must be close to the main meeting hall stage.

"My colleagues, I am here to welcome you to this series of educational seminars and to demonstrate what damned good guys we all are," he said. Loud good-natured laughter echoed from the hall. Endicott was winning them over again.

"Before we begin, I would like to recite something that is a bit of a personal statement for me, something many of you have heard before. It was composed by my father many years ago, and it is something I have tried to live by. If I may have your attention for a moment."

The Endicott corporate credo. Donald had told Liz about it, how the sight had galled him of the kindly old man reading his statement of principles, surrounded by his unscrupulous and mercenary staff. Endicott began to speak.

"We shall endeavor to serve those in our charge with the utmost sense of righteousness and respect for their dignity," he intoned. "And we shall not forget our responsibility to be good citizens of the realm. As individuals and as a collective whole, our duty shall be to the betterment of the American way of life: over time, over financial profit, and over personal gain."

Liz sipped on her orange juice and listened to the applause from the audience. From what she knew of Malcolm Endicott, he lived up to his words: what you saw was what you got. Unfortunately, in his advanced age, he seemed to have lost some of his ability to judge people. Kerry Nordstrom was a case in point.

As she mused over this, the blue of an Endicott employee uniform appeared in the corner of her eye. It wasn't a security guard; it was one of the older women in skirts who ran the information booths. The woman began to haggle with the chef over where and when lunch was to be served.

Liz decided to escape before she was noticed and asked what her business was in the kitchen. She had lost all sense of direction, but she thought that she was on the end of the building that faced Jefferson Street, a busy thoroughfare lined with shops and restaurants. She ducked into a hallway that ran off the kitchen, continuing her progress away from the loading docks and the restrooms.

After stepping through a door into silence and pitch blackness, Liz realized she was completely lost. She wondered briefly if she was legally trespassing. Another voice begin to speak, and the hallway outside produced a ringing echo. The ballroom was near, but it was hopeless to try to figure out precisely where. She felt through the blackness toward a light, hoping that she was moving toward an exit.

She fought back her fear of darkness by considering her options, one of which was to threaten to release the tape to the police or the medical board. Perhaps it had come to that. Nordstrom's reaction would be interesting, and he might be bluffed into revealing the tape's importance.

A stumbling step through a doorway left Liz completely confused. She couldn't determine the dimensions of the room she had entered or what it contained. Vague, indistinct shapes loomed in the murky stillness. This didn't seem to be a highly used part of the building.

Another voice had begun to speak, but she couldn't tell who it belonged to. The ballroom speakers must have been nearby, because she heard the echo and static of the sound system. The person's words dissolved into a cacophonous jumble.

The voice and the hiss of the amplifiers continued, completely disorienting her. She spun on her heels, trying to find something recognizable, somewhere to go. To her relief, she saw the shape of a door, its edges illuminated by light from the other side. If it was sunlight, it must be the exit to Jefferson Street.

Liz walked through the door onto a wooden surface, realizing with disappointment that she was still indoors. She looked to her right and involuntarily gasped. Sitting at tables, aligned in neat rows, were the two thousand surgeons attending the conference: she had stumbled onto the stage. There was a sudden silence, and she realized that she had stepped out into the plain sight of the audience and the panel. At the podium was Irwin Ross, and behind him were five men sitting at a long oak table. Kerry Nordstrom looked at her coolly, revealing no emotion.

A soft chuckle echoed through the sound system. Ross removed his reading glasses and held up his hand to pause the video monitors suspended above the stage.

"Can that be Dr. Danny?" he said in a farcically whimsical manner. "I think it is. Ladies and gentlemen, one of our brightest and most attractive young stars. Unfortunately, she seems to have become lost on her way to the ladies' room."

The entire crowd burst into spontaneous laughter, led by Ross, who stepped away from his podium and gallantly walked to take Liz's hand. He led her down the stairs and into the audience. There was an open seat in the front row, and when he released her hand he said, "I would like to talk to you later," the smile still affixed to his face. "If you don't want to talk to Kerry, perhaps you can deal with me."

He walked back to the stage, leaving Liz shocked by his unmistakable tone of menace. She sat down and refused to look at anyone around her, though she could feel their stares. At least she was out in the open, safe in the numbers of the crowd. It would be easy to slip out at some point during the seminar.

Ironically, when she relaxed enough to listen to what Ross was saying, she couldn't help but wish she were just an anonymous audience member. There was no denying the man's brilliance. He spoke at length about assessment of the severity of acid-peptic disease, citing research that he had performed while serving as a consultant at a large Spokane city hospital. The diagnostic efficacy of several techniques were contrasted against a control group, and Ross had developed an entirely new method of gauging the disease.

Liz listened intently, borrowing a pen and paper from her neighbor to take notes. This was information she could use. When Ross left the stage, she applauded the man in spite of herself, forgetting her worries and the strange intimation of what he had said to her.

This is what initially attracted me to medicine, she thought. The level of inquiry and intellectual curiosity, the devotion to developing new methodology and treatments that would save or lengthen countless lives. Here was all of the good of medicine displayed right before her eyes, and for a moment it did not matter who was on the stage making the presentation.

This train of thought was derailed when the applause of the crowd died down and Kerry Nordstrom took the stage, introduced by the renowned South African surgeon who was panel moderator. Nordstrom coughed into the microphone, peering at the audience. "Please turn that spotlight down right now," he said petulantly. "It's blinding me up here."

The light was dimmed, and Nordstrom began to speak on his research series of laparoscopic vagotomies with red dye testing, the very procedure that had run afoul in Indianapolis. He pressed a button, and a slide appeared on the large screen above him: it was a picture of the research facilities in Minneapolis where he and Donald had worked together.

"I brought this along out of nostalgia," he began. "Since my tenure there and as a result of my subsequent achievements, I have since moved to Med-Tek, the jewel in the corporate crown of Endicott International. Some of you may wonder why I took this position at the facility." Nordstrom pressed the button again, and a large green dollar sign appeared against a field of hundred-dollar bills. He hastily pressed the button again, and an aerial shot of Med-Tek filled the screen.

"Ah, there we are," Nordstrom said, feigning confusion. "I don't know how that last one got in there." The audience tittered with laughter and mumbled comments. Ross and Endicott sat at the table with long-suffering expressions.

Nordstrom continued his presentation, outlining the red dye testing, vagotomy, and seromyotomy procedures. He illustrated his description with video footage that prominently featured Endicott instruments. The tapes must have been recorded in the brief time that had elapsed since the death of Ray Barker, Liz thought.

As if reading her mind, Nordstrom brought up a graphic illustrating his success rate at Med-Tek. The death at Donald's hands had been the sole fatality.

"If you will look here," he said, "you will see that we have had fourteen successes and only one failure." He shot a pointed look at Liz, who avoided his gaze.

She watched footage of Nordstrom performing an effective seromyotomy. The operation was in its closing stages, and the tape ran on without comment from Nordstrom. A single Endicott laser moved from branch to branch of the remaining sections of vagus nerve, cauterizing them with brief pulses down to the crow's-foot junction at the stomach. The laser flashed a red beam, and smoke came from the burning tissue.

There was a pause in the video action, as if the surgeon were looking around for a particularly difficult section. Then the laser stopped and held firm: Nordstrom had found what he was looking for.

On the giant screen, twenty feet above the audience, the laser did a small loop-the-loop in the patient's abdominal cavity, finally moving in and activating a beam that resumed the operation. Liz's mind flashed back to the videotape and the move that had killed Barker: it was precisely the same motion. The operation on the screen was a success, but the surgeon's hand was the same as the one that had killed Ray Barker. That surgeon was Kerry Nordstrom.

Liz gasped loudly, attracting attention all around her. A low round of conversation began in reaction. Kerry Nordstrom paused, holding his pointer unsteadily in the air. He looked in the darkness for Liz, then saw her.

They stared at each other for a moment. She knew.

CHAPTER ELEVEN

IT WAS IMPOSSIBLE TO SIT STILL. NORDSTROM CONTINUED HIS presentation, as if nothing had happened, while Liz listened to his voice with the knowledge that he was worse than a common manipulator or liar: he was a murderer. He had killed Ray Barker and driven Donald to suicide.

"In conclusion," he said, his voice firm, "we feel that we have perfected a laparoscopic technique for ulcer patients that permanently alleviates their suffering. Med-Tek is in the process of developing an instrument kit and an instructional course that will make the procedure accessible and attainable for the experienced surgeon."

The crowd applauded his presentation, awed by the glossy video footage and extensive data. Liz sat with her arms folded, her eyes beginning to well up with stinging tears.

"Before I leave the stage," Nordstrom continued. "I would like to make an announcement. Med-Tek has recently assembled technology that will revolutionize medical data transferal well into the twenty-first century." He completely ignored Liz now, his voice growing loud and boastful.

"I had to fight a little with my superiors to get funding on this one," Nordstrom said, glancing back at Ross and Endicott. "But they saw the light."

Liz covered her eyes with her hand, waves of realization and shock washing over her. Nordstrom wanted the videotape so he could destroy all possible evidence of his crime: he was trying to assure that Donald would always be blamed for an error he hadn't made.

"At twelve noon on November fourth, I will oversee a global satellite link with a selected medical site in Asia or the Middle East. It will be a demonstration attended by a very select audience. In other words, people, if you don't know if you're coming, you ain't."

The audience tittered with laughter. "But this link will be a pioneering event. We have the capacity to tailor our transmissions to match the language and technical sophistication of each receiving site. I will be sending random data from Med-Tek as a test of the system. Within the week, Endicott will be the first truly global medical facility."

The room buzzed with conversation after Nordstrom stepped from the stage. The more thoughtful members of the audience expressed apprehension at the idea that the corporation was activating a global network of data exchange: they could consolidate a monopoly on the technological market and dictate the terms of surgery's future. Many in the audience, however, were simply impressed with the spectacular outlandish nature of the idea.

Liz stayed in the ballroom halfway through the next speaker's presentation. Everett Sanders, a portly southern man dressed in a lurid red jacket and bow tie, spoke on laparoscopic management of perforated ulcers. Normally, she would have been fascinated by his video footage and the test series of ninety-seven patients he had assembled in Augusta, Georgia, but she realized when her stomach lurched that it was time to get away. She kept an eye on Nordstrom, but he sat still and emotionless, interjecting once when Sanders turned to request comparative data from Med-Tek.

While Nordstrom was busy trying to recall the relapse rate on his cases, Liz quietly stood and walked down the wide aisle. Away from the stage, she was enveloped in darkness, lost amid the crowd of thousands.

She left the huge room without looking back. The bright afternoon sun outside the convention center momentarily stunned her with its brightness. She looked to the street while walking down the empty stairs: only a few of the surgeons were around, those who had sneaked out of the seminar to grab a quick cigarette. A long row of taxis and a line of shuttle buses waited to transport the doctors back to the hotels and the evening dinners and parties. Liz hailed the first cab she saw and hopped into it.

At first she planned to go back to her hotel to grab her things: this idea was quickly jettisoned. It was time to face the full reality of what was happening: she had evidence that could be used to end Nordstrom's career, even land him in jail. He wasn't the kind of man to allow such a loose end to remain dangling.

"Take me to the airport," she ordered the cab driver, a Middle Eastern man who had stuck handwritten Arabic phrases to his dashboard. He nodded, staring at Liz in his rearview mirror, then drove slowly through the downtown streets to the freeway.

Liz leaned back in the seat and tried to calm herself with deep, measured breaths. She was in a state of panic and had started to hyperventilate. She looked down at her dress and saw her heart beating through the thin fabric.

All of the hours blankly and obsessively reviewing the video from the vagotomy had given her a special knowledge. At first glance, no one would have detected the signature motion with the laser that Nordstrom employed; it was too slight, too idiosyncratic. Yet it was absolutely ingrained in her memory, and she had found a smoking gun that could be used as evidence against Nordstrom. The generous offer from Kerry was a way of making a deal. She hadn't even known.

The cab slowed on the freeway as they entered heavy traffic. Liz cursed her luck: the last thing she expected to find in Phoenix was this simulation of Los Angeles gridlock. They rode stop-and-go for several miles, eventually finding some open road. She remembered from her trip into town that morning that the airport was only a few miles away.

The cabbie expertly wound through the thinning traffic. Liz's mind ached with the realization that she had sold her husband short. Everyone's first reaction, including hers, had been to blame Donald. She felt a pain in the depths of her heart: she should have defended Donald's skills, his reputation. No one had truly considered that there was no absolute concrete evidence that Donald's laser had perforated the stomach—only Nordstrom's immediate exclamation and Donald's subsequent silence.

Perhaps Donald hadn't even known that he didn't sever the artery. He had been disheveled and confused and may indeed have been operating under negligent conditions. Nordstrom had seized an opportunity to ruin a man who was a threat to him.

But how? Donald was no threat: he had remained silent about Nordstrom's manipulation of data, hadn't threatened his job or his reputation or his renown. It didn't make sense that Nordstrom would do something so damaging to his corporation on the outside chance that Donald would one day reveal old secrets. Who would have believed Donald so late after the fact?

The cab picked up speed after entering the wide-open lanes of the airport. With good timing, Liz thought, I could be in the air in fifteen or twenty minutes. When they reached the terminal, she threw a twenty over the seat at the cabbie, telling him to keep the change. His expression remained stoic as he pocketed the money and pulled away.

Walking toward the terminal, Liz hoped she wouldn't seem conspicuous. She continued her deep breathing to calm herself down, looking around for signs of blue Endicott jackets. Her image in the glass door—disheveled and walking too fast—showed her that she hardly appeared calm.

Behind her, a black Cadillac pulled up the the curb and two men in suits and sunglasses stepped out. Liz looked at them over her shoulder. They had seen her. One man yelled to the other, pointing at her through the thin crowd of travelers.

Inside the terminal, she saw that she had a lucky break: the airline had installed an automatic ticket vendor. She had only to run her credit card along a slot, punch in her destination, and the machine coughed out a ticket with a seat assignment. The entire process took seconds, in which time the two men jogged into the building, pacing through the ticket lines. They finally spotted her but immediately bumped into a large family who stood directly in their path, sending luggage and baby strollers careening across the floor.

She checked her ticket and saw that the flight left in ten minutes at Gate 7. Walking faster, without looking over her shoulder, she passed through the metal detectors and found her gate. The men finally caught up with her as she hastily stepped over the tunnel threshold leading to the plane. One of them tapped her on the arm, still wearing sunglasses over a clean-shaven inscrutable face.

"Liz Danny?" he asked. "I'm here to inform you that there's been a robbery of medical equipment at the Civic Plaza and that you're under suspicion. I have orders to bring you back to the scene."

The airline employee, a young man of about twenty, looked at Liz quizzically. "This plane is leaving immediately, ma'am," he stammered, intimidated by the presence of the two men. With their stern bearing, they could easily have been detectives or federal agents.

Liz knew she would have to brazen it out. "I have a medical emergency in Los Angeles," she said, stepping toward the tunnel. "Unless you have some kind of identification, I have to catch this plane." It was a bluff: for all she knew, Nordstrom had called the police with a phony charge.

The man flashed a badge that read, "Endicott Security Captain." Liz smiled and walked into the tunnel.

"Seems you have no jurisdiction here, gentlemen. You can contact me at my office if you have any questions." It was another bluff: she had no idea what law-enforcement jurisdictions applied in an airport, but she guessed that two security guards couldn't bring someone into custody on their word alone.

She was right. Walking into the plane, she heard the ticket clerk and the Endicott captain yelling at each other. The clerk said, "But you can't go any further without a ticket, and I'm afraid this plane is full. If you'd like to go to the ticket counter . . ."

The flight attendant closed the door of the plane and locked it. Within minutes, they were airborne.

By the time the plane landed in Los Angeles, Liz had a plan: she would simply call Nordstrom and tell him to leave her alone. She would tell him that she had a copy of the tape in a safe place, and if anything happened to her he would be exposed.

Then she would call Detective Willers in Cincinnati and tell him everything she knew. Even if she couldn't help solve his string of murders, he could advise her how to deal with Nordstrom. All right, it isn't much of a plan, she thought. But it beats waiting for something to happen to me.

She caught a cab at LAX and gave the driver her address. They rode quickly on the six-lane freeway, the city whizzing by outside the windows, unaware of the danger she faced. Never in her life had she felt the palpable presence of her own death, and it frightened her. Anything could have happened in that convention center. Anything.

The cab exited the freeway and slowly wound through the quiet residential roads of Santa Monica. The cabbie became momentarily confused by a series of one-way streets and had to depend on Liz's directions to find her house.

They were only a block away when an alarm sounded through Liz's mind like a blast of electricity: if they had followed her to the airport, they certainly could have someone waiting for her at home. She surprised the cabbie by ducking low in her seat and giving him a new address, tossing a twenty-dollar bill onto the front seat and telling him to drive faster.

* * *

Ten minutes later, Hank Mancini arrived in his black Oldsmobile. He had been called back to the case an hour after being instructed to return to Chicago. After complaining that he had business at home and would lose money by staying longer, he had earned himself a fifty percent raise. Not bad.

Today he'd wait for her around the corner: he didn't want to be spotted after hanging out on the street for three nights in a row. No matter—with the electronic bugs he had installed when he stole that stupid tape, he would know when she came home. Finishing the job would take only minutes. In fact, he wouldn't have long to wait. According to his anonymous client, she would arrive from Phoenix any minute.

The elevator in John's building rose unimpeded to the sixteenth floor. No one was in the lobby except for the doorman, and as far as Liz could tell, no one had followed her cab. She relaxed a bit as she walked down the long carpeted corridor to the apartment. The frantic din of a TV game show exploded through the door of one of the apartments. The sound of quiet boring stable life filled Liz with an almost nostalgic longing.

She rang the doorbell, then knocked loudly on the thick door. The TV set next door was quickly turned down, so Liz quit knocking: she didn't want to draw any attention. Kneeling down on the floor, she hunted under the frayed corner of the carpet, where John had said he kept his spare key. Finding it, she let herself in and locked the door behind her.

The apartment was deathly still, and all the curtains

were drawn. She turned on every light she could find to drive away the eerie feeling of solitude. Then she sat by the phone, considering what to do. Nordstrom was at the convention, so she couldn't call him until later; anyway, there was no point in trying to make a Faustian deal with him. She thought about the Western-themed gala Endicott was throwing at the Ritz-Carlton hotel that night. It sounded dreadful.

"I guess I won't have the pleasure of seeing you in spurs and chaps, Kerry," she said aloud.

She needed to talk to someone in her own profession, someone she could use as a sounding board. At the moment, Lawrence Cooke didn't seem like a good option. She had been harangued by him enough for one week. She took a deep breath, her nose stung of disinfectant. John was a bit of a neat nut, she realized, and smiled. How cute. She picked up the phone again and dialed a local number.

Hal Bergman answered on the seventh ring. His sons yelled at each other in the background over the electronic screeches and discordant music of a video game.

"Liz," Hal said, "aren't you in Phoenix at the nefarious corporate gathering?" She could picture his easy smile by hearing his voice. Hal was a family man and a good colleague. And unlike Ben Wilder, he owed nothing to Endicott.

"Hey, David. You share that game with your brother," he said, sounding irritated. Then the laughter returned to his voice. "Sorry, Liz. Just playing zookeeper. What can I do for you?"

She couldn't bring him into this. He had a family and children, too much to lose. "Nothing really, Hal. I wanted to request a leave of absence."

"A leave? Why? Are you sick?"

"No. I want to visit my mother. The strain of the last couple months has finally caught up with me."

"Liz, Liz," he said. His voice was caring and compassionate. "That's fine. Take a couple of weeks. In fact, I was going to suggest you do something like this. Things need to cool out for a while, especially after that board meeting. You call me up if there's anything I can do for you."

"Thanks, Hal. Good-bye." She sat in the quiet living room for several minutes, then went to the kitchen for a glass of orange juice. Sipping the drink, she walked to the window and peeked out the curtains. Wilshire Boulevard, sixteen stories below, hummed and pulsed with a continuous stream of racing traffic. Across the street were two more high-rise buildings, making the street look like a concrete canyon. Atop the taller building, a great jack-o'-lantern balloon floated and bobbed in the light breeze.

It was Halloween. She hadn't even thought of it. Normally, she and Donald would be at home giving candy to the neighborhood children. This year, her house would be dark and empty.

It was almost eight o'clock: probably too late to call Willers with the three-hour time difference. Liz walked to the kitchen and found a tin of chocolate chip cookies. Her hands shook with frayed nerves as she grabbed a handful to take back to the sofa.

Suddenly there was a commotion in the hall. Someone rattled the knob and kicked the apartment door, which opened with a crash. A vase in the entryway fell from its stand to the floor and shattered. A low voice cursed.

Liz crouched down on the linoleum and listened. The intruder stayed in the doorway for a moment, as if trying to tell if anyone was inside. She remained completely still and quiet, trying to guess which drawer contained the knives. Then a figure rounded the corner. Liz screamed out in fear, throwing her hands in the air and backing into the sink.

John Rogers stood in the doorway of his kitchen and cried out as well, his face contorted with shock. He dropped the bag of groceries he was holding and tensed up, relaxing only when he saw that Liz was the source of his fright.

"Liz," he said, observing the growing puddle of milk at his feet. "For God's sake. You scared the shit out of me. I knew I turned the lights off when I left. I expected to find someone holding a gun on me."

"Happy Halloween," she said, smiling through the tears that flowed down her cheeks.

They looked at each other for a moment, both panting with the rush of adrenaline they had experienced, then they began to laugh. Liz knelt to pick up John's groceries, and he walked back to the vestibule to survey the wreckage of his vase. "You know, I always bump into this stupid thing. I figured one of these days it would take a tumble," he said.

After Liz placed the perishables in the refrigerator and John swept up the fragments of his vase, they sat down to talk. Liz told him everything: about the burglary in her apartment, witnessing Nordstrom's signature surgical move, and her eluding Endicott's security guards.

John sat running his hands through his hair, then went to his kitchen for a glass of water. He returned, rolled up the sleeves of his white cotton shirt, loosened his yellow silk tie, and began to pace the floor. "My God. So you came here instead of going to your place? Because you think they might have followed you?"

"That's right," Liz said. She put on a baggy blue

sweater that John had fetched from his hall closet. "I let myself in with your extra key. I hope you don't mind."

"I don't mind at all. I'm glad you thought to come here. God, let me think. Your house was burglarized, but you never saw the burglar? You were very lucky. You could have been hurt. Why the hell didn't you call me?"

"My first impulse is not necessarily to run to a man for help," Liz said, her anger flaring. She reconsidered, her tense features softening. "Sorry. I was scared and didn't know what to do. I didn't even know anything was missing until the next morning. I guess I should have called the police."

"That's right," John said. "Then you'd have an official complaint. That could be important if this videotape thing amounts to anything." He completed another circuit of pacing the far end of his living-room carpet. Each trip took some time, and Liz was growing tired of keeping up. It was like watching a tennis match.

"John, could you please stop pacing? It's making me dizzy," she said.

"Oh. Sorry." He sat down on the sofa, recreating their positions of two nights before. "You think those goons were really going to do something to you?"

"I wasn't sure. I think it was just an intimidation tactic, but at the airport it was more serious. They actually accused me of stealing before they backed off."

He nodded gravely. "You're absolutely sure Nordstrom killed that patient and that Donald was innocent? How could you see that on a videotape?"

"What do you mean?" Liz asked. She sat forward in her seat and finished what was left of her second orange juice.

"I don't know. It just seems . . . convenient. It's precisely what one would want to believe. I just wonder if there's a little wishful thinking involved on your part.''

Liz's jaw began to tremble with anger. It was all she could do to stay seated on the chair and talk reasonably. ''Damn it, John. I'm telling you that he has a distinctive, completely unique move that he makes with the laser. It looks like he's taking aim. Anyway, no concrete evidence was ever brought out to implicate Donald. He used drugs, but that's circumstantial. I know he could have fought it, if only he hadn't killed himself.''

It was the first time she had used such a blunt term to describe what Donald had done. Her words sounded strange and surreal as she spoke them.

''And another thing, John. I'm coming to you for help. You've acted like I'm a hysterical woman since I came here the other night. Like I'm going off the deep end because I can't stand the pressure of what's happened. I'm sad, John, because I lost my husband. But I'm in command. Look at me. I've been through hell, and I'm still in control. Why don't you drop the attitude and really listen to me?''

Shocked by her intensity, he looked at her face and into her eyes. She was tense and nervous but completely in control. Her long black hair hung unfettered, cascading around her neck and shoulders. Somehow the fire of her anger had made her even more stunning.

''Would it help if I said you're beautiful when you're angry?'' he said sheepishly.

''Thanks. And no, it doesn't help much.''

''All right,'' he said, looking into her eyes. ''What we need to do is get that tape out of your security box. We'll take it to the police and spill our guts.''

Liz shook her head. He hadn't thought it through. ''No. Not yet. I don't think I have anything good enough to press charges with—just more circumstantial evidence. At the most, I could sue those Endicott security men for making false charges at the airport. But they're not the ones I'm after. I need to have more to bring Nordstrom down."

The soft patter of raindrops began to fall on the window. John started to open the blinds to look at the rain but stopped himself. If he was to take her word for what was happening—which he had begun to do—then she might have been followed over to his apartment. They could be outside watching.

"I think we should go somewhere else. We don't want to be found until this is cleared up," he said. I have to believe her, he said to himself. She needs me.

"But where?" Liz asked. "I guess the Midwest would be a good place to start. We could try to get into Med-Tek. I could talk to Willers in Cincinnati. The copies of those autopsy records are probably waiting for me in my office by now."

The rain had begun to beat a steady soothing rhythm. It rarely rains in Los Angeles, and its sound often brings about a rare meditative state. It seemed impossible, but Liz and John began to relax. In minutes, though, the shower slowed to a nearly imperceptible drizzle.

"I have to show you something," John said, nervously stroking his chin. "I'll be back in a minute."

He walked out in the direction of his bedroom. Liz pulled up the sleeves of the sweater and tried to get comfortable. She hadn't slept properly in over a week, and her vision was blurred with the spotty debris of fatigue. She had almost dozed off by the time he returned with a large manila envelope.

"I've been trying to decide whether or not to show this

to you," he said. "I'm not supposed to. I'm not even sure what it means, but I think you need to know about it."

Liz looked at the return address on the envelope. There was no name, but her address was written across the corner in Donald's distinctive doctor's scrawl. "When did he send you this?" she asked.

"The day before he died, I think. That's when it's postmarked. It came to me after his death with instructions to keep its contents to myself. He wrote me a note saying that he thought about destroying it, but he couldn't. He said the contents of this envelope were one of the things that were going to kill him." As he said this, he dropped his gaze to stare at the carpet.

John had neatly unsealed the envelope with a letter opener. Its flap had been covered with sealing tape, as if Donald had been afraid that the contents might spill out. Liz removed what was inside: several clipped-together parcels of newsprint and paper, along with a small stack of booklets. She began to look everything over while John resumed his pacing circuit of the room. He remained completely silent, looking at his watch and staring at the floor. After she's seen the papers, he thought, we have to get out of here.

The first bundle was a stack of newspaper clippings. The newest and least yellowed was from a 1993 edition of the *Los Angeles Times*. It was a small notice about a series of murders in Cincinnati. Police suspected a single killer because of the distinctive technique: the bodies had been eviscerated through a tiny series of abdominal incisions. Police and the Hamilton County Coroner's Office were at a loss.

Underneath was a series of clippings from the *Cincinnati Enquirer*. The stories were considerably longer, dating from early 1992 to mid-1993. They traced the progress of the murder series, beginning with the first clumsily mutilated corpses found in the Ohio River. Later stories contained quotes from Homicide Detective Carlton Willers, who said that the killer was clumsy and inept but deadly.

A rather large and sensationalistic article, the last in the series, recounted the story of Evan Rose, a lumberyard night watchman, who disappeared for a day with no memory of what had happened to him. Police discovered him wandering in a field and returned him to his family.

After twelve hours, Rose fell ill and began to hallucinate. He was taken to the county hospital, where he fell into a coma and died within a day. An autopsy report revealed that he had no kidneys: without them, he was almost the walking dead. The case was ruled a murder pending investigation. Willers's name appeared again, along with a small snapshot of him at a press conference.

Liz looked closely at the photo, finally matching a face to the voice. He was a stocky black man, about forty-five, and he looked severely aggravated as he fielded questions from the press. He wore a long raincoat and smoked during the questioning, telling the press that speculation could not be yet confirmed that this was the latest in the series of "Keyhole Killings." The story went on to explain that the killings were so named because the coroner had remarked that the removal of a victim's internal organs was akin to a burglar's "stealing your refrigerator through the keyhole of your house."

"Why in the world would Donald have saved these? He had to go to a lot of trouble to get these articles from an out-of-town newspaper," said Liz. John didn't answer. He quickened his pacing, once peeking through the blinds as he passed the window.

The second stack was all in Spanish, from Mexican

newspapers. Above the headlines were translations of the stories' contents in Donald's handwriting. Donald had taken some rudimentary Spanish in college and, with the aid of a dictionary, must have been able to glean the over-all sense of the articles. Certain passages had been underlined in a different-colored ink.

One article's headline translated: "Strange Rumors in Rural Maya Population." Another read: "Yucatán Mayans Speak of Abductions, Unsolved Killings." Liz asked John if he could read it.

"Unexplained mutilations involving mysterious cuts have been blamed on ghosts. Others think it is a maniac on the loose," John said. "I looked up some of the difficult words in my Spanish dictionary and pieced together the meaning. The next paragraph reads: 'Medical examiners report that the victims' abdominal cavities were emptied through tiny incisions.' "

The dates on the clippings indicated that they all had been printed within the last year. A few were from the *Diario de Yucatán*, printed in the city of Mérida, and looked sleek and professional. Others were from smaller publications and were printed on cheaper paper with ink that had already begun to fade.

"Why in the world would Donald collect these?" Liz asked. "Some of these look like tiny rural newspapers. I mean, we hadn't been to Mexico in almost five years."

"I don't know," John said. He stopped pacing and stood with his back to the window. "He must have had someone send them to him. He probably subscribed to a clipping service; they might have regular access to some off-the-wall newspapers. They're original copies, clipped from the source. They weren't compiled out of a library, where you would have to photocopy them."

Spread out on the coffee table, the clippings ran together like a grisly chronicle of human depravity. The unexplained fatal mutilations had all occurred in the Indian Mayan population, which had superstitiously assumed that there was a supernatural explanation. Next to the Cincinnati clippings, though, the connection was too obvious to miss. The same killer, or killers, had to be responsible.

"How familiar would they be with laparoscopy in Mexico?" Liz asked.

"I'm not sure," John said. "Quite familiar in the cities. But in the rural areas, high-technology surgery would be unknown. There would be a space of quite a few miles between hospitals out there. And—think about it—Detective Willers in Cincinnati only made the connection this week. It's just a matter of who hears about the cases and who had access to the evidence. If you just read the headlines, you might assume that a garden-variety slasher was on the loose."

John sat next to Liz on the sofa and took her hand, feeling her warmth. "Donald didn't want you to see those clippings," he said gravely.

"Why not, John? Why did he send them to you? Did he explain anything: why had had them, what he was going to do with them?"

"Not really. He attached a short note that told me to do what I wanted with them as long as I didn't show them to you. To tell you the truth, I was at a loss, so I just held on to them. After you told me about Willers, I knew there had to be a connection."

"But why didn't you say anything?" Liz asked, her voice rising in a mixture of confusion and anger. "I came over here in shock because that detective called me, and you just kept your mouth shut."

John pulled his hand away from Liz, staring at it as if it

had done something offensive. "The note from Donald told me never to let you look at them. I obviously couldn't ask him why. I respected the request of a dead friend, but at this point it would be irresponsible of me to hide them from you."

His voice had grown cold and formal, which shocked Liz. He seemed profoundly saddened by the entire set of circumstances. "I'm sorry to have kept them from you," he said.

Perhaps what bothered Liz the most was that this collection of clippings, which represented an expenditure of time and effort for reasons she couldn't guess, was yet another secret her husband had kept from her. A dormant sense of loss and betrayal began to eat away at the edges of her emotions, a feeling that had become far too familiar. Come on, Danny, keep it together, she told herself. There will be time to let go when all of this is over.

"It's all right, John. Really. I can understand your situation. The important thing now is that I contact Willers first thing in the morning. I'll call him at seven, which is four here. Do you mind if I stay over?" she asked, now all business.

John turned a little pale. "Yes. I mean, no, but we need to get out of here. We'll get a hotel room for the night."

They sat in silence for a moment, both agreeing they were too worked up to sleep anytime soon. Liz looked at the final items from the envelope, a brochure from Endicott Mexico—the very one that Nordstrom had sent to her as an enticement—and an envelope full of letters.

"The Mexico facility," she said. "This is where Nordstrom offered to send me. Donald never spoke to me about it."

She pulled out the letters and began to look at them. To her surprise, they were a series of correspondence between Donald and Nordstrom. Donald routinely made photocopies of the letters he wrote, and he had saved both sides of his contacts with Nordstrom.

"Listen to this," she said. *"Dear Kerry, It has come to my attention that you have made an unusually large request of fluocil supplies at my hospital, as well as the other twelve in the U.S. that have the substance in stock. I am disappointed that less fluocil will be available for my use, but I understand you have offered a handsome price. In light of our past research into fluocil, particularly in combination with experimental laser frequencies, I respectfully request information on how you plan to use these massive reserves."*

"What was the response?" John asked.

"Dear Donald, I know your curiosity is aroused by my need for fluocil. I am using it for my research at Med-Tek, and this explanation should be sufficient. You may speculate on the nature of this research, but such a line of inquiry would be fruitless and unnecessarily detrimental to your own work and livelihood. In time, the nature of my research will become public knowledge."

"Nordstrom was warning Donald not to dig into the Med-Tek research. It sounded like it was an outgrowth of work they did together. You knew them then. What were they working on?" John asked impatiently.

"They were working on fluocil's oxygenation potential. That's about all I know; it was pretty esoteric stuff. God, in Med-Tek—" she said, putting her hand over her mouth.

"What?" John said.

"Nordstrom had a pig breathing in fluocil. It was so disgusting that I haven't even thought of it since then, but Kerry said he had made recent breakthroughs. God, Donald would have wanted to know about that. I never had a chance to tell him. I thought he might be jealous to know Nordstrom had the means to continue research they started together. They were using early model lasers to treat fluocil years ago."

She read the next letter aloud: *"Dear Kerry, As usual, your response speaks volumes about your intentions. You must know that my memory is not so short that I don't have a good idea what you're developing. If you've achieved our old dream, it is an amazing thing. Please, Kerry, don't use this as another way to make money. Our debt to humanity as doctors is to bring this to the world, not just those whom we choose. I enclose copies of American and Mexican newspaper clippings to show you that I know what has begun. Events in Mexico cannot continue. It is against all the laws of God and nature. I will not act on this information until we have had a chance to talk."*

"This letter is dated three months ago," Liz said. Her face had turned a chalky white, and she felt a sore dryness in her throat. "This must have been what they were talking about at the hotel in Indianapolis. Nordstrom must have lied to Donald somehow."

A loud slam came from the hallway. Liz and John looked at each other in alarm until they heard the sound of childish voices raised in laughter. It was just a bunch of kids playing around on Halloween.

"I'm going to Mexico," Liz said suddenly. "I'm going to see for myself what the hell is going on there. I owe it to Donald."

John clapped his hands in anger. "Liz, be reasonable. Look at what we're talking about: conspiracy, unknown technology, maybe even mass murder."

"Exactly," Liz said. "That's why I'm going. You're welcome to stay here if you want, but I'm leaving for Valladolid tomorrow morning. It's the last place anyone would think to look for me, and I might be able to find out what Nordstrom is doing with laser technology that's so valuable that it was worth destroying my husband.''

John put his head in his hands.

"It is your favorite vacation destination, after all," Liz said. "Have you ever been to the Yucatán?"

"Many times." He sighed. "What are we going to do, go up to Endicott Mexico and ring the front doorbell?"

"It might work," Liz said, standing up. It made her feel light and giddy to have a course of action, away from her fears, away from her feelings.

"God," John said. "I'd better go with you. I'd never be able to live with myself if I let you go down there alone." He looked at Liz tenderly, trying to reconcile his fear with his feelings for her. Of course he would go. He would go anywhere to be with her.

Several miles away, Hank Mancini walked from the pay phone in front of the convenience store to his beat-up black Oldsmobile. The doctor never came home. He had let himself in and introduced himself to the dog, but there was no sign of Liz Danny. He had filled up the dog's water dish and sat on the floor for a while petting it. Having a lifelong soft spot for animals, he was always glad to meet a dog that was so friendly he didn't have to kill it.

He called in to update the client. Hank mentioned the last place the doctor had gone to before leaving town the other night: the high-rise home of the dark-haired Casanova. The client said to take care of it, and to make it look like a bungled burglary if things got rough. Sources at the police department said that his little break-in two nights ago—the one he had twice been royally chewed out for—

had never been reported. That meant the police weren't involved yet.

Nineteen years of experience, from busting kneecaps in the parking lot of Soldier Field to assassinations in the posh houses of Lake Shore Drive, told Mancini that the doctor was at Rogers's house. It would be a snap to finish the job and head back to Chicago, away from the irritation of L.A. smog and the pushy anonymous client with his southern accent.

CHAPTER TWELVE

11 P.M., October 31, Los Angeles.

HOT WATER AND A LOOFAH-SPONGE SCRUB IN JOHN'S SHOWER woke Liz up a bit, though her back and neck still deeply ached from stress and exhaustion. While John called to book a flight to Mexico, she tried to clear her mind of everything, if just for a moment. She allowed the hard spray to pound her shoulders and the smell of the scented soap to fill her nose. It was hard to tell when she would be able to sleep or even to relax again: certainly not that night.

In the next room, John packed a bag for the trip. He called the number that Liz had given him and spoke to Samantha, Liz's neighbor. John told her that Liz was going to Virginia to see her mother. Samantha was surprised by the call but agreed to feed Daisy and take her for walks with her own cocker spaniel.

He packed his camera and passport. They could buy clothes and other necessities when they got to Mexico. In the meantime, John set aside a blue gabardine shirt and a collared cotton oxford for Liz. If she tucked the clothes in and rolled the sleeves up, they would look as if they belonged to her.

Liz stepped out of the shower and began to dry herself. She toweled off a spot on the steamy mirror and had a look at what she saw: she looked tired and gaunt. She had lost too much weight in the last few weeks. When this was all over, she thought, it would be time for a couple weeks of rest and rich meals. Wrapping the towel around her hair, she ran water to brush her teeth.

She heard voices coming from John's living room, under the gurgling of the bathtub drain and the sound of the running tap. At first she thought her mind was playing tricks, so she turned off the water and listened more closely.

Two men were speaking: John and a stranger. Quickly putting on the clothes she had worn before the shower, she pressed her ear to the door to hear what they were saying.

" . . . don't know who you think you are, coming in like this, but I'm telling you, the woman in the bathroom is not the one you're looking for. She's my date, and we're going out for dinner."

"Oh, I see," the second man said in a rough mocking voice. He sounded as if he were conducting an interrogation. "Kind of late for dinner, ain't it? I'm sick of talking to you, mister. You're gonna take me in there to meet your date. I have something to tell you both, and I'd rather not say it twice."

"At least be a gentleman and give her a minute to get dressed," John said. "I'm sure we can get this cleared up in no time at all."

Liz opened the door a crack and peeked down the hall. She could see only John. He calmly continued to talk, holding his hands in the air and standing very still while he spoke. He was being held at gunpoint.

"I've had enough of this," the man said. "I don't care if she's dressed or not. In fact, I might like it better if she's undressed, if you know what I mean. Come on, we're going in there together. And slowly."

Through the crack, Liz could see John take a couple of steps toward the bathroom. His expression betrayed nothing of the fear he had to be feeling, and his hands were still held in the air as he entered the long hallway.

She didn't wait to see the man behind him, quickly covering her face with the towel, opening the bathroom door, and running into John's bedroom. A trail of droplets watered the carpet behind her. She heard the deep voice of the man cursing at her from the hall.

"What've you got in your room? A gun or something? You people are real stupid, you know that? You're about a minute away from dying, buddy, so you'd better call her out here."

Liz looked around the bedroom in a panic. There was no way out except the way she had come in, and the windows were sixteen stories above the pavement. She had about thirty seconds to act: the door was locked behind her, and it would take at least that long to kick it in. From the sound of the man's voice, he had only one intention: killing them both. A terrible sadness mixed with her panic, a feeling of profound regret that she had brought John into all this.

The bedroom closet door banged shut with a clatter. Mancini put the gun to John's chest. "Call her out, big guy. You don't want to make me more pissed off than I already am. I've been a nice guy so far, but I might get real unpleasant."

The man had rung the doorbell while Liz was in the

shower, claiming to be from building maintenance. He said that the apartment above John's had a busted pipe and that he needed to inspect the ceiling. The man was dressed in a sweatshirt and jeans, with a three-day beard growth, and John had let him in. He simply wasn't used to thinking like a fugitive. After he pulled a gun, the man had said he needed to talk to Liz Danny. Nothing personal, he had added, warning John against playing the hero.

A line of sweat ran down John's forehead. He couldn't stop looking at the gun, his thoughts racing in search of an option. The man was about forty and heavyset, with thinning, receding hair cropped short in a military-style fashion. He was big and acted as if he had been in situations like this before. John would have thought twice about resisting even if a gun hadn't been pointed at his heart.

"Uh, Danielle, honey?" John called through the door. "We seem to have a case of mistaken identity. There's a man here who thinks you're someone else."

Mancini and John listened at the door. There was no sound. John shrugged his shoulders. "What can I say? I just met her tonight at a bar. I don't even know her, really. Liz, I think, is at a medical conference in Phoenix. If you want to talk to her, I'm sure you could find her there at one of the big hotels."

"Sure," Mancini said. "That's good enough for me. I'll just run along and leave you folks to your date. I know a little Italian place downtown that I can recommend."

With sudden and brutal force, he hit John on the side of the head with the butt of the gun. John dropped to the floor bleeding and lay there motionless.

"What an asshole," Mancini said. "I'm gonna do you, man, and the lady doctor too. Just for the hell of it. Stay put for a minute, and I'll be right back."

He tried the bedroom doorknob. Locked. There was still no sound from inside: she must have gone into the closet and frozen with fear. That would make her an easy stationary target.

The thin wood door splintered with the force of a hard kick from Mancini's steel-toed shoes. Only a thin strip remained hanging from the cracked hinges.

He turned on the light and walked into the room with his gun raised, opening the closet door. It was a walk-in, deep and filled with all manner of clothes, boxes, old sports equipment, and an array of shoes. He couldn't even see the back wall. She must huddled in there with all that junk.

It took seconds to roughly grab about a quarter of the closet's contents and throw them to the middle of the room. Mancini took his gun and moved it through the rows of shirts and suits that remained. God, he thought, this guy is a clothes horse.

She wasn't in the closet. His eyes scanned the room for hiding places. There was only one: under the bed.

"Hang on a minute, Dr. Danny," he said, pulling a metal cylinder from his jacket pocket. "Make yourself comfortable." He screwed the silencer onto the gun, calculating: two doctors, a high-rise apartment. It would be easy to make this seem like a burglary, and he might pick up a few bonus items in the process. The entertainment center in the living room must be worth a few grand alone.

The bed was on rollers. A swift kick sent it flying to the wall, where its impact knocked loose a piece of plaster. She wasn't there. Mancini's head swiveled from side to side; he thought for a second that he had missed her sitting in plain sight. Then his glance caught the open window, where a pair of women's shoes sat below the sill.

He threw open the curtains and stuck his head outside. A moment of vertigo took his breath away, and he tightly closed his eyes. Damn it, he thought. That fear of heights is going to do me in one of these days.

Mancini opened his eyes and looked to the right. A long ledge trailed off to the corner of the building, a cement line broken only by several balconies coming off the apartments. She could have walked along the ledge and hidden on one of them, among the plants and furniture. It made sense. He rested his elbow on the ledge and peered at the nearest patio. It was too dark to really see anything.

A jarring kick to his jaw momentarily stunned him. He shook his head violently in an attempt to rid himself of the haze of pain. There was just time enough to register that he had been kicked from behind, when another blow to his head pitched him forward.

He hung out the window from the waist up. For a moment the street far below surged into his vision. Tiny cars raced along what looked like a child's racing track, and the minute glow of lights illuminated the pavement. It looked as if he were miles above the hard stony sidewalk.

It was the doctor, the Danny woman. She was on the ledge to his left. He turned and pointed his gun, but another swipe to the jaw turned his head in the opposite direction. The gristle in his neck audibly clicked as he straightened his head, his eyes burning and the blood pounding in his ears. She had a good kick: focused on its target to maximize impact. He respected that. Now he would have to kill her.

The first shot glanced off the side of the building, chipping away a small piece of stone that fell down into the darkness. The bullet hissed through the air and vanished.

Liz tried to kick Mancini again but missed, her leg extended into the air. She comically whirled her arms about her, trying to regain her balance. Hank grabbed for her stockinged foot and touched it before she pulled back, clinging to the wall. The motion left him leaning farther out the window, and he grabbed for the frame with a moment of phobic panic.

Mancini would have cursed but he didn't have the energy. His ear had begun to bleed from the kicks, and it was all he could do to not look down. Still, he was in luck: Liz regained her balance and backed away from him on the ledge, a look of pure fear on her face. He had her. It would be an obvious case of murder when her body was found on the sidewalk with a bullet in it, but at that point he didn't care. She had hurt him. Killing her would bring personal satisfaction.

He extended the gun over the crook of his elbow to steady his aim. She would go down with a single shot, and there was absolutely nothing she could do about it but stand there and take it. Clinging to the wall for support, Liz had finally run out of options.

She closed her eyes and braced for the impact, hoping at least not to fall when the bullet hit. The last picture she saw was the endless cascade of headlights far below, surging to and fro in the night. Then she heard a bang and a man's scream. The shot rang out, somehow louder than the first, and a high whining hiss passed close to her ear. She pressed her face to the wall, waiting for the pain, and opened her eyes.

John had shut the window down hard on the man's ribs, making him drop the gun and cry out in pain. He had missed her. From the way her assailant's upper body jerked, she could tell that he was trying to kick John. The window quickly opened and shut again, harder this time.

Liz could hear the sound of breaking bones, and the man turned ghastly white. Hands reached out from the apartment and grabbed the man's shoulders. He screamed in pain as he was dragged inside.

Liz tried to hear what was happening in the apartment, but her ears were filled with the wind. It blew her skirt into the air and covered her eyes with her hair. She looked down: several people had gathered at the entrance of the building, looking up and pointing. They were so small that they appeared in her vision as little specks of motion and action.

A voice called her name. Her knees shook as she edged along the precipice back to the open window, where a hand appeared and pulled her in. John stood, blood caked on his ear and forehead. He smiled a ridiculous grin.

"Thank God you're all right. I was so worried," he said, as if they hadn't seen each other in years.

On the floor, the man was bound by a bed sheet knotted around his hands and feet. A sock was stuffed into his mouth, and his eyes watered with pain and rage. John rolled him over to pull out his wallet, bringing forth a round of muffled exclamations.

"Hank Mancini," John said, riffling through the wallet's contents. "Or Leonard Williams. Or Michael Wagner. He sure has a lot of ID in here. Well, what is it, mister? Who the hell are you? What did you want with Liz?" he yelled, nudging the man hard with his foot. Hank lay motionless, his eyes shut.

"I think he has a broken rib," John said, then turned to take Liz in his arms. "Thank God you're all right. He broke in here, or rather, I let him in like an idiot. Then he knocked me out."

She pulled the sock out of Mancini's mouth, tensing

when he began to struggle with his bonds. "Who are you? What do you want with me?"

Spittle mixed with blood poured from Mancini's mouth when he opened it. "Fuck you," he said. "I'm not telling you anything. You're the doctor—call the damned police so I can get some medical attention."

Liz replaced the sock, narrowly avoiding Mancini's teeth as he tried to bite her. "We have to leave. Now," she told John. "There are people downstairs who saw what happened, and we'll lose time explaining everything to the police. We may have bought time to get away. If he came alone."

John looked doubtful but picked up his jacket and put it on. "I can't talk you out of going?" he asked, careful not to mention their destination in front of Mancini.

"This guy has to have been sent by Nordstrom, John. Who else would want to kill me? This just proves that I'm getting close to the truth. Guys like this play in the big leagues," she said, motioning to Mancini on the floor.

"All right," John said. He grabbed his overnight bag. "If you're in danger, then I don't want you to be alone. I care too much about you to let anything happen to you."

Liz looked at him: at the determined set of his mouth, at his empathic eyes. She knew what she was asking of him: that he risk his life to be with her. He was willing to, and without a moment's hesitation. There was something else in his eyes: something deeper and more urgent. It shocked her, and she didn't know how to respond.

She tried to think of something to say to him, some way to thank him. Before she could speak, sirens began to wail from the street below. Time was running out. They left Mancini in the bedroom, alone and disgusted at his own failure.

NOVEMBER

November 1, 1995
Satellite Microwave Transmission—Scrambled and Restricted Code. **_Do not transcribe. Commit to Memory._**

Executive Office, United States National
Security Council
The White House, by Permission and Acknowledgement
of the President of the United States of America

To:
All Active Intelligence/Security Operatives
South-Central Asia

Information expressed by prior communiqué expanded, clarified. President orders military staff, strategic personnel on full tactical stand-by pending final developments concerning Nation Eleven.

Nation Eleven has outbid other nations for technological discovery originating in continental U.S.

Parties developing technology unknown. Attempts to trace source unsuccessful. Lifebank discovery thought to inoculate humans to known poisons, radiation sickness.

Nation Eleven regime will use technology to initiate tactical strike against neighbor to the west (review border dispute: 89-92, if necessary).

Exchange of Lifebank technology to occur on November 4. Internal intelligence in Nation Eleven express low confidence that exchange can be prevented.

Motivation for selling technology unclear, as is level of the seller's knowledge of the region's instability.

Nations in region must be informed of projected advantage possessed by Nation Eleven when transfer takes place. Projected diplomatic breakdown, regional conflict is expected. United States currently clarifying options vis-á-vis nuclear/conventional strikes for own protection, that of allies.

Each operative receiving this transmission expected to sacrifice goods, safety, undercover roles for purpose of stopping transmission. Prepare emergency evacuation of region.

Transmission complete. Reset receiving and scrambling equipment to standard security settings. Out.

CHAPTER THIRTEEN

8:00 A.M., November 1, Mexico.

THE MEXICO CITY AIRPORT BUSTLED WITH ACTIVITY EVEN IN THE early-morning hours. The last-minute red-eye special Liz and John had booked required a one-hour stopover before a connecting flight. She was able to sleep on the plane but became wide awake when they hit the ground and found herself in the heart of another culture. She looked doubtfully through the wad of pesos she had purchased in Los Angeles, wondering how much a soda would cost.

She walked on with John behind her. He was distant, lost in thought, and she was still charged with the fear and danger of the last twenty-four hours. The airport was safe, she figured: who would think to look for her there, and how would they find her?

The long airport concourse looked like a shopping mall, though the stores were shallower and narrower than their American counterparts. Outside the high glass terminal doors, traffic careened by on a narrow street. High-rise buildings jutted high into the smoggy sky.

Liz entered a shop in search of something to drink. She went to the cashier after selecting an orange soda. The young dark-haired woman eyed Liz with studied indifference as she extended the bottle and reached for her money.

The woman said something incomprehensible to her, and Liz handed over several bills, receiving a small handful of change in return. She had always been terrible at foreign languages and currency: on college vacation in Greece many years ago, she had accidentally bought a rowboat at an Aegean market, thinking she was purchasing leather sandals.

She sipped the soda and walked out of the store, looking around for John. She found him at a ticket counter, talking to an agent of Aeromexico. When she was closer, she heard them conducting a rapid conversation in Spanish. John, his back still turned to Liz, said something in a friendly tone of voice that made the ticket agent's face break into a toothy grin. They shook hands and John walked away, nearly bumping into her.

"What were you talking about with that man?" Liz asked.

"I was finding out what time our flight leaves, and at what gate," John said defensively.

"It sounds like your Spanish is pretty good. That's another reason I'm glad you're coming along: my language skills are hopeless. I just overextended myself buying this soda."

John's face flushed red. "Well . . . he was helping me out quite a bit," he said. "If you make an effort to speak their language, people are very friendly."

Liz noticed the strange exasperation and distance in John's voice but decided to ignore it. She was far too grateful that he had insisted on coming along. His quiet, protective presence gave her a sense of warmth and safety she hadn't felt in years.

They walked to a bank of chairs near their gate and sat down. Liz sighed and drank her soda in silence. John crossed his legs and began to twitch his foot nervously. He was obviously agitated.

"John, what's the matter?" she asked.

"To begin with, I'm worried about that thug we left in my apartment. I'll be wanted for questioning as soon as he's discovered, you know. In a way, I'm a fugitive."

"For God's sake, John, he was going to kill us. People will have heard the shots fired, and they'll find the gun. You have me as a witness. Anyway, the police will have more on their hands than a tied-up man when we get back."

He looked at Liz with a dubious expression. She really expected to solve this mass murder, he thought, searching his heart for the reasons he had come with her. Was he in Mexico only because he was falling in love? Was he indulging her in a crazy dangerous course of action, when he should be taking her straight to the police? He found no comfortable answers.

Liz marveled at the people and action around them. This wasn't much like an American airport: people seemed less protective of their personal space and privacy. Strangers sat next to each other and struck up conversations, sharing cigarettes. It had become more crowded as the early morning wore on. The usual assortment of foreign tourists wandered about, clutching their tickets and looking bewildered as they checked their departure times.

They had fetched Willers's autopsy reports from her office at Community Hospital on the way to the airport, a fearful and paranoid errand that turned out to take an easy five minutes. They were almost surprised that no one was there waiting to kill them. Liz reached into John's duffel bag and pulled out the large envelope. Each packet was held together by a black binder clip.

She began to read: The first victim had been found in the Ohio River late the night of November 20, 1992. He was listed at first as an unknown "John Doe," but later was identified as Lawrence Jackson, an indigent whose last known address was the downtown rescue mission.

This information came from the police report. On the next page began the summation from the medical examiner's office. The autopsy was conducted by a G. Simpson, who determined that the body had been in the river for several hours before being discovered. The corpse's flesh had rotted extensively, but no trauma wounds to the head were evident. The fingernails were unbroken, which suggested that the victim hadn't been in a fight. The only sign of damage to the body was a series of small incisions across the abdomen, not consistent with haphazard stab wounds. It was when the traditional Y-shaped incision was made to open the body that the greatest surprise came.

The body had been eviscerated. The kidneys, liver, spleen, appendix, gall bladder, stomach, and intestines were missing. The heart and lungs were intact. After tilting the body, Simpson found a lateral incision, approximately six inches in length, along the victim's side. Lawrence Jackson's cause of death was listed as "gross trauma and removal of vital organs through unknown means."

Simpson added below: "The victim was disemboweled, the organs apparently removed through the small incision in the side. The means are unknown to me. Incidental damage to the visceral cavity indicates that the organs were removed one by one, possibly left intact in the process, and with only moderate damage to surrounding tissue.''

Liz examined the diagram that the examiner had drawn to show the pattern of incisions. A one-inch cut had been made under the navel, with two of equal size approximately five inches from the navel. Two more cuts had been made higher up, under the ribs. She nudged John and showed him the drawing.

He leaned over and studied it intently, his eyes suddenly wide with shock. ''My God,'' he said. ''This is exactly the same as the pattern of incisions used in a laparoscopic endometriosis operation. Or for ruptured ovarian cysts. I've used it a hundred times.''

Liz nodded. ''It's similar to the pattern I would use for a laparoscopic hernia operation. See, there was also an incision along the side. That's the only difference. They must have severed the organs through the abdominal ports and carried them out through the victim's side.''

''What did the toxicology results say?'' John asked, taking the diagram from Liz and staring at it.

''Well, they're not the most complete in the world. I suspect they didn't use all of their resources because the victim was homeless. Still, I don't see why this didn't raise some questions in the medical examiner's office. Here's something—carbon dioxide and pentathol.''

John's eyebrows lifted as he leaned over to read the document in Liz's lap. ''Anesthesia. What serial killer uses anesthesia?''

Liz, busy scanning the rest of the reports, didn't respond. She saw that two more murders were committed before the end of 1992. Both were indigents: one had been identified, and the other remained anonymous. One was a man and the other a woman. The stories were much the same: missing organs, consistent incision patterns, and anesthesia in the toxicology report. It must have been at this point, when it became apparent that the killings were related, that Willers came onto the case.

A difference appeared in the next case: a twenty-five-year-old woman. "Jane Doe" had suffered the same evisceration, but there was no mention of damage to the surrounding tissue. The report on the previous killing, in contrast, noted damage to tissue and arterial structures, as well as tearing around the lateral incision in the patient's side.

"Whoever he was, he got better at what he was doing," Liz said, flipping through the stack of reports. They had forty minutes until their flight would begin to board passengers.

"There aren't any photographs in here," she said. "But by the fourth case the peripheral damage was reduced to almost nothing. Of course, I have to assume that these reports are reliable: the cases were done by three different examiners."

"What about the man we found out about through the computer bulletin board?" John said. "Evan Rose. The guy with no kidneys."

"It's the last one here. August 1994. Evan Rose, twenty-nine years old, in good health. He disappeared from work and was found the next morning with no recollection of what had happened. His family brought him to the hospital the next morning, after he lapsed into a coma. Just like the newspaper said."

Liz examined the report and read it aloud. "Same as the others. Five small abdominal incisions, one lateral incision in the side. In this case, though, only the kidneys were taken. Surrounding tissue and organs were undisturbed, which is why the victim lived as long as he did. Here's a difference: the wounds were stitched shut with standard sutures, and the renal arteries were clipped to keep him from bleeding to death.''

John grabbed the report. ''They found hospital implements in the body? If that isn't a clue, what is?''

''I guess so,'' Liz said doubtfully. ''But even if they found the make of the silk and the clips, it wouldn't mean much. Anyone could order them from a medical supply house. They could even steal them from a hospital.''

''We need to talk to Willers,'' John said. ''I don't know what kind of investigation they're running there, but the medical examiner should have been able to work with this.''

''I think we're going to be able to do more in Mexico than on the phone to Willers,'' Liz said. ''Donald knew something was happening down there, the same thing as in Cincinnati, and he knew Kerry Nordstrom was involved somehow. All Willers can say is that he has no clues.''

John stood up and stretched his legs. ''Assuming we can get access to any information at Endicott Mexico, I'm at a loss as to what to look for. What are we supposed to do, ask them politely if they're behind a string of mutilations and killings in the Yucatán?''

''We can find that out in other ways,'' Liz said. She was bothered by something in John's voice, a note of sarcasm. He kept subtly undermining her plan to go to Endicott Mexico. A faint glimmer of doubt played in her mind. Maybe she had been under too much strain. Maybe she should stop here while she was still alive. No, she thought. She hadn't believed in Donald while he was alive, but now she could do something for him.

''Look, John. If we can get lists of doctors who have practiced laparoscopy there in the last year or so, we. might have a solid lead. Maybe a surgeon who worked in Cincinnati moved to Mexico and took a job at Endicott.

Or maybe a nurse or a technician—anyone with access to the technology. If we take that to the police, we can give them something to work with.''

''Still, it doesn't mean that Nordstrom is involved in the killings. He might have no idea what's going on,'' John said. ''Look, I'm ready to buy the idea that he hired a goon to scare you after you figured out that he rigged the vagotomy operation. I'm not sure the man's a killer.''

Liz's full lips turned down in a determined frown. She set her soda on the carpeted floor. ''John, Donald knew something. It might have to do with the fluocil or with something else, but it was enough for Nordstrom to ruin him. I trust Donald's judgment, I know that now. I have an obligation to do this one last thing for him.''

John was silent. Liz's tone saddened him: it was the first time since Donald's death that she had spoken of him so affectionately. He worried that she was due for a breakdown when her walls of denial came down.

Still, she had a point. Donald had made a connection that no one else had. And John had broken his trust and brought Liz into the affair. Juan Rodriguez looked around him at the whirl of people and accents. This was his home of sorts, the home of his ancestors and living relatives. He felt confident here, strong enough to protect Liz. He knew in his deepest feelings that he would give his life to keep her from harm.

The plane to Valladolid was markedly different from the jumbo jet they had taken from Los Angeles to Mexico City, two of the largest metropolises in the hemisphere. It was a twin-engine Cessna, occupied by only a dozen passengers. They made two stops on the way before finally landing on a small strip nestled in a clearing outside of town. Liz and John both secretly breathed a sigh of intense relief when they landed: while the landscapes had been spectacular as the land shifted from the brown hills of Central Mexico to the thick foliage and wide vistas of the Yucatán, the aircraft's rocking and its low altitude made the nearness of the ground more of a threat than a thing to behold in wonder.

There was no line to rent a car. The only vehicle available was a decrepit two-seater Volkswagen, for which they left an exorbitant deposit. As they drove through the roads leading out of the airport, Liz cried out in recognition.

"That jet," she said, pointing at a sleek plane housed in the field's largest hangar. "Look at the logo on the side."

John slowed the car, taking a welcome break from struggling with its stripped gears. "Endicott. Look at that thing. It looks like Air Force One."

"Looks like we came to the right place," Liz said, squinting in the afternoon sun. "Maybe we can hijack it for the ride home." She looked over at John, who didn't seem to appreciate the joke.

As they drove on, Valladolid surprised Liz with its atmosphere of easygoing languor. It was an old town: many of its buildings were constructed of faded brick, and the narrow streets required that what little car traffic passed through do so carefully. At times, only one vehicle at a time could traverse an avenue, the other car waiting its turn.

They passed through the city square, which was dominated by a huge Spanish mission that had fallen into disrepair but maintained its air of Old World grandeur. The square was the most populated part of the city and was filled with well-maintained benches and rows of bright flowers. Small children swarmed around a few tourists, trying to sell articles of homemade clothing and packets of chewing gum.

The car rental attendant had recommended a small, out-of-the-way hotel, and they found it perched on a low grassy hill facing away from town. John talked at length with the desk clerk, asking for directions to Endicott Mexico. The conversation was rapid, but John's diction and accent were perfect.

Liz looked at John as they walked to their room, a bungalow separate from the main body of the hotel. "It's a good thing you're here to translate," she said. "Come on, tell me the truth. Where did you learn to speak Spanish so well?"

Opening the door to the small room, occupied by old mismatched furniture, John smiled ruefully. "I guess I need to talk to you about that," he said. "It's something I should have trusted you with before now." He closed the door behind them and shut the drapes. A tranquil hush settled over the room.

Liz immediately fetched a clean shirt from John's bag and made for the bathroom. "What do you mean by that? Were you a spy or something?" she asked in a teasing voice.

Before he could answer, a knock at the door destroyed the moment. Liz was alarmed, but John peeked through the drapes and motioned for her to relax. "It's just the desk clerk. Go ahead and change."

She came out of the bathroom dressed in John's shirt, which gave her a boyish slender appearance. "What did he want?"

"He wanted a deposit for the radio," John said. They looked at the dusty radio in the corner, an ancient appliance with missing knobs and a threadbare electrical cord running to a wall socket. "I don't even think I'll have the nerve to plug that thing in."

"What were you about to say when he knocked, John?" Liz said, searching about in the duffel back for clean socks. As she leaned forward, the sight of her lithe figure caught his attention. He quickly looked away, embarrassed.

"Nothing. I'll tell you later." He stretched out on the bed and growled, his back popping with stiffness from the pair of plane rides.

Liz looked at him curiously. He was hiding something, but she decided not to push him. She wondered if, as Donald had thought, John was gay. It would be a shame, she thought, realizing how attractive she found him. It was more than his good looks: he was respectful and supportive, and there was something old-fashioned and sexy in his protective chivalrous attitude.

"It's getting late in the afternoon," she said, slipping into her shoes. "I want to get to a market somewhere and buy some better walking shoes. I also want to call Endicott and try to get an appointment to tour the hospital tomorrow."

John was incredulous. "Liz, we have to talk," he said. "If you call them, you might as well send Nordstrom a card telling him where you are. Don't be ridiculous." He walked to the window and looked through the curtains, as if he expected to find a gang of assassins outside.

"John, I think we're all right. This is the last place anyone would expect to look for us. When that man in your apartment is found and the news gets out, Kerry will probably lie low for a while. He'll probably just be relieved that we didn't call the police."

John stared down the hill at a row of small homes,

single-room structures with open doors and windows. The countryside looked incredibly poor and underdeveloped.

"Look, Liz," he said. "There are other reasons for us to keep a low profile here. If anything is going on with Endicott International, it plays right into the local people's worst fears."

"What do you mean?" Liz asked, folding her arms.

"There have been rumors in this part of the world for years about child kidnapping. I don't know if you've kept up with the news, but there has been some brutal violence directed at Americans in Mayan parts of Guatemala."

Liz searched her memory. "I did hear something about that. There were several riots, weren't there?"

John nodded. "And the objects of people's anger were American. American women, specifically. The crowds were acting on reports that Mayan children were being kidnapped to become organ donors for wealthy patients in America."

"God," Liz said, shuddering involuntarily. "Children—that's horrible. Is it true?"

John shrugged. "Probably not, but who knows. No one has found any direct evidence that children are being taken for that purpose, but you can't reason with an angry mob."

Suddenly terrible images filled Liz's mind, of a report she had seen on the news. Nearly entire villages had turned violent in a couple of cases, burning buildings and leaving their victims near death. "Why would they believe this?" she asked.

John's face turned grim. "In a way I can't blame them. You have to understand, children are in danger in this part of the world. I know that infant mortality among the Mayans in Guatemala is in the area of five hundred per thousand live births, and it isn't much better in Mexico."

"I had no idea it was so high," Liz said.

"And there are a lot of Westerners coming to this part of the world for adoptions. Not all of them are legal. So you can see how Americans can be viewed as a threat to already endangered children."

Liz's thoughts wandered to the children she had seen in town, the impoverished youths staying close to their mothers. Had the people there seen Liz as a potential menace to their young?

"It's not a new fear for them," John said. "It goes all the way back to their myths. All through Latin America, children are warned about La Llorona, who was Cortez's lover and drowned the child she bore for him after his betrayal of the Indians. They say she wanders the riverbanks at night, howling and looking for children to take away with her."

"That's worse than the bogeyman," Liz said.

John smiled ruefully. "I think so."

"But the murder victims here have been adults," she said. "Not children."

"And thank God for that," John said grimly. He looked out the window again. "Anyway, I just wanted you to know. The Mayans have been made the victims of a lot of historical forces, from Cortez to the modern dictatorships, and their folklore has come to reflect that."

"Thanks for telling me," Liz said quietly. "I'll keep it in mind."

John stepped away from the window. "I'm going to the hotel office and try to talk to the clerk about the Endicott hospital. It's so big, everyone must know about it. While I'm at it, I'll see if he's heard about the murders. They must be quite famous around here. In the meantime, don't call the place. It's crazy: just because we're in another country, don't think that we can't be followed. Whoever is after you, for whatever reason, isn't going to give up.''

''All right,'' Liz said irritably. She was grateful for John's presence and protection. The problem was the flip side of his chivalry. He thought he automatically had to be in charge.

After John left, Liz stepped outside. She walked to the pay phone at the edge of the parking lot and dropped in a coin. ''Endicott Mexico,'' she said repeatedly to the queries of the operator. The line began to ring.

After all, they were visiting surgeons. They could say they were tourists. John was right to worry, but he was being overly cautious. If they were too scared to act, then they would find out nothing. And she knew she could never go home without being armed with evidence. Death awaited her there.

The sun set on Indianapolis, but in the basement studio where Kerry Nordstrom had been ensconced all afternoon, artificial light gave the room a sterile timeless feeling. Here he indulged a passion, the one he turned to when he had reached a momentary impasse with his research: music.

He sat on a stool with an electric guitar, trying to master the chord change he had come up with that morning. When he was ready, he would call in one of the technicians from promotions to man the sound board and record the song. It would join all the others he continually sent to agents and promoters in Nashville.

His labors were interrupted by a red telephone on the wall, which emitted a brittle electronic tone. The secretarial voice on the line informed him that Roberto Calderon was calling. After several clicks and beeps, a long-distance hiss filled his earpiece.

"Roberto, what can I do for you?" Nordstrom asked, impatient. He had hoped for word from Los Angeles on the success of the job he had commissioned, not another round of Calderon's whining and chest-beating over the Mexican operation.

"Dr. Nordstrom," the voice began, deep and rich, with a cultured Spanish accent. Calderon had been handpicked by Nordstrom for the job as managing director of Endicott Mexico. He had been a soft-spoken surgeon from Mexico City when they met at a Med-Tek seminar. He was also in serious trouble with the Mexican drug cartels after becoming involved in some extracurricular smuggling. Calderon's price had been easy to meet.

"In regards to our earlier conversation," Calderon said, "I had ordered our operators to report to me when we receive calls from Americans. I have received such a call today."

The guitar chimed a discordant note when Nordstrom dropped it to the floor. He hadn't heard from the middleman in Los Angeles, he realized, because the job had been a failure.

"You have my attention, Roberto," he said. "Go ahead. Tell me what you have."

"An American doctor, Rosalyn Campbell, called to say that she was in town on a tourist package and wanted to visit our facilities. She said that she would bring along a man she traveled with, who was a doctor as well."

Nordstrom remained silent. He had received the report on Rogers before the Phoenix conference. They must have reunited when Danny returned to Los Angeles. This was disturbing; he wanted Liz roughed up, even killed, if she had the wrong attitude, but the thought of her with another man filled him with searing jealousy. Seeing her in the past month had rekindled the unsatisfied lust for her that he had harbored for years. It was a shame that she was getting too dangerous. "When did she say she wanted to visit?"

"Tomorrow. She was told that she could come between the hours of one and three in the afternoon."

"Did she say where they were staying?"

"No, but I can easily find out."

"Then do it. Use all your resources to find out where they are." He paused for a moment. "Then send our security people to eliminate them."

Now Calderon was silent. When he spoke, it was in a halting voice. "Dr. Nordstrom, I want to be sure of what you are saying."

"Just do your job, Calderon. That's what you were hired for. I will explain the reasons when I visit in April," Nordstrom said with harsh finality. This was a new test of Calderon's loyalty, different from the surgeries. Nordstrom had no worries: Calderon would be a dead man if he strayed too far from the hospital's heavy security. If hired killers from the cocaine cartels didn't find him, a suspicious and hateful populace would.

"Of course, Doctor. I understand what is required of me."

Nordstrom reached down and inspected his guitar for nicks and scratches. He dusted off its body with the edge of his sleeve. Sudden light footsteps from behind made him turn around: she was there, finished with her shower in the luxury living quarters built into the studio. She stood naked to his appraisal, her long hair hanging damp over her young perfect body, a cold smile playing across her delicate features. He enjoyed her company, which cost him five hundred dollars an evening, plus extras.

"There will be rewards," he said. "Irwin Ross is with me on this. The two of you can sip cognac and talk about poetry when this is all over. But listen, Roberto, they are a serious threat. I don't want them to survive the night."

Nordstrom hung up the phone and strummed his guitar. A man can't have it all, he thought. It's a shame to have a beautiful woman killed, but she deserved it. Everything she did brought her closer to the truth, which was greater than her or Donald, or the trifling events of a faked surgical accident.

In two days, it would all be irrelevant. The satellite worked, the data and the product were ready for shipping. The bids had been delivered in total secrecy, and the winner had been decided. Endicott, Med-Tek—it could all go to hell. History would change, but even that didn't matter.

"Come over here, darling," he said to the nude young woman, extending his hand. "There's still time on the meter."

She stood behind him, rubbing his shoulders. "What were you talking about on the phone, Doctor?" she asked.

"Nothing. Just pinning down some details."

As her hands moved downward his thoughts raced. How would he go about spending a billion dollars?

CHAPTER FOURTEEN

9:00 P.M., November 1, Valladolid.

"YOU *WHAT*?"

"I called Endicott Mexico from the pay phone outside and scheduled an appointment for a tour. Come on, John, don't be so upset. I used a phony name. You can't really think that—"

John pulled hard on the towel around his neck, feeling the rough fiber against his bare skin. He had been about to take a shower when Liz dropped the news on him.

"I think that we don't know what we're up against, Liz. There's a guy in Los Angeles, who no doubt has been found by the police, who was going to kill me, until I inflicted internal injuries on him of unknown severity. Now you've called the hospital run by the man who hired that maniac. My God, Liz, you're being reckless!"

"I figured we could take their little tour, catch them off guard. You're a computer hacker. If we could just get you online for a few minutes, you could access the files we need."

She ran her hands through her long hair, a habitual gesture that increased in frequency as she grew more nervous. She slouched back in the threadbare hotel room chair, with her hair pulled away from her features, the slender oval of her features stood out stark in the dim light thrown off by the desk lamp. It was hard to stay mad at her, he thought, but he was damn well going to try.

"I'm going to take a shower," he said, "and try to figure out what the hell to do. I'm almost ready to say we should turn around and go back home."

"Do it, and you're going home alone," Liz yelled at his back as he stormed into the bathroom, slamming the door shut behind him.

She looked out the window at the deserted parking lot, then tightly shut the curtains. The sound of angrily jerked faucets, followed by a trickle of running water, echoed from the bathroom. For a moment, it had almost felt that they were who they pretended to be: a married couple on a leisurely trip through Mexico, shopping and eating and taking in the sights. Not to mention arguing.

When they had gone to town that afternoon to buy Liz a skirt and Mexican blouse, followed by a delicious dinner of fresh tortillas and seafood trucked in from the Caribbean coast, they forgot the sense of danger that had followed them to Mexico. But soon, she had noticed, they attracted the attention of the local people, who hung back in small groups and openly observed her. Liz felt conspicuously American and certainly under suspicion. They had quickly returned to their hotel.

Maybe she had made a mistake in calling the hospital, she thought, pulling out Donald's file and the Cincinnati medical examiner's reports. At the very least, she should have told John earlier. She realized that she shouldn't have let her temper flare; after all, John was putting himself in danger on her behalf. An inability to admit when she was wrong was a character trait that had followed her since childhood, one that she wasn't particularly proud of.

John finally emerged from his shower, dressed in the jeans and turtleneck he had bought at the market. His wet hair was slicked back away from his dark angular face, and his brown eyes were full of worry and fatigue.

"How was the water pressure?" she asked.

"Fine," John said. He walked to the small table in the corner of the room with a careful nonchalance that somehow showed her he wasn't angry. "Have you had a chance to look over these medical examiner's reports in greater detail?"

"Somewhat. The victim with the missing kidneys is probably the most fascinating. He entered the hospital in a state of psychocoma, with skin discoloration and loss of motor function. The initial diagnosis was some kind of poisoning, perhaps from rotten food or an overdose of nonprescription medicine. Naturally, the emergency room staff had never seen a case like that before."

"I'll bet they hope they never see one like it again," he said.

They didn't speak for a time. The bungalow was entirely silent, the surrounding units vacant. It appeared that the obscure location of the hotel, while perfect for someone wishing to hide out, kept it from doing much business.

"What would help," Liz said, "would be an examiner's report of one of the killings that took place down here. If there's a concrete correlation with the Cincinnati cases, we would be the most qualified to see it."

John sighed. "One thing I do know is that the people here don't want to talk about the killings. The desk clerk here told me that it had only happened to the Mayan Indians in the countryside, and that a lot of people thought there was some kind of ritual sacrifice involved. I got the impression that the townspeople are prejudiced against the Indians.''

''I forgot you talked to the clerk,'' Liz said. She stretched out on the bed, watching John begin his inevitable floor pacing. ''What did he say about Endicott?''

''At first, he told me, the local people were very happy the American company decided to set up shop in Valladolid. They provide basic medical care on a walk-in basis and perform laparoscopies gratis on patients who need them. They also employ a large number of people from the area as janitors, maintenance men, groundskeepers, security that kind of thing.''

''Security?'' Liz asked.

''Apparently the Endicott mania for security is the same down here as in the States. When I asked, the clerk told me that Endicott employed the roughest men in the area as a security force.''

''What else did he say?''

John tapped on the table. ''Well, I told him that I thought something might not be right at Endicott. He looked at me like I was crazy, then made the sign of the cross. He said that people around here know there's something strange and dangerous about the place. Then he asked me to leave.''

''That's comforting,'' Liz said. She closed her eyes and tried to relax. Thinking about tomorrow, she tried to envision herself and John walking into the complex for the tour. She thought harder, trying to determine what exactly she hoped to find in the nondescript building on the outer edge of the town.

''When we go back to Los Angeles, I'll have some explaining to do,'' he mused. ''I hope that man wasn't injured too severely.''

"You amaze me, John. That lunatic tried to kill us, and you're still worried about his health."

"I guess it's a weakness of mine," he said.

"No, no. I admire you for it," Liz said.

"I'm sorry I was angry at you," he said. "Who knows? Maybe your approach is best. Nordstrom may have gotten scared and given up after we took care of his man." He picked up the Endicott Mexico booklet from the nightstand.

Liz patted the empty spot on the bed next to her. Taking the cue, John lay down beside her. "It may have been the wrong thing for me to do," she said. "Maybe I am getting reckless. Since Donald died, I've felt kind of lost. Maybe it's clouded my judgment a little." She wrinkled her nose. "Enough of that. I've yet to meet the gunman who could withstand the John Rogers slammed-window treatment."

"You're impossible," he said, opening the booklet. "At least let me see where they keep the computers."

As he flipped through the pages, a small folded stack of paper fell out onto the bedspread. They were photocopies of letters on Community Hospital and Endicott International stationery.

"What are those?" John said as Liz grabbed them.

"It's a letter from Donald to Kerry, written right before we went to the seminar in Indianapolis: *Kerry, This has gone too far. You have bought almost all fluocil supplies in the United States. Now I hear you have obtained a laser frequency modification unit developed at our old labs in Minneapolis. You have to have known that I would hear about it. What do you expect me to do?*

"My conscience won't allow me to continue this charade. You try to hide your work in Mexico; you're disgusting. I know what you're developing: I know because we inaugurated the research before laparoscopy changed our careers. I can't fool myself into thinking you will use this discovery for the betterment of humanity. Your global satellite information network (yes, I know about it) is a sham. All you care about is getting more money. Tell me you won't make the mistake of a lifetime when the link is made on November 4, and I'll believe it. But then, you can't tell me that. You were always a greedy bastard.''

John whistled softly, taking the letter from Liz's hand. ''It looks like their correspondence got nastier,'' he said.

''There's a response,'' Liz said. *''Donald, there's no need for you to accuse me of greed in that silly, self-righteous tone. To listen to you, one would think I'm the only man in history to ever be interested in getting rich. Sure, I have the technology. I can't hide the substance of my ideas from you. And it is true that the satellite link could be used to transmit certain data in a manner that would be untraceable. The problem is: I'm not going to do it. The link won't be ready November 4, and in any case, maybe I'll surprise you and actually release the data to the world free of charge. I'm due for some charity work, right? Bear with me, old friend. Come to the seminar (info attached), and you'll see the light. Maybe you'll let an old friend do you a favor.''*

Liz turned the page over. ''That's it,'' she said, her hands shaking. ''This was the invitation to the conference. Kerry lured Donald into a trap.''

''They were still talking about the fluocil,'' John said. He edged closer to Liz on the bed to look at the letter. ''But what in the world is this about a satellite? I haven't heard anything—''

Liz snapped her fingers. ''Phoenix,'' she said.

John looked up from the letter. ''What are you talking about?''

"In Phoenix. Kerry was bragging about a medical satellite network he was inaugurating at noon on November 4. He told Donald it wasn't going to happen, but he was lying. It is going to happen!"

John grabbed her hand as if to calm her, but his expression quickly turned from one of reassurance to haunted concern. "Wait a minute. If it is happening, then some kind of data is going to be transferred through the system. It has to be the information that Donald said Nordstrom is going to profit from."

A gust of wind rattled the window, causing them to look up in alarm. The reassuring atmosphere of the quiet deserted hotel began to be replaced by an indistinct dread. John read the letters again, searching for meaning.

"This could be big," he said. "From the sound of it, he plans to transmit the data using an irretrievable link-up. The information is lost to the sender once it's sent. If he's selling something important, that means the buyer has a guaranteed exclusive. The rest of the world would miss out. But what in the world . . ."

"Whatever it is, we have to stop him," Liz said. "We have to get back to America by the fourth. That means we have only a couple days to find out what's going on. Unless we have some concrete evidence, we couldn't even get on the grounds of Med-Tek, much less stop the transmission from taking place."

John reached over Liz's sitting figure to the nightstand and dimmed the light a notch. He sighed deeply. "I'm with you. One way or another, we'll find out what's going on."

Liz folded the letters and replaced them in the booklet. "Donald knew all of this," she said. "And he never said a thing. He trusted Kerry Nordstrom. Damn it, he knew better."

She spoke calmly and rationally, but tears fell from her eyes and ran down her cheek. The soft curves of her face glowed radiantly in the low luminance of the room. John took her hand and held it to his chest. It had grown dark outside.

"Too many secrets," she said. "These needless deaths . . ."

John stared up at the ceiling for a long time, saying nothing. The room was silent save for the occasional sound of a car passing by on the road below.

"Liz," he began. "I have to tell you something about myself."

She nodded, a little alarmed at his grave tone of voice.

"My name is Juan Rodriguez. I grew up in East Los Angeles." Liz began to speak but he hushed her. "Please, let me go on," he said.

"I grew up in a large Mexican family. My father worked as a laborer in a bottling plant, and my mother cared for the kids. She even baby-sat other people's children to bring in money. We did all right, but it was still very much the barrio.

"My father wanted more for me than he had. I enrolled in the pre-med program at Cal State L.A. and worked full time waiting tables to keep up with the tuition. At the time, I looked forward to the day when I would become a doctor. . . . I wanted to return to my family and my community as a provider, as someone to look up to and be proud of.

"I couldn't get into an American medical school—the long hours at my job kept my grades down—but I was able to enroll in the University of Guadalajara. The U.S. Army helped me out with the cost of my education, but required that I serve five years in the military when I was finished. I was a Mexican-American, schooled in Mexico, who became an American army doctor.

"The real education came about when I was in the army. I served in Texas, where my name alone made me a second-class citizen. I was called a spic, a wetback. I was told that the men at the base didn't want their wives going to a Mexican gynecologist. Even when I delivered their babies, it was still as if there were something permanently wrong with me. I thought about going home, but that was closed off to me somehow. I had changed—I was neither here nor there, and I felt that I was part of nothing anymore.

"So I changed my name at the county courthouse. It was easy, just a matter of filling out a few forms. I worked in Houston for a while, then came to Community Hospital in L.A. As John Rogers, I've been able to be recognized for my work alone. I'm a damned good doctor, you know.

"The irony is that I've shut myself off from the world by living this lie. I can't get close to anyone. I—I never thought it would be this way."

Liz sat in shocked silence as he spoke, watching his thin lips quiver with anxiety. When he was finished, she took his hand and looked into his eyes.

"Do you still see your family?" she asked.

"My father died when I was in medical school, but my mother still lives in East L.A. I try to visit her as often as I can, bring her money and presents. She's been very proud of me ever since I started school. You know, I was the first member of my family to make it past high school."

"Does she know that you changed your name?"

"She knows, but she never mentions it. She thinks I did it because I'm embarrassed about my background, which isn't true." He mused for a moment, his face locked in concentration and memory. "My brother, Jorge, is very angry with me. He was jealous when I went away to school, and since he found out about my name, he's had nothing to do with me. He calls me his 'white brother,' as if that were the greatest insult he could think of.''

"But he lives in L.A.?''

"Yes, with his family. I've only met his oldest child, and that was when she was born. He has three others that I've never seen. I think I'm more jealous of him than he is of me. He has a normal life: a wife, children. Things that I've wanted but haven't been able to have.''

"Why didn't you ever tell me?'' Liz asked.

John exhaled heavily and rose to his feet. He shoved his hands into his pockets and looked around the room.

"You have to understand, Liz. It's difficult for me. It was a decision I made a long time ago, when I was younger and didn't know who I was. Now I have Latino colleagues, you know, and I have to pretend to be a gringo from suburban America. People now wouldn't care who I am, but if they knew what I did, they'd think I was a coward and a traitor to my own race. And they might be right.'' He walked to the wall and pressed down on a loose piece of wallpaper, his expression at once grieved and angry.

"I would hope that people would realize that what you had to do is a comment on our society more than any duplicity on your part,'' Liz said. Her voice sounded strained and formal in her ears. John, the man she thought she knew, now seemed like a completely different person. "Besides,'' she said, "this is America. Everyone's blood-lines and nationalities are so intermingled, I don't see how anyone can maintain any kind of prejudice.''

"But they do,'' John said sadly. "Or they did. Maybe now it would be easier, I don't know. I almost told you when we ate together in Venice, the night of Donald's death. Since then I've felt that you had enough to worry about.''

''I suppose I haven't talked about what's inside me, either,'' Liz said. ''I haven't felt clear enough with my own feelings to share them. I have a friend, a psychologist, who warned me about the highs and lows I would have. But I haven't had any, just a sense that my emotions are blocked inside of me. When I lost Donald, I simply shut down. In a weird way, I've been almost relieved for all the things that have happened lately; they've kept me from thinking too much.''

John sat beside her and put his arm around her shoulders. ''I know it must still be hard.''

''The worst part is that he was lying to me,'' Liz said. She could feel warm tears streaming down her face. ''And not just about Nordstrom. If he was in such despair that he turned to drugs, I should have been the person he came to. I should have been able to do something. He was so good at hiding it, and I never asked him how he was really doing, what he really felt. He was older than me. Somehow I thought he knew more about the world. I always assumed he would be all right.''

She rested her head on John's chest, finally crying the tears that she had held back for weeks. Mingled with her feeling of loss and sadness was rage at the injustice of Donald's professional ruin, and the terrible fear that she was going to die next. With a finality that racked her body with sobs, she realized that her old life was gone forever.

''You can't blame yourself,'' John said in a whisper. ''The things that happened to Donald just happened. We can do justice to his memory in the next two days. Just remember, life is for the living.''

He cradled her face in his hand. His touch was warm

and tender, as if it were the embodiment of his purest
emotions. She looked up into his eyes, which also welled
with tears. His face spoke of his own suffering, as well as
the intense compassion and growing love he felt for her.

Their lips met with a tender touch, barely grazing at
first. She touched his chest and felt his heartbeat through
the thin fabric of his shirt. A shiver passed through one,
then the other, as they kissed with more force, their hands
working through each other's hair. They pressed close
together, pulled tight in an embrace composed of equal
parts desire, relief, and need. An excitement coursed
through Liz's body that she couldn't remember feeling
since she was younger and first experienced the touch of
another.

John reached over to the lamp on the nightstand and
turned it off. They lay down together in the darkness,
trembling as they kissed again. John circled his arm
around her waist and pulled her closer. She quietly
moaned at the pressure against her body.

He unbuttoned her blouse and touched the soft skin of
her belly and breasts, then leaned over to kiss her again.
She became more excited, exploring his body with her
hands, lying underneath him with her eyes closed to the
world. Their movements lost their grace and light touch, a
mutual desperation overwhelming them as they undressed
and pressed their warm bodies together. In the rhythm of
their movements was an unspoken plea: for safety, for a
return to their lives, for feelings of wholeness and forgive-
ness.

Their lovemaking was awkward and rough, their unfa-
miliarity with each other making each moment distinct
and alien. The sounds they made were new, their grasping
hands and pressing legs like those of strangers. They finished in unison, their fingers locked together and their

faces buried in each other's, as if they tried to break beyond the isolation of their skin and bodies, straining to become one.

The room became quiet again, the enveloping darkness and still of the night as it was before they touched. Neither could find anything to say as their minds returned to the danger and the brief time they had to accomplish a task they couldn't define. John pulled a blanket over their bodies, pulling Liz close to him. After a time they began to kiss again, this time softly, without hurry or panic.

The sound of the doorknob turning made them freeze. Their eyes met in the darkness. It turned again with an audible creak. They had locked and bolted the door upon entering, so it didn't open. For a moment, there was no sound from outside.

Liz pulled away from John, trying to remain silent as she hastily grabbed her clothes from the floor and put them on. Her mind filled with images of the men and women she had seen in town; they had watched her openly, as if waiting for her to make a move toward their children. She also had felt a palpable jealousy from some of them, the resentment of the poor who had to make their lives throughout the year in a place where Americans came to play. Ironically, unlike most tourists, Liz and John had brought little worth stealing.

Before there was a chance to act, the door burst open with a loud crash, the bolt's chain flying into the air. A ray of moonlight entered the room, illuminating the shapes of three men. They wore black, and their faces were covered with ski masks. The steel barrel of a gun glinted in the faint light. The man in front aimed his weapon and fired, the gun hissing with the muffled report of a silencer.

The pillow next to Liz's head flew back into the wall as

it was hit, a small snowfall of feathers filling the air. The men remained silent, and the one in the rear turned to shut the door behind them, restoring the room to complete darkness. The second man held a gun before him, firing another muffled shot that barely missed the scrambling Liz, who dove behind the bed. The men clearly were aiming at her.

John reached to the nightstand next to him as all eyes adjusted to the sudden darkness. The man who had shut the door began to grope around the wall trying to find a switch, not knowing that the only source of light in the room was the lamp next to the bed. In the moment of confusion, John held his camera before him, repeatedly pushing the triggering button that activated the high-powered flash.

The three men yelled out in confusion and fired their guns blindly. A hail of hissing bullets riddled the room, and an odor of gunpowder permeated the air. When the men stopped shooting and finally found the bedside lamp, Liz and John were gone.

John had had to pull roughly at Liz's arm to guide her out the bathroom window, where only an hour before he had showered and idly noticed that its low height and broad width would make it easy to climb through. Then he had been worried about a burglary; now, as they fell onto the dirt outside, he was grateful for the hotel's lack of security-conscious design.

They ran around the building to the road. Angry voices cursed in Spanish behind them, but there was no time to look back to see how close their pursuers were. The hotel office was dark and closed. When John started the engine of their rental car and pulled out to the road, Liz cursed aloud.

"We left the clippings and examiner's reports inside," she said. "We need those."

"We're certainly not going back for them," John said, picking up speed on the narrow road leading back to town. Traffic was almost nonexistent at that hour, and the men had yet to appear in the rearview mirror. They must have come on foot, or have left their car some distance away so they wouldn't be heard approaching. This afforded Liz and John a slight lead.

The car shook and rattled on the rutted road as they picked up speed. Small single-room houses flashed by on either side, perched perilously close to the road. Inside them, the illumination of a small electric light or even a fire provided a brief glimpse of hammocks and plain spare tables. Liz marveled that so many people lived so close to the road, where a tiny mistake on the poor surface could easily send a car careening into someone's bed.

"They're coming," John said, looking in the mirror. He reached down to buckle his pants, the only garment he'd had time to put on. "It's a single car, and they're driving fast. I can only get so much speed out of this damned Volkswagen."

Liz turned to look behind her. The car's headlights bounced up and down as the vehicle bobbed on the rough pavement.

"Where are we going?" Liz asked. John was driving recklessly fast, maintaining enough of a lead on the men that they hadn't yet tried to shoot at their car.

"I don't know," he said, his arms extended and braced against the steering wheel. "I can get us back to town, but once we're there I'm not sure."

"We need to get to the police," Liz shouted as the car shook violently over a particularly deep pothole. The men were getting closer: their headlights illuminated the interior of the rental car. When she looked back, the glare momentarily blinded her.

"Maybe, maybe not," John yelled over the whine of the Volkswagen's engine. "If those men were sent from Endicott, then we don't know for sure that the police will be on our side." He glanced briefly at Liz, who looked shocked. "This is a poor part of the country. Money can buy a lot."

A pair of headlights appeared at a bend ahead of them, high and far apart. In horror, Liz realized that it was a truck straddling the center of the road. It was on them in seconds. John veered to the right, skidding in gravel and making the rear end of their car swerve and fishtail wildly. The engine caught and started to stall as the large truck passed by within inches, its horn blaring.

John managed to pull the car back on the road and keep the engine running, gunning it to keep it from dying. A few seconds later, the truck's horn sounded again. Liz looked back and saw the pursuing car veer to the left, crashing through a row of bicycles parked too close to the road. The bikes pitched up into the air, scattered, and wrecked as the car moved through them, pulling back into the lane without stopping.

When they reached the heart of the city, the road narrowed considerably. Luckily, the sleepy town had almost as little traffic at that hour as the more rural route they had arrived on. John took a series of sharp turns to try to lose the car behind them, the tires squealing as he and Liz were violently tossed from side to side. An old man appeared in their headlights at a sharp turn, then dived from their path before they raced around another corner.

The noise of their car and their pursuers' sounded louder in the brick streets of the town, echoing off the stone buildings. Lights turned on in windows all along their path. As John swerved through an intersection, barely avoiding a parked car, their back window shattered with a great noise of breaking glass. Liz screamed and ducked as the fragments flew over the backseat. John cut onto a side road, momentarily losing the other car.

They drove on until their headlights showed a wall of brick at the end of a narrow alley. John drove halfway into the alley before realizing that they were trapped. He cut the engine.

"Get out, we have to run for it," he said, trying to sound calm. He looked down and realized that he had brought the camera along with him in his panic.

The soles of Liz's bare feet were cut and scraped by the rough stones in the alley. She limped and bit her lip as they ran deeper into the dead end. There was as yet no sign of the car behind them. In the moonlight, they could see overflowing cans of trash lining the walls of the surrounding buildings.

The building to their right was brick, with no doors or windows facing the alley. John grabbed Liz's hand and pulled her toward a portal to their left, which emerged from a white stone structure. Over the door was a small portico built of painted wood. A cross was inlaid with brass to the right of the door.

It opened to John's push. They entered and stood in darkness: ahead was a large high-ceilinged room, the sanctuary of a church. From the gloom, a man wearing the black tunic of the clergy emerged with a worried look on his face. He talked to them in an annoyed voice. Liz imagined how they must have looked to him: two crazed people breaking in from the alley, one shirtless and the other barefoot.

John responded in perfect Spanish, speaking rapidly and pointing back to the alley. The priest, a heavyset youngish man with thick black hair, looked at him warily as he spoke. His eyes widened as John continued to talk, grabbing the priest's sleeve to pull him away from the door. The father motioned for them to be quiet and led them into an adjoining hallway.

"What's going on?" Liz asked. "Is he going to help us?"

The priest leaned over, grunting and working at the edges of a piece of wooden floorboard. He pulled it back, exposing a dark space underneath, and motioned for them to enter.

Stairs led into the damp darkness, and all light vanished when the panel was shut above them. Their ears rang with the sound of the priest's foot stamping on the trap door to restore its place flush in the floor. Liz looked around, but her eyes were useless. After climbing down for about six feet, they ran out of stairs at a cramped dirt square, barely wide enough for both of them to sit down.

"This kind of thing seems to have happened before," Liz said, reaching out to take John's hand.

"This is an old church. This part of the world has been pretty wild in the past."

"In the past? If it were any wilder now, I don't think I'd be able to stand it," Liz said.

John hushed her, hearing voices above. They seemed to come from outside, where the priest's high even voice answered questions from a man who spoke in an abusive growl. He seemed to be threatening the priest, who continued to speak calmly. Finally the voices disappeared.

"What did he say to them?" Liz whispered.

"They asked him if he had seen us. They know we're nearby because our car is still in the alley. Basically, the priest told them: 'They went thataway.' "

They shared a quiet laugh of relief in the darkness,

waiting for the priest to come for them. After an indeterminate period of time, the hatch finally opened. They squinted and held their hands before their eyes, trying to adjust to the light as they came from the hiding place.

The priest led them up a flight of stairs, where they emerged onto a balcony overlooking the sanctuary; then he disappeared. It was a small poor country church: the plaster walls and ceiling were webbed with a network of cracks. A chandelier hung from the ceiling, dusty and aged. The pews in the balcony, like those below, were made of hard unpolished wood, with straight backs.

Bearing blankets, the priest returned and serenely draped them over the pews. He spoke a few words to John and stared at them expectantly.

"He says his name is Father Diego, and he will provide us with protection for the night. He wants me to tell him what's going on, which may take a while. You can go ahead and get some rest while we talk."

"*Gracias*, Padre," Liz said, exhausting her Spanish vocabulary. Speaking in English, she said: "Maybe he knows something about the murders or about Endicott."

John spoke to the priest for a moment, nodding. The priest gestured to the ceiling, then walked out, leaving Liz and John alone.

"He's going to make sure the place is locked up properly," John said. He sat heavily on a blanketed pew and motioned for Liz to join him.

Liz sat close to John and held her hand over her chest. "My heart is pounding," she said.

John put his arm around her and pulled her close. "We'll be safe for the night." He looked around the balcony, peering over the rail to the sanctuary. "I visited a church like this one time when I was a kid. My parents brought me down to Mexico to meet relatives."

She detected a fairy-tale quality in his voice and realized that he was trying to calm her. "Was it anywhere around here?" she asked, grateful to speak of happier things.

"No, not at all. Both my parents' families are from a little town close to Lake de Chapala, not too far from Guadalajara. They're country people."

"Have you seen them since you"—she paused, not sure how to refer to his identity change—"since you became an adult?"

"Since I changed my name?" he said quickly. "No. I send them money from time to time."

"We should visit them one day soon. Together."

John tightened his embrace, kissing her hair delicately. "I'd like that. I was always a favorite of the family."

"Why, because of your brains and charm?" Liz said lightly, smiling up at him. She felt a distant warmth, the fingers of exhaustion tingling under her scalp.

"Actually, I think it was my skin color. Both sides of my family have European and Indian ancestry—not Mayan, but descendents of the Central Mexican empires like the Aztecs, and the Zapotecs before them. In many families, brothers and sisters can show very different aspects of that heritage."

She listened to his voice, to his dispassionate explanation, sensing some hurt that lay beneath. "So you looked European, and they liked that?"

He nodded. "Many times the children who look most white are favored, perhaps because they stand a better chance of 'passing' in the white world. Children such as myself would have more options, would face less prejudice."

Liz pondered this, considering how easily Juan had changed his identity, how she could see his Latino ancestry now after being blind to it for as long as she had known him. Then she heard footsteps coming up the balcony stairs. Father Diego joined them again.

John leaned down and whispered, "And that's why my brother hates me. Because I was lucky enough to look white when he was unmistakably Mexican, and because I took the cowardly step of denying who I was."

Father Diego stood ten feet away, waiting to be invited to join them. Liz took John's hand. "He's your brother," she said. "You have to go to him, you have to bring your family together again."

John smiled ruefully. "Maybe so," he said. He turned to Father Diego and waved him to the pew. "I think the father deserves an explanation for all this," he said warmly. "Why don't you get some rest."

Seeing that John no longer wanted to talk about his family, Liz stretched out on a pew in the row behind him and Father Diego, listening to their hushed conversation as she drifted off to sleep. The sound of their voices speaking melodic Spanish was comforting and reassuring. She noticed again that John's accent was impeccable, and she pondered all that he had told her that evening. Though he had grown up in America, he must feel at home here, truly himself. In a strange way, it was the only place where he could live without artifice.

Her body relaxed, several days of tension sliding away as she felt the cool evening air blowing down through a skylight above them. Outside, the town was quiet. Consciousness faded, and she dreamed of the warmth and comfort of her childhood home. She was a little girl again, carried around on her father's shoulders, confident that the world was safe and that things would always stay the same.

* * *

A bright beam of sunlight shining in her eyes abruptly woke her. John, asleep in the pew in front of her, slept heavily, his chest rising and falling in a placid regular rhythm. Suddenly, a peal of voices from below stirred her from her blankets.

Looking down to the sanctuary, she saw fifteen or twenty young boys and girls, dressed in the ragtag clothes that all the town children wore. Their eyes were closed as they began another verse in high wavering voices, which coalesced into a sweet harmony, a hymn that rose and continued until it reached its end, when they began another. Father Diego stood at the front of the stage, issuing commands and compliments in a quiet voice to his choir.

John woke up and joined her at the edge of the balcony, wiping his sleepy eyes.

"It sounds beautiful," Liz said.

"That's the sound of my childhood," John said, resting his chin on the back of Liz's head. They listened for a few moments, then walked down the steep stairs, both entranced by the sound of the music.

"I gave Father Diego my camera," John said. "It was all I had to give him. He said he'd use it to take pictures of the children."

"That's wonderful," she said as they reached the foot of the stairs.

They stood and listened to another hymn, both entranced by the music and dreading the moment when they would have to leave the church. It was dangerous out there. They had two days to find out the secret that its owner was willing to kill for.

CHAPTER FIFTEEN

8 A.M., November 2, Indianapolis.

THOUGH LIZ DANNY'S PRESENCE IN MEXICO WAS WORRISOME TO Kerry Nordstrom, at least it gave him the opportunity to watch Irwin Ross's reaction. He selectively edited the story, omitting elements that pertained to the vagotomy, but her mere presence at the site of their facility was enough to rattle the younger man. Of course, in two days Nordstrom would be gone, leaving Irwin holding the bag. Now *that* was something to worry about, but of course the kid had no idea.

The hired thug had been found in Los Angeles, but that wouldn't be a problem. There was no way to trace the contract back to Nordstrom or Endicott, so there was no reason to tell Ross. The botched hit last evening in Valladolid was another matter. At least the pair of American doctors had been positively identified by appearance, after the desk clerk at their hotel had been persuaded to talk. They were indeed Liz Danny and John Rogers.

Ross turned pale, his hand shaking as he put down his cup of coffee. Lately, Nordstrom loved having the kid come in from the Endicott headquarters downtown. It was his pleasure to make Irwin's last days of freedom as uncomfortable as possible.

"Come on, kid. Don't get weak on me now," Nordstrom said. "We have the airports covered and the roads out of town under surveillance. Our security is blanketing the area. Everything is completely under control. Besides, they don't know anything." And neither do you, he thought.

Ross burned with anger at being referred to as a "kid." Nordstrom sat behind his enormous pretentious desk, a balding, arrogant mass of a man who took any opportunity to insult and intimidate everyone in his path. Ross appraised him coolly for a moment before speaking, trying to regain the edge in the conversation.

"Look, Kerry. Let me remind you that you still work for me."

"How could I forget, Irwin? You come out here every day to remind me."

"In my opinion you've overplayed our hand. I heard about your display of force at Phoenix, which was completely unnecessary and stupid. You're the one who has put us in the situation of becoming murderers." He punctuated his words by jabbing at the air with his finger, an effect that was actually quite comical in the slender bespectacled man.

Nordstrom stood up from his desk and walked to the window. He looked over the sprawling white compound of Med-Tek. It was always breathtaking from above, the high roof of the animal lab standing out over the surrounding buildings like an ivory bunker. In the distance, a crew of workmen and technicians were finalizing the electronic information link, checking the satellite dish connections for feedback or unintentional scrambling.

"Listen, Irwin," he said, "if you think you aren't a murderer already, you're fooling yourself."

Ross ran a hand through his immaculately groomed blond hair. "I prefer not to think of it that way," he said weakly.

"You know the threat they could pose to us," Nordstrom said. "I only asked our men in Phoenix to detain her. I have reason to believe that she has suspected us for some time."

"But what if something went wrong? Think about the publicity," Ross said. "And what is this so-called threat? Is it enough to kill Rogers as well? They know nothing specific. All of this could have been handled with a great deal more subtlety."

"Subtlety? If you're worried about publicity, wait until they get to the hospital and start finding out more than they need to know. With all of the child-snatching rumors going around Central America, we would be history if we were wrongly associated. We could kiss Mexico good-bye, not to mention the Uruguay facility next year. Do I have to remind you of the profits I'm bringing to—"

"All right, all right," Ross interrupted. He always prided himself on being unflappable, but these conversations with Nordstrom inevitably got under his skin. He cradled his chin in his hands and looked at Nordstrom thoughtfully. "Your detective is calling me now," he said coolly.

"Who, Willers?" Nordstrom said. Ross nodded. "What's he talking to you for? I offered him a tour of the place, told him that I'd cooperate fully. The last damned thing we need is for him to start making connections. What did he say to you?"

"Well, Kerry," Ross said. "First of all, he told me that he didn't like you. Off the record, of course," he chuckled. "He found me far more agreeable. I took the liberty of sending him some of the basic manuals on exploratory laparoscopy so that he could see for himself if there were any connections to his Keyhole Killings."

Nordstrom began to pace in front of the window. He pulled a cigarette from his shirt pocket and lit it, taking a long intense drag. He always backslid on the smoking when something big was going to happen. "Where did he say he was going with the case?" he asked.

"You tell me. He gave me his Columbo act, pretending to be stupid and clueless. My feeling is that he's going to start questioning health care workers in the Cincinnati area. That should keep him busy for a while."

"Long enough, hopefully," Nordstrom muttered.

"What do you mean by that?" Ross asked. He gripped the arms of the chair and peered at Nordstrom suspiciously. "Kerry, did you hear me? What did you mean by that?"

"Nothing, kid. Willers is a fool. We have nothing to worry about."

Ross picked up a pencil and began nibbling on the eraser. Nordstrom stared at this act in disgust. "Would you stop eating the office supplies, Irwin?"

"Never mind that. If Willers starts compiling lists, he might find the name of our man. I knew that was a bad idea. We should have done it here."

Nordstrom sighed. "We've been through that, you idiot. It was a smokescreen. I've diverted Willers—he won't find out about our man."

"Could they trace it back to us? They couldn't, could they?" Ross said. His voice took on a sudden note of vulnerability.

I wish I could be around to see them come for you,

Nordstrom thought. "No way," he said. "I took care of it. Wasn't that one of the conditions when I cut you in?"

They pondered in deep silence. Nordstrom smoked his cigarette down to a smoldering nub. He looked out the window again, at the fortress under his charge. That very day, another five hundred surgeons would arrive from all over the world to take seminars at his lab. They had all been profiled and worked over, and contracts would be offered to those with the most lucrative practices.

It would all be irrelevant in a couple of days. So would the work in Cincinnati and the perfected process in Mexico. Ross would soon find out what his role in the plan was: to take a fall. He still thought that he had discovered Nordstrom's early work by accident. Ross should have known that nothing happened by accident. This conversation was beginning to bore him, but it was important to keep up appearances.

"Again, Kerry, I'm worried about the publicity. Even if we can protect our man and keep him hidden, the fact that laparoscopy was involved will soon become very clear. Malcolm Endicott—who, I might remind you, is my employer and yours—has invested phenomenal resources in high-tech surgery. I'd hate to see his name dragged into this kind of thing."

"Don't worry about the old man," Nordstrom said, his voice calm. The cars had begun to arrive for the morning session. "I know how to keep him happy."

"By botching vagotomies in front of a global audience?" Ross said, his eyebrows arched.

Nordstrom appraised his superior, his partner, his antagonist. There was no way Ross could know what had happened at the vagotomy. No way. He had no doubt that

Irwin Ross would turn on him, given the opportunity. Of course, to destroy a man, you have to be able to find him.

"Accidents will happen," Nordstrom said.

9:30 A.M., November 2, Valladolid.

Liz and John sat at an umbrella-shaded table on a Valladolid cantina's stone patio. It was an out-of-the-way place they had found on a side street away from the center of town. They had to travel on foot: their rental car was gone when they emerged from the church in the morning. It had been stolen or removed by the men who had tried to kill them.

They were in a part of town that was almost completely deserted. The sidewalks and buildings were in an obvious state of disrepair, and no one seemed to be doing much of anything. It was as close to disappearing as they could manage.

John wore walking shorts, sunglasses, and an obnoxious floral print shirt he had bought at a tiny store, and Liz wore slacks and a long-sleeved shirt, along with a wide-brimmed straw hat. She opened a paper bag and pulled out a pair of scissors with a mock air of ceremony.

"Well, this is it. Let's get it done before breakfast comes," she said, snipping at the air with an attitude of bravado.

"Are you sure about this? It might be enough just to wear the hat," John said, looking up and down the deserted street. Only a trio of children could be seen, chasing each other with water pistols around an aged American car.

"What if I want to take off the hat? Come on, before I

chicken out," Liz said with an ironic smile. "We'll do it in the bathroom."

They walked past the watching waiters, who had little else to do but stare. Liz and John were the only customers to arrive at the restaurant so early in the day. It wasn't a place that seemed likely to serve many tourists. Visitors to town rarely ventured this far away from the safety and relative commercialism of the town square.

Liz latched the bathroom door behind them and stood over the sink. The mirror was clouded and dirty, so she would have to trust John's hands. She nodded for him to go ahead and closed her eyes while he cut off long strands of her straight black hair. He snipped quickly but carefully. When he was finished, the sink was full of her dark tresses, most of them over a foot long. She picked them up and pursed her lips.

"Well, there goes my vanity. Hopefully this will work as a disguise." She looked into the mirror, her image distorted and obscure. Her hair had a short boyish look. "You didn't do a bad job, Rogers. Maybe you can do this for a living someday."

John leaned over and kissed her lightly on the lips. "You're still very beautiful," he said.

Liz looked away from him, embarrassed, then threw the hair into a garbage pail. They returned to the patio, glad to leave the bad-smelling bathroom for the fresh air outside. The children had gone elsewhere to seek out entertainment, leaving the street quiet and deserted.

Their food arrived: sweet rolls and tropical fruit, along with a pot of strong coffee. They ate heartily, though their stomachs were knotted with anxiety.

John picked up a newspaper and looked at it blankly. Suddenly something caught his interest, and he folded the page to an article.

"What is it?" Liz asked.

"An editorial about Mayan children. It says that American practices of illegal adoption, combined with the unproved possibility of children being kidnapped for medical purposes, have created a state in which Mayan parents must watch their children carefully."

"Against Americans?" Liz asked somberly.

"Specifically, American women," John replied. He put down the paper. "Hopefully people will know this is an attempt by political interests to work them up into an anti-American state of mind."

"But there might be some truth to it, right? I mean, these people have a right to their anger, even if the abductions are a fiction. I know if I were a mother, having people lining up to adopt my child would make me want to do anything to prevent it."

"I wonder how difficult it's going to be to get out of here when it's time to leave," John mused, obviously trying to change the subject. "My suspicion is that Endicott security will be waiting for us when we try to leave town."

"I'm not worried about that at the moment," Liz said, biting into a slice of pineapple. "My first priority is getting into that hospital."

John sighed heavily. "I agree, but I don't like it. Don't you think they'll shoot us on sight?"

"Only if they see us. Like you said, they probably expect us to try to get the hell out of town as quickly as possible. They might not expect us at the hospital itself."

The Caribbean sun rose quickly in the morning: its rays already baked the stones on the small street. Liz fanned herself with a spare menu, feeling the air's caress on her neck and ears for the first time since high school, when she had cut her hair short after breaking up with a boy-friend.

"The more I think about it, the more I wonder," she said. "Nordstrom's going to a lot of trouble to kill me. Us, I mean. But sending three guys can't be the limit of what he could do, given the resources he must have down here. He must not think we have any idea about the satellite transmission. If he did, he'd probably try to drop a nuclear bomb on this place."

"Well, that could work in our favor," John said. "If he's preoccupied elsewhere, your knowledge of the vagotomy would be secondary."

"Unless he's mixed up with the killings. I mean, really involved," Liz said. "Then he'd want to keep us quiet."

John tapped the table nervously. "Sure. Wouldn't you want to keep it quiet? We're talking about a sadistic killer, whether it's Nordstrom or someone else. He kills people in Cincinnati, then comes here when things get hot to continue in anonymity. And he's probably an employee of Endicott International, a reputable firm with billions of dollars invested in serving people through advancing surgical technology, which makes it all the more perverse."

"My friend Ronnie, the psychologist," Liz said, "once told me that sociopaths can be among the most charming people you'd ever want to meet. He could have been hired and trained by Endicott, worked in Cincinnati for a time, and then been transferred down here. That's my guess."

"There's such a thing as legal information requests," John said. "We could have obtained employee rosters in the States, or Willers could have. For that matter, we could have brought in the FBI."

"No," Liz said, shaking her head. "That's the problem. You don't know Kerry Nordstrom. Even if he were harboring a vicious psychopath, he would hold back information just to maintain his control and power. He would never cooperate, especially now that he knows I could wreck his career.''

''But why would Nordstrom be involved?'' John said, beginning to nervously shred his paper napkin. The conversation had made them both anxious. ''The man's not insane. What could he want?''

Liz stared at an elderly couple who emerged from a house across the street. The woman carried a broom and began to sweep the sidewalk as her husband knelt to examine his small flower garden.

''It must have to do with that sickening fluocil tank he put that pig in. I can't get the image out of my mind of that poor animal breathing that liquid, staring at me like it was looking for an explanation. It doesn't seem to mean anything, but Kerry was certainly proud of it.''

''Maybe he was trying to impress you,'' John said. He leaned back in his chair and chuckled. ''Chicks are pretty impressed by animal research, you know.''

Liz punched him in the arm, barely able to suppress her own laughter. ''Yeah, John. It was a real turn-on. There's nothing sexier than a man with his pigs.''

The waiter brought them their check; breakfast was twelve thousand pesos. Liz tried to calculate the cost in dollars, finally giving up and placing a twenty-thousand-peso note on the table.

''We need to try to get a layout of the building,'' Liz said as they walked out to the sun-drenched street. ''If we go in tonight, when it's dark, we can get back to America tomorrow. There has to be a way to sneak into the place.''

''Hold on a minute,'' John said. He jogged back into the restaurant and emerged after a moment.

''I asked where the hall of records is,'' he said. ''They

should have a blueprint of the hospital building, since it appears to be a converted structure."

They walked in the shaded side of the street, moving toward the center of town. "What are you smiling at?" Liz asked, noticing John staring at her.

"I did a pretty good job on your hair," he said, reaching out to run his hands through it. "You look good."

"Thanks," she said, playfully knocking his hand away. "I've been meaning to do it for a while, hired gunmen or no hired gunmen."

"Liz, about last night . . ." John said, suddenly turning serious.

She reached out and put her finger over his lips. "It was wonderful. And it made me very confused. I need to take it slow with you, John. I mean, I had no idea that . . . and Donald and I . . ."

"Don't worry, Liz," John said. "I can wait. I just wanted you to know it was very special to me."

They looked into each other's eyes for a moment, then turned shyly away from each other as they crossed the street. She was telling the truth; she was confused, and she still owed a debt to Donald. Something like love for John was already growing inside her, but it was like a flower growing in the shadow of a boulder. Life felt strange and unreal to her, and she was frightened by a deep numbness within. Every day she waited for feeling to return.

John took Liz's arm when they reached a more populated section of town. A series of shops and small businesses lined either side of the street.

"Father Diego told me that Endicott is the main hospital in the area," he said. "After they moved in here, the existing hospital transferred its staff to the facility."

"So all local medical records are at Endicott?"

John nodded and led Liz to a storefront, pretending to

look at a window display of baskets and blankets as a police car passed.

The Valladolid Hall of Records was little more than a dingy, high-ceilinged room, tucked away in a second-floor corner of the old brick building that housed the entire city government. It was a block away from the city square, a conspicuous place close to Father Diego's church. Hoping not to be seen, Liz and John tried to mix with the small sleepy tourist crowd, which gathered around a large outdoor restaurant next door to the government building.

They stepped inside to find that it was even hotter there than on the street. A clerk sat at a small desk in front of a portable fan, reading a newspaper and adding to a pile of cigarette butts in an old metal ashtray.

John spoke a few words to him in Spanish. The man pointed to a flight of stairs, then returned to reading his newspaper.

The air upstairs was even hotter and more stifling than below. A thin fog of stale cigarette smoke hung in the long corridor, making Liz feel faint even before they reached the records room at the end of the hall. The door was propped open by a wooden crate, which seemed to accomplish little but to allow smoky air to fill the hall as well as the records room. They stepped inside to see a jumble of old gray metal filing cabinets and desks, a ceiling fan vainly trying to stir the stale atmosphere.

At the front desk, a young man sat amid a huge pile of papers, which he had stacked into neat fastidious rows. He had a rubber stamp and a pad of black ink and examined each document briefly before vigorously stamping it and dropping it in a basket. He seemed annoyed when John interrupted him to ask about architectural blueprints.

Liz stood by the door and tried to make out what they were talking about. She heard a reference to Endicott, which was met by a knowing nod. Finally, John handed the man some money and motioned for Liz to follow him past a waist-high wooden gate into the rear section of the office.

"I told him we're on vacation and that I'm interested in converted colonial structures. He tried to offer me a look at the plans for the big mission, but I insisted on seeing the Endicott building. He was suspicious, so I bribed him," John said.

"You're kidding," Liz said. "We have to pay to see public records?"

The clerk walked to one of the filing cabinets and dug through its contents until he found a long folded blueprint. *"Cinco minutos,"* he said, holding up five fingers.

John unrolled the document on a vacant desk and began to examine it. He and Liz seemed to be the most interesting thing to occur in the office on that particular day: the clerks all stopped their work and conversations to stare openly at them. Liz tried to ignore them, concentrating on the complicated floor plan.

"This is even better than I thought," John said. "It contains the basic layout but also the renovations that Endicott International performed to bring the place up to snuff as a hospital. They didn't do that much: knocked out a few walls here and there, partitioned off the large common area. But you can see here how they added a series of corridors built around a newly constructed loading dock."

"How can you tell? It looks like hieroglyphics to me."

"I worked part-time construction in medical school. But look; there are ways we could access the back of the building."

"So we don't have to walk up and knock on the front door?" Liz said.

"Precisely."

John turned and addressed the nearest clerk. He might as well have been talking to the entire room, for everyone was still staring at them with intense interest. The clerk shrugged and pointed at an older man with gray hair and suspenders, who had been standing in the back of the office.

He appeared to be the manager: he stood near the largest desk and wore well-fitting pressed clothes that contrasted sharply with the more ragged attire the rest of the staff wore. John talked to him in a tone of politeness, pointing to Liz and smiling. The manager shook his head and turned away.

"I told him that you collect blueprints and that you want a photocopy," John said. "I think he expects me to bribe him now."

John peeled off several bills and passed them around the manager's shoulder. The older man took the bills without comment, pointing John to a small side room. Inside it was an antiquated photocopier, covered with dust but plugged in and operational. It creaked and moaned as it copied the main plan, but it produced a reasonably readable duplicate.

Liz and John left to eat lunch at a restaurant several blocks from the center of town. The afternoon tours had begun to bring in the one-day tourist arrivals. Reading the photocopy at a table in the rear, John realized that the blueprint revealed nothing about the hospital's security measures. Surveillance and human security would be their greatest threats.

"Look here," John said, pointing at the floor plan. "There are two corridors coming off the entrance from the loading docks. Assuming we can enter that way, we could take this lesser passage, which winds around to the administrative area. It's as good a bet as any. From there, the operating rooms and computer rooms are nearby. All the offices and patient beds are upstairs, so we can stay on the ground floor. With any luck, they maintain a skeleton crew at night."

Liz sipped on a beer with a slice of lime, staring at a small park across the street. A family stood at the edge of a little pond, the mother carrying a small baby. Her children were trying to get a kite airborne in the light wind.

"We'll need to buy dark clothes," Liz said. "It's a shame we don't have a gun or something."

"Forget it," John said. "That would bring us more trouble than it's worth. At least this way, we might be able to talk our way out of it if we're caught. The night crew might not have heard about us."

Liz nodded. "I've seen enough guns in the last few days to last me a lifetime."

They ate their light lunch in tense silence. Darkness was only two hours away.

"John," Liz said, "what do you think will happen to us if we're caught? Do you really think the police wouldn't help us?"

"Let's just hope it doesn't come to that," said John. "I think we should consider ourselves alone here."

Across the street, a little boy with dark features and a wide, gap-toothed grin had succeeded in getting his kite aloft in the slight afternoon breeze. He exclaimed in triumph, calling out to his mother. A small crowd of children gathered around him to watch, commenting and cajoling as he tried to keep the line taut.

Liz smiled and stood up from the table. It must be a wonderful thing to have children. Maybe one day, she thought, she would feel well and whole again. She could start her life over. She could see the love in John's eyes every time he looked at her. They might have a future together.

She walked onto the restaurant porch, looking up at the kite and watching the children. The kite had lost wind and was dangerously close to careering to the ground. Liz stepped forward, ready to try to catch the kite if it fell.

A Mayan woman ran out of a small windowless building, pulling her hair out of her face. She yelled harshly at the child with the kite, motioning toward their house. Then she fixed a questioning look at Liz, as if trying to peer into her soul and determine her intentions. The boy, complaining, reeled in the kite and made for home.

Two men in straw hats moved out from the shade of a nearby bar, staring at Liz and speaking to each other in low voices. Suddenly, Liz realized that everyone on the small street was staring at her.

Liz felt a hand at her back. "Come back inside," John said.

"But I was just—"

"I know. Come inside. It's natural for them to wonder. In a few days we won't have to worry about anything."

If she lived through the next few days. They had come here to unravel a mystery and found themselves the object of suspicion. How long would it take, how difficult would it be to explain this to the men—who now withdrew, casting glances over their shoulders as they walked back to the bar?

Whatever secrets were to be found at Endicott Mexico were obviously so valuable to Kerry Nordstrom that a couple of lives might be meaningless. They could always try to just walk away, pretending they knew nothing.

But it was too late to walk away. It was too late to be selfish.

They had less than forty-eight hours.

CHAPTER SIXTEEN

10:30 P.M., November 2, Valladolid.

By sticking to the side streets of Valladolid, Liz and John were able to kill time walking from cantina to cantina, never staying in any one place for long. A couple of hours after darkness fell, they hired a cab to drop them off at a street corner about a half mile from Endicott Mexico.

It was one of the last proper street corners in Valladolid, which tapered off into a series of overgrown vacant fields lining either side of the highway leading west. A few one-room dwellings hugged the outskirts of town, but all signs of habitation vanished as they neared the hospital. Finally, the road branched off in two directions: one led farther into the Yucatán interior, the other was a recently built access road that led to their destination.

Liz walked silently next to John in the inky country darkness, trying to quell her feelings of fear. She felt guilty in John's strong, protective presence, as she had as a child when she drew a playmate into trouble by her own impetuousness. Their only visibility was afforded by a metal flashlight bought at a dusty hardware store in town. She hoped the batteries were fresh.

John had called the airport that afternoon and booked a flight to Mexico City under their real names, hoping to fool whoever might be following them into waiting for them there. This measure, while reassuring, hadn't kept either from continually looking furtively about for the rest of the day, trying to anticipate an attack.

The future was an idea that she couldn't visualize. It felt as if there were no tomorrow, until she thought of John. Feeling his presence next to her, she thought of what had begun to happen between them. Their lovemaking had been reckless and abandoned; the growing bond between them felt real and lasting. Gradually, she felt that there might be life beyond murderers and bullets, beyond global schemes and perverted medicine. And she wished they'd had a chance to make love again before going to this dangerous and unfamiliar place.

Lost in these thoughts, Liz was shocked when they reached a clearing and the hospital became visible. She looked at Endicott Mexico, a squat bunker tucked into the wild countryside. From the brief history accompanying the blueprints, they had learned that the structure had been used as housing and schoolrooms by missionary priests during the Spanish colonial period, and that they had built additions and upper levels as time wore on.

As it stood now, the building was a large three-story box, with remnants of Spanish-style architectural adornment largely painted over with dull white. In sharp contrast to the imperial style of Med-Tek, Endicott Mexico was a plain unassuming structure that one would never see unless he or she took a wrong turn on the highway.

More important at the moment, most of the windows were darkened. The place appeared to have shut down for the night. John walked off the road, his shoes loudly crunching in the dry vegetation. He stopped under a tree.

"Here we are," he said. The darkness was so pervasive that Liz could barely make out his features in the moonlight.

"Where else would we be?" She smiled at him in the darkness. The moon above was a thin crescent, and the facility appeared to utilize only minimal outdoor lighting. A first lucky break: their approach might go without notice.

"There's not even a fence around it," she said. "Where is all the famous security?"

"Busy elsewhere, I guess," said John.

"Out looking for us, or kidnapping Mayans." Her words hung in the quiet blackness like a fearful prediction. Until she had seen the place, she hadn't fully contemplated what happened there. If she was right, it was a place of calculated unconscionable murder.

"I think we can walk through this underbrush," he said, pointing at an obscured path leading in the direction of the building. "If I'm right, it should lead us behind the building to the loading docks. Remember, if there's trouble, don't be afraid to run and leave me behind."

"Oh, shut up, John. I mean it," she said. She was worried enough without his playing silent-movie hero. She knew she could never desert him.

He looked irritated for a moment, then smiled grimly, sensing the meaning of her words. They were in it together, each silently dreading to think what they would do without the other.

With John leading the way, they walked as quietly as possible under short trees through a path of dried grass. The city dweller in Liz came to the fore: she had immediate visions of snakes and spiders, perhaps wild dogs. She thought she heard footsteps deep in the brush but decided she was hearing things. Her imagination had fertile material to work with. They had walked five minutes from the road to find themselves in a wild untamed patch of country.

Their cover ended a hundred feet from the building. John's calculation was correct: they were in a direct line with the loading docks. Only a single bulb shone above the windowless steel door, and there was no sign of any activity. On that side of the building, only one light glowed inside, high up on the third floor.

Liz held her breath as they jogged quietly to the rear of the building. They had done it—they were there. They were alone, standing in the shadows of the high wall, waiting. No sirens, no attack dogs—nothing came forth to announce their intrusion. John turned to the steel door and pulled the horizontal bar that served as a latch. It was locked. He walked, crouching, to the normal-size door ten yards away, finding that it was also locked.

"So much for that plan. I guess I shouldn't give up my day job and become a spy," he whispered in the darkness.

"Come on," Liz said, leading them along the back of the hospital. "There has to be some way inside."

They had to pass under the lone light above the loading dock door, walking low and fast as they did so. Pausing near a window, they waited, both breathing heavily with fear. Maybe John was wrong, Liz thought. Maybe they should have brought a gun or some kind of weapon. It was strange that this complex, if it was indeed the site of murders and mutilations, would be so unguarded, even at night. With every second that passed, she feared that armed men would step from the shadows and train their guns on her, ending the hope of stopping Nordstrom, ending her life.

She looked up over her shoulder at the window: it was partially ajar, practically inviting a break-in. "This is too weird,'' she whispered. "Where's the guard tower? Where are the dogs? It's almost as if they don't expect anyone to try to get in."

"Maybe they don't," John said, his features tight with tension. "We can't see the front of the building. Maybe they only post a guard there. After all, how could the locals pose a threat? By stealing medical supplies? From what I understand, Endicott provides everything for free."

He stood up and put his ear to the open crack of the window, heard nothing inside, and opened it. It creaked loudly, making Liz grit her teeth. She stared at the ground in paralyzed fear, noticing cigarette butts and candy wrappers littering the clearing. Someone had been around recently. She immediately corrected herself. Forget about the landscaping. Don't get distracted.

John pulled the folded blueprint out of his pocket and held it under the moonlight. "I can't read the legend on this," he said. "It's too blurry. My best guess is that the room inside is either a storeroom or a restroom."

Without further comment, he pulled himself up onto the windowsill and disappeared inside. Liz waited for a moment, listening for sounds, staring out into the darkness until she saw spots dancing before her eyes. She tried not to let her imagination drive her to panic when she heard a branch break in the woods nearby. It was the country, after all. There would be lots of animals. In a sense, humans were the intruders.

An arm brushing against her hair nearly caused her to cry out, but she bit her lip and turned around. It was John, offering a hand to pull her up. She waved him away, pulling herself up and into the window with a swift graceful motion.

"I'm glad you're so tall," he said. "I was wondering if I was in good enough shape to pull you up."

"What are you trying to say?" she whispered, smiling to fight off the urge to run away. "That I'm too heavy?"

"Not at all, but I let my health club membership expire a year ago. I've been meaning to tell you: don't expect superhuman strength from me."

He turned on the flashlight, cupping his hand over it to dim and diffuse the beam. They were inside a storeroom filled with crates of medical supplies. One wall was stacked high with boxes of disposable Endicott trocars, graspers, and other implements of laparoscopic surgery. It appeared that they had laid in enough supplies to last through several years of routine surgeries.

The door was unlocked, and John tentatively opened it to peer outside the storeroom. The hallway was quiet and dark, lit only by a row of bulbs placed at floor level, giving it a gloomy pall. Closed doors lined either side, but in the strange light, it was impossible to tell how far the hall extended, or whether all the doors were shut.

From what they could see as they stepped out, the building's interior was as modern as the promotional brochure had claimed: it appeared that Endicott had redone the walls and ceilings, making the place look like any modern American hospital.

"I think these are all storage rooms," John said. "See, on the schematic, they ran the heavy-duty power lines to the center and south side of the building. That's where the computers and ORs must be. Hopefully they keep the paper files nearby."

"So which way do we go?" Liz asked, looking nervously behind her. The extreme quiet of the place was even more unsettling than if it had been a beehive of activity. The polished tile hall floor was conducive to echoes, and she felt that her every step made a noise that carried throughout the entire building.

"We keep going ahead," John said. "There should be a door up there to the right that leads to the building's administrative center."

"Where are the ORs?" she asked.

"On the far side of the computers. I think. You can check them out while I try to access the employee records. Remember, we have to work fast and get the hell out of this place."

"You don't have to remind me," she whispered. "We'll take what we can and check out the files later. We just need something, anything that we can use to justify stopping that satellite transmission from taking place."

What they saw at the end of the hallway was encouraging. It branched off in two directions, both lit only by the same floor lights. This part of the ground floor was also silent and unoccupied. They walked unhindered through a doorless entryway into a small room that, in the darkness, looked like a reception area or perhaps a surgical lounge.

A sudden clatter of metal echoed on the tile floor behind them. John pushed Liz into the room, diving in behind her. She fell to the floor in the darkness, bumping her knee on something hard. John peeked through the doorway into the hall, his body trembling with shock and fear.

"It's a cleaning lady," he whispered with wary relief. "She came out into the hall to get something from a storage closet, then she went into . . . let's see now." He consulted the diagram in the glow of the flashlight. "The elevator. Good. She's going upstairs."

Liz took the flashlight from John and shone it around the room. She saw that she had bumped into a steel typewriter tray, one of several scattered through the room in front of desks piled with typical hospital paperwork: reports, files, rotation schedules.

"That door leads to the computer room," John said, pointing to a side exit.

Some light seeped under the door and through a tinted-glass transom: it didn't appear that the room was completely lit but that some low-energy source was in use. They listened at the door and heard nothing inside.

"It's probably the glow from the computers," John whispered. "They might process data through the night."

"Still, we have to watch out," Liz said. "Those cleaning people would notify security if they saw us. And they could be anywhere."

Liz reminded herself that, corrupt or not, the police would definitely take issue with her and John's presence in the hospital. In addition to trespassing, they could be charged with corporate espionage or even petty theft. She had no idea how the Mexican justice system would treat an American convicted of such crimes. Probably not kindly.

She took the lead and cracked open the door. The room was occupied only by a long row of desktop computers, most of them running. Swirling patterns flitted across their faces: screen savers, designed to keep a static image from imprinting itself on the monitors. The bright play of the automated patterns had been visible through the transom.

"Let me go first," John said. "This is my part. Hopefully, they're all networked into a mainframe data base. I'll see if I can break into the system. If I can, it won't take me long."

He walked in quietly and sat at one of the terminals. With the press of a button, the screen obligingly broke off from its display pattern and showed a menu of administrative functions. He turned to whisper to Liz.

"This will take a few minutes, but I know what I'm

looking for. Why don't you check the adjacent room for hard files? Look at the ORs if you can. Don't go too far, all right? I'll be ready to get out of this place in about five minutes."

John leaned over the computer and began type rapidly at the keyboard, creating a clatter in the room that set Liz's nerves on edge. She took a deep breath, rubbing her hands on the knots of tension that had appeared in her neck, and walked into the adjoining room. It was darker, bereft of the computer screens' electronic glow. She shone the flashlight and saw a row of filing cabinets. To her amazement, they were unlocked.

She had to work quickly. The subject headings on the cabinets were in Spanish, and she found nothing to indicate that any of the files contained personnel records. Cursing her luck, she pulled open a drawer labeled: *"Enero–Julio 1993."* It would contain information of some kind pertaining to January through July of that year, she knew, remembering a little rudimentary Spanish.

The files were alphabetized. Within them were standard patient reports: X rays, data compiled on admittance, doctors' scribbled diagnoses and prescriptions. She had no idea what any of them indicated, save for those containing diagrams of broken bones or physical defects. Apparently, the files were from the general-care side of the hospital's operations. She put the records back in order and closed the cabinet. There was nothing useful here, just typical hospital paperwork.

The next cabinet opened as easily as the first. The top three drawers contained the same day-to-day information found in the other files. When she reached the bottom shelf, though, she found something different: files written in English.

It was a shallow drawer, containing perhaps a hundred

thin hanging folders. They were organized by date, and she opened one from the middle of the bunch. Brief rows of typed data had been imposed over a grid of dates. The patients were identified only by number.

She peered closely at the sheet. Following the row marked December 4, 1993, she saw an entry: "A-level isotope, anthrax virus. Fluocil-treated tissue sample administered promptly."

"Anthrax?" she whispered softly. That was primarily a disease that afflicted cattle. It was rare in humans. "Some nations have bred supplies of anthrax for germ warfare. And an isotope? There's nothing here about cancer."

The final entry was even more puzzling: "December 6 —Immunization complete. Fluocil accountable for destroying toxic elements." Restoring the file to its place, she tried to account for the cryptic data. If she had read the sheet properly, the isotope and perhaps the anthrax virus were purposefully introduced into the patient, followed by fluocil treatment to prevent death. That was impossible. Fluocil had never been used as any kind of antibacterial or antiradiation cure.

Liz peeked back into the computer room, where John continued to type away on the computer keyboard. He was moving quickly through a series of menus and lists of data. A small stack of printouts was in his lap. At least he's finding something concrete, she thought.

He was deep in concentration, so she decided to venture farther into the hospital. From the moisture on the tile floors, it appeared that the cleaning crew had already worked in that section of the building.

She walked through double doors to a darkened hallway. The doors lining the hall had to be the operating rooms, she thought. Equipment lined the walls: respirators, crash kits, spare gurneys, boxes of Endicott surgical devices. The diagram had indicated that nine ORs were installed when the building was renovated. They were all in this wing and apparently were unoccupied that night.

Fighting off the fluttering in her stomach, Liz peeked into a door. The first operating room looked like any top-line American facility. The steel operating table was equipped with hydraulic lifts to tilt the patient, and along one wall spigots piped in gas from a central source. High-powered lights, now dormant, hung from the ceiling.

It must have cost Endicott a fortune to adapt this place, she thought. It was strange that construction wasn't undertaken on a larger scale, so that greater numbers of Latin American surgeons could be trained and recruited to bring in higher profits. Unless, of course, Nordstrom wanted the place to be inconspicuous, visited by as few outsiders as possible.

Liz left the OR and walked farther down the hall. She knew she should rejoin John and leave the place while they were still lucky enough to remain undiscovered, but the possibility of finding out something valuable was too great a lure to go back. Her fear was replaced by a tenuous giddy sense of exhilaration. We might actually not be caught, she thought. We might get out of here and make it back to America tomorrow.

Through the windows on the other doors in the wing, Liz saw that all the other rooms were like the first: well appointed, well equipped, and sparkling clean. The people of Valladolid were fortunate to have such a facility so close to their town. Less fortunate were the Yucatán's Mayan Indians.

She had decided to rejoin John, feeling there was no more to see, when she saw that one room had no window on the door, making it impossible to look in. It was locked and wouldn't budge when she pushed her weight against it.

Ducking into the adjacent OR9, she saw that she was in luck: there was a door that looked as if it led into the locked room. It was secured only by a latch, which she was able to break with a surgical hammer that had been left on an instrument tray.

The door was extremely thick and insulated and opened only when Liz threw her body against it. She saw OR lamps hanging from the ceiling in the darkness.

This room hadn't appeared on the blueprint, which had indicated only nine operating suites on the wing. This was a tenth. The insulation on the doors was airtight: once she closed the door, she could turn on the light and not be seen from the hall. Grasping along the wall for a switch, she realized that the OR was colder and much larger than the others. A low hum, which sounded like an air-conditioning unit, came from all around her.

She found the lights and turned them on. Her eyes were slow to adjust to the glare from the fluorescent ceiling bank. She could only see that the room was filled with surgical tables and indistinct shapes. Luckily, she hadn't hit any of the other switches: the room was filled with high-beam lamps and surgical devices. She could have inadvertently activated any of them.

Liz's vision finally focused. She instantly realized that she wasn't alone. It was too much for her: she cried out in alarm, her hand instinctively moving to her mouth to muffle the sound. She dropped the flashlight with a loud clatter, reaching out to grab a table to keep herself from fainting. Her hand glanced across a tray of surgical utensils, sending an electrocautery flying to the floor, where it broke into several pieces with a hollow smash of shattering plastic and metal.

There were twelve steel surgical tables in the room, aligned neatly along two rows. Upon them, half-covered by sheets, were the nude bodies of six men and six women. Their dark features were instantly recognizable as common among the Mayan Indians.

Intubation tubes, disconnected from respirators, jutted haphazardly from their mouths, and she could see that they had been restrained with straps across their chests and legs, most of which had been unbuckled. The corpses' abdomens were covered with blood, which soaked through the white sheets thrown over them.

Checking pulses would be pointless: they were all dead, their skin already gray. She pulled the sheet off the nearest body, a young woman. Her belly showed five open wounds, each only about an inch wide, consistent with the pattern of laparoscopic surgical incisions.

Liz gingerly rolled the woman over on her side, where she found a lateral incision just under the rib cage that had been left open to bleed until the heart's stoppage had ceased the flow of blood. From the small amount of blood on the table, Liz guessed that the woman had been almost dead when brought into the room.

Her heart pounding in her ears, she pulled the covering sheet away from another, smaller body. A young boy, he also demonstrated the same pattern of wounds. Liz looked into his dark child's features, his mouth half-open in death. Several of his teeth were missing, leaving gaps that in life must have made an endearing charming smile. With a wave of nausea she realized it was the boy with the kite she had seen earlier in the day, the boy pulled away from Liz by his concerned mother. She closed her eyes tightly for a second, fighting back hot tears.

After closing the boy's eyes and covering him completely with the bloody sheet, Liz put her head in her

hands, trying to fight back her revulsion. She knew what
had happened to these poor people: they had been ab-
ducted, probably surprised and sedated with scopolamine
hydrobromide or some other hypnotic agent, and brought
to the hospital, where they were eviscerated and left in the
open air of this horrible room. Whoever had done this was
around, probably in the building. She took a quick look
around her, her panic growing.

There was some surgical equipment in the room: gas
and suction hoses, an open cabinet filled with scissors,
cauteries, sutures, and surgical thread. Behind the tables
was a white filing cabinet. Liz shuddered at the thought of
the kind of surgery performed in the room, with its dozen
tables filled like a macabre assembly line. She wondered:
Did these people ever wake up? Did they ever have any
idea what was being done to them?

She walked to the cabinet, knowing that every second
she stayed brought her closer to her own death. Surely she
wouldn't be allowed to live after seeing this. Opening a
drawer, she pulled out a pile of documents. They were all
identical forms, much like standard post-op reports.

They were ordered by date instead of name. In fact,
none of the reports listed patient names: they were all
anonymous. Looking down the form, she saw that the
usual lines of information had been left unfilled, replaced
by new categories: "living matter," "date of retrieval,"
"destination."

The reports were filled out in English. The first section,
under "living matter," indicated: "splenic tissue, kidney." After the date of retrieval, the "destination" cate-
gory indicated: "17255, Pakistan." A brief glance at the
other reports reinforced the pattern: the unnamed patients,
like the ones in the room, had been used as donors of
living tissue and organs that were subsequently shipped to

foreign destinations. Many of the receiving nations were notorious dictatorships, outlaw nations known for their disregard for law and human life.

Liz had heard about the profit to be made from black-market trade in human organs for transplant: it was huge, in direct proportion to the vileness and depravity of the practice. The list of organs sold was horrifically extensive and specific: kidneys, livers, splenic tissue, intestinal tissue, bone marrow, even a few hearts. Apparently, all bases had been covered at Endicott Mexico, for the files revealed that numerous samples of each organ type had been taken through involuntary surgery.

For a second, it felt as if there was someone behind her; she turned quickly, bumping into the body of a mustached man atop one of the surgical tables. Liz ignored the contact and feel of the cold flesh, entranced by what had been behind her since she entered the room.

How did I miss this? she thought, walking up to a five-foot-high, fifteen-foot-long glass tank nestled in the dark between a pair of tall filing cabinets. It looked like a large aquarium, until Liz noticed the strange light infusing the murky liquid within. The dancing hues of green and orange originated from four lasers installed at the containers. They were the precise colors she had seen at Med-Tek, when Nordstrom revealed to her the pig immersed in fluocil.

She couldn't see the tank's contents. From the viscous movement of the liquid, though, she could tell that it was probably fluocil. Nordstrom's experiment had been duplicated here, in a secret room in Mexico. But what was inside? she thought. Surely not another pig.

A computer, linked to the tank and the lasers with thick black cables, displayed a shifting table of numbers that rose and fell within the same range. It must have been an automatic regulator. She found a control panel built into the tank's housing and began flipping switches, trying to illuminate its contents.

The first lever sent a gas, probably oxygen, bubbling and roiling into the tank. The second did nothing. With the third, a row of lights came on within the tank, lighting it with the eerie evanescence of a fish-tank bulb.

Housed in neat rows on a series of racks was an assortment of human organs: oblong kidneys, pancreases, livers, open trays of tissue, loops of intestine. It was a horrid butcher shop of human components, anatomy stolen from unwilling victims and displayed like a trophy case.

Liz looked closer: something was wrong here. There were perhaps five to six hundred separate organs in the case. They couldn't possibly have come from the dozen victims on the tables behind her. Amassing this number of human organs in one night was impossible, even with the assembly-line technique the surgeon or surgeons had obviously used.

Also, storing organs in fluocil was unheard of. Organs were normally iced in a special solution and shipped immediately: depending on the sample, the surgeon had only twelve to twenty-four hours to work, after which the organ became unsuitable for transplant.

There was only one answer: the laser-treated fluocil had properties that enabled human organs and tissue to be stored longer than a day, perhaps indefinitely. "Jesus Christ," Liz whispered, extending her hands to keep her balance as her stomach swam in a wave of nausea.

She stared into the tank. The shelves were coded, using waterproof stickers to indicate tissue type. The stickers indicated dates ranging back almost a year—to the opening date of the hospital. By common standards these organs were far too old to be of any use, but they looked to be in pristine condition. Kerry Nordstrom had developed a means of indefinitely keeping them alive.

My God, she thought, this is incredible. This technology could forever alleviate waiting lists for organ transplants. She thought about the planned satellite link-up: Nordstrom was going to sell the formula. He could transmit the laser frequencies and fluocil chemistry to a receiving computer, making its owners the sole possessors of the greatest medical secret of the century.

Another thought struck her. The files. Technicians at Endicott Mexico were experimenting with the treated fluocil as a means of immunization from deadly viruses and radiation. It took a genius to do this, she thought, and he's going to sell the process to the highest bidder.

Footsteps echoed in the hall outside. Startled, Liz scrambled to switch off the lights on the ceiling and in the tank. She held her flashlight in the air: if need be, it could serve as a weapon. For an excruciating moment, she waited to hear another noise.

The footsteps resumed in the adjacent operating room. She was trapped: the hallway door was bolted from the outside. The only exit was through OR9. It could have been John out there, but it was impossible to know without risking running into an armed guard. The footsteps idly circled the room, and Liz heard the sound of a match being struck and a long drag on a cigarette. It couldn't be John: he didn't smoke.

In the darkness, Liz tried to reconstruct the room in her memory. She knew that there were no windows, no closets, no possible hiding place. She would have to wait to be discovered—and then what? Would she meet the same fate as the luckless people on the surgical tables?

Then she had an idea. The old mission building had high ceilings. They weren't expedient for operating rooms, which had to be lit and heated, so modular ceilings had been installed in rooms like this. She removed her canvas shoes and stuffed them into her pockets, hoping that bare feet would make less noise as she climbed atop the operating table. She felt the cold flesh of a corpse against her foot as she felt around the ceiling for one of the removable tiles.

If she could push out a ceiling tile, she figured, she might be able to move along the supports between the old and new ceilings. Then she could get to John, and they could try to escape into the wild darkness of the countryside.

Her arms trembled as she pushed out a tile and pulled herself up to the ceiling with a strength borne out of fear. Locks of her newly-shorn hair dropped to her forehead and stuck with sweat. The ceiling tile made a slight clatter as she replaced it under her feet, hoping that the noise hadn't been loud enough to be heard in the next room.

The space between the new and the old ceilings was cramped: Liz barely had room to crawl. She untucked her shirt and pulled it up to her face, trying to wipe off the perspiration that collected around her neck and eyes. The air was stale and still, and blackness extended in all directions.

Lights were visible directly to her right, where the stranger had turned on the overheard light in OR9, and about thirty feet ahead, which she had to guess was the glow from the computer screens. She hoped that John had been able to print out some kind of evidence, knowing that what she had seen would sound insane if she recounted it to the police.

The door beneath her opened: footsteps entered the tenth operating room. The light came on, followed by the sound of switches being flipped on the fluocil tank. The door closed with a heavy slam, followed by silence.

Inch by inch, foot by foot, Liz crawled to the second source of light. Please, God, just let John be safe, she thought. And don't let him go searching for me. We can be out of this awful place in five minutes.

Liz repeated these thoughts to herself as she crawled, her knees and back aching from the strain of trying to stay balanced on the supporting beams—the fake ceiling tiles could never contain a person's weight, and would easily break under any kind of strain. She had to extend her leg to regain her balance as her sweaty hand slipped on the beam. For a moment, she allowed herself to rest, her vision blurred and cloudy in the stale space.

Finally she was close enough to the light source to see shapes in front of her. The crawl space was mostly empty, but a few rows of thick cable branched out to her left. Those must be the computer wires, she thought with excitement. I must be directly above John. There were no cracks between the tiles and their fittings sufficiently wide enough to peek through, but she would have to gamble that her sense of direction was sound. Suddenly, she heard several voices speaking in Spanish. One of them was John's.

In her haste, Liz had crawled away from the security of the bracing beam; too late, she realized that she had ventured out onto one of the tiles. It creaked under her. And she vainly tried to grab something to hang on to, but there was nothing. The support gave way, along with four surrounding tiles, and Liz fell through the ceiling with a deafening crash. Her body came to a stop, and her vision went red. It felt as if her back were broken.

It took a moment for the haze of pain to clear. When it did, she realized that she had fallen onto a desk in the middle of the computer room. She was flat on her back, covered with dust from the destroyed tiles, staring up at the hole in the ceiling. A tilt of her head to have a look around brought an even more painful shock: John sat in a chair against the wall, a bruise on his forehead. Two men dressed in identical uniforms stood on either side of him, holding him down so he couldn't come to her assistance.

Two guards rushed to her, wearing stunned expressions at her sudden appearance. They were called off by another man. Their lips were moving, Liz realized, but she couldn't hear what they were saying. For the first time, she wondered if she had been badly hurt in the fall. My God, she thought. I could be paralyzed. She wiggled her toes and her fingers, feeling them respond. That was a good sign.

Hearing began to return. John's voice, speaking in Spanish, argued bitterly with the person standing over her. She looked up at the dark-haired man, who wore a white lab coat over a natty floral tie and oxford shirt: he was muscular and carried himself with an air of vitality. He would have been handsome if he didn't have such a surplus of worry lines and wrinkles about his face. Liz thought that he had a look of perpetual anxiety and fretfulness. He bent over her and spoke to her in accented English.

"My name is Dr. Roberto Calderon. I am the chief physician and administrator at this hospital. Let me see if you are hurt."

His voice was low and tremulous. She distrusted him instantly. She looked around at the four men; their blue jackets were emblazoned with the Endicott logo, and each carried a gun in a shoulder holster. They looked at her prone form with expressions of undisguised appraisal. She realized that her shirt had nearly torn off in the fall and pulled it around her as she sat up. To her surprise, she was able to, though her legs were afire with stabbing pain. She could barely straighten her spine.

Calderon pressed his fingers against the small of her back. She cried out as a red-hot tendril ran from her tailbone to her shoulder blades. He pressed firmly down the length of her legs and arms, checking for reflex responses, then flashed a penlight into her eyes.

"You appear to be scraped and bruised but not seriously injured," he said. "I am afraid that your back injury will take some time to show its severity."

He left her sitting on the edge of the desk, in the middle of the wreckage she had created.

"I believe you called to arrange a tour, Dr. Rosalyn Campbell," he said. "That would have been possible, Dr. Danny. We are very proud of our facility. What we do not enjoy so much are people who come in and illegally access our computer files and destroy our property."

Liz laughed aloud. This was a splendid act on his part, there was no doubt about it: he was the offended party, his hospital had been invaded. "Please," she said, trying to keep up her bravado. "Spare me."

Calderon ignored Liz and picked up the stack of printouts from the table where John had been working. He looked at them and shook his head.

"Why would you need knowledge of our staff, visitors, and distribution of surgical privileges? If you wanted to work here, it could have been arranged. You, Dr. Danny, are familiar with laparoscopy. And you, Dr. Rogers, have a thriving practice in gynecological procedures. We need an OB/GYN man here. I've heard all about both of you. You could have done some good instead of breaking in and making fools of yourselves." His voice carried both anger and a genuine note of regret. It was the latter quality that sent a chill down Liz's spine.

"Then tell me, Doctor," John said. He stared straight ahead as he spoke, apparently still smarting from a blow to the head. His shirt was ripped at the collar, his hair hanging wildly over his face. "Why is it that you've tissue-typed everyone who came in here for treatment, regardless of the severity of their case? I was astounded to see in your computer the cost Endicott has incurred in doing so. Surely you don't call that standard procedure."

"Obviously, that is an unusual practice," Calderon said. "We are dealing with people who have little prior medical documentation."

"That doesn't explain—"

"You are the one who has to explain, Dr. Rogers," Calderon interrupted. "This has gone on long enough. Please excuse me for a moment. Make yourselves comfortable, and don't give the guards any reason to cause you harm."

Calderon left the room. John tried to go to Liz but was forcibly restrained in his chair. Finally he sat back, rubbing the bruise on his head. "Are you all right?" he asked.

"I've felt better," she said. "What happened?"

"They were watching us all the time," John said. "They picked us up on a laser motion detector when we came into the building. They even cleared the ground-floor areas so we'd come in and entrap ourselves."

"John, I have to tell you something," Liz said, shivering at the memory of the bodies and the tank filled with the disembodied organs.

John nodded. "They're harvesting human organs. I know. When I saw that they were tissue typing the populace, it all fell into place. No one's lab needs that much practice work. They have files on more than ten thousand people, along with their home addresses, such as they are. Some of these people can be located only between mile markers on the highway.''

''It's more than that, John. They've found a way to store organs indefinitely, and I think they're combining the tissue supply with the use of fluocil as an inoculating agent. Kerry Nordstrom is planning to sell the secret through that satellite link-up, I'm sure of it. It's the only answer. They have a tank full of hundreds of organs back there.''

''You saw this?'' John asked. Liz nodded. He sat back in his chair with an expression of defeat. ''You know, if I were them, there's no way I'd let us walk out of here alive,'' he said.

''Stop it, John. We don't know what's going to happen.''

A woman walked to the doorway and peeked inside. She was about thirty, with the wide dark features of the Yucatán people. She wore a nurse's white dress and asked one of the guards where Calderon was. The guard pointed upstairs and resumed staring at Liz. The nurse paused in the doorway.

''You know, I think they rigged the computers so I could access them. I was able to reach what should have been restricted menus without a password. I'm good, but I'm not that good. It was a complete setup.''

Liz didn't listen to John. Instead, she looked into the nurse's eyes. They were weary and sad, reflecting the horrible things she had seen or suspected in the hospital. She stared at Liz for a moment, then turned on her heels and left the room. A moment after she was gone, Calderon quickly stormed back in and began issuing orders.

CHAPTER SEVENTEEN

12:05 A.M., November 3, Valladolid.

THE FOUR GUARDS HELD GUNS—TWO HAND PISTOLS AND TWO semiautomatic assault rifles—trained on Liz and John. The firepower at Endicott Mexico was formidable, and the rumors about the security guards were true. They were very rough-looking men, scruffy and bearded, and they carried themselves as if they were used to violence. Roberto Calderon picked up a phone and dialed a number, then barked a series of commands in Spanish into the mouthpiece.

"What's he saying?" Liz said to John. She tried to stand to stretch her back, feeling her injured muscles beginning to tighten up, but sat down again when a rifle butt poked her in the ribs.

"He called a nurse and told her to assemble a surgical team," John said. "They're all in the building but were cleared out when security saw us coming."

Calderon turned to John as if to speak but thought better of it. To Liz, the man had looked irritated and tense since he returned to the room moments ago. She wondered where he had been: on the telephone to America, asking for orders?

"You talked to Kerry Nordstrom, didn't you, Dr. Calderon? You called him up and asked him what to do with us. There are a few things you should know before you do what he tells you," Liz said.

"There is nothing I should know," Calderon said, standing with his hands on his hips. "You were stupid to come here. What did you expect to find?"

"American police are investigating murders in the United States that are identical to what you are doing here. Sooner or later, they'll make the connection that leads them straight to you," Liz said.

One of the young gunmen said something to Calderon in Spanish, motioning with his pistol. Calderon shook his head.

"Go ahead and talk," he said to Liz.

"I don't know how you got involved in this abomination, Dr. Calderon, and I don't care. As a surgeon, you have to realize that what you are doing is a perversion. You can put a stop to it right now. I have evidence in Los Angeles that could ruin Nordstrom. You could walk away from all of this," Liz said, holding Calderon's curious gaze.

Calderon began to laugh. "Really, Dr. Danny. You tell me I can walk away. That is impossible. Unfortunately, I will never be in a position to walk away from here."

"How many people are in on this?" John asked. "How can you hide what's going on?"

"We have a small core of trusted people who know what is happening. I perform the surgery personally." He paused to adjust his tie with a strange incongruous delicacy.

"The people here are terrified that their children are in

danger," John said. "You have to know that. You're making these poor people's worst nightmares come true, and they'll eventually respond with anger."

Calderon shook his head. "Ridiculous rumors. We're doing nothing to the children of the area. Of that you have my word. People have suspicions but nothing to link us to their folklore and rumor. Nothing will come of it."

"You're lying," Liz said. "I saw a boy in your operating room—a boy I saw alive in town earlier today."

"I . . . I didn't know," Calderon said, genuinely surprised.

"You didn't know? Your people kidnap children and you know nothing about it?" John said bitterly.

"I am sure you understand, Doctor, that one cannot control every action of those under their employ. It is regrettable, but . . ." He paused. "I will see to it that it never happens again.

"My employer mentioned you to me very recently, Dr. Danny. He said you are an idealist. You must realize that our activities here are not all bad: we provide health care to the needy people of the Yucatán. Without us, there would be much suffering."

Calderon sat on one of the vacant desks, speaking in a thoughtful and abstracted fashion. Liz could see that he had convinced himself that the ends justified the means: though they randomly murdered innocents by the score, they also ministered to the needs of others. She couldn't believe that this perspective was enough to ease his conscience.

"I am just a country doctor," Calderon said with an air of finality, "who helps as many people as I can. There are always sacrifices, but I also know that the work I do will one day revolutionize medicine. I have no choice but to continue with my work."

Liz tried to speak but Calderon held up his hand in the air, an authoritative gesture with unmistakable meaning. The guards tightened their grips on the guns: the conversation was over.

Two Mexican women in white nurse's uniforms warily stepped into the room, obviously uncomfortable around the guards. Liz saw the nurse who had walked in before, but the woman now avoided Liz's gaze, focusing in a businesslike fashion on Calderon. The other nurse, older and matronly, quietly stared at her shoes, waiting for orders.

The young nurse spoke in Spanish to Calderon in a harsh tone of voice. "What's she saying?" Liz asked John.

"She's saying that the other nurse shouldn't be here. That she is innocent and shouldn't be brought into these things. That Calderon is involving too many people."

Calderon returned the verbal volley with an even stronger tone of command and exhortation—including an evocation of Nordstrom's name, which quieted the younger woman. She turned and walked out of the room in the direction of the surgical suites, motioning for the older nurse to follow her.

"They're going to prep for surgery," John said in an incredulous voice. "The patients are going to be us."

Liz's heart began to beat rapidly as she and John were led out of the room and down the hall, which was now lit with bright fluorescent bulbs. They were taken into OR9, which was lit by surgical lamps. The door to the tenth room was tightly closed, but Liz vividly pictured its contents when she saw the two vacant steel tables awaiting her and John.

She tried to speak, but her voice died in the back of her throat. Everything else that had happened was nothing.

Compared to this, it had been harmless fun. Having her body carved up and stored in that tank, to be distributed to the highest bidder—this was far worse than violent danger.

I've never had surgery before, she suddenly realized. I'm a surgeon, but I've never felt this absolute submission to the doctor's power. This is what my patients must feel like, she thought, at least somewhere deep inside their minds. Anything could happen to them. They were trusting someone who would cut them open and, hopefully, perform acts that would prolong their lives.

She was made to lie down on a surgical table; John was forced onto the second, just feet away from her. Liz felt the pressure of a gun at her head and tried to remain motionless. She felt her legs and arms being strapped to the table, the nylon cords abrading the scrapes from her fall. Then the final strap was tightened across her breasts, making her immobile. Her back began to burn with pain, the useless but natural reaction of a body unaware of its impending death.

Suddenly several people walked into the room. Liz pushed against her restraints to see who they were. She was surprised to see another pair of guards enter with a young Mexican man. They half carried, half led him into the room. He appeared to be heavily drugged and barely awake, taking only the slightest interest in his surroundings.

The older nurse bustled into the room wheeling a portable steel table, which she set up next to Liz's. The young man was stripped naked, forced to the table, and strapped down in the same fashion as Liz and John. His head rolled to the side, and he looked at Liz without any sign of comprehension. She saw that he barely had a wisp of mustache above his upper lip.

The younger nurse wheeled in a cart of laparoscopic surgical instruments, including two video monitors and a tray of trocars, microscissors, and some instruments that looked unfamiliar. Liz tried to get a closer look, but the tray was placed out of her line of vision. The deep hum of a laser scalpel generator sounded out, breaking the silence.

"John, talk to me," Liz said. She felt a grip like a tight hand within her chest, keeping her from breathing properly. "What are they doing?"

"Please, Dr. Danny. This is not something that any of us relish. Let us proceed with dignity," Calderon said as he entered the room. He wheeled a video monitor next to Liz. The screen was placed in an unorthodox place: by her side, where she could clearly see it. Though she tried to contain her voice, she cried out. He was going to operate on her and make her watch it. That meant she would have to remain conscious.

"You call yourself a doctor," John said. "You're a lapdog of the devil, you son of a bitch. You'll burn in hell for this."

Calderon hesitated for a moment, then moved to John's table, where he fastidiously placed a video screen within John's vision. He donned a surgical mask.

The nurses were scrubbing up at a sink in the corner. Liz caught a glimpse of the older nurse: only her eyes showed over her mask, and her forehead and eyes were tensed with an expression of confusion. From now on, she would be part of the evil at Endicott Mexico, implicated in something that no sane person could rationalize or consider anything less than a sin. Liz felt sorry for her.

Calderon addressed the team with cold terseness. "What is he saying?" Liz asked John.

"He says they will take tissue-type samples from us

during the operation, but they have records on the young
man. Evidently he goes first. Calderon also told the crew
that they would all go to prison if we were allowed to
live.''

Liz heard the rattle of instruments on a tray and had a
horrible thought: Which of them would go first? Her or
John?

"I love you, Liz,'' she heard John say in a weak voice.

She tried to turn to look at him, but a spasm of hot pain
erupted in her neck. She thought that she might have serious muscle damage. Of course, it didn't matter now.

"John?'' she said, feeling hot tears run down her face.
She wasn't able to wipe them away, which felt strangely
humiliating. "John . . . I love you, too, darling. I always
will.'' A wave of emotion surged over her as she spoke:
she hadn't realized the depth of her feelings. She felt a
terrible profound sadness that they would never be together.

The surgical team assembled around the young man's
table. Liz could only partially see what was happening:
Calderon administered what she assumed was a local anesthetic. A nurse draped the nude body and slathered viscous orange jelly over his exposed flesh. He didn't cry
out, instead dozing, his eyes lidded with sleep.

Calderon plunged a Veress needle into the boy's abdomen and activated a gas switch. The patient's belly slowly
inflated. Swiftly piercing the distended skin with four trocars above the navel, Calderon then inserted the microcamera. With a swift motion, he made an incision with a
scalpel on the boy's right side, under his ribs.

On the video monitor, Liz could see the camera plunge
through the tube of the trocar and into the patient's body.
The boy's anatomy appeared vividly on the screen: whole,
intact, and healthy.

Liz watched in horrified fascination as an unfamiliar instrument was passed through the trocar and into the abdominal cavity. Joining a conventional laparoscopic grasper, it looked like a regular laser but had a slim silver curve of metal and a hook attached at its base.

The curiosity was too much. "For God's sake, Calderon, what is that instrument you're using?"

Her quavering voice betrayed her fear, but Calderon responded to the question with a certain pride, as if he were giving a lecture.

"This is a special instrument developed and delivered to me by Kerry Nordstrom," he said. "It removes the organ from its housing while placing a thin coat of treated fluocil on the connecting tissue. The organ's preservation begins before it is even removed from the body. These laparoscopic techniques are essential to achieving the highest degree of lasting power in the lifebank you stumbled upon. Dr. Nordstrom informed me that the instrument was developed through trial and error and only after several unsuccessful attempts."

Several unsuccessful attempts, Liz thought. In those first murder cases in Cincinnati, the bodies had been more damaged—it had to have been Nordstrom, trying to perfect his instruments.

She watched as the young nurse pushed a retractor through the fourth trocar, isolating and pulling back the liver. Calderon moved in with the instrument, an electronic buzz sounding out as he pressed a foot pedal. Slowly the laser burned the liver away from the supporting ligaments and hepatic duct. As it cut, the thin sliver of metal slid across the severed surfaces, coating them with the treated liquid.

Calderon moved to the patient's side and inserted a large grasper. It appeared on the screen, grabbing the liver and pulling it out of the boy. He held the organ aloft for a moment, then unceremoniously dropped it into a waiting tray of thick liquid. The older nurse, silent and expressionless, took the tray into the tenth room, where it would join many others of its kind.

"What's going on, Liz? I can't see," John said. She still couldn't turn to look at him, and she closed her eyes so she wouldn't have to watch the carnage Calderon was inflicting on the innocent boy. "Liz? Can you hear me? Talk to me," John said.

"I'm here, John." She felt weak and nauseous: the antiseptic odor of the orange jelly and the pain in her back were overwhelming. When she realized she was blacking out, it was with a sense of gratitude. Maybe she would wake up to find it was all a dream.

The rubber-gloved hand was strangely cold and wet on her skin until Liz realized that the clammy feel was the jelly being applied to her bare stomach. She hadn't been anesthetized, she knew, because she felt the chill of the room and the steel beneath her touching her bare flesh. Though her body had been draped, she lay naked on the table. Her back and neck ached so severely that she gritted her teeth in pain when she ineffectually struggled against the straps. She looked for the table where the boy had been: it was gone, wheeled away. The boy had vanished.

John. What had happened to John?

"John," she called out in a whisper. Her throat was raw and dry, her voice a brittle scratch. "Juan. Are you still there?" A nurse she hadn't seen before appeared at her head, pressing down on her shoulders to keep her motionless.

"John?" she cried out, louder this time. Fear of being

alone overcame her, more powerful now than fear for her own life.

"I'm here, honey. I'm here."

I won't cry, she thought. I won't lose control. "John, the boy is gone. They killed him, John."

"I know. You blacked out. I was worried about you."

Roberto Calderon's masked face suddenly appeared, hovering over Liz. "It's unfortunate," he said, his dark eyes reflecting the light of the overhead lamps.

"I had hoped you would remain unconscious. I'm not a cruel man, Dr. Danny. Perhaps it will be some small comfort for you to realize that your sacrifice is part of a great plan. One day the world will benefit from the technology you have seen here. Unfortunately, you saw it too early. The time is not yet right."

"Who told you that," Liz said. "Nordstrom? Do you really think he's going to give this gift to the world, after the crimes he's committed? Don't you realize that you and everyone else here and at Med-Tek are expendable to him? In just—"

Calderon put his gloved hand over Liz's mouth. "Enough," he said. "There will be no more talking."

There was a clatter from the instrument tray, and Calderon was handed a Veress needle. He held it up to the light for a moment, inspecting it, then lowered his hand to Liz's skin. She felt the cold, painful touch of the needle and screamed. John began yelling epithets at Calderon from beyond her vision, cursing him alternately in Spanish and English.

Calderon activated the gas switch, and Liz's belly began to fill. As her stomach inflated like a flesh balloon, she felt the painful pressure of her expanding nerve endings and skin. She tried to scream but couldn't; nothing emerged but a hollow scratchy whisper.

The young nurse stepped forward, adjusting the video screen so that Liz could see it. Hot tears coursed down Liz's cheek as Calderon deftly made a series of incisions across her exposed flesh. The cuts were small, but the scalpel burned like fire. He didn't cut her side, and she realized why: he had to tissue-type her first. He was going to remove a slice of her inner anatomy for laboratory analysis.

Within a minute Calderon shoved four trocars through the incisions, stretching her skin. The pain increased, but consciousness wouldn't leave her. The video screen image was black and empty. Calderon then picked up the microcamera and activated it, causing the monitor to flash with a magnified image of his hand.

Finally he shoved the camera through a trocar. Liz couldn't see it, but she knew it was being inserted just below her navel. John screamed again from somewhere in the room. He was watching it all happen: the microcamera's path down the shining white trocar tube into Liz's abdominal cavity, the insertion of the retractor and the strange hybrid instrument.

Liz opened her eyes to look at the screen. She had seen this sight a thousand times, but now it was different—the violet sac of the gall bladder, the reds and whites of the arteries and ligaments, the fleshy purple lobe of the liver — this was her own body. The brilliant, diffuse hues looked to her like Monet's garden.

She realized with horror that Calderon was moving toward her liver with the fluocil laser. He stepped on the foot pedal, and a hum preceded the yellowish beam. Wisps of smoke trailed through her body as a small slice of liver was cut out and retrieved for analysis. The instrument instantly cauterized the wound. Strangely, she felt little pain; her organs, unlike her skin and muscle, did not react to the intrusion by sending flashes of pain to the brain of their host.

After the young nurse took the sample out of the room, apparently bound for the laboratory, Calderon again picked up the scalpel. He was going to cut into her side, she realized, as John began to scream.

She couldn't make out what he was saying: she felt her hold on consciousness fading again as the blade neared her exposed flesh. Suddenly, more voices started to yell: Calderon's joined the din, asking panicked questions of a security guard who had just barged through the operating-room doors.

Calderon hastily began to pull the trocars from her belly. The gas escaped with a loud hiss, and the older nurse stepped forward to efficiently press down on Liz's stomach, forcing out the remaining CO_2. Calderon, cursing softly, pulled the metal tray toward him and quickly stitched each incision. They were small; each cut took only seconds to close.

She felt her restraints being unfastened. The older nurse came forward with Liz's clothes and, after applying adhesive bandages over her wounds, sat her up and hastily began to dress her. There wasn't much pain, just a stinging feeling from her belly. Liz was confused but grateful to be alive.

John was being released from his bonds as well. He sat up, snarling at Calderon. "Liz, honey, are you all right?" he said as security guards came forward to keep him on the table.

Before she could respond, a bustle of bodies and voices erupted into the room. Liz tried to turn to see as the nurse helped her on with her shirt, but a spasm of pain in her neck forced her to pull her head back. She caught a brief glimpse of two men in black uniforms. They addressed their questions to Calderon, but their presence obviously unnerved the nurses and guards.

"The police," John whispered to Liz. "Those are the police."

"My God, I don't believe it!" she exclaimed. "Please get us out of here, officers. These people were going to—"

"Hold on," John interrupted, holding his hand out to caution her. "I don't know what's going on here."

The police ignored Liz's outburst and continued to talk to Calderon. An older officer did most of the talking: a short man with a thin black mustache, holding a club in his hand and tapping it against his leg as he spoke.

Calderon pulled off his surgical mask and nodded respectfully to the officer. He spoke to his security guards, who immediately retreated to the back of the room, leaving John and Liz free for the moment.

"They're here on a burglary call," John said. "Someone must have spotted us outside. Calderon is telling them that they caught us and restrained us and were about to call the police. Which doesn't explain the surgical setup, but the police don't seem to care about that."

The senior police officer, who wore a sergeant's stripe on his shoulder and clearly outranked his younger silent partner, looked at John. It seemed that he had understood what John said, but he turned and continued talking to Calderon in Spanish.

"They're taking us to the police station," John said, a hint of glee creeping into his voice. He crossed from his table to Liz's, holding his hands in the air in a posture of surrender. The police immediately grabbed him, cuffing his hands behind him. They then did the same to Liz, looking at her in alarm as she cried out in pain when her hands were pulled behind her.

"The cop is asking Calderon if he's going to press charges," John said, trying to distract Liz from her discomfort.

John chuckled quietly as they were led out to the computer room. Liz was frightened of going to a Mexican jail for burglary, but she was so relieved to be freed from the operating table that her eyes filled with uncontrollable tears of emotion. She had a fleeting thought: the nearest United States embassy must be in Mexico City, hundreds of miles away.

She had no idea what kind of legal recourse they might have, or whether anyone would listen to what they had found; in all likelihood, they could be detained indefinitely. If they were, then Nordstrom would win: he would transmit the data, making his fortune and cheating society of the benefits of his research. A great feeling of helplessness overcame her; the source of her tears turned from relief to sadness.

They were ordered to stand still in the computer room as Calderon asked the policemen a question. In a tired voice, the senior officer began to explain something, tapping his fingers in his palm as if enumerating a list of points or instructions.

No one was looking at Liz. John, on the other hand, had the full attention of the younger officer. The security guards stared at their boss as if transfixed by this unexpected turn of events. Taking advantage of the fleeting moment, Liz felt around on the desk behind her, finding a pile of papers. She knew that these were the printouts John had made. Calderon had left them there after ordering the operating room to be prepped.

Liz quietly folded the small bundle and shoved it into the back of her pants, covering it with her shirt. It was difficult with the handcuffs. One of the security guards spotted her, then looked away again when she pretended to strair- -ust her bonds as if trying to stretch her back. The pr- -e cost her a moment of sharp pain, but it worked: the guard was afraid of the police and no longer wanted any bu- -ess with her or John. Calderon pointed at the pile of rubble made by her fall, motioning toward her and shaking his head like an aggrieved crime victim.

The police led John and Liz out to a waiting police car. The blue and red lights on its roof made rotating swaths of color that shone into the dark forest around the hospital.

Liz looked back at Calderon as the door shut, locking her in the car. He looked ashen and sick. He slowly shook his head, as if cognizant of his failure and the many ways that his life could be destroyed by what had happened. She thought, for a second, that she detected a flicker of relief in his features.

Liz and John spoke very little during the trip from the Endicott hospital back to the center of town. They sat close together, her feeling of relief tainted by the pain in her body: in her neck and back, and in the tingling cuts where Calderon had inserted the trocars. At least the aborted surgery had been laparoscopic, she thought. She wouldn't have walked away from a deep muscle-tearing incision.

"Something went very wrong for them back there," John said, turning on his side to ease the pressure from the handcuffs. "Calderon was truly surprised that we were taken away. He laid some very broad hints that we were to remain in his custody. My guess is that Endicott has some kind of agreement with the police here, and that the officers who arrested us unknowingly violated it."

"I never thought I'd be relieved to be taken to jail,"

Liz said. She looked at John. The idea that the police might have left her there on that table was too terrifying to contemplate.

Evidently the police station wasn't used to a lot of action. Several prisoners idled in a small cell at the rear of the room; only a clerk and another officer were there, both smoking and talking. They looked up when Liz and John were brought in, then returned to their conversation.

After their passports were taken, they were uncuffed and made to sit down on a pair of folding chairs. The officer who had arrested them took a cigarette from the clerk and joined in their talking, laughing in a deep throaty voice. Finally he walked over and asked John a question.

He responded tersely, nodding at Liz. *"Mi esposa solo habla inglés,"* he said. The officer looked at her and nodded.

The questioning that followed was excruciating for Liz: she heard Los Angeles and Endicott mentioned, and something about their being doctors and tourists, but the rest eluded her. The officer, a small compact man with a black mustache and unkempt hair tucked under his cap, listened impassively, writing down notes on a clipboard.

"What's going on?" Liz asked.

"I told him that we were looking for medical records on a relative. He doesn't believe me. He told me we'll go to jail if Calderon presses charges. I think it was the first time he met Calderon, but he certainly knew a lot about him."

"Is that good or bad?" Liz said.

"I have no idea. He seems to have no problem with the fact that he found us in an operating room."

The officer finally led them to the tiny cell. Liz tried to protest when she realized that she was being locked in with the men, but she was ignored. The room was relatively clean, but an open toilet in the center of the room was dingy and uninviting, and a smell of stale liquor permeated the room. The walls were painted a depressing faded beige.

John led her to a seat on a narrow bench, where she became the object of a number of interested stares. A couple of men were asleep in the corner. They looked like plain working people in jeans and straw hats: they probably were being held for public drunkenness and would be released in the morning. Another man, small and old and wrinkled from decades in the harsh sun, sneaked looks at Liz and John as if trying to hide his fascination. Her gaze caught the stares of the young men sitting on the opposite bench: they were dirty and rough-looking and smirked when she turned away.

John didn't notice: instead, he began to inspect the abrasions on her arms that she had received from falling. "Those bruises don't look as bad as I thought they would. You came down on that desk pretty hard." He tried to lift her shirt to look at her belly, but she pushed his hand away. "Why don't you let me look at you?"

"I'm fine. It's just a few cuts. We got out of there before any real damage could be done. Anyway, that's what I get for acting like I'm in a spy movie," she said.

John had a look around the room, catching the gaze of the young men. They stared at each other for a moment, then turned away. "What did you see there?" he asked. "How are they able to store the organs they're stealing?"

"It's disgusting," she said, shaking her head at the memory. "They're kept in a huge tank under constant laser treatment. There must have been hundreds of them, and the bodies . . . John, they killed over a dozen people tonight."

John stared ahead, a stunned look in his eyes. "They've tissue-typed everyone. They have the entire rural populace catalogued like a mail-order business, so they must be able to fill a request instantly. The money must be staggering."

"Not as much as what Nordstrom will get when he sells the formula. And if it also acts as an inoculating agent," Liz said, "it's priceless. It's all falling together, and we're the only people who know about it. He's going to win, John."

The three men in the corner continued to stare at Liz. They spoke to each other in low voices and smiled.

"Hold on a minute," John said, walking over to them. He bent over and whispered to them in a low voice, pointing back at Liz. The men were defiant at first, then looked agape at her over John's shoulder. They turned their bench sideways, resuming their conversation with their backs to her.

"What did you say to them?" she asked.

"I told them you killed someone tonight with an ax," John said.

"You're having too much fun," she said with a tired smile. An idea came to her. "What were those documents you were printing out?"

"Staff lists from the last eighteen months, surgical assignments and privileges, fatality rates. It's a damned shame we couldn't bring them with us. I think we might have some hard evidence to correlate with Cincinnati. It could be his fatal mistake: starting up his operation in the States, rather than down here where he could hide his work."

"I have them with me. I stuffed them in the back of my pants while we were being arrested."

John smiled and leaned back on the bench. "You amaze me," he said.

She allowed herself to smile back, reclining against the wall. She felt nauseated from her wounds but realized that she wasn't permanently harmed. I hope they let me out of here soon, she thought. In addition to wanting to save the world from Nordstrom, I really don't want to have to use that toilet in the middle of the room.

"John," she said, "I'm sorry I dragged you into all this. I really am. I should be alone down here."

"I couldn't have lived with myself if I didn't try to help," John said, taking her hand. "We're going to be all right."

"I hope you know what you're talking about," she said.

"I've been praying like a monk since we got here. Something good will happen."

"It had better happen fast," Liz said. "I've been thinking about it: when Kerry sells the formula, he'll be richer than we can imagine. An outlaw nation would pay anything to have an infinite supply of preservable human tissue with enhanced immunogenic properties. After the sale, he's going to disappear. There's no doubt in my mind. He'll be gone when the evidence falls together. Calderon, and who knows who else, will take the fall for him."

"Maybe he'll go to live in the country that buys the formula," John said.

"I doubt it. From looking at the places the organs were shipped to, it looks like he's mostly dealing with military dictatorships: not the most pleasant places to live."

"They must use that jet we saw at the landing field to transport the organs," John said. "That thing could fly anywhere in the world. But what would anyone do with the preservation formula?"

"Think about what a despot could do with the ability to store obscenely vast numbers of treated organs, John. They could perpetuate their own lives and those of their heirs, using their subjects as a sort of crop to harvest. They could use the technology in war, patching up internal injuries with transplants. And they could inoculate themselves and their soldiers from biological, maybe even nuclear warfare, with the stolen tissue. Thousands, maybe millions of people would die because of the evil and greed of a despot ruler."

John looked out at the station. The police had returned to their sedate conversations. "I hadn't thought about that," he said. "They could use the populace as a sort of spare-parts source, reaping from their bodies and hoarding human supplies."

"I'm sure Nordstrom doesn't care," she said. "As long as there's some part of the world he can go to enjoy his fortune."

"And the suffering—" John said, reflexively making fists. "People like the Mayans here, used like they were pieces of meat. They were once a great people. They were advanced astronomers and mathematicians. They had an empire. Now they're helpless, like other people throughout the world, to keep themselves from being butchered."

She had never seen him like this: his anger was palpable, coming off him in waves.

"The world could change tomorrow," he said. "And we're stuck in this fucking jail."

They sat for a while without speaking, the silence broken only by the sound of a typewriter slowly clacking. They had been given no clue as to their fate.

"John," Liz said. "If we get out of this jail, we have to

run for it. Damn the consequences. I don't care if we have to hijack a plane—we're getting back to America.''

"We need to get to Willers," John said. "He knows the case. We couldn't stop the transmission without someone to get us past Nordstrom's security."

"He has to believe us. When we get there—if we get there . . ." Her voice trailed off.

Liz lay out on the bench and rested her head on John's lap. "I'm going to try to sleep for a few minutes," she said, then looked up at his forehead. "They cut you, you poor thing."

"Clubbed in the head twice in two days. It has to be some kind of a record," he said. "You go ahead and sleep. I'll keep watch."

She fell asleep instantly. He stayed awake, staring at her sleeping face. She was beautiful as her body relaxed under his protective presence. She had told him she loved him, he realized.

A picture of Donald's face came to his mind, embarrassing him. He had liked Donald, even admired him, which made John's guilt over his feelings for Liz sting all the more. He had been in love with her almost from the moment they met, never imagining that she would return his feelings one day. He would go through it all again, and more, to hear her say it again.

7:00 A.M., November 3, Valladolid.

John woke with a start as the bright morning sun hit his eyes through the cell window. He looked around him, trying to figure out where he was. On the far bench, the three rough young men slept: they looked far younger and less dangerous in the light of day.

A police officer unlocked their cell and motioned for Liz and John to come out. She jumped when John woke her, a look of panic and fear in her eyes. Taking John's hand, she walked with him to the station's booking area, her steps heavy and labored. Her back muscles and belly were tight and painful.

They were sat down at a desk, where their passports sat before them. John picked them up and spoke with an officer in shoulder stripes and cap. Finally John turned to talk to Liz.

"The sergeant informs me that he went to Endicott early this morning. Calderon is not pressing charges. We're free to go," he said.

"I don't understand," she said. "Calderon must have talked to Nordstrom. I thought they would press charges and keep us in jail."

"I think I know," John said. "And I don't like it. Maybe they don't trust us to the justice system. We could be extradited to the States, or we could find someone to listen to our story. I think the cops made a deal with Calderon to allow him to take care of us himself."

"Oh, God," Liz said, stunned. Her heart began to race. She couldn't go back there—never. Not back to that operating room. "Isn't there anywhere we can go for help?" she asked in a high voice.

"I'm thinking. If we could get to . . ."

The sergeant stood up. "You are free to go," he said, flashing a smile as they reacted with surprise to his speaking in English.

"Wait," she said to John. "We'll use their phone. We can call Willers, or we could call the American embassy. There's got to be something we can do."

"You are free to use our phone," the sergeant said, brushing lint from his uniform shirt. "But no long-distance calls. You will have to make those from a pay phone."

"Listen to me," Liz said. She heard a note of entreaty in her voice. "Let me tell you what's going on. You have to protect us."

"Dr. Calderon has explained the situation. Now I must ask you to leave us to our business," the sergeant said. He was becoming irritable and impatient.

Liz looked out the station window, immediately recognizing where they were: near the center of town, only a block from the pretty, flower-laden town square. Even at this early hour, scattered tourists had begun to wander the streets in search of bargains and experience, blissfully unaware of the evil taking place around them.

She had a last look back at the police station as John took her arm to lead her out. One of the young prisoners caught her eye and waved at her with a gentle smile. She waved back at him.

The satellite transmission would happen tomorrow. They had perhaps thirty hours to stop it, but they would never be allowed to leave.

Outside the police station, a black sedan idled across the dusty, stone-paved street. The morning was warm and already sunny, the little town springing to life under the Caribbean sky. As they emerged, two young men in Endicott security uniforms and dark sunglasses stepped from the car. Spotting Liz and John, they reached deep into their jackets and strode toward them.

CHAPTER EIGHTEEN

7:30 A.M., November 3, Valladolid.

LIZ BECAME DISORIENTED AS THE YOUNG MEN APPROACHED THEM: the relative brightness inside the police station had given way to the dusty gloom of the early morning street. She looked desperately around, but there was no place to run: they were completely trapped and exposed. The police station door closed loudly behind them, and the young Endicott guards discreetly flashed guns at their bellies, motioning toward the car. It was over.

They stepped into the sedan without exchanging a word with the men. A couple of onlookers watched from a sidewalk café but did nothing. They must have thought the situation was somehow under control; after all, they were directly in front of the police station.

The car windows were tinted a deep smoky black. Once inside, Liz and John were invisible to the world. One man leaned into the car and handcuffed them together after threading the chain through a metal loop installed on the floor. The young men, expressionless behind their dark glasses, slammed shut the car doors and jumped into the front seat, gunning the engine.

The doors had no handles on the inside. Liz started to pull at her cuffs in frustration but found that doing so only increased the pressure on John's hand. Her back ached from the base of her skull to her legs.

"Looks like we're in the hands of professionals," she said.

John merely nodded. He looked exhausted, a dark stubble developing on his cheeks and under his lip, his dark eyes ringed with red. He looked as if he were giving up, letting the fatigue and the threat of death overtake him. She knew they had to fight. Until the satellite transmission had taken place, until they had failed, they couldn't stop.

"We've got to think," she said angrily. "This whole thing was a setup. We weren't meant to be arrested at all, not if the police are turning us over to these goons."

"There's no law here," he said, turning to face her. "Endicott has corrupted everything. I remember my mother telling me about Valladolid when I was a child. She said it was a wonderful place. It makes me sick to see what they've done."

"They're so young," Liz said, nodding toward the guards, who paid no attention to their passengers. The driver, a short and stocky kid, had a dark trace of a mustache over his upper lip. The passenger looked a couple years older but had a similar childish pudginess to his face. They looked like brothers, and neither could have been much older than twenty.

The driver craned his head toward them and yelled back angrily.

"He said to shut up and enjoy the ride," John said, "or they'll shoot us now. He's scared, I think. They have the firepower, but they're not comfortable doing this."

Within ten minutes they had driven out of the Valladolid city limits. They were going east, out into the rugged terrain of the Yucatán countryside. The driver took the turns in the poorly paved road with practiced ease and familiarity.

Liz watched the small dwellings on either side of the road pass by, tiny one-room houses with doors and windows thrown open to the dust and debris from the road. The poverty saddened her, but also intensified her fear: they were in the middle of nowhere and heading deeper in. Their bodies might never be discovered.

A small meat market passed by their window. Liz examined it intently before they left it behind, hungry for life's details. Carcasses hung from hooks in the open air, and a small crowd of people bartered with butchers. Trying to deny her fear, she fixated on all the tiny elements, all the minutiae of a life she had never imagined.

Farther down the road, they passed a gas station and tourist trap, where a large bus had parked and unleashed its dozens of pale tired-looking travelers. A large painted sign asked the tourists in English not to give money to the beggar children, claiming that it kept them out of school and "encouraged a life of idleness and crime."

Soon all signs of civilization disappeared. It was hard to tell how far they had gone; the road twisted and turned, and she couldn't see the speedometer to tell how fast they were moving. The path was very narrow, and when cars passed in the other direction she could see only a foot or so of space between them and the colorful shapes racing by. John was silent, alertly looking all around them for landmarks. She nudged him with her free hand.

"Quite a way to get a tour of the countryside, isn't it?" she said. He nodded and smiled imperceptibly.

"When this is all over we should open a school or something," he said. "We could teach people how to deal with masked marauders and hired killers. We're certainly getting enough experience.''

"When we stop, you have to talk to them," Liz said, suddenly serious. "It might be our only chance. They're so young—maybe we can talk them out of it. I can't believe they like to take strangers out and murder them."

"I'll talk to them, of course," John said, shaking his head. "But I don't think they'll listen. They probably make five times as much money doing Endicott's dirty work as they would through an honest job, even if they could find one. They probably support their entire extended family by taking orders and not asking questions."

The young man in the passenger seat turned and pointed his gun at Liz, a childish pout on his face. She closed her eyes and quit talking.

She felt a profound release of pressure within her, as if her emotions and fears were uncoiling like a spool of thread. The threat of death had become ever-present, unavoidable. A feeling came from within her, something like courage but more extreme. She knew she would take any risk to get away from these young men.

Suddenly, John leaned over and whispered in her ear. "Liz, listen. I'm going to jump one of them when they uncuff us, and try to take his gun. When you see me make my move, I want you to run into the underbrush and don't stop until you can't run anymore. You have to stop Nordstrom—alone if neccessary.''

Tears welled up in her eyes. "Shut up, John. We're going to get out of here together." He looked away from her.

The car veered abruptly off the highway, the brakes whining and gravel flying from under the tires as the driver adeptly maneuvered down a narrow dirt road. Trees and high grass enclosed the path on either side. They truly were in the wilderness, in an uninhabited part of the countryside. A small flock of white birds rose to the sky in a flustered mass as the car raced forward, pitching up and down on the ragged surface of the road. Liz's arm ached from the handcuff, and she was almost tossed out of the seat by the violent lurching of the vehicle. She felt that she could have begged for a time-out, a chance to stretch her aching muscles.

After about a mile, the road branched off in two directions. The young guard in the passenger seat held a gun trained on Liz and John, his face betraying only a trace of dismay at the rough ride. After about another quarter mile, the driver pulled the car into a row of sparse hedges and killed the engine, which rattled in protest of its rough treatment even after it was turned off.

The sudden silence made all four pause for a moment to regain their senses. Liz tried to guess how long the ride had lasted: fifteen minutes? A half hour? Birds sang in the surrounding trees, and the sun had baked the grasses into a golden brown. The foliage looked too thick to run through: the only clear way back was the road they had taken.

The young man released Liz and John from the handcuffs. John tensed to move, but a gun was instantly shoved against Liz's temple. He paused, and the younger brother freed the cuffs from the metal loop on the car floor and shackled him to Liz.

Without speaking, his older brother pointed to a path through the trees, leading them to a small clearing. The high rattling chirp of locusts could be heard all around, and the gurgling of a small stream sounded from behind them. It's a beautiful place, Liz thought. Then she felt a rough hand at her back push her into a kneeling position on the ground, pulling John down with her. The older brother stood before them, his gun pointed at John's head.

"Talk to them, John. Say something. They're going to kill us right here," Liz said. Her breath began to catch in her throat as she realized that she might have only moments to live.

John spoke rapid Spanish to the young men. He was silenced by the older brother, who stepped closer and pressed the revolver barrel to John's forehead.

For a moment, nothing happened. Liz turned and saw the black metal of the gun against John's head. The brothers took off their sunglasses and began to speak quietly to each other. The older of the pair dominated the conversation, exhorting his partner in a commanding tone.

"They're arguing about their family," John whispered. "It's something about their mother—"

The harsh report of the gun sounded out next to Liz. She screamed as John's words were cut off, and she closed her eyes to the world. A hand reached around from behind her and clamped over her mouth. She struggled, but he was too strong. Then the gun fired again, the acrid smell of gunpowder burning her nostrils. Her ears rang from the close range of the blast, and she waited, suspended in time for a moment, for death to take her.

It's so unfair, she thought. Nordstrom will escape with his money, untold thousands will die to serve the needs of greedy evil men. John, poor John, who had nothing to do with this . . .

"Liz," John said quietly. "Liz, open your eyes."

She looked to her side. John was there, unhurt. They were alive.

The older brother walked to John and knelt in front of him, their eyes only feet from each other. He kept the gun pointed at John's head and began to speak. At first John winced, then a sort of relieved wonder filled his features.

"His name is Bernard. He wants me to tell you what he's saying," John said, nodding at the young man. As Bernard spoke, John rapidly translated. "He and his brother, José, have been paid to take us out here and kill us. They even brought shovels to bury us. Our bodies might never be discovered."

Liz winced, her heart racing. Were they toying with them? Then why had they fired the gun? John continued to speak, a faint smile lighting his features.

"But they're not going to do it," he said. "They're going to let us go. They have something to ask of us. They are going to take off our handcuffs, but if we try to run, they will have to kill us."

The younger brother, his face contorted with worry, leaned over Liz and released her hand. She rubbed the abraded flesh of her wrists, rising to her feet and stepping away from the young men.

"Don't run," John said as his end of the shackle was unlocked. "I believe them." He stood with his arms folded, nodding rapidly as the older brother began to talk too rapidly to translate. He produced an envelope from his jacket's inner pocket and handed it to John. The young man pointed through the brush, and John responded in a grave serious tone. They shook hands, and the brothers walked warily back to the sedan, sitting inside and watching John and Liz.

"What's going on?" Liz asked. "Are they serious? They're really letting us go?"

John took Liz's hand. "There's no time to explain. We have to get out of here right now: Can you walk with your injuries? I can carry you if I have to."

"I can walk," Liz said, looking back at the car. The

engine raced loudly. John ventured a final wave and led Liz into the high grass in the direction where Bernard had pointed.

"There's a road less than a mile in this direction," John said. "Bernard said that a bus will run through here in about a half hour, which will take us to Cancún. From there we can take an airplane back to the United States. I have their word that we won't be followed."

He pulled harder on Liz's wrist, making her walk faster. Their pace was too quick for conversation, but Liz saw an expression on John's face that mirrored her own feelings: they had to move fast. In spite of what she had been told, she still feared that they would be shot in the back while they tried to escape.

Soon they found the path, which led in a circular fashion to another highway, much like the road they had taken out of Valladolid. Several hundred feet to their right, a small group of people waited on the side of the road. Liz and John joined them.

From the quizzical expressions on the people's faces, Liz knew that she must have been quite a sight. Her pants had been ripped around the ankles by sharp branches in their hurried flight to the road, and the dust from the countryside mingled on her clothes and hair with shards of the wall tile she had fallen through and shattered the night before.

John looked disheveled and exhausted; he had unbuttoned his shirt while they walked, and his jeans were dirty and sported a large rip in one knee. They were both coated in sweat and were still in shock from another brush with death.

"I guess we don't look like the average tourists," she said with a soft laugh.

John looked down at his torn clothes. "I guess not. But you're still beautiful."

"Flatter me later, sweetheart," she said, taking his hand, "after we save the world."

The wait for their ride was interminable. John muttered something about the buses always being late, looking up and down the road as if he still expected to be followed. Liz didn't ask him what the boy had said: she wanted to think of something other than death, if only for a few moments.

She passed the time by trading ugly faces with a giggling young boy who sat shyly close to his mother, venturing away from time to time to approach Liz. When he neared her, he would step away with an uproarious burst of laughter.

John noticed this game and finally smiled, beginning to relax. The bus came moments later. They boarded, paying the driver from their dwindling roll of pesos. Liz was glad John had the money. In her state, she would simply have thrust the roll of bills at the driver: anything just to get on and away from Valladolid. They sat in the rear of the packed bus, elbowing past a crush of people and luggage.

Inside was a sensory overload that did little to calm Liz's nerves. She estimated that the smallish bus contained seventy-five passengers; included in that number were about twenty small children, the more vocal of whom emitted ear-piercing wails of anxiety that could be heard from the front seat to the back. One elderly lady had brought along a small wooden cage that contained a pair of clucking chickens.

"This is no tourist special," John said, noticing Liz's wearied appraisal of the crushing crowd around them.

She nodded in agreement. "All right, John," she said. "It's going to be a few hours before we get to Cancún.

What in the world did Bernard say to you? Why did they let us go?'' She realized that she was almost yelling, drawing the attention of the other passengers. Putting a hand over her mouth, she took a deep breath: I'm getting by on adrenaline and nerves, she thought. I'm going to collapse if I'm not careful.

''They've had to kill people before,'' John began. He looked out the window of the bus at the landscape rushing by. This was yet another narrow highway, though it felt more secure to be in the bus than in a small two-seater car.

''They're poor Mayan Indians, and they grew up here,'' John continued. ''They came to work for Endicott in the last year, and they did whatever was asked of them to help their family. They didn't know anything about the real dirty business, but they dealt with people who posed any sort of threat.''

''Like us,'' Liz said, nervously running her hands through her hair.

''Like us. Recently their uncle had an 'accident.' He disappeared for thirty-six hours and was found by the side of the road about a mile from their family's house. He had no memory of what had happened to him and was largely unharmed, except that he had a series of small incisions on his abdomen and side.''

Liz gasped. ''Their relative was kidnapped by Endicott? They would do that to their own staff?''

''Maybe. It's more likely that it was a mistake. They probably had different last names. But it made them suspicious, because they had seen characteristic laparoscopic surgical scars at the hospital. Instead of taking their uncle to Endicott for an examination, they drove him to Mérida, where there's a big government hospital. The examining physician found that the uncle was missing a kidney, as well as a good amount of splenic tissue.''

"But they left him alive," Liz said. "Now they're killing the people outright and taking everything. It means that they've recently stepped up business.''

"I think Nordstrom's planning to cash out of the operation in style," John said. "But think about the people who lived: they would never miss a kidney or some other tissue. They might think they were just stabbed. A lot of people might be walking around in that state.''

"How horrible," Liz said. "Those poor people could be prone to all kinds of health problems in the future.''

The bus stopped to allow passengers to disembark and enter. John peered around anxiously at the road, but it was empty. They hadn't been followed.

"Those boys risked their lives letting us go," John said as the bus gained speed again. "And it's only because of what they found out that they did it. I know they wouldn't have hesitated to kill us otherwise. We also have their mother to thank.''

"What do you mean?''

"She was the older nurse in Calderon's OR. She hadn't been involved in the surgeries before, but she knew about them. The man with the missing tissue was her brother.''

Liz gasped. "So she called in the burglary complaint that got us arrested?''

"And bought us some time," said John.

He pulled the long envelope out of his pocket and unsealed it. It contained a thick stack of documents in an array of colors. Some appeared to be forms, some were photocopies of X rays. Liz looked over John's shoulder as he riffled through them.

"Doctors' reports, photographs, all the evidence of what happened to their uncle. This is better than what we found, you know. We have staff lists, but this directly incriminates Endicott Mexico. Nordstrom runs the place from the United States, so he's directly implicated.''

"These are exactly what we need,'' Liz said, her enthusiasm building as she took a small stack of the papers. "These are internal documents from Endicott Mexico: shipping destinations, operating reports. We can match them up with the Mérida doctor's examination to create an airtight case. John, this is wonderful.''

"I'll think it's wonderful when we get to Indianapolis and put a stop to it all," John said. He looked over the forms in his lap. "Hong Kong. They shipped the uncle's kidney and splenic tissue to Hong Kong. Incredible.''

The forms fell to the floor as the bus hit a jarring bump. Liz leaned over to retrieve them.

"What about the brothers?'' Liz asked. "Do they have any idea what they're going to do? They took enough of a chance stealing these papers, much less releasing us. It'll only be a while until word gets back that we're still alive.''

"They are going to say they did the job,'' John said, shrugging. "They've killed before, so there's no reason for Calderon not to believe them. There won't be any suspicion for at least twenty-four hours. They're thinking about packing up their families, stealing an Endicott van, and driving to Guatemala, where they have relatives. It's only about an eight- or ten-hour drive from here.''

"I hope they make it,'' Liz said. She remembered how young they were. To them, life and death were still just fantasy. It took the suffering of someone close to them to jar their conscience enough to find out what evil they worked for.

"Bernard demanded my word that I would take this information to American authorities,'' John said. "He's heard of Nordstrom and knows that he controls Calderon. He also told me what I already know: that the local police are in the pocket of Endicott.''

John's voice trailed off, and he took Liz's hand as she rested her head on his shoulder. There was nothing more to say. Ironically, Nordstrom's disregard for human life had come back to haunt him. He had been betrayed by two young Mexican men he probably had never heard of: they were just two of the faceless horde he employed to fulfill his goal.

Her watch face caught a beam of the sun through the bus window. The morning was passing; soon it would be afternoon. They had a day, maybe less, to stop the transmission in Indianapolis. It has to be enough time, she thought. It has to.

Then she caught herself. She pictured Kerry Nordstrom in her mind, heard his voice whispering in her ear. The glint of monstrous greed and ambition shone in his eyes. He would stop at nothing.

She shuddered, even in the close heat of the bus. As she drifted off to a fitful slumber, she thought: he has done the unspeakable. What price would he make the world pay for trying to stop him?

CHAPTER NINETEEN

12:15 A.M., November 4, Cincinnati.

IT HAD BEEN A NIGHT LIKE ANY OTHER FOR CARL WILLERS. HE sat in the kitchen with his son, David, going over the Reds' baseball schedule for next season. David was up past his bedtime, but they were having too much fun circling the dates when the best National League teams were coming to town. His son had been eager and happy to look past the coming winter and the school year to the carefree days of summer vacation. Carl, for his part, was happy as well. He never had enough time to spend with the boy.

The Keyhole Killings were the last thing on his mind. He had done some investigation recently, calling up a couple of surgeons, but in his heart he didn't expect to make any breakthroughs. Leaving the case unsolved bothered him and preyed on his mind when he was at the job, but he had been learning to try to relax and leave his worries at the station. After a terrible stress-test reading during a mandatory insurance physical, Carl's doctor had told him he had to slow down. Plenty of men had heart attacks at forty-six, and Carl fit the high-risk profile.

His relationship with Claudia had improved when he adopted his new attitude, and he had even taken himself off the nighttime duty rotation three nights a week. But when the electronic pulse of his phone rang out in the kitchen that night he knew what it was: work, pulling him again into the netherworld of homicide. Claudia, as usual, would have to put David to bed.

He pondered all this in Hatfield's Coffee Shop, extinguishing his cigarette in a dirty ashtray. The all-night, downtown greasy spoon was a place he had haunted many times. He knew all the waitresses and the owner and was easily able to reserve the back booth for his meeting with Liz Danny.

She wouldn't say where she was calling from, just that she had arrived from Mexico and was at an American airport. Somehow she had managed to get his home number from the precinct, or else she had called the operator. Carl thought that she had lost her mind at first, until she insisted that she had information to link Kerry Nordstrom at Med-Tek with the Keyhole Killings.

That got his interest. Since his first phone conversation with the officious director of the sprawling medical complex, Willers had a suspicion that something wasn't right with the man. It didn't mean Nordstrom was a killer, but Carl would have bet his badge that he knew something he wasn't telling.

Dr. Danny had insisted that she was flying to Indianapolis to "put a stop to" some technological transfer that was taking place the next morning. Hearing this, Willers knew it was time for him to step in. Meet me in Cincinnati, he reasoned, and we'll figure out how to stop Nordstrom. If we have to get to Indianapolis quick, it's only a little over a hundred miles away. They could requisition emergency use of the department plane if it was necessary.

He regretted the part about the plane. As far as Carl knew, only the commissioner ever used it. Grunts on the force took commercial flights, and only when they absolutely had to, and then they were raked over the coals by department bean counters for their expense accounts. At that point, though, Willers would have said anything to keep Danny from flying off half-cocked to mess with the prominent director of a prestigious medical firm. He had given her directions to Hatfield's and made plans to meet there at midnight.

"Norma, can I get a slice of that lemon pie?" he asked of a middle-aged waitress as she walked by. "And another cup of coffee?"

"Sure, Carl, but I hate to add any more tread to that spare tire of yours," she said, laughing and making her way behind the front counter.

Willers reached down and buttoned his sport jacket, tugging on and straightening his plain blue tie. "That's why I keep coming back, Norma. It's not just the fine food, it's also the atmosphere."

Norma shot him a look over her shoulder as she cut the pie for Carl, and both shared a laugh. He had been coming to this downtown institution since he first joined the force, but Norma had worked there for years before he even enlisted in the academy. She ran the night shift like a benevolent queen bee.

The street outside was bathed in the glow of old-fashioned streetlights, the meager traffic moving by at a leisurely pace. This is a mellow middle-of-the-road town, he thought, with not much crime for a city of its size. Maybe that's why the Keyhole Killings had seemed so shocking and off the wall. In New York, all right. But Cincinnati . . .

A yellow Checker cab pulled up outside the restaurant, dislodging two passengers: a pretty woman with short hair, dressed in a floral skirt and novelty T-shirt; and a dark unshaven man wearing ridiculously ill-fitting walking shorts and a short-sleeve shirt with a tropical fruit motif. The midwestern late-autumn chill had begun to show hints of wintery bluster, and the pair looked absurdly out of place.

They strode purposefully into Hatfield's. Willers followed them with his gaze through the window and into the place. The woman recognized Carl, waving and walking to the back booth.

"Detective Willers, I'm so glad to meet you. You look just like your photographs. I know my phone call must have seemed insane."

"A little," Carl said. "Who's your friend?"

"Dr. John Rogers," he said, extending his hand.

"I don't want to be rude," Willers said, "but you people look like you just got in off the boat. What in the hell have you been doing?"

They sat down. Liz and John ordered coffee and hamburgers, which they ravenously consumed as they told their story. Liz did most of the talking. As she began to reveal one aspect of what had happened, she would recall another and have to backtrack to another element of the story. She brought up Donald's clippings and correspondence with Nordstrom, bringing in elements of the failed vagotomy and her husband's suicide. Then she moved on to what had happened in Mexico.

When she had finished, Willers sat in stunned silence, staring at the end of the cigarette he had just lit. He had listened to the entire story impassively, without comment.

"You mean to tell me that Endicott International, which even I know about—I mean, I feed my baby daughter their crushed peaches and infant formula—is involved in body snatching and international trade of black-market organs?" He held his hands out before him, as if pleading for it not to be true. Liz and John simply nodded.

"It's Nordstrom that's the real criminal. He's using Endicott money for his own purposes. Tomorrow—I mean, today—" Liz said, glancing up at a wall clock, "he's going to send technological data to a client nation that will give that country the power to harvest and store human organs and tissue. Here, look at these."

Liz placed the packet of documents on the table, going through each individually and explaining its significance. Willers's interest was piqued when he saw the diagram of wounds suffered by the young brothers' uncle.

"That's exactly what we saw here," he said. "Looks like a damned basketball play. Only the people here didn't live. Except one, and he didn't make it long without his kidneys."

"Detective Willers," John said, leaning forward, "why didn't you tell Liz everything about that case? We had to find out more about it by hacking around on a national computer bulletin board."

Willers looked at Liz. "Do you really want to know?"

She nodded, holding out her mug for Norma to fill.

"You were a suspect. Nothing personal: everyone was a suspect because I didn't have any solid leads. I was waiting for someone to trip up and reveal information they shouldn't have known."

Norma listened to what Carl was saying and rolled her eyes at Liz before she walked away. "Listen to James Bond over here," she said, giving Willers a nudge with her hip.

"So you no longer think I'm a suspect?" Liz asked.

"No, I don't. I never really did, I was just grabbing at straws. And after what you say you've been through, you're not a suspect. You know, you've been doing my job." Willers patted down his short Afro, looking at his haggard features in the window. It was after one in the morning.

"So where does this leave us, Detective?" Liz asked. She was exhausted: only the little sleep she had stolen on the connecting flight from Dallas to Cincinnati kept her going. "I think the data transmission is taking place around noon: that's only eleven hours. If we don't stop him, one of the greatest medical advances of the century might be lost to the world."

"Except for some murderous dictator," John added. "I'm telling you, if he's selling exclusive rights to one nation, then he'll send an irretrievable data stream. No trace, no nothing. Lost forever. And we have reason to believe that there's another side to this technology: the possibility of inoculation against nuclear radiation and bacterial strains used in germ warfare."

Willers arched his eyebrows at the pair, again harboring the doubt that he was wasting his time listening to crazies. A moment of silence passed, as Liz and John stared him down.

"Let me get this straight," Willers finally said. "Nordstrom has developed a means of freezing organs?"

"No, not freezing them," Liz said. "Submerging them in a laser-treated fluocil solution. He and my husband did some work on tissue preservation years ago, but they never developed anything substantial. Now that Nordstrom has the resources, he's seen the research through. I'm sure of it, Detective. I've seen it."

"You've seen what? Listen, Dr. Danny. You're tired.

From the sound of it, you've been running yourself ragged. What I can do is take the evidence you've given me —especially the medical reports and these shipping destination forms— and try to get a warrant to bring in Nordstrom for questioning. In terms of this big high-tech satellite link, I don't really see—''

"Look, Detective," John said. His loud voice got the attention of the other diners, who turned around to look. "This is no joke. We had letters exchanged between Nordstrom and Liz's late husband that made direct mention of this exchange. A man lost his life because he knew Nordstrom was selling the formula. That in addition to the lives that have been lost since Nordstrom began selling organs. After the sale is made, Nordstrom is going to be gone. No suspect, no nothing. You'll be made a fool of, just like the rest of us.''

Willers took a sip of his coffee, looking up at John through the steam flowing off the cup. "Dr. Rogers, you need to chill out," he said. "First of all, the only evidence you have comes from Mexico. That's way out of my jurisdiction. I don't have any say in what happens to a bunch of Mexicans.''

"I'm one of those Mexicans," John said calmly. "So what are you trying to say?''

They faced each other with a moment of icy tension, staring into each other's eyes. Willers was angry with himself for his choice of words: he had been bucking prejudice his entire life. There was no excuse for his attitude.

"Sorry, Rogers," he said in a conciliatory tone. "That came out wrong." He leaned back in the booth, stretching his arms. "But my point is the same. It will take time to get a warrant on Nordstrom, and maybe even longer to get a search-and-seizure to go into Med-Tek. The jurisdictional headaches will be unbelievable. Those are the facts. Look, from what you've shown me, I believe that Nordstrom was involved in the killings, both here and in Mexico. I've suspected something like that for a long time. But until I have something to directly link him to what happened here—"

"What about these?" Liz said, pulling out the creased and worn sheets she had taken from the Endicott Mexico computer room. "There's a duty roster here, as well as a list of everyone who ever took a class or even visited on official medical business. Maybe there will be some connection."

"Give me those," Willers said. His sleepy eyes brightened for the first time since listening to Liz's story. "Now these I might be able to do something with."

Willers reached to the floor under the table and pulled out a worn ragged leather briefcase. He riffled through a stack of papers and reports within, fishing out a spare pack of cigarettes to replace the rapidly dwindling one next to his ashtray. Finally he produced a folder.

"Kerry Nordstrom gave me a list," Willers said matter-of-factly. "A charming guy."

"You've got to be kidding," Liz said, pushing her papers toward him.

"Pretty much. I thought he was a pompous ass and a snake in the grass, to tell you the truth. But he helped me out. He acted like he didn't want to, but I didn't give him much choice. This," he said, laying out a computer printout from the file, "is a list of doctors who have practiced laparoscopic surgery in the greater Cincinnati area since 1990. Most of them checked out."

"But not all of them?" John said.

Willers mumbled and brought Liz's list closer to him.

He put on a pair of tiny reading glasses, which looked strangely delicate and professorial on his broad face.

He looked through the documents for ten minutes, ignoring Liz and John. Nodding his head from time to time and crossing names off his list with a blunt pencil, he began to whistle softly.

Liz rolled her eyes at the ceiling. Willers was whistling the theme from *Dragnet*. John, growing impatient, went to the counter to order dessert.

"Hello," Willers finally said.

"What?" Liz asked, growing irritated at the delay.

"I said hello. Come to Papa."

His face was obscured behind the long sheet of computer paper; Liz could only see a curl of smoke coming from behind it. He put the form down and placed it next to his own, staring at it intently as if looking at something that might vanish if his attention were distracted.

"Interesting," he said. "Very interesting. What do you make of that?"

He didn't seem to be addressing Liz, or John, who had returned with a slice of pie. "What are you talking about?" Liz finally asked.

"Look at this." Willers took his pencil and underlined a name on the staff list from Endicott Mexico. "It's funny," he said, lighting another cigarette. "It's like this a lot. One little loose end, you know. You can't do anything with it, and it seems to be nothing at the time, but it always comes back to you when you least expect it."

Liz looked at the underlined name, craning her neck to read it upside down. Her muscles sent a flash of pain in protest. "Henry Chambers. So what does that mean?"

"Well, he wasn't on Nordstrom's list. Surprise, surprise. I trust that kind of guy about as far as I can throw him. He thinks he can bullshit a dumb cop like me. When he gave me his list of laparoscopic surgeons, I took the liberty of compiling my own. I went through the files at all the local hospitals.''

"I didn't know the police could access secret hospital files," Liz said.

"Let's just say I've been around a while, made a few friends. Anyway, the list I made jibed with the one Nordstrom gave me. Except in one case."

"Henry Chambers," Liz said. "I've never heard of him."

"You're not alone. He's had operating privileges at Cincinnati General for the last three years, but no one there has ever met him. He has no local practice. According to records, he's never done surgery at the hospital."

"What are you saying?" John asked.

"I'm saying that he's a fictional character. He had credentials to get in the door, but he could be anyone. He could be several people, if you think about it. I want to ask you something. Is it possible that someone could operate on a patient without a report being filed?''

"No, not really," Liz said. "A surgeon files reports to account for the time of the entire team, not just herself."

"What if you operated alone? Would anyone know about it?"

"Well, they'd think it was strange, as well as unsafe" Liz said, waving her hand in the air to ward off Willers's smoke. This guy is a health hazard, she thought.

Willers mumbled in assent. "Strange. Out of line. Against the rules. Unorthodox. That's what I thought. But not impossible."

He turned the papers around for Liz and John to see. "I did some snooping around at Cincinnati General," he said. "I found out that they have operating rooms they don't even use anymore. They're out of date but still functional. They're situated next to an old loading dock that's also unused. The security alarm there is easy to bypass. Did it myself and found that it led out to a platform facing out on an alley. No one ever goes back there.''

"So someone, if they had operating privileges, could go into the old wing, open the door to the old loading docks, and—"

"And do whatever they wanted," Willers said. "Bring in someone they picked up off the street and do their business with them. No one would notice if they did it in the middle of the night. I hung around there for a while; the security's lax, and the nurses are so overworked that they don't have time to patrol the halls of an old unused wing. In addition, the surgical library is set up on the same floor. Someone could come in, flash their credentials, and say they're going to the library. Instead, they rip someone's guts out, keep the guts, and dump the body in the river.''

Liz looked at the list. "Henry Chambers. He's on the list at Endicott Mexico.''

"But this Chambers could be anywhere," John said. "We don't know that he even knew Nordstrom.''

Willers took a sip of cold coffee. "You weren't listening. Chambers doesn't exist, except on these two pieces of paper. The interesting thing is that Nordstrom signed out the request and reference authorization for Chambers to work in Cincinnati. They're one and the same man.''

"But why would he be on the staff list in Mexico?" Liz said. "Unless Nordstrom were leaving a trail to be found eventually. Maybe he has people working with him that he wants to destroy. He leaves the country, and his associates take the fall when the evidence is finally put together.''

"You're not bad," Willers said, smiling for the first

time that evening. "Maybe you should think about changing careers."

"Let's just cut to the chase, Detective," Liz snapped. She heard the harsh sound of her words and winced. "I'm sorry, Carl. Really. I'm wrapped a little too tight right now."

"It's all right, Doctor," Willers said, his smile vanishing. "You're right, though. Here's what it all boils down to: I have enough to move on Nordstrom. I can even subpoena the surgical team on that operation your husband took the fall for. As soon as the courts open, we'll get started."

"No, we have to do it now," Liz said, her hand trembling as she beat it on the Formica tabletop. "I'm telling you, we only have until noon."

Willers sighed. "Please believe me, Detective," Liz said.

They sat in silence for a moment. "I'm going to have to wake up a judge in the middle of the night to sign the warrant," Willers said. "And that bit about the jet was bullshit. When I call the lieutenant and ask him for authorization, he's going to reach through the phone line and strangle the shit out of me. Of course, he does owe me a favor. I took his kid with mine to a few ballgames. . . ."

They could see the Indianapolis skyline come into view from their small plane. It was surrounded by the orderly placid glow of the city lights. The sun had almost risen, and John and Liz hadn't slept. After riding to department headquarters in Willers's station wagon, Liz and John had little to do but wait while the detective made a series of frantic, cajoling, persuading phone calls to line up all the elements of a spur-of-the-moment warrant delivery. Somehow all the pieces fell together.

As they neared the small municipal landing field, Willers chewed disconsolately on his pencil eraser, having been forbidden permission to smoke on the brief flight from Cincinnati. A group of local police and detectives would meet them at the airstrip. He looked through the Byzantine stack of forms that would allow him jurisdiction to work with local cops to make the arrest.

"Carl," Liz said, moving across the aisle to sit next to him, "thank you. You'll see, stopping the satellite transmission is even bigger than solving the murders. Thousands of people's lives will be spared."

"Don't thank me," Willers said. "My motivation in going through all this shit is purely selfish. I finally have a chance to break open the Keyhole Killings, even if I'll never be able to ask for another favor for the rest of my career. You have to understand, I feel personally responsible for every single death that I'm assigned to solve. I feel like I let those poor people down."

A hint of vulnerability in the large, gruff man made Liz feel strangely affectionate, almost protective of him. This is a side of him that few people must know, she thought: the man driven by compassion and emotion, feeling the suffering of the victims as if it were his own.

Soon after the plane landed, it became immediately obvious that the police were running the show, and that Liz and John were mere spectators. They were met by the Indianapolis cops, and Willers immediately fell into a long consultation with plainclothes officers, going over background and evidence and their goals in conducting the arrest. By the time transportation was arranged and the information passed on to the local police, it was almost nine in the morning.

"Detective Willers," Liz called out, sipping coffee out of a paper cup. A chill wind blew across the quiet airport. She and John had passed the time by walking around amid the antique aircraft parked in rows along the landing strip's periphery. "When are we going? We're going to be too late."

Willers looked up from a diagram of Med-Tek that he had been consulting over with one of the detectives. The Indianapolis officers, who had been aiming quizzical looks at the tropically attired Liz and John, looked over at them with impatient expressions. Willers, however, nodded grimly, motioning toward the unmarked vans parked in a row along the outer fence of the airstrip.

"The lady knows what she's talking about," he said. "We have to roll on it."

They drove along the circular freeway that encased Indianapolis like a great concrete belt, heading into the area of industrial parks and shopping centers that Liz recognized from a little over a month before. She and John held hands, dressed in black jumpsuits emblazoned with the Indianapolis Police logo, which had been given to them only after they had shivered on the runway for nearly an hour.

"I'll tell you what's going to happen," Willers said, leaning over the seat to speak to Liz and John in the rear of the police van.

"Me and Detective Simmons, the tall blond guy riding in the van ahead of us, are going to take the lead. We're going to deal with the security at the gate so we can make a surprise arrest. You people don't have much of a role. I went out on a limb even bringing you along, so I want you to lie low and keep your eyes open. If you see any pertinent evidence, tell me. Otherwise, stay out of trouble and let us work."

He finished his speech with a stern look at Liz. He had a bad feeling about bringing her along, but he felt he owed it to her. Without the evidence she had brought him, he would have been at home in bed, no closer than before to solving the case. He just hoped he hadn't cashed in a dozen favors for nothing.

Med-Tek was alive with activity when they finally arrived: the parking lot was filled with employees' cars, and Endicott vans drove about the grounds, transferring equipment from the labs to the production lines. Their caravan of five vehicles drove quickly through the outer grounds, over the gray waters of the moat and to the main security checkpoint. Willers hopped out of the van with vigorous purpose, followed by Simmons, a muscular crew-cut man with the manner of an ex-Marine.

"My God, there's the satellite dish," Liz said, pointing out the van's window at an area deeper inside the complex. "And there's no one around it. That must mean we still have time."

"Maybe," John said, craning his neck to see. "It's probably all remote-controlled from inside Med-Tek. The transmission could be made at any time. We just have to hope that he hasn't done it yet."

An Endicott guard, wearing the blue coveralls of the security staff, picked up a phone in his booth after talking with Willers and Simmons. Carl drew his revolver from his holster and shouted at him. Liz couldn't hear what they were saying; their words were muffled by the safety glass of the kiosk. The guard dropped the phone and put up his hands, looking around for help.

He, along with another guard who approached the booth, were discreetly handcuffed and loaded into one of the vans. Their detainment escaped the notice of the workmen, who drove past with single-minded efficiency. The metal gate blocking off the driveway opened as Simmons threw a switch from within the structure.

Willers clambered back into the van, looking over the seat at Liz as the driver pulled deeper into the complex. "These guys are well trained. They weren't going to co-operate unless they could call Nordstrom first. You'd damned well better be right about this satellite link, Doctor, or I'm going to have a lot of explaining to do for pulling a gun on those guys."

Liz was about to respond, but they had already reached the building's front entrance. They, along with the dozen Indianapolis police officers, wedged into the door as a blue-coated security guard exited, probably checking out why the main desk didn't respond. He was immediately cuffed and detained by three officers.

Willers and Simmons strode boldly up to the front desk, their badges held before them. "I need to see Dr. Kerry Nordstrom. Now," Willers said.

"I'll have to phone his office and see if I can locate him, officer," said the receptionist, an attractive woman who acted as if there were nothing unusual about what was happening.

"You're not listening," Simmons said, leaning over the desk. "We have to see him now. You're going to take us to him, or you're gonna find yourself charged with obstructing justice."

Simmons's brusque manner attracted the attention of about twenty-five surgeons in the lobby, who were standing about poring over the schedule for the day's seminar. Apparently Med-Tek business continued as usual, even though Nordstrom was somewhere in the building planning to execute an exchange that could throw modern medicine into a state of turmoil.

"Give me a security pass to get me around this place,"

Willers said, looking at the electronic locks to the right of every door leading out of the lobby. "And give me one that works for all these doors. We need to ask Dr. Nordstrom some questions, then we'll be out of your hair. All right?"

She handed Willers a key card, which dangled on the end of a nylon cord. "This is the best I have," she said, her tone softened by Willers's kind attitude. "It's only good enough to get to the cafeteria and the employee lounge. I think Dr. Nordstrom is in the labs."

"Fuck this," Simmons said, jogging out of the lobby to the vans outside. He returned with a silver metallic key card. "I got this from one of the guards out there. He said we can go anywhere with it except the highest-level security areas."

Liz looked at John, who was warily watching the surveillance cameras in the corner of the lobby. "He must be still preparing the transfer," she said, "or he wouldn't still be here. It would make sense to compile the data at the last minute, so there wouldn't be any prior evidence of what he plans to do."

"Take us there," Willers said, turning away from the reception desk. He gave Liz the electronic pass. "And you people just go on about your business," he added, addressing the staff and the befuddled surgeons, who had been intently watching the police.

Liz opened the door leading to the labs, flashing the key card in front of the invisible beam. The door automatically opened with a hiss, allowing their group to pass through. They found themselves in the long antiseptic hallway that led to the restricted parts of the building.

"Nordstrom's private lab is situated just off the animal testing room, across from the amphitheater," Liz said to Willers. "My guess is that he's there."

She took the lead, leaving John amid a small phalanx of police officers. They strode through another door, which opened with Liz's pass. To their right was a large lounge, filled with about a hundred surgeons dressed in blue papery scrubs for a morning surgical session. A few of them noticed the group of uniformed figures passing by outside and crowded against the glass.

"This way," Liz said, striding to a glass door marked "Restricted Access." She held the card in front of the electronic eye, and it opened with a hiss and a click.

"All right," Simmons said. "Looks like that guard wasn't shitting me." Liz walked through the passage, looking down the long empty hallway.

Willers halted the group at the doorway. "Dr. Danny, listen up," Willers said. He peered over his shoulder. "And you too, Rogers. When we get to Nordstrom, I'm serving him with the warrant. I want you two to stay out of the way. Don't touch anything, don't say anything. We can check out the—"

Suddenly the door closed with a matter-of-fact clatter of steel and glass. Liz, trapped alone on the other side, pushed uselessly against the portal's clear surface. Willers yelled to her, but the thickness of the glass muffled his words to an indistinct murmur. John was in the back of the group, pushing his way forward, an expression of alarm on his haggard sleepy features.

Liz looked at her watch: it was 11:35. Simmons turned away from the group, at the apparent behest of Willers, and stalked angrily back to the reception area. Liz still had the card; they had no way to get into the restricted area.

She began to turn away from the door, ignoring Willers and John's silent entreaties for her to stop. There was no time to wait, and she didn't think that the door had closed by accident. Nordstrom must have seen them on the surveillance camera and taken the opportunity to separate her from the group.

Above her head, the inanimate eye of a camera steadfastly blinked. She looked up at it. "I'm coming, Kerry. This is how you want it, right? You and me?"

Slowly, deliberately, she walked down the hall to the labs, her soft step making the only noise in the eerily quiet hall. She reached the pig lab door, opening it with a swipe of the card.

Inside were the familiar rows of tables, each occupied by a pig. In the darkened room, the only light came from the life-support monitors and surgical lamps activated above the tables. Unlike before, there were no technicians, no attendants, no surgeons. A smell of electricity permeated the air.

Her heart began to beat heavily in her chest, and her hands shook as she stepped farther into the room. Where had everyone gone? They couldn't leave the animals unattended for long, she thought. The door closed behind her, leaving her alone and isolated. Only the rhythmic beep of the pigs' life-support devices could be heard in the unnatural silence.

The door to Nordstrom's private lab was shut but yielded with a pass of the key card. When it opened, she stepped in, feeling the passing breeze behind her as the door closed to seal her inside. She felt the perspiration on her forehead and a terrible lurch within her heart as she looked inside.

"Don't move a fucking muscle," Nordstrom said from behind his computer console. He wheeled around in his chair to face her, the shiny black metal of his gun reflecting the bright light of the lab. "Step over here," he said, a contemptuous look on his face.

Liz walked slowly toward him, measuring out each

pace in an attempt to stay in control. She looked around: the single tank was there, wired in to the activated lasers and awash in glowing treated fluocil. There was no pig inside, just the hallucinatory play of the green and red colors as a gentle current passed within. The high platform of a hydraulic lift stood next to the liquid's surface, a thin metal ladder leading up to it.

"What are you doing here, and with that ridiculous haircut?" he said in a mocking voice. She stared at the cylinder, her attention fixed on the bizarre hues.

"Your timing is amazing," Nordstrom said, pulling her attention away from the tank. She stopped where she was, looking at the gun. She felt no real fear; instead, she felt a glacial unfamiliar calm. It had all been leading up to this, she thought.

"It truly is," he continued, standing up and brushing off his white lab coat with his free hand. "I'm about twenty minutes from getting away from all this bureaucratic bullshit, and look who comes waltzing up with the Roman legions. It's laughable, really. When they told me you were dead, I believed them."

He began to chuckle softly, turning to look at his tank. Liz tensed, ready to spring at him, but he turned again to face her, pointing the gun at her heart.

"You're not going to send that data, Kerry. It's all over," she said. Her own voice surprised her with its calm sense of purpose.

"So you know about my little secret," Nordstrom said, truly surprised. "Imagine that. How in the world—"

"You're a braggart and a loudmouth, Kerry. That's how I know. You popped off in Phoenix about your satellite, and you were idiotic enough to play cat-and-mouse with Donald."

"You read the letters, I take it? That's interesting. Donald told me that you didn't know anything about the fluocil solution. He was trying to keep you out of trouble." He took a couple steps toward her. "Of course, I spiked him with so many drugs that he probably didn't know what he was saying. Ironic, isn't it? I spiked a junkie with drugs. I should have just let him take care of himself. It would have happened eventually, you know."

Liz felt heat in her eyes and pinched her leg to stanch the tears that were welling up within her. "Don't you even care, Kerry? You and Donald were colleagues and friends. You destroyed him."

"Indirectly, I suppose. I could have had him killed when he first suspected, but I was too much of a gentleman. My plan to simply ruin him worked quite well, but now you're here because I let him live too long. You live and learn, don't you?"

She walked toward the tank. "How did you do this?" she asked. "It's incredible."

Nordstrom followed her over, keeping the gun trained on her. "You're stalling, aren't you? Waiting for reinforcements, appealing to my sense of hubris?"

"I'm trying to keep from throwing up at the sight of you, you bastard," she said. Now she did feel as if she were going to cry: not for her own life or for Donald's. This perversion of all the noble possibilities of medicine, the inhumanity of this man's planning, suddenly superseded all.

"Hmm," Nordstrom said. "I suppose inviting you to come along with me for a sexy billionaire's life on the run is out of the question. I'll admit that you haven't lost your attractiveness to me." He looked up and down her body, practically caressing her with his eyes. She visibly recoiled.

"Fine," he said. "I'd get tired of you, anyway. You're

far too unimaginative." He stepped away from her to his computer bank. She stood opposite, helpless amid the rows of high-technology generators, lasers, and computers. None of the machinery looked at all familiar to her; his research was truly beyond anything she had seen, in an advanced realm of experimental science that appeared utterly unique.

Nordstrom looked at his watch. "It's eleven fifty-two," he said. "My clients will be prepared to receive the information at twelve. At the same instant, one billion dollars will be deposited to a secret account in a Caribbean bank. I will leave here through the subbasement and live out the rest of my life in supreme luxury. By the time your cops get in here, I'll be gone forever." His thoughts appeared to drift with the idea of his new life.

Liz dug her fingernails into the palms of her hands, using the pain to keep her calm. "Can you really inoculate humans against radiation and disease?" she said.

Nordstrom looked surprised for a moment, then regained himself. "You figured that out? Amazing. The answer is yes. At first I set up the organ-harvesting operation and left it at that. However, I grew tired of sharing the money with Irwin Ross and pressed ahead. I did experiments. It turns out that a small amount of treated tissue can go a long way. Even I don't know all that it can do."

"Who did you sell it to, Kerry?" Liz said, looking around for anything that could be used as a weapon. There was nothing.

"That doesn't matter, Liz. If you've seen one strong-arm fanatic general, you've seen them all. I'm making them happy, though. I've arranged for delivery of the Endicott Mexico organ bank as a sort of goodwill gesture. We run them from a jet out of Valladolid, you know. It's very expensive."

"How do you expect to get out of here?" Liz said, trying to keep Nordstrom talking, and his concentration away from the gun. "They've come to arrest you."

"This is my kingdom, Danny," he said, frowning at a readout on one of several screens before him. "I can do whatever I want. This land is the site of an old milling plant. There are tunnels that lead on for miles. I know them—no one else does."

He walked to a bank of blinking television screens: the surveillance monitors. "You really should see this," he said, bending over to take a closer look. "The big black guy just threw a chair against the door. Probably broke it, the idiot. And now D'Amato's there, that fat fool. Works here everyday and has no idea what's really going on. Now the cop is yelling at—that reminds me, who is this Rogers fellow? You're a little freshly widowed to be running around, aren't you?"

She turned her back, her eyes burning with anger. There was nothing she could use against that gun. Nothing.

"Oh, that was uncalled for, Liz. You'll have to pardon me. I don't intend to be unnecessarily cruel."

He walked to his main bank of computers, near the fluocil tank, wiping the lenses of his glasses on his brilliant red tie. "If it's any consolation to you, I plan on letting you live," he said. "A few more minutes and I'm out of here. You won't be a threat to me any longer, Liz. You were simply too late."

Liz walked nearer to Nordstrom and the computer bank. "Seeing as how I'm out of the loop, why don't you tell me what's happening with the data transfer?" she said. She had no plan of action, no idea of what to do. The transfer would take place in minutes.

Nordstrom looked at her skeptically. His eyes narrowed

through his glasses, and he reached for a spray bottle of alcohol sitting on a computer monitor.

"Damn glasses," he said. "I should have gone into ophthalmology. Could have figured out a way not to rely on them." He sprayed a fine mist of alcohol on the glasses' lenses, wiping them clean with a chamois cloth.

"All right, here it is," he said, putting down the cloth. "Come closer, but don't forget that I'll shoot you if I have to. I grew up in the South, you know. My father gave me a pistol for my fifth birthday."

Liz nodded and stepped closer, pretending to be transfixed by the computer screen, which played out an automated sequence of ever-changing numbers against a green and black map of the world. She saw that a spot in Asia was highlighted: it must be the destination. At the same time she kept an eye on the gun, remembering Kerry's aversion to physical violence. She wondered if he had changed, if she should gamble that this tendency hadn't gone away.

"As you can see, my role is quite scant at this point," Nordstrom said, resting the gun on his lap. "I had my technicians run an automatic sequence tying into a United States government satellite, which we bought time on at an exorbitant rate."

He stared into the screen. "The Arab sheikhs aren't as loose with their money as you might think, you know. They were lowball bidding on the fluocil formula. My current clients were much more visionary. They saw the value of my creation. They and their heirs will live out exquisitely long life-spans. The same might not be true for their neighbors, unfortunately. But I never cared for politics."

A timer sounded in the computer casing. "There we have it," Nordstrom said. "Three minutes to go. At the precise time this data is sent, an Endicott jet will lift off, prepared to deliver the previous human tissue supplies, as well as an abundant array of the special instruments I created. And the formula will be gone: the computer will erase the laser frequency settings. This room will contain nothing more than a tank of garden-variety fluocil.''

Liz stepped closer. "You're a brilliant man, Kerry."

Nordstrom looked up through fogged glasses: he was breathing so heavily in his excitement that the lenses were steamed. "I'm glad to hear you finally admit it," he said, reaching for the chamois cloth and taking off his tortoise-shell frames. "These goddamned glasses—"

As he reached for the cloth, Liz grabbed the alcohol bottle, a gasp of panic escaping from her lips as Nordstrom lifted the gun into the air. Before he could shoot, she squirted a stream of the liquid into his eyes. His face contorted into a grimace as she sprayed him again, the clear alcohol running in a stream down his face, mingling with tears of shock and pain.

"You damned bitch!" he said, squealing and reaching for his eyes. His words were garbled into a half-scream as he pointed the gun at the air. He couldn't see to aim, and Liz took the opportunity to run behind him.

The timer sounded again, and a large digital number appeared in the corner of the screen, counting down the seconds until the data transfer. Nordstrom fell to the floor, cursing and furiously rubbing his eyes.

Keep rubbing your eyes, she thought. That should keep them irritated. The timer on the computer counted down to fifty seconds. She looked all around her for something to use as a weapon—not against Nordstrom but against the damned computer.

Forty-five seconds. Nordstrom crawled toward her with amazing speed, grabbing at her leg. She kicked him away, running to a surgical tray behind the surveillance monitors. *Thirty-five seconds.* She looked at the instruments and found nothing: trocars, graspers, conventional small-beam lasers. Nordstrom had kept his word and shipped out all the organ-harvesting instruments.

Thirty seconds. Nordstrom made it to his knees, his eyes red and tearing. He still held the gun before him, his finger on the trigger, but he didn't shoot. If he misfired, he would destroy the equipment that was going to make him a billionaire. Then she looked under the tray, finding a bucket of muddied viscous fluid. It had to be fluocil, but it was dirty, the by-product of the tank's filtration system. *Twenty seconds.*

She picked up the bucket. Some of its contents sloshed over the edge; mixed with the fluocil were spiky hairs and other debris. It must have come from the immersed pigs, she thought. *Ten seconds.* She lifted the bucket above her head, stealing a last glance at Nordstrom, whose hands were over his eyes. With a heave, she emptied the heavy contents of the pail directly onto the computer console.

"Christ, no!" Nordstrom exclaimed, pulling his hands away from his eyes in time to see, through intermixed tears of agony and rage, his entire computer bathed in the thick dirty solution. The liquid seeped into the keyboard and the floppy disk drive, running through the broad cracks in the machine's casing. A generous portion ran off and onto the kneeling Nordstrom, soaking his gun hand and covering his coat. A few sparks shot out of the machines.

The screen read "*Five seconds,*" then went dead. More sparks flew from the computer, along with plumes of caustic smelly smoke. The liquid had filled the interior of the machine and begun to drip from its casing. It was ruined; its delicate circuitry was completely soaked.

"Damn you!" Nordstrom yelled. His eyes were red and swollen, but he had regained his vision and disgustedly tried to wipe the fluocil from his lab coat. "You fucked up my computer! The data can't have gone through. They're going to think I screwed them! I'm dead!"

Liz ignored his ranting, moving quickly away from the computer. Orange tongues of flame had begun to emerge from it, mingled with smoke from its burning interior. She glanced at the surveillance monitors; they fluttered with static, apparently because a power surge was going through the room. Before the image broke up, she saw John and Willers with an acetylene torch, cutting a hole in the thick glass of the outer hallway door. D'Amato stood with them, running his hands through his hair with an expression of concern. They were coming for her. She had to just stay alive.

Nordstrom walked quickly, almost maniacally toward Liz, stopping just feet away from her. He pointed the gun at her head and, without a word, pulled the trigger. The barrel clicked loudly, and Liz winced from the expected impact.

Nothing happened. The gun had been soaked in the fluocil solution and jammed up. Nordstrom sneered and threw it away from him, a snarl on his lips. "Do you know what you just cost me, you idiot bitch?" he screamed, his voice cracking like a teenager's. "A billion dollars. Is your life worth a billion dollars?"

He moved toward her, his outstretched hands forming claws. He was going to murder her with brute force. She gasped, feeling the pulse of fear for the first time since entering the room. Before he could reach her, she grabbed a standing instrument tray and threw it in his path. He brushed it aside, a row of scissors and clamps falling to the floor with a metallic smash.

They were beyond talking: he was in a murderous rage. He kept walking toward her, backing her into the rear of the room. She grabbed whatever she found as she stepped away from him: a thick notebook, an unattached computer keyboard. She hit him both times, but he held his hands out to deflect the objects. If anything, he grew angrier.

She ran around the tank, feeling the low electronic pulse of the surging lasers. The computer had completely caught fire, and the other equipment in the room had begun to hum with an electrical backsurge. The lights dimmed and brightened: the entire room was on the verge of shorting out. She heard the distant sound of sirens from somewhere outside the building.

From the other side of the tank, Nordstrom howled out in rage. She saw him through the oscillating, hypnotic swirl of reds and yellows, colors that seemed to intensify as sparks flew from other equipment in the room. The lights had gone completely berserk; they alternated between a weak gray luminance and a blinding glare. Sparks began to fly from wall sockets, and she looked down to her feet in time to see a blue flame sputter from the laser bank.

There was nowhere to run. In utter panic, she grabbed a fire extinguisher installed in the tank's casing, stepping onto the thin metal rungs of the hydraulic lift. Her body screamed in protest as she lifted the heavy object up the first several steps, straining to reach the platform above her. Nordstrom stepped around the tank, slapping it hard with his clenched fist.

Now she was above him. An internal alarm sounded from his computer bank, the last gasp of a ruined system. Its high-pitched wail grated against Liz's ears as she climbed higher alongside the tank, waiting until Nordstrom was entirely under her. She reached the platform above the fluocil, looking down into the roiling solution. It had brightened incredibly, becoming a stew of vivid swirling color and tidal motion.

Nordstrom stepped onto the bottom rung of the ladder, looking up as the metal fire extinguisher plunged hard into him, glancing off his shoulder and hitting the floor with an explosion of noise. He screamed out but held tight to the rung above him. Liz looked down at his face: his reddened eyes seethed above his scarlet jowly cheeks. He looked at her with a terrifying homicidal rage.

There was nowhere to run from him. She had given her best shot and hadn't been able to stop him. He quickly climbed the ladder, his fleshy bulk animated by an almost supernatural energy. They stood facing one another on the narrow metal platform, half over the tank and half suspended above the lab floor, ten feet below.

He struck her with all his strength, a punch to her cheek that sent her reeling back into the metal bar around the platform. She kept from blacking out only by sheer instinct, holding on to the rail for purchase. She kneeled just as Nordstrom kicked her solidly in the ribs, sending a blinding flash of pain through the fresh wounds on her abdomen.

She collapsed on the platform as he moved toward her. Looking down into the fluocil, which surged crazily and was suffused with an intense, almost blinding glow from the out-of-control laser bank, she felt the grip of death. He stood behind her, his hands around her throat. The strength in his hands instantly cut off her oxygen supply.

"Bitch!" he yelled, jerking her neck in his hands. Her eyes bulged with pressure, and her vision faded to red, mixed only with the mad laser colors. "You took the one thing away from me that I cared about! You took my money away! I earned it, you bitch! I made the solution, it was mine!''

Finally he quit shaking her, tightening his grip to snap her neck. He pushed her forward, immersing her head in the fluocil. Her eyes opened to the brilliant colors, her nose filled with a chemical odor. The substance had gone out of balance—she couldn't breathe in it. She gurgled as the final traces of consciousness faded, seeing a great blast of light. Thinking it was only her brain sending a panicked message as it expired, she relaxed, finally giving up the fight. At least I stopped him, she thought. At least . . .

The flash wasn't an illusion; instead, a great wave of electricity shot through the room as the power system expressed its outrage. A row of fluorescent lights exploded above the tank, the bulbs shattering and raining glass on the room. A heavy metal casing fell from its moorings and tumbled wildly down, striking Nordstrom and Liz before crashing into a computer terminal below.

Liz felt the impact, though Kerry had taken most of it. His hands loosened from around her neck. She pulled her head out of the liquid, gagging as she looked up at him: he was bleeding profusely from his head, and his eyes showed all white. He reached out for the metal rail, but his hand slipped off it as he pitched forward, tumbling headlong into the tank.

She stood up, rubbing her neck and feeling terrible pain from where he had struck her. Thinking that she might have a broken rib, she propelled herself by pure force of will to climb down the ladder to the laboratory floor. There her vision returned to full focus as she fought to stay conscious and keep her injuries from overcoming her.

The room had become a burning chaotic nightmare. Bulbs broke above her head, plunging the room into near darkness. The main computer bank was completely afire, and the entire array of equipment was blackened and beginning to burn completely. She turned to look at the tank, pressing her face to it to try to see inside.

At first, there was only color. The laser bank buzzed menacingly, itself spewing off great plumes of smoke. Then the shape of Kerry Nordstrom became visible. His face was contorted with pain as it rammed forward through the bright liquid, crashing into the side of the tank. Bubbles of air poured from his mouth and nose. For a brief second, he and Liz stared into each other's eyes, but his sudden thrashing pulled him into the center of the tank, where he vainly struggled to reach the surface.

She turned to the lasers. They were overcharged, completely haywire, destroying the delicate combination of current and frequency that made the fluocil vital to preserving organs. It would be impossible to breathe in the out-of-balance tank. Stepping to the machines, trying to find a way to at least switch them off, she was thrown to the ground by an electrical explosion. She smelled the disgusting scent of her own burned hair.

The lasers were now on maximum charge. They sparkled from the tank's surface, shooting glistening beams of orange and yellow toward the ceiling. Liz looked up in time to see Nordstrom appear again in the tank; this time, he showed no sign of life. His hands dangled uselessly, his tie floated up into his face. Singed strands of flesh hung from his scalp and hands: he had burned alive in the liquid.

She shouted out as the next explosion hit, which threw her violently away from the tank and the computers. A fireball engulfed the tank, shattering it with a horrible roar. Liz crawled toward the door of the lab, trying to get away. Finally, unconsciousness claimed her.

The air outside was cold and biting. She awoke in the company of strangers, two men in masks who were strapping her down. Struggling against her bonds, she relaxed when John Rogers's face appeared over hers. He leaned over to kiss her, and she tasted the soot that covered and blackened his features.

"You're all right, honey. We're all fine," he said, taking her hand. "Just don't try to move. They're going to put you in this ambulance. You're going to be fine."

He kept repeating those words like a litany of hope and love, leaning over her and crying through his smile. The tears ran through the soot and ash, creating broad streaks down his cheek.

A huge blast erupted far away from them, causing a chorus of shouts all around. Liz turned her head to see: it was the animal lab, exploding with incredible fury. Glass and metal shot high into the air, chased by flame and black smoke. Med-Tek was burning.

Sirens filled her ears, making her wince. A red fire truck raced past, its horn barking out an order to let it pass. Before it got any closer, another explosion rocked the complex.

"We got to you just in time," John said, holding her hand tighter. "The flames had just about taken out the entire lab."

"What about Nordstrom?" Liz asked, tensing. "He tried to—"

"He's gone, Liz," said John, pressing down gently on Liz's shoulder. "Just sit still. We did it. We stopped him."

Another face appeared in Liz's restricted field of vision. She felt groggy: they must have drugged her. This grimly smiling black man, who was he . . . ?

"Carl," she said.

"Looks like you were right about everything, Dr. Danny," he said, gently touching her cheek.

"Liz."

"Liz. Anyway, I'll be seeing you in the hospital. I'm afraid I'm a little busy at the moment. Nordstrom left tape-recorded conversations between him and Irwin Ross. We're reviewing them right now. It looks like Nordstrom wanted to take his partner down with him. "

"Thank you for everything, Carl," she said, her words becoming slurred as the tranquilizers took hold.

"Don't mention it," he said, standing up. "But there's something I've been meaning to mention. See, I have this pain in my guts, and I was worrying that it might be a hernia."

She laughed as he leaned over her again, a childish grin on his face.

"Free of charge, Carl. Come see me sometime."

"Thanks," he said. He clapped John hard on the shoulder. "This guy pulled you out of the fire, you know. Showed more guts than I've seen in a long time." He stepped away from them, heading toward the burning complex.

She looked into John's eyes. "Thank you, too," she said. "Thank you so much, Juan."

"Don't thank me, Liz. Just stay with me." His gentle eyes shone out of the mask of soot, rimmed with hopeful tears.

"I'll stay with you, honey," she said. "You want to know something weird?"

"Weird has become a very relative term to me lately," he said, looking over his shoulder at Med-Tek.

"I think my back is better. Really. All that running around must have helped it. You know, we might have to do something like this again. . . ." Her voice began to fade.

"Not on your life, sweetheart," he said, leaning over to kiss her again. "From now on, I'm looking out for you."

She looked again at his kind loving face, then up at the sky. It was dark, painted with black and gray hues of smoke. Somewhere within Med-Tek was Kerry Nordstrom's secret, a discovery that could have changed the future. Instead, it burned, destroyed along with its creator.

A strong breeze blew over the parking lot, sweeping away the smoke. She smelled the bitter chill of the air, and loved it.